THE DOOMSDAY CONSPIRACY

Books by Sidney Sheldon

THE DOOMSDAY CONSPIRACY

MEMORIES OF MIDNIGHT

THE SANDS OF TIME

WINDMILLS OF THE GODS

IF TOMORROW COMES

MASTER OF THE GAME

RAGE OF ANGELS

BLOODLINE

A STRANGER IN THE MIRROR

THE OTHER SIDE OF MIDNIGHT

THE NAKED FACE

THE DOOMSDAY CONSPIRACY

Sidney Sheldon

WILLIAM MORROW AND COMPANY, INC.
NEW YORK

It is the policy of William Morrow and Company, Inc., and its imprints and affiliates, recognizing the importance of preserving what has been written, to print the books we publish on acid-free paper, and we exert our best efforts to that end.

Library of Congress Cataloging-in-Publication Data

Sheldon, Sidney.
The doomsday conspiracy / by Sidney Sheldon.
p. cm.
ISBN 0-688-08489-3
I. Title.
PS3569.H3927D66 1991
813′.54—dc20 91-12109
CIP

Printed in the United States of America

First Edition

1 2 3 4 5 6 7 8 9 10

This is for
Jerry Davis

Acknowledgment

I wish to express my appreciation to James J. Hurtak, Ph.D., and his wife, Desirée, for making available to me their invaluable technical expertise.

May you live in interesting times.
—ancient Chinese curse

Prologue

Uetendorf, Switzerland
Sunday, October 14, 1500 Hours

The witnesses standing at the edge of the field were staring in horrified silence, too stunned to speak. The scene that lay before them was grotesque, a primeval nightmare dredged up from some deep, dark depths of primitive man's collective unconscious. Each witness had a different reaction. One fainted. A second one vomited. A woman was shaking uncontrollably. Another one thought: *I'm going to have a heart attack!* The elderly priest clutched his beads and crossed himself. *Help me, Father. Help us all. Protect us against this evil incarnate. We have finally seen the face of Satan. It is the end of the world. Judgment Day has come.*

Armageddon is here. . . . Armageddon . . . Armageddon . . .

BOOK ONE

THE HUNTER

Sunday, October 14, 2100 Hours

FLASH MESSAGE

TOP SECRET ULTRA

NSA TO DEPUTY DIRECTOR COMSEC

EYES ONLY

SUBJECT: OPERATION DOOMSDAY

MESSAGE: ACTIVATE

NOTIFY NORAD, CIRVIS, GEPAN, DIS, GHG, VSAF, INS.

END OF MESSAGE

Sunday, October 14, 2115 Hours

FLASH MESSAGE

TOP SECRET ULTRA

NSA TO DEPUTY DIRECTOR—

NAVAL INTELLIGENCE 17TH DISTRICT

EYES ONLY

SUBJECT: COMMANDER ROBERT BELLAMY

ARRANGE TEMPORARY TRANSFER THIS AGENCY,

EFFECTIVE IMMEDIATELY.

YOUR CONCURRENCE IN THE ABOVE IS ASSUMED.

END OF MESSAGE

Chapter One

Day One
Monday, October 15

He was back in the crowded hospital ward at Cu Chi Base in Vietnam and Susan was leaning over his bed, lovely in her crisp white nurse's uniform, whispering, "Wake up, sailor. You don't want to die."

And when he heard the magic of her voice, he could almost forget his pain. She was murmuring something else in his ear, but a loud bell was ringing, and he could not hear her clearly. He reached up to pull her closer, and his hands clutched empty air.

It was the sound of the telephone that fully awoke Robert Bellamy. He opened his eyes reluctantly, not wanting to let go of the dream. The telephone at his bedside was insistent. He looked at the clock. Four A.M. He snatched up the instrument, angry at having his dream interrupted. "Do you know what the hell time it is?"

"Commander Bellamy?" A deep, male voice.

"Yes—"

"I have a message for you, Commander. You are ordered to report to General Hilliard at National Security Agency headquarters at Fort Meade at oh six hundred this morning. Is the message understood, Commander?"

"Yes." *And no. Mostly no.*

Commander Robert Bellamy slowly replaced the receiver, puzzled. What the devil could the NSA want with him? He was assigned to ONI, the Office of Naval Intelligence. And what could be urgent enough to call for a meeting at six o'clock in the morning? He lay down again and closed his eyes, trying to recapture the dream. It had been so real. He knew, of course, what had triggered it. Susan had telephoned the evening before.

"Robert . . ."

The sound of her voice did to him what it always did. He took a shaky breath. "Hello, Susan."

"Are you all right, Robert?"

"Sure. Fantastic. How's Moneybags?"

"Please, don't."

"All right. How's Monte Banks?"

He could not bring himself to say "your husband." *He* was her husband.

"He's fine. I just wanted to tell you that we're going to be away for a little while. I didn't want you to worry."

That was so like her, so Susan. He fought to keep his voice steady. "Where are you going this time?"

"We're flying to Brazil."

On Moneybags's private 727.

"Monte has some business interests there."

"Really? I thought he owned the country."

"Stop it, Robert. Please."

"Sorry."

There was a pause. "I wish you sounded better."

"If you were here, I would."

"I want you to find someone wonderful and be happy."

"I did find someone wonderful, Susan." The damned lump in his throat made it difficult for him to speak. "And do you know what happened? I lost her."

"If you're going to do this, I won't call you again."

He was filled with sudden panic. "Don't say that. Please." She was his lifeline. He could not bear the thought of never speaking to her again. He tried to sound cheerful. "I'm going to go out and find some luscious blonde and screw us both to death."

"I want you to find someone."

"I promise."

"I'm concerned about you, darling."

"No need. I'm really fine." He almost gagged on his lie. If she only knew the truth. But it was nothing he could bring himself to discuss with anyone. Especially Susan. He could not bear the thought of her pity.

"I'll telephone you from Brazil," Susan said.

There was a long silence. They could not let go of each other because there was too much to say, too many things that were better left unsaid, that had to be left unsaid.

"I have to go now, Robert."

"Susan?"

"Yes?"

"I love you, baby. I always will."

"I know. I love you too, Robert."

And that was the bittersweet irony of it. They still loved each other so much.

You two have the perfect marriage, all their friends used to say. What had gone wrong?

Commander Robert Bellamy got out of bed and walked through the silent living room in his bare feet. The room screamed out Susan's absence. There were dozens of photographs of Susan and himself scattered around, frozen moments in time. The two of them fishing in the Highlands of Scotland, standing in front of a Buddha near a Thai *klong,* riding a carriage in the rain through the Borghese gardens in Rome. And in each picture, they were smiling and hugging, two people wildly in love.

He went into the kitchen and put on a pot of coffee. The kitchen clock read 4:15 A.M. He hesitated a moment, then dialed a number. There were six rings, and finally he heard Admiral Whittaker's voice at the other end of the line. "Hello."

"Admiral—"

"Yes?"

"It's Robert. I'm terribly sorry to wake you, sir. I just had a rather strange phone call from the National Security Agency."

"The NSA? What did they want?"

"I don't know. I've been ordered to report to General Hilliard at oh six hundred."

There was a thoughtful silence. "Perhaps you're being transferred there."

"I can't be. It doesn't make sense. Why would they—?"

"It's obviously something urgent, Robert. Why don't you give me a call after the meeting?"

"I will. Thank you."

The connection was broken. *I shouldn't have bothered the old man,* Robert thought. The admiral had retired as head of Naval Intelligence two years earlier. *Forced* to retire, was more like it. The rumor was that as a sop, the Navy had given him a little office somewhere and put him to work counting barnacles on the mothball fleet, or some such shit. The admiral would have no idea about current intelligence activities. But he was Robert's mentor. He was closer to Robert than anyone in the world, except, of course, Susan. And Robert had needed to talk to someone. With Susan gone, he felt as though he were living in a time warp. He fantasized that somewhere, in another dimension of time and space, he and Susan were still happily married, laughing and carefree and loving. *Or maybe not,* Robert thought wearily. *Maybe I just don't know when to let go.*

The coffee was ready. It tasted bitter. He wondered whether the beans came from Brazil.

He carried the coffee cup into the bathroom and studied his image in the mirror. He was looking at a man in his early forties, tall and lean and physically fit with a craggy face, a strong chin, black hair, and intelligent, probing dark eyes. There was a long, deep scar on his chest, a souvenir from the plane crash. But that was yesterday. That was Susan. This was today. Without Susan. He shaved and showered and walked over to his clothes closet. *What do I wear,* he wondered, *Navy uniform or civilian clothes? And on the other hand, who gives a damn?* He put on a charcoal gray suit, a white shirt, and a gray silk tie. He knew very little about the National Security Agency, only that the Puzzle Palace, as it was nicknamed, superseded all other American intelligence agencies and was the most secretive of them all. *What do they want with me? I'll soon find out.*

Chapter Two

The National Security Agency is hidden discreetly away on eighty-two rambling acres at Fort Meade, Maryland, in two buildings that together are twice the size of the CIA complex in Langley, Virginia. The agency, created to give technical support to protect United States communications and acquire worldwide electronic intelligence data, employs thousands of people, and so much information is generated by its operations that it shreds more than forty tons of documents every day.

It was still dark when Commander Robert Bellamy arrived at the first gate. He drove up to an eight-foot-high Cyclone fence with a topping of barbed wire. There was a sentry booth there, manned by two armed guards. One of them stayed in the booth watching as the other approached the car. "Can I help you?"

"Commander Bellamy to see General Hilliard."

"May I see your identification, Commander?"

Robert Bellamy pulled out his wallet and removed his 17th District Naval Intelligence ID card. The guard studied it carefully and returned it. "Thank you, Commander."

He nodded to the guard in the booth, and the gate swung open. The guard inside picked up a telephone. "Commander Bellamy is on his way."

A minute later, Robert Bellamy drove up to a closed, electrified gate.

An armed guard approached the car. "Commander Bellamy?"

"Yes."

"May I see your identification, please?"

He started to protest and then he thought, *What the hell. It's their zoo.* He took out his wallet again and showed his identification to the guard.

"Thank you, Commander." The guard gave some invisible sign, and the gate opened.

As Robert Bellamy drove ahead, he saw a third Cyclone fence ahead of him. *My God,* he thought, *I'm in the Land of Oz.*

Another uniformed guard walked up to the car. As Robert Bellamy reached for his wallet, the guard looked at the license plate and said, "Please drive straight ahead to the administration building, Commander. There will be someone there to meet you."

"Thank you."

The gate swung open, and Robert followed the driveway up to an enormous white building. A man in civilian clothes was standing outside waiting, shivering in the chill October air. "You can leave your car right there, Commander," he called out. "We'll take care of it."

Robert Bellamy left the keys in his car and stepped out. The man greeting him appeared to be in his thirties, tall, thin, and sallow. He looked as though he had not seen the sun in years.

"I'm Harrison Keller. I'll escort you to General Hilliard's office."

They walked into a large high-ceilinged entrance hall. A man in civilian clothes was seated behind a desk. "Commander Bellamy—"

Robert Bellamy swung around. He heard the click of a camera.

"Thank you, sir."

Robert Bellamy turned to Keller. "What—?"

"This will take only a minute," Harrison Keller assured him.

Sixty seconds later, Robert Bellamy was handed a blue and white identification badge with his photograph on it.

"Please wear this at all times while you're in the building, Commander."

"Right."

They started walking down a long, white corridor. Robert Bellamy noticed security cameras mounted at twenty-foot intervals on both sides of the hall.

"How big is this building?"

"Just over two million square feet, Commander."

"What?"

"Yes. This corridor is the longest corridor in the world—nine hundred and eighty feet. We're completely self-contained here. We have a shopping center, cafeteria, post exchange, eight snack bars, a hospital, complete with an operating room, a dentist's office, a branch of the State Bank of Laurel, a dry-cleaning shop, a shoe shop, a barbershop, and a few other odds and ends."

It's a home away from home, Robert thought. He found it oddly depressing.

They passed an enormous open area filled with a vast sea of computers. Robert stopped in amazement.

"Impressive, isn't it? That's just one of our computer rooms. The complex contains three billion dollars' worth of decoding machines and computers."

"How many people work in this place?"

"About sixteen thousand."

So what the hell do they need me for? Robert Bellamy wondered.

He was led into a private elevator that Keller operated with a key. They went up one floor and started on another trek down a long corridor until they reached a suite of offices at the end of the hall.

"Right in here, Commander." They entered a large reception office with four secretaries' desks. Two of the secretaries had already arrived for work. Harrison Keller nodded to one of them, and she pressed a button, and a door to the inner office clicked open.

"Go right in, please, gentlemen. The general is expecting you."

Harrison Keller said, "This way."

Robert Bellamy followed him into the inner sanctum. He found himself in a spacious office, the ceilings and walls heavily soundproofed. The room was comfortably furnished, filled with photographs and personal mementos. It was obvious that the man behind the desk spent a lot of time there.

General Mark Hilliard, deputy director of the NSA, appeared to be in his middle fifties, very tall, with a face carved in flint, icy, steely eyes, and a ramrod-straight posture. The general was dressed in a gray suit, white shirt, and gray tie. *I guessed right,* Robert thought.

Harrison Keller said, "General Hilliard, this is Commander Bellamy."

"Thank you for dropping by, Commander."

As though it was an invitation to some tea party.

The two men shook hands.

"Sit down. I'll bet you could do with a cup of coffee."

The man was *a mind reader*. "Yes, sir."

"Harrison?"

"No, thank you." He took a chair in the corner.

A buzzer was pressed, the door opened, and an Oriental in a mess jacket entered with a tray of coffee and Danish pastry. Robert noted that he was not wearing an identification badge. *Shame*. The coffee was poured. It smelled wonderful.

"How do you take yours?" General Hilliard asked.

"Black, please." The coffee tasted great.

The two men were seated facing each other in soft leather chairs.

"The director asked that I meet with you."

The director. Edward Sanderson. A legend in espionage circles. A brilliant, ruthless puppet master, credited with masterminding dozens of daring coups all over the world. A man seldom seen in public and whispered about in private.

"How long have you been with the 17th District Naval Intelligence Group, Commander?" General Hilliard asked.

Robert played it straight. "Fifteen years." He would have bet a month's pay that the general could have told him the time of day when he had joined ONI.

"Before that, I believe you commanded a naval air squadron in Vietnam."

"Yes, sir."

"You were shot down. They didn't expect you to pull through."

The doctor was saying, "Forget about him. He won't make it." He had wanted to die. The pain was unbearable.

And then Susan was leaning over him. *"Open your eyes, sailor, you don't want to die."* He had forced his eyes open and through the haze of pain was staring at the most beautiful woman he had ever seen. She had a soft oval face and thick black hair, sparkling brown eyes and a smile like a blessing. He had tried to speak, but it was too much of an effort.

General Hilliard was saying something.

Robert Bellamy brought his mind back to the present. "I beg your pardon, General?"

"We have a problem, Commander. We need your help."

"Yes, sir?"

The general stood up and began to pace. "What I'm about to tell you is extremely sensitive. It's above top secret."

"Yes, sir."

"Yesterday, in the Swiss Alps, a NATO weather balloon crashed. There were some experimental military objects aboard the balloon that are highly secret."

Robert found himself wondering where all this was leading.

"The Swiss government has removed those objects from the balloon, but unfortunately, it seems that there were some witnesses to the crash. It is of vital importance that none of them talk to anyone about what they saw. It could provide valuable information to certain other countries. Do you follow me?"

"I think so, sir. You want me to speak to the witnesses and warn them not to discuss what they saw."

"Not exactly, Commander."

"Then I don't under—"

"What I want you to do is simply track down those

witnesses. Others will talk to them about the necessity for silence."

"I see. Are the witnesses all in Switzerland?"

General Hilliard stopped in front of Robert. "That's our problem, Commander. You see, we have no idea where they are. Or who they are."

Robert thought he had missed something. "I beg your pardon?"

"The only information we have is that the witnesses were on a tour bus. They happened to be passing the scene when the weather balloon crashed near a little village called . . ." He turned to Harrison Keller.

"Uetendorf."

The general turned back to Robert. "The passengers got off the bus for a few minutes to look at the crash and then continued on. When the tour ended, the passengers dispersed."

Robert said slowly, "General Hilliard, are you saying that there is *no* record of who these people are or where they went?"

"That is correct."

"And you want me to go over and find them?"

"Exactly. You've been very highly recommended. I'm told that you speak half a dozen languages fluently, and you have an excellent field record. The director arranged to have you temporarily transferred to the NSA."

Terrific. "I assume I'll be working with the Swiss government on this?"

"No, you'll be working alone."

"Alone? But—"

"We must not involve anyone else in this mission. I can't stress enough the importance of what was in that balloon, Commander. Time is of the essence. I want you to report your progress to me every day."

The general wrote a number on a card and handed it to Robert. "I can be reached through this number day or night. There's a plane waiting to fly you to Zurich. You'll be escorted to your apartment, so you can pack what you need, and then you'll be taken to the airport."

So much for "Thank you for dropping by." Robert was tempted to ask "Will someone feed my goldfish while I'm gone?" but he had a feeling the answer would be "You have no goldfish."

"In your work with ONI, Commander, I assume you've acquired intelligence contacts abroad?"

"Yes, sir. I have quite a few friends who could be of use—"

"You're not to get in touch with any of them. You are not authorized to make any contacts at all. The witnesses you're looking for are undoubtedly nationals of various countries." The general turned to Keller. "Harrison—"

Keller walked over to a filing cabinet in the corner and unlocked it. He removed a large manila envelope and passed it to Robert.

"There's fifty thousand dollars in here in different European currencies and another twenty thousand in U.S. dollars. You will also find several sets of false identifications that may come in handy."

General Hilliard held out a thick, shiny black plastic card with a white stripe on it. "Here's a credit card that—"

"I doubt if I'll need that, General. The cash will be enough, and I have an ONI credit card."

"Take it."

"Very well." Robert examined the card. It was drawn on a bank he had never heard of. At the bottom of the card was a telephone number. "There's no name on the card," Robert said.

"It's the equivalent of a blank check. It requires no

identification. Just have them call the telephone number on the card when you make a purchase. It's very important that you keep it with you at all times."

"Right."

"And Commander?"

"Sir?"

"You must find those witnesses. Every one of them. I'll inform the director that you have started the assignment."

The meeting was over.

Harrison Keller walked Robert to the outer office. A uniformed marine was seated there. He rose as the two men came in.

"This is Captain Dougherty. He'll take you to the airport. Good luck."

"Thanks."

The two men shook hands. Keller turned and walked back into General Hilliard's office.

"Are you ready, Commander?" Captain Dougherty asked.

"Yes." *But ready for what?* He had handled difficult intelligence assignments in the past, but never anything as crazy as this. He was expected to track down an unknown number of unknown witnesses from unknown countries. *What are the odds against that?* Robert wondered. *I feel like the White Queen in Through the Looking Glass. "Why sometimes I've believed as many as six impossible things before breakfast." Well, this was all six of them.*

"I have orders to take you directly to your apartment and then to Andrews Air Force Base," Captain Dougherty said. "There's a plane waiting to—"

Robert shook his head. "I have to make a stop at my office first."

Dougherty hesitated. "Very well. I'll go there with you and wait for you."

It was as if they didn't trust him out of their sight. Because he knew that a weather balloon had crashed? It made no sense. He surrendered his badge at the reception desk and walked outside, into the chill, breaking dawn. His car was gone. In its place was a stretch limousine.

"Your car will be taken care of, Commander," Captain Dougherty informed him. "We'll ride in this."

There was a high-handedness about all this that Robert found vaguely disturbing.

"Fine," he said.

And they were on their way to Naval Intelligence. The pale morning sun was disappearing behind rain clouds. It was going to be a miserable day. *In more ways than one,* Robert thought.

Chapter Three

Ottawa, Canada
2400 Hours

His code name was Janus. He was addressing twelve men in the heavily guarded room of a military compound.

"As you have all been informed, Operation Doomsday has been activated. There are a number of witnesses who must be found as quickly and as quietly as possible. We are not able to attempt to track them down through regular security channels because of the danger of a leak."

"Who are we using?" The Russian. *Huge. Short-tempered.*

"His name is Commander Robert Bellamy."

"How was he selected?" The German. *Aristocratic. Ruthless.*

"The commander was chosen after a thorough computer search of the files of the CIA, FBI, and a half dozen other security agencies."

"Please, may I inquire what are his qualifications?" The Japanese. *Polite. Sly.*

"Commander Bellamy is an experienced field officer who speaks six languages fluently and has an exemplary record. Again and again he has proved himself to be very resourceful. He has no living relatives."

"Is he aware of the urgency of this?" The Englishman. *Snobbish. Dangerous.*

"He is. We have every expectation that he will be able to locate all the witnesses very quickly."

"Does he understand the purpose of his mission?" The Frenchman. *Argumentative. Stubborn.*

"No."

"And when he has found the witnesses?" The Chinese. *Clever. Patient.*

"He will be suitably rewarded."

Chapter Four

The headquarters of the Office of Naval Intelligence occupies the entire fifth floor of the sprawling Pentagon, an enclave in the middle of the largest office building in the world, with seventeen miles of corridors and twenty-nine thousand military and civilian employees.

The interior of the Office of Naval Intelligence reflects its seagoing traditions. The desks and file cabinets are either olive green, from the World War II era, or battleship gray, from the Vietnam era. The walls and ceilings are painted a buff or cream color. In the beginning, Robert had been put off by the Spartan decor, but he had long since grown accustomed to it.

Now, as he walked into the building and approached the reception desk, the familiar guard at the desk said, "Good morning, Commander. May I see your pass?"

Robert had been working here for seven years, but the

ritual never changed. He dutifully displayed his pass.

"Thank you, Commander."

On his way to his office, Robert thought about Captain Dougherty, waiting for him in the parking lot at the river entrance. Waiting to escort him to the plane that would fly him to Switzerland to begin an impossible hunt.

When Robert reached his office, his secretary, Barbara, was already there.

"Good morning, Commander. The deputy director would like to see you in his office."

"He can wait. Get me Admiral Whittaker, please."

"Yes, sir."

A minute later Robert was speaking with the admiral.

"I presume you have finished your meeting, Robert?"

"A few minutes ago."

"How did it go?"

"It was—interesting. Are you free to join me for breakfast, Admiral?" He tried to keep his voice casual.

There was no hesitation. "Yes. Shall we meet there?"

"Fine. I'll leave a visitors' pass for you."

"Very well. I'll see you in an hour."

Robert replaced the receiver and thought, *It's ironic that I have to leave a visitors' pass for the admiral. A few years ago, he was the fair-haired boy here, in charge of Naval Intelligence. How must he feel?*

Robert buzzed his secretary on the intercom.

"Yes, Commander?"

"I'm expecting Admiral Whittaker. Arrange a pass for him."

"I'll take care of it right away."

It was time to report to the deputy director. Dustin fucking Thornton.

Chapter Five

Dustin "Dusty" Thornton, deputy director of the Office of Naval Intelligence, had won his fame as one of the greatest athletes ever to come out of Annapolis. Thornton owed his present exalted position to a football game. An Army-Navy game, to be precise. Thornton, a towering monolith of a man, had played fullback as a senior at Annapolis in Navy's most important game of the year. At the beginning of the fourth quarter, with Army leading 13–0, two touchdowns and a conversion ahead, destiny stepped in and changed Dustin Thornton's life. Thornton intercepted an Army pass, pivoted around, and charged through the Army phalanx for a touchdown. Navy missed on the extra point but soon scored a field goal. After the ensuing kickoff, Army failed to make a first down and punted into Navy territory. The score stood at Army 13, Navy 9, and the clock was running.

When play resumed, the ball was passed to Thornton,

and he went down under a heap of Army uniforms. It took him a long time to get to his feet. A doctor came running out onto the field. Thornton angrily waved him away.

With seconds left to play, signals were called for a lateral pass. Thornton caught it on his own ten yard line and took off. He was unstoppable. He charged through the opposition like a tank, knocking down everyone unlucky enough to get in his way. With two seconds to go, Thornton crossed the goal line for the winning touchdown, and Navy scored its first victory against Army in four years. That, in itself, would have had little effect on Thornton's life. What made the event significant was that seated in a box reserved for VIPs were Willard Stone and his daughter, Eleanor. As the crowd rose to its feet, wildly cheering the Navy hero, Eleanor turned to her father and said quietly, "I want to meet him."

Eleanor Stone was a woman of large appetites. Plain-faced, she had a voluptuous body and an insatiable libido. Watching Dustin Thornton savagely plow his way down the football field, she fantasized what he would be like in bed. If his manhood was as big as the rest of his body . . . She was not disappointed.

Six months later, Eleanor and Dustin Thornton were married. That was the beginning. Dustin Thornton went to work for his father-in-law and was inducted into an arcane world he had not dreamed existed.

Willard Stone, Thornton's new father-in-law, was a man of mystery. A billionaire with powerful political connections and a past shrouded in secrecy, he was a shadowy figure who pulled strings in capitals all over the world. He was in his late sixties, a meticulous man whose every movement was precise and methodical. He had razor-sharp features and hooded eyes that revealed nothing. Willard Stone believed in wasting neither words nor emotions, and he was ruthless in obtaining what he wanted.

The rumors about him were fascinating. He was reported to have murdered a competitor in Malaysia and to have had a torrid affair with the favorite wife of an emir. He was said to have backed a successful revolution in Nigeria. The government had brought half a dozen indictments against him, but they were always mysteriously dropped. There were tales of bribes, and senators suborned, business secrets stolen, and witnesses who disappeared. Stone was an adviser to presidents and kings. He was raw, naked power. Among his many properties was a large, isolated estate in the Colorado mountains where every year scientists, captains of industry, and world leaders gathered for seminars. Armed guards kept out unwanted visitors.

Willard Stone had not only approved his daughter's marriage, he had encouraged it. His new son-in-law was brilliant, ambitious, and, most important, malleable.

Twelve years after the marriage, Stone arranged for Dustin to be appointed ambassador to South Korea. Several years later, the President appointed him ambassador to the United Nations. When Admiral Ralph Whittaker was suddenly ousted as acting director of ONI, Thornton took his place.

That day Willard Stone sent for his son-in-law.

"This is merely the beginning," Stone promised. "I have bigger plans for you, Dustin. Great plans." And he had proceeded to outline them.

Two years earlier, Robert had had his first meeting with the new acting director of ONI.

"Sit down, Commander." There was no cordiality in Dustin Thornton's voice. "I see by your record that you're something of a maverick."

What the hell does he mean? Robert wondered. He decided to keep his mouth shut.

Thornton looked up. "I don't know how Admiral Whittaker ran this office when he was in charge, but from now on we're doing everything by the book. I expect my orders to be carried out to the letter. Do I make myself clear?"

Jesus, Robert thought, *what the hell are we in for here?*

"Do I make myself clear, Commander?"

"Yes. You expect your orders to be carried out to the letter." He wondered whether he was expected to salute.

"That's all."

But it was not all.

A month later, Robert was sent to East Germany to bring in a scientist who wanted to defect. It was a dangerous assignment because *Stasi,* the East German secret police, had learned about the proposed defection and was watching the scientist closely. In spite of that, Robert had managed to smuggle the man across the border, to a safe house. He was making arrangements to bring him to Washington when he received a call from Dustin Thornton telling him that the situation had changed and that he was to drop the assignment.

"We can't just dump him here," Robert had protested. "They'll kill him."

"That's his problem," Thornton had replied. "Your orders are to come back home."

Screw you, Robert thought. *I'm not going to abandon him.* He had called a friend of his in MI6, British Intelligence, and explained the situation.

"If he goes back to East Germany," Robert said, "they'll chop him. Will you take him?"

"I'll see what can be done, old chap. Bring him along."

And the scientist had been given haven in England.

Dustin Thornton never forgave Robert for disobeying his instructions. From that point on, there was open animosity between the two men. Thornton had discussed the incident with his father-in-law.

"Loose cannons like Bellamy are dangerous," Willard Stone warned. "They're a security hazard. Men like that are expendable. Remember that."

And Thornton had remembered.

Now, walking down the corridor toward Dustin Thornton's office, Robert could not help thinking about the difference between Thornton and Whittaker. In a job like his, trust was the sine qua non. He did not trust Dustin Thornton.

Thornton was seated behind his desk when Robert walked into his office.

"You wanted to see me?"

"Yes. Sit down, Commander." Their relationship had never reached the "Robert" phase.

"I've been told you've been temporarily transferred to the National Security Agency. When you come back, I have a—"

"I'm not coming back. This is my last assignment."

"What?"

"I'm quitting."

Thinking about it later, Robert was not sure exactly what reaction he had expected. Some kind of scene. Dustin Thornton could have shown surprise, or he could have argued, or been angry, or relieved. Instead, he had merely looked at Robert and nodded. "That's it then, isn't it?"

When Robert returned to his own office, he said to his secretary, "I'm going to be away for a while. I'll be leaving in about an hour."

"Is there some place where you can be reached?"

Robert remembered General Hilliard's orders. "No."

"There are some meetings you—"

"Cancel them." He looked at his watch. It was time to meet Admiral Whittaker.

They had breakfast in the center yard of the Pentagon at the Ground Zero Café, so named because it was once thought that the Pentagon was where the first nuclear-bomb attack against the United States would take place. Robert had arranged for a corner table where they would have a degree of privacy. Admiral Whittaker was punctual, and as Robert watched him approach the table, it seemed to him that the admiral looked older and smaller, as though semiretirement had somehow aged and shrunk him. He was still a striking-looking man with strong features, a Roman nose, good cheekbones, and a crown of silvered hair. Robert had served under the admiral in Vietnam and later in the Office of Naval Intelligence, and he had a high regard for him. *More than a high regard,* Robert admitted to himself. Admiral Whittaker was his surrogate father.

The admiral sat down. "Good morning, Robert. Well, did they transfer you to the NSA?"

Robert nodded. "Temporarily."

The waitress arrived, and the two men studied the menu.

"I had forgotten how bad the food here was," Admiral Whittaker said, smiling. He looked around the room, his face reflecting an unspoken nostalgia.

He wishes he were back here, Robert thought. *Amen.*

They ordered. When the waitress was out of earshot, Robert said, "Admiral, General Hilliard is sending me on an urgent three-thousand-mile trip to locate some witnesses who saw a weather balloon crash. I find that strange. And there's something else that's even stranger. 'Time is of the essence,' to quote the general, but I've been ordered not to use any of my intelligence contacts abroad to help me."

Admiral Whittaker looked puzzled. "I suppose the general must have his reasons."

Robert said, "I can't imagine what they are."

Admiral Whittaker studied Robert. Commander Bellamy had served under him in Vietnam and had been the best pilot in the squadron. The admiral's son, Edward, had been Robert's bombardier, and on the terrible day their plane had been shot down, Edward had been killed. Robert had barely survived. The admiral had gone to the hospital to visit him.

"He's not going to make it," the doctors had told him. Robert, lying there in agonizing pain, had whispered, "I'm sorry about Edward. . . . I'm so sorry."

Admiral Whittaker had squeezed Robert's hand. "I know you did everything you could. You've got to get well, now. You're going to be fine." He wanted desperately for Robert to live. In the admiral's mind, Robert was his son, the son who would take Edward's place.

And Robert had pulled through.

"Robert—"

"Yes, Admiral?"

"I hope your mission to Switzerland is successful."

"So do I. It's my last one."

"You're still determined to quit?"

The admiral was the only one Robert had confided in. "I've had enough."

"Thornton?"

"It's not just him. It's me. I'm tired of interfering with

other people's lives." *I'm tired of the lies and the cheating, and the broken promises that were never meant to be kept. I'm tired of manipulating people and of being manipulated. I'm tired of the games and the danger and the betrayals. It's cost me everything I ever gave a damn about.*

"Do you have any idea what you're going to do?"

"I'll try to find something useful to do with my life, something positive."

"What if they won't let you go?"

Robert said, "They have no choice, have they?"

Chapter Six

The limousine was waiting at the river-entrance parking lot.

"Are you ready, Commander?" Captain Dougherty asked.

As ready as I'll ever be, Robert thought. "Yes."

Captain Dougherty accompanied Robert to his apartment so he could pack. Robert had no idea how many days he would be gone. *How long does an impossible assignment take?* He packed enough clothes for a week and, at the last minute, put in a framed photograph of Susan. He stared at it for a long time and wondered if she were enjoying herself in Brazil. He thought, *I hope not. I hope she's having a lousy time.* And was immediately ashamed of himself.

When the limousine arrived at Andrews Air Force Base, the plane was waiting. It was a C2OA, an Air Force jet.

Captain Dougherty held out his hand. "Good luck, Commander."

"Thanks." *I'll need it.* Robert walked up the steps to the cabin. The crew was inside finishing the preflight check. There was a pilot, a copilot, a navigator, and a steward, all in Air Force uniforms. Robert was familiar with the plane. It was loaded with electronic equipment. On the outside near the tail was a high-frequency antenna that looked like an enormous fishing pole. Inside the cabin were twelve red telephones on the walls and a white, unsecured phone. Radio transmissions were in code, and the plane's radar was on a military frequency. The primary color inside was air force blue, and the cabin was furnished with comfortable club chairs.

Robert found that he was the only passenger. The pilot greeted him. "Welcome aboard, Commander. If you'll put on your seat belt, we have clearance to take off."

Robert strapped himself in and leaned back in his seat as the plane taxied down the runway. A minute later, he felt the familiar pull of gravity as the jet screamed into the air. He had not piloted a plane since his crash, when he had been told he would never be able to fly again. *Fly again, hell,* Robert thought, *they said I wouldn't live. It was a miracle—No, it was Susan. . . .*

Vietnam. He had been sent there with the rank of lieutenant commander, stationed on the aircraft carrier *Ranger* as a tactics officer, responsible for training fighter pilots and planning attack strategy. He had led a bomber squadron of A-6A Intruders, and there was very little time away from the pressures of battle. One of the few leaves he had was in Bangkok for a week of R and R, and during that time he never bothered to sleep. The city was a Disneyland designed for the pleasure of the male animal. He had met an exquisite Thai girl his first hour in town, and she had stayed at his side the whole time and taught him a few Thai phrases. He had found the language soft and mellifluous.

Good morning. *Arun sawasdi.*
Where are you from? *Khun na chak nai?*
Where are you going now? *Khun kamrant chain pai?*

She taught him other phrases too, but she would not tell him what they meant, and when he said them, she giggled.

When Robert returned to the *Ranger,* Bangkok seemed like a faraway dream. The war was the reality and it was a horror. Someone showed him one of the leaflets the marines dropped over North Vietnam. It read:

Dear Citizens:

The U.S. Marines are fighting alongside South Vietnamese forces in Duc Pho in order to give the Vietnamese people a chance to live a free, happy life, without fear of hunger and suffering. But many Vietnamese have paid with their lives, and their homes have been destroyed because they helped the Vietcong.

The hamlets of Hai Mon, Hai Tan, Sa Binh,

> Ta Binh, and many others have been destroyed because of this. We will not hesitate to destroy every hamlet that helps the Vietcong, who are powerless to stop the combined might of the GVN and its allies. The choice is yours. If you refuse to let the Vietcong use your villages and hamlets as their battlefield, your homes and your lives will be saved.

We're saving the poor bastards, all right. Robert thought grimly. *And all we're destroying is their country.*

The aircraft carrier *Ranger* was equipped with all the state-of-the-art technology that could be crammed into it. The ship was home base for 16 aircraft, 40 officers, and 350 enlisted men. Flight schedules were handed out three or four hours before the first launch of the day.

In the mission planning section of the ship's intelligence center, the latest information and reconnaissance photos were given to the bombardiers, who then planned their flight patterns.

"Jesus, they gave us a beauty this morning," said Edward Whittaker, Robert's bombardier.

Edward Whittaker looked like a younger version of his father, but he had a completely different personality. Where the admiral was a formidable figure, dignified and austere, his son was down-to-earth, warm and friendly. He had earned his place as "just one of the boys." The other airmen forgave him for being the son of their commander. He was the best bombardier in the squadron, and he and Robert had become fast friends.

"Where are we heading?" Robert asked.

"For our sins, we've drawn Package Six."

It was the most dangerous mission of all. It meant

flying north to Hanoi, Haiphong, and up the Red River delta, where the flak was heaviest. There was a catch-22: They were not permitted to bomb any strategic targets if there were civilians nearby, and the North Vietnamese, not being stupid, immediately placed civilians around all their military installations. There was a lot of grumbling in the allied military, but President Lyndon Johnson, safely back in Washington, was giving the orders.

The twelve years that United States troops fought in Vietnam were the longest period it has ever been at war. Robert Bellamy had come into it late in 1972, when the Navy was having major problems. Their F-4 squadrons were being destroyed. In spite of the fact that their planes were superior to the Russian MiG's, the U.S. Navy was losing one F-4 for every two MiG's shot down. It was an unacceptable ratio.

Robert was summoned to the headquarters of Admiral Ralph Whittaker.

"You sent for me, Admiral?"

"You have the reputation of being a hotshot pilot, Commander. I need your help."

"Yes, sir?"

"We're getting murdered by the goddamned enemy. I have had a thorough analysis made. There's nothing wrong with our planes—it's the training of the men who are flying them. Do you understand?"

"Yes, sir."

"I want you to pick a group and retrain it in maneuvers and weapons employment. . . ."

The new group was called Top Gun, and before they were through, the ratio changed from two to one to twelve to one. For every two F-4's lost, twenty-four MiG's were shot down. The assignment had taken eight weeks of intensive training, and Commander Bellamy had finally returned to his ship. Admiral Whittaker was there to greet him. "That was a damned fine job, Commander."

"Thank you, Admiral."

"Now, let's get back to work."

"I'm ready, sir."

Robert had flown thirty-four bombing missions from the *Ranger* without incident.

His thirty-fifth mission was Package Six.

They had passed Hanoi and were heading northwest toward Phu Tho and Yen Bai. The flak was getting increasingly heavy. Edward Whittaker was seated on Robert's right, staring at the radar screen, listening to the ominous bass tones of enemy search radars sweeping the sky.

The sky directly ahead of them looked like the Fourth of July, streaked with white smoke from the light guns below, dark gray bursts from the fifty-five-millimeter shells, black clouds from the hundred-millimeter shells, and colored tracer bullets from heavy machine-gun fire.

"We're approaching target," Edward said. His voice through the headphones sounded eerily far away.

"Roger."

The A-6A Intruder was flying at 450 knots, and at that speed, even with the drag and weight of the bomb load, it handled remarkably well, moving too fast for enemies to track it.

Robert reached out and turned on the master armament switch. The dozen 500-pound bombs were now ready to be released. He was headed straight for the target.

A voice on his radio said, "Romeo—you have a bogey at four o'clock high."

Robert turned to look. A MiG was hurtling toward him, coming out of the sun. Robert banked and sent the plane into a steep dive. The MiG was on his tail. It loosed a missile. Robert checked his instrument panel. The missile was closing in rapidly. A thousand feet away . . . six hundred . . . four hundred . . .

"Holy shit!" Edward yelled. "What are we waiting for?"

Robert waited until the last second, then released a stream of metal chaff and went into a steep climbing turn, leaving the missile to follow the chaff and crash harmlessly into the ground below.

"Thank you, God," Edward said. "And you, pal."

Robert continued the climb and swung behind the MiG. The pilot started to take evasive action, but it was too late. Robert loosed a Sidewinder missile and watched it crawl up the tail pipe of the MiG and explode. An instant later, the sky was showered with pieces of metal.

A voice came over the intercom. "Nice work, Romeo."

The plane was over the target now. "Here we go," Edward said. He pressed the red button that released the bombs and watched them tumble down toward their target. Mission accomplished. Robert headed the plane back toward the carrier.

At that instant, they felt a heavy thud. The swift and graceful bomber suddenly became sluggish.

"We've been hit!" Edward called.

Both fire-warning lights were flashing red. The plane was moving erratically, out of control.

A voice came over the radio. "Romeo, this is Tiger. Do you want us to cover you?"

Robert made a split-second decision. "No, go on to your targets. I'm going to try to make it back to base."

The plane had slowed down and was becoming more difficult to handle.

"Faster," Edward said nervously, "or we're going to be late for lunch."

Robert looked at the altimeter. The needle was dropping rapidly. He activated his radio mike. "Romeo to home base. We've taken a hit."

"Home base to Romeo. How bad is it?"

"I'm not sure. I think I can bring it home."

"Hold on." A moment later the voice returned. "Your signal is 'Charlie on arrival.' "

That meant they were cleared to land on the carrier immediately.

"Roger."

"Good luck."

The plane was starting to roll. Robert fought to correct it, trying to gain altitude. "Come on, baby, you can make it." Robert's face was tight. They were losing too much altitude. "What's our ETA?"

Edward looked at his chart. "Seven minutes."

"I'm going to get you that hot lunch."

Robert was nursing the plane along with all the skill at his command, using the throttle and rudder to try to keep it on a straight course. The altitude was still dropping alarmingly. Finally, ahead of him, Robert saw the sparkling blue waters of the Tonkin Gulf.

"We're home free, buddy," Robert said. "Just a few more miles."

"Terrific. I never doubted—"

And out of nowhere, two MiG's descended on the plane with a thunderous roar. Bullets began thudding against the fuselage.

"Eddie! Bail out!" He turned to look. Edward was

slumped against his seat belt, his right side torn open, blood spattering the cockpit.

"No!" It was a scream.

A second later, Robert felt a sudden, agonizing blow to his chest. His flight suit was instantly soaked in blood. The plane started to spiral downward. He felt himself losing consciousness. With his last ounce of strength, he unfastened his seat belt. He turned to take a final look at Edward. "I'm sorry," he whispered. He blacked out and later had no recollection of how he ejected out of the plane and parachuted into the water below. A Mayday call had been sent out, and a Sikorsky SH-3A Sea King helicopter from the U.S.S. *Yorktown* was circling, waiting to pick him up. In the distance, the crew could see Chinese junks rapidly closing in for the kill, but they were too late.

When they loaded Robert into the helicopter, a medical corpsman took one look at his torn body and said, "Jesus Christ, he'll never even make it to the hospital."

They gave Robert a shot of morphine, wrapped pressure bandages tightly around his chest, and flew him to the 12th Evacuation Hospital at Cu Chi Base.

The "12th Evac," which served Cu Chi, Tay Ninh, and Dau Tieng bases, had four hundred beds in a dozen wards, housed in quonset huts arranged around a U-shaped compound connected by covered walkways. The hospital had two intensive-care units, one for surgery cases, the other for burns, and each unit was seriously overcrowded. When Robert was brought in, he left a bright red trail of blood across the hospital floor.

A harried surgeon cut the bandages from Robert's chest, took one look, and said wearily, "He's not going to make it. Take him in back to cold storage."

And the doctor moved on.

Robert, fading in and out of consciousness, heard the

doctor's voice from a far distance. *So, this is it,* he thought. *What a lousy way to die.*

"You don't want to die, do you, sailor? Open your eyes. Come on."

He opened his eyes and saw a blurred image of a white uniform and a woman's face. She was saying something more, but he could not make out the words. The ward was too noisy, filled with a cacophony of screams and moans of patients, and doctors yelling out orders, and nurses frantically running around administering to the savaged bodies that lay there.

Robert's memory of the next forty-eight hours was a haze of pain and delirium. It was only later that he learned that the nurse, Susan Ward, had persuaded a doctor to operate on him and had donated her own blood for a transfusion. Fighting to keep him alive, they had put three IV's into Robert's ravaged body and pumped blood through them simultaneously.

When the operation was over, the surgeon in charge sighed. "We've wasted our time. He's got no more than a ten percent chance of pulling through."

But the doctor did not know Robert Bellamy. And he did not know Susan Ward. It seemed to Robert that whenever he opened his eyes, Susan was there, holding his hand, stroking his forehead, ministering to him, willing him to live. He was delirious most of the time. Susan sat quietly next to him in the dark ward in the middle of the lonely nights and listened to his ravings.

". . . The DOD is wrong, you can't head in perpendicular to the target or you'll hit the river. . . . Tell them to angle the dives a few degrees off target heading. . . . Tell them . . ." he mumbled.

Susan said soothingly, "I will."

Robert's body was soaked in perspiration. She sponged

him off. ". . . You have to remove all five of the safety pins or the seat won't eject. . . . Check them. . . ."

"All right. Go back to sleep now."

". . . The shackles on the multiple ejector racks malfunctioned. . . . God only knows where the bombs landed. . . ."

Half the time Susan could not understand what her patient was talking about.

Susan Ward was head of the emergency operating-room nurses. She had come from a small town in Idaho and had grown up with the boy next door, Frank Prescott, the son of the mayor. Everyone in town assumed they would be married one day.

Susan had a younger brother, Michael, whom she adored. On his eighteenth birthday, he joined the Army and was sent to Vietnam, and Susan wrote to him there every day. Three months after he had enlisted, Susan's family received a telegram, and she knew what it contained before they opened it.

When Frank Prescott heard the news, he rushed over. "I'm really sorry, Susan. I liked Michael a lot." And then he made the mistake of saying, "Let's get married right away."

And Susan had looked at him and made a decision. "No. I have to do something important with my life."

"For God's sake! What's more important than marrying me?"

The answer was Vietnam.

Susan Ward went to nursing school.

She had been in Vietnam for eleven months, working tirelessly, when Commander Robert Bellamy was wheeled in and sentenced to die. Triage was a common practice in emergency evacuation hospitals. The doctors would examine two or three patients and make summary judgments as to which one they would try to save. For reasons that were never truly clear to her, Susan had taken one look at the torn body of Robert Bellamy and had known that she could not let him die. Was it her brother she was trying to save? Or was it something else? She was exhausted and overworked, but instead of taking her time off, she spent every spare moment tending to him.

Susan had looked up her patient's record. An ace Navy pilot and instructor, he had earned the Naval Cross. His birthplace was Harvey, Illinois, a small industrial city south of Chicago. He had enlisted in the Navy after graduating from college and had trained at Pensacola. He was unmarried.

Each day, as Robert Bellamy was recuperating, walking the thin line between death and life, Susan whispered to him, "Come on, sailor. I'm waiting for you."

One night, six days after he had been brought into the hospital, Robert was rambling on in his delirium, when suddenly he sat straight up in bed, looked at Susan, and said clearly, "It's not a dream. You're real."

Susan felt her heart give a little jump. "Yes," she said softly. "I'm real."

"I thought I was dreaming. I thought I had gone to heaven and God assigned you to me."

She looked into Robert's eyes and said seriously, "I would have killed you if you had died."

His eyes swept the crowded ward. "Where—where am I?"

"The 12th Evacuation Hospital at Cu Chi."

"How long have I been here?"

"Six days."

"Eddie—he—"

"I'm sorry."

"I have to tell the admiral."

She took Robert's hand and said gently, "He knows. He's been here to visit you."

Robert's eyes filled with tears. "I hate this goddamn war. I can't tell you how much I hate it."

From that moment on, Robert's progress astonished the doctors. All his vital signs stabilized.

"We'll be shipping him out of here soon," they told Susan. And she felt a sharp pang.

Robert was not sure exactly when he fell in love with Susan Ward. Perhaps it was the moment when she was dressing his wounds, and nearby they heard the sounds of bombs dropping and she murmured, "They're playing our song."

Or perhaps it was when they told Robert he was well enough to be transferred to Walter Reed Hospital in Washington to finish his convalescence, and Susan said, "Do you think I'm going to stay here and let some other nurse have that great body? Oh, no. I'm going to pull every string I can to go with you."

They were married two weeks later. It took Robert a year to heal completely, and Susan tended to his every need, night and day. He had never met anyone like her, nor had he dreamed that he could ever love anyone so much. He loved her compassion and sensitivity, her passion and vitality. He loved her beauty and her sense of humor.

On their first anniversary, he said to her, "You're the most beautiful, the most wonderful, the most caring human being in the world. There is no one on this earth with your warmth and wit and intelligence."

And Susan had held him tightly and whispered in a nasal, chorus-girl voice, "Likewise, I'm sure."

They shared more than love. They genuinely liked and respected each other. All their friends envied them, and with good reason. Whenever they talked about a perfect marriage, it was always Robert and Susan they held up as an example. They were compatible in every way, complete soul mates. Susan was the most sensual woman Robert had ever known, and they were able to set each other on fire with a touch, a word. One evening, when they were scheduled to go to a formal dinner party, Robert was running late. He was in the shower when Susan came into the bathroom carefully made up and dressed in a lovely strapless evening gown.

"My God, you look sexy," Robert said. "It's too bad we don't have more time."

"Oh, don't worry about that," Susan murmured. And a moment later she had stripped off her clothes and joined Robert in the shower.

They never got to the party.

Susan sensed Robert's needs almost before he knew them, and she saw to it that they were attended to. And Robert was equally attentive to her. Susan would find love notes on her dressing-room table, or in her shoes when she started to get dressed. Flowers and little gifts would be delivered to her on Groundhog Day and President Polk's birthday and in celebration of the Lewis and Clark Expedition.

And the laughter that they shared. The wonderful laughter . . .

* * *

The pilot's voice crackled over the intercom. "We'll be landing in Zurich in ten minutes, Commander."

Robert Bellamy's thoughts snapped back to the present, to his assignment. In his fifteen years with Naval Intelligence, he had been involved in dozens of challenging cases, but this one promised to be the most bizarre of them all. He was on his way to Switzerland to find a busload of anonymous witnesses who had disappeared into thin air. *Talk about looking for a needle in a haystack. I don't even know where the haystack is. Where is Sherlock Holmes when I need him?*

"Will you fasten your seat belt, please?"

The C2OA was flying over dark forests, and a moment later, skimming over the runway etched by the landing lights of the Zurich International Airport. The plane taxied to the east side of the airport and headed for the small General Aviation building, away from the main terminal. There were still puddles on the tarmac from the earlier rainstorms, but the night sky was clear.

"Crazy weather," the pilot commented. "Sunny here Sunday, rainy all day today, and clearing tonight. You don't need a watch here. What you really need is a barometer. Can I arrange a car for you, Commander?"

"No, thanks." From this moment on, he was completely on his own. Robert waited until the plane taxied away, and then boarded a minibus to the airport hotel, where he collapsed into a dreamless sleep.

Chapter Seven

Day Two
0800 Hours

The next morning Robert approached a clerk behind the Europcar desk.

"Guten Tag."

It was a reminder that he was in the German-speaking part of Switzerland. "*Guten Tag*. Do you have a car available?"

"Yes, sir, we do. How long will you be needing it?"

Good question. An hour? A month? Maybe a year or two? "I'm not sure."

"Do you plan to return the car to this airport?"

"Possibly."

The clerk looked at him strangely. "Very well. Will you fill out these papers, please?"

Robert paid for the car with the special black credit card General Hilliard had given him. The clerk examined it, perplexed, then said, "Excuse me." He disappeared into an office, and when he returned, Robert asked, "Any problem?"

"No, sir. None at all."

The car was a gray Opel Omega. Robert got onto the airport highway and headed for downtown Zurich. He enjoyed Switzerland. It was one of the most beautiful countries in the world. Years earlier he had skied there. In more recent times, he had carried out assignments there, liaising with Espionage Abteilung, the Swiss intelligence agency. During World War II, the agency had been organized into three bureaus: D, P, and I, covering Germany, France, and Italy, respectively. Now its main purpose was related to detecting undercover espionage operations conducted within the various UN organizations in Geneva. Robert had friends in Espionage Abteilung, but he remembered General Hilliard's words: *"You're not to get in touch with any of them."*

The drive into the city took twenty-five minutes. Robert reached the Dübendorf downtown exit ramp and headed for the Dolder Grand Hotel. It was exactly as he remembered it: an overgrown Swiss château with turrets, stately and imposing, surrounded by greenery and overlooking Lake Zurich. He parked the car and walked into the lobby. On the left was the reception desk.

"Guten Tag."

"Guten Tag. Haben Sie ein Zimmer für eine Nacht?"

"Ja. Wie möchten Sie bezahlen?"

"Mit Kreditkarte." The black and white credit card that General Hilliard had given him. Robert asked for a map of Switzerland and was escorted to a comfortable room in the new wing of the hotel. It had a small balcony that overlooked the lake. Robert stood there, breathing in the crisp, autumn air, thinking about the task that lay ahead of him.

He had nothing to go on. Not one damned thing. All the factors to the equation of his assignment were completely unknown. The name of the tour company. The number of passengers. Their names and whereabouts. *"Are the witnesses all in Switzerland?" "That's our problem. We have no idea where they are, or who they are."* And it wasn't enough to find some of the witnesses. *"You must find every one of them."* The only information he had was the place and date: Uetendorf, Sunday, October 14.

He needed a handle, something to grab onto.

If he remembered correctly, all-day tour buses left from only two major cities: Zurich and Geneva. Robert opened a desk drawer and took out the bulky *Telefonbuch. I should look under M, for miracle,* Robert thought. There were more than half a dozen tour companies listed: Sunshine Tours, Swisstour, Tour Service, Touralpino, Tourisma Reisen . . . He would have to check each of them. He copied down the addresses of all the companies and drove to the offices of the nearest one listed.

There were two clerks behind the counter taking care of tourists. When one of them was free, Robert said, "Excuse me. My wife was on one of your tours last Sunday, and she left her purse on the bus. I think she got excited because she saw the weather balloon that crashed near Uetendorf."

The clerk frowned. "*Es tut mir viel leid.* You must be mistaken. Our tours do not go near Uetendorf."

"Oh. Sorry." *Strike one.*

The next stop promised to be more fruitful.

"Do your tours go to Uetendorf?"

"Oh, *ja.*" The clerk smiled. "Our tours go everywhere in Switzerland. They are the most scenic. We have a tour to Zermatt—the Tell Special. There is also the Glacier Express and the Palm Express. The Great Circle Tour leaves in fifteen—"

"Did you have a tour Sunday that stopped to watch

that weather balloon that crashed? I know my wife was late getting back to the hotel and—"

The clerk behind the counter said indignantly, "We take great pride in the fact that our tours are *never* late. We make no unscheduled stops."

"Then one of your buses didn't stop to look at that weather balloon?"

"Absolutely not."

"Thank you." *Strike two.*

The third office Robert visited was located at Bahnhofplatz, and the sign outside said Sunshine Tours. Robert walked up to the counter. "Good afternoon. I wanted to ask you about one of your tour buses. I heard that a weather balloon crashed near Uetendorf and that your driver stopped for half an hour so the passengers could look at it."

"No, no. He only stopped for fifteen minutes. We have very strict schedules."

Home run!

"What was your interest in this, did you say?"

Robert pulled out one of the identification cards that had been given him. "I'm a reporter," Robert said earnestly, "and I'm doing a story for *Travel and Leisure* magazine on how efficient the buses in Switzerland are, compared with other countries. I wonder if I might interview your driver?"

"That would make a very interesting article. Very interesting, indeed. We Swiss pride ourselves on our efficiency."

"And that pride is well deserved," Robert assured him.

"Would the name of our company be mentioned?"

"Prominently."

The clerk smiled. "Well, then I see no harm."

"Could I speak with him now?"

"This is his day off." He wrote a name on a piece of paper.

Robert Bellamy read it upside down. *Hans Beckerman.*

The clerk added an address. "He lives in Kappel. That's a small village about forty kilometers from Zurich. You should be able to find him at home now."

Robert Bellamy took the paper. "Thank you very much. By the way," Robert said, "just so we have all the facts for the story, do you have a record of how many tickets you sold for that particular tour?"

"Of course. We keep records of all our tours. Just a moment." He picked up a ledger underneath the counter and flipped a page. "Ah, here we are. Sunday. Hans Beckerman. There were seven passengers. He drove the Iveco that day, the small bus."

Seven unknown passengers and the driver. Robert took a stab in the dark. "Would you happen to have the names of those passengers?"

"Sir, people come in off the street, buy their ticket, and take the tour. We don't ask for identification."

Wonderful. "Thank you again." Robert started toward the door.

The clerk called out, "I hope you will send us a copy of the article."

"Absolutely," Robert said.

The first piece of the puzzle lay in the tour bus, and Robert drove to Talstrasse, where the buses departed, as though it might reveal some hidden clue. The Iveco bus was brown and silver, small enough to traverse the steep Alpine roads, with seats for fourteen passengers. *Who are the seven, and where have they disappeared to?* Robert got back in his car. He consulted his map and marked it. He took Lavessneralle out of the city, into the Albis, the start of the Alps, toward the village of Kappel. He headed south, driving past the small hills that surround Zurich, and began the climb into the magnificent mountain chain of the Alps. He drove through Adliswil and Langnau and Hausen and nameless hamlets with chalets and colorful picture-postcard scenery until almost an hour later, he came to Kappel. The little village consisted of a restaurant, a church, a post office, and twelve or so houses scattered around the hills. Robert parked the car and walked into the restaurant. A waitress was clearing a table near the door.

"Entschuldigen Sie bitte, Fraulein. Welche Richtung ist das Haus von Herr Beckerman?"

"Ja." She pointed down the road. *"An der Kirche rechts."*

"Danke."

Robert turned right at the church and drove up to a modest two-story stone house with a ceramic tiled roof. He got out of the car and walked up to the door. He could see no bell, and knocked.

A heavyset woman with a faint mustache answered the door. *"Ja?"*

"I'm sorry to bother you. Is Mr. Beckerman in?"

She eyed him suspiciously. "What do you want with him?"

Robert gave her a winning smile. "You must be Mrs. Beckerman." He pulled out his reporter's identification card. "I'm doing a magazine article on Swiss bus drivers, and your husband was recommended to my magazine as having one of the finest safety records in the country."

She brightened and said proudly, "My Hans is an excellent driver."

"That's what everyone tells me, Mrs. Beckerman. I would like to do an interview with him."

"An interview with my Hans for a magazine?" She was flustered. "That is very exciting. Come in, please."

She led Robert into a small, meticulously neat living room. "Wait here, *bitte.* I will get Hans."

The house had a low, beamed ceiling, dark wooden floors, and plain wooden furniture. There was a small stone fireplace and lace curtains at the windows.

Robert stood there thinking. This was not only his best lead, it was his *only* lead. *"People come in off the street, buy their ticket, and take the tour. We don't ask for identification. . . ." There's no place to go from here,* Robert thought grimly. *If this doesn't work out, I can always place an ad: Will the seven bus passengers who saw a weather balloon crash Sunday please assemble in my hotel room at oh twelve hundred tomorrow. Breakfast will be served.*

A thin, bald man appeared. His complexion was pale, and he wore a thick, black mustache that was startlingly out of keeping with the rest of his appearance. "Good afternoon, *Herr—*?"

"Smith. Good afternoon." Robert's voice was hearty. "I've certainly been looking forward to meeting you, Mr. Beckerman."

"My wife tells me you are writing a story about bus drivers." He spoke with a heavy German accent.

Robert smiled ingratiatingly. "That's right. My magazine is interested in your wonderful safety record and—"

"Scheissdreck!" Beckerman said rudely. "You are interested in the thing that crashed yesterday afternoon, no?"

Robert managed to look abashed. "As a matter of fact, yes, I am interested in discussing that too."

"Then why do you not come out and say so? Sit down."

"Thank you." Robert took a seat on the couch.

Beckerman said, "I am sorry I cannot offer you a drink, but we do not keep schnapps in the house anymore." He tapped his stomach. "Ulcers. The doctors cannot even give me drugs to relieve the pain. I am allergic to all of them." He sat down opposite Robert. "But you did not come here to talk about my health, eh? What is it you wish to know?"

"I want to talk to you about the passengers who were on your bus Sunday when you stopped near Uetendorf at the site of the weather-balloon crash."

Hans Beckerman was staring at him. "Weather balloon? What weather balloon? What are you talking about?"

"The balloon that—"

"You mean the spaceship."

It was Robert's turn to stare. "The . . . *spaceship*?"

"*Ja,* the flying saucer."

It took a moment for the words to sink in. Robert felt a sudden chill. "Are you telling me that you saw a flying saucer?"

"*Ja*. With dead bodies in it."

"Yesterday, in the Swiss Alps, a NATO weather balloon crashed. There were some experimental military objects aboard the balloon that are highly secret."

Robert tried hard to sound calm. "Mr. Beckerman, are you certain that what you saw was a flying saucer?"

"Of course. What they call a UFO."

"And there were dead people inside?"

"Not people, no. *Creatures*. It is hard to describe them." He gave a little shiver. "They were very small with big, strange eyes. They were dressed in suits of a silver metallic color. It was very frightening."

Robert listened, his mind in a turmoil. "Did your passengers see this?"

"Oh, *ja*. We all saw it. I stopped there for maybe fifteen minutes. They wanted me to stay longer, but the company is very strict about schedules."

Robert knew the question was futile before he even asked it. "Mr. Beckerman, would you happen to know the names of any of your passengers?"

"Mister, I drive a bus. The passengers buy a ticket in Zurich, and we take a tour southwest to Interlaken and then northwest to Bern. They can either get off at Bern or return to Zurich. Nobody gives their names."

Robert said desperately, "There's *no* way you can identify any of them?"

The bus driver thought for a moment. "Well, I can tell you there were no children on that trip. Just men."

"Only men?"

Beckerman thought for a moment. "No. That's not right. There was one woman too."

Terrific. That really narrows it down, Robert thought. *Next question: Why the hell did I ever agree to this assignment?* "What you're saying, Mr. Beckerman, is that a group of tourists boarded your bus at Zurich, and then when the tour was over, they simply scattered?"

"That's right, Mr. Smith."

So there's not even a haystack. "Do you remember *anything* at all about the passengers? Anything they said or did?"

Beckerman shook his head. "Mister, you get so you don't pay no attention to them. Unless they cause some trouble. Like that German."

Robert sat very still. He asked softly, "What German?"

"*Affenarsch!* All the other passengers were excited about seeing the UFO and those dead creatures in it, but this old man kept complaining about how we had to hurry up to get to Bern because he had to prepare some lecture for the university in the morning. . . ."

A beginning. "Do you remember anything else about him?"

"No."

"Nothing at all?"

"He was wearing a black overcoat."

Great. "Mr. Beckerman, I want to ask you for a favor. Would you mind driving out with me to Uetendorf?"

"It's my day off. I am busy with—"

"I'll be glad to pay you."

"Ja?"

"Two hundred marks."

"I don't—"

"I'll make it four hundred marks."

Beckerman thought for a moment. "Why not? It's a nice day for a drive, *nicht*?"

They headed south, past Luzern and the picturesque villages of Immensee and Meggen. The scenery was breathtakingly beautiful, but Robert had other things on his mind.

They passed through Engelberg, with its ancient Benedictine monastery, and Brünig, the pass leading to Interlaken. They sped past Leissigen and Faulensee, with its lovely blue lake dotted with white sailboats.

"How much farther is it?" Robert asked.

"Soon," Hans Beckerman promised.

They had been driving for almost an hour when they

came to Spiez. Hans Beckerman said, "It is not far now. Just past Thun."

Robert felt his heart beginning to beat faster. He was about to witness something that was far beyond imagination, alien visitors from the stars. They drove through the little village of Thun, and a few minutes later, as they neared a grove of trees across the highway, Hans Beckerman pointed and said, "There!"

Robert braked to a stop and pulled over to the side of the road.

"Across the highway. Behind those trees."

Robert felt a growing sense of excitement. "Right. Let's have a look."

A truck was speeding by. When it had passed, Robert and Hans Beckerman crossed the road. Robert followed the bus driver up a small incline into the stand of trees.

The highway was completely hidden from sight. As they stepped into a clearing, Beckerman announced, "It is right there."

Lying on the ground in front of them were the torn remains of a weather balloon.

Chapter Eight

I'm getting too old for this, Robert thought wearily. *I was really beginning to fall for his flying-saucer fairy tale.*

Hans Beckerman was staring at the object on the ground, a confused expression on his face. "*Verfalschen!* That is not it."

Robert sighed. "No, it isn't, is it?"

Beckerman shook his head. "It was here yesterday."

"Your little green men probably flew it away."

Beckerman was stubborn, "No, no. They were both *tot*—dead."

Tot—dead. That sums up my mission pretty well. My only lead is a crazy old man who sees spaceships.

Robert walked over to the balloon to examine it more closely. It was a large aluminum envelope, fourteen feet in diameter, with serrated edges where it had ripped open when it crashed to earth. All the instruments had been removed, just as General Hilliard had told him. *"I can't stress enough the importance of what was in that balloon."*

Robert circled the deflated balloon, his shoes squishing in the wet grass, looking for anything that might give him the slightest clue. Nothing. It was identical to a dozen other weather balloons he had seen over the years.

The old man still would not give up, filled with Germanic stubbornness. "Those alien things . . . They made it look like this. They can do anything, you know."

There's nothing more to be done here, Robert decided. His socks had gotten wet walking through the tall grass. He started to turn away, then hesitated, struck by a thought. He walked back to the balloon. "Lift up a corner of this, will you?"

Beckerman looked at him a moment, surprised. "You wish me to raise it up?"

"Bitte."

Beckerman shrugged. He picked up a corner of the lightweight material and lifted it while Robert raised another corner. Robert held the piece of aluminum over his head while he walked underneath the balloon toward the center. His feet sank into the grass. "It's wet under here," Robert called out.

"Of course." The *Dummkopf* was left unsaid. "It rained all yesterday. The whole ground is wet."

Robert crawled out from under the balloon. "It should be dry." *"Crazy weather," the pilot said. "Sunny here Sunday." The day the balloon crashed. "Rainy all day today and clearing tonight. You don't need a watch here. What you really need is a barometer."*

"What?"

"What was the weather like when you saw the UFO?"

Beckerman thought for a moment. "It was a nice afternoon."

"Sunny?"

"*Ja*. Sunny."

"But it rained all day yesterday?"

Beckerman was looking at him, puzzled. "So?"

"So if the balloon was here all night, the ground under it should be dry—or damp, at the most, through osmosis. But it's soaking wet, like the rest of this area."

Beckerman was staring. "I don't understand. What does that mean?"

"It could mean," Robert said carefully, "that someone placed this balloon here yesterday after the rain started and took away what you saw." Or was there some saner explanation he had not thought of?

"Who would do such a crazy thing?"

Not so crazy, Robert thought. *The Swiss government could have planted this to deceive any curious visitors. The first stratagem of a cover-up is disinformation.* Robert walked through the wet grass scanning the ground, cursing himself for being a gullible idiot.

Hans Beckerman was watching Robert suspiciously. "What magazine did you say you write for, mister?"

"Travel and Leisure."

Hans Beckerman brightened. "Oh. Then I suppose you will want to take a picture of me, like the other fellow did."

"What?"

"That photographer who took pictures of us."

Robert froze. "Who are you talking about?"

"That photographer fellow. The one who took pictures of us at the wreck. He said he would send us each a print. Some of the passengers had cameras, too."

Robert said slowly, "Just a moment. Are you saying that someone took a picture of the passengers here in front of the UFO?"

"That's what I am trying to tell you."

"And he promised to send you each a print?"

"That's right."

"Then he must have taken your names and addresses."

"Well, sure. Otherwise, how would he know where to send them?"

Robert stood still, a feeling of euphoria sweeping over him. *Serendipity, Robert, you lucky sonofabitch!* An impossible mission had suddenly become a piece of cake. He was no longer looking for seven unknown passengers. All he had to do was find one photographer. "Why didn't you mention him before, Mr. Beckerman?"

"You asked me about passengers."

"You mean he wasn't a passenger?"

Hans Beckerman shook his head. *"Nein."* He pointed. "His car was stalled across the highway. A tow truck was starting to haul it away, and then there was this loud crash, and he ran across the road to see what was happening. When he saw what it was, the fellow ran back to his car, grabbed his cameras, and came back. Then he asked us all to pose in front of the saucer thing."

"Did this photographer give you his name?"

"No."

"Do you remember anything about him?"

Hans Beckerman concentrated. "Well, he was a foreigner. American or English."

"You said a tow truck was getting ready to haul his car away?"

"That's right."

"Do you remember which way the truck was headed?"

"North. I figured he was towing it into Bern. Thun is closer, but on Sunday, all the garages in Thun are closed."

Robert grinned. "Thank you. You've been very helpful."

"You won't forget to send me your article when it's finished?"

"No. Here's your money and an extra hundred marks for your great help. I'll drive you home." They walked over to the car. As Beckerman opened the door, he stopped and turned toward Robert.

"That was very generous of you." He took from his pocket a small rectangular piece of metal, the size of a cigarette lighter, containing a tiny white crystal.

"What's this?"

"I found it on the ground Sunday before we got back on the bus."

Robert examined the strange object. It was as light as paper and was the color of sand. A rough edge at one end indicated that it might be part of another piece. *Part of the equipment that was in the weather balloon? Or part of a UFO?*

"Maybe it will bring you luck," said Beckerman, as he placed the bills Robert had given him in his wallet. "It certainly worked for me." He smiled broadly and got into the car.

It was time to ask himself the hard question: *Do I really believe in UFOs?* He had read many wild newspaper stories about people who said they had been beamed up into spaceships and had had all kinds of weird experiences, and he had always attributed those reports to people who were either looking for publicity or who should have thrown themselves on the mercy of a good psychiatrist. But in the past few years, there had been reports that were less easy to dismiss. Reports of UFO sightings by astronauts, Air Force pilots, and police officials, people with credibility, who shunned publicity. In addition there had been the disturbing report of the UFO crash at Roswell, New Mexico, where the bodies of aliens had purportedly been discovered. The government was supposed to have hushed that up and removed all the evidence. In World War II, pilots had reported strange sightings of what they called Foo fighters, unidentified objects that buzzed them and then disappeared. There were stories of towns visited by unexplainable objects that had come speeding through the sky. *What if there really are aliens in UFOs from another galaxy?* Robert wondered. *How would it affect our world? Would it mean peace? War? The end of civilization as we know it?* He found himself half hoping that Hans Beckerman was a raving lunatic, and that what had crashed was really a weather balloon. He would have to find another witness either to verify Beckerman's story or to refute it. On the surface, the story seemed incredible, but yet, there was something nagging at Robert. *If it was only a weather balloon that crashed, even if it did carry special equipment, why was I called into a meeting at the National Security Agency at six o'clock in the morning and told that it was urgent that all the witnesses be found quickly? Is there a cover-up? And if so . . . why?*

Chapter Nine

Later that day, a press conference was held in Geneva in the austere offices of the Swiss Ministry of Internal Affairs. There were more than fifty reporters in the room and an overflow crowd outside in the corridor. There were representatives from television, radio, and the press from more than a dozen countries, many of them loaded down with microphones and television gear. They all seemed to be speaking at once.

"We've heard reports that it was not a weather balloon. . . ."

"Is it true that it was a flying saucer?"

"There are rumors that there were alien bodies aboard the ship. . . ."

"Was one of the aliens alive?"

"Is the government trying to hide the truth from the people? . . ."

The press officer raised his voice to regain control.

"Ladies and gentlemen, there has been a simple misunderstanding. We get calls all the time. People see satellites, shooting stars . . . Isn't it interesting that reports of UFOs are always made anonymously? Perhaps this caller really believed it was a UFO, but in actuality it was a weather balloon that fell to the ground. We have arranged transportation to take you to it. If you will follow me, please . . ."

Fifteen minutes later, two busloads of reporters and television cameras were on their way to Uetendorf to see the remains of a weather-balloon crash. When they arrived, they stood in the wet grass surveying the torn metallic envelope. The press officer said, "This is your mysterious flying saucer. It was sent aloft from our air base in Vevey. To the best of our knowledge, ladies and gentlemen, there are no unidentified flying objects that our government has not been able to explain satisfactorily, nor to our knowledge, are there any extraterrestrials visiting us. It is our government's firm policy that if we should come across any such evidence, we would immediately make that information available to the public. If there are no further questions . . ."

Chapter Ten

Hangar 17 at Langley Air Force Base in Virginia was locked in complete and rigid security. Outside, four armed marines guarded the perimeter of the building, and inside, three high-ranking Army officers stayed on alternate watches of eight hours each, guarding a sealed room inside the hangar. None of the officers knew what he was guarding. Besides the scientists and doctors who were working inside, there had been only three visitors permitted in the sealed chamber.

The fourth visitor was just arriving. He was greeted by Brigadier General Paxton, the officer in charge of security. "Welcome to our menagerie."

"I've been looking forward to this."

"You won't be disappointed. Come this way, please."

Outside the door of the sealed room was a rack containing four white, sterile suits that completely covered the body.

"Would you please put one on?" the general asked.

"Certainly." Janus slipped into the suit. Only his face was visible through the glass mask. He put large white slippers over his shoes, and the general led him to the entrance of the sealed room. The marine guard stepped aside, and the general opened the door. "In here."

Janus entered the chamber and looked around. In the center of the room was the spaceship. On white autopsy tables at the other side lay the bodies of the two aliens. A pathologist was performing an autopsy on one of them.

General Paxton directed the visitor's attention to the spaceship.

"We're dealing here with what we believe to be a scout ship," General Paxton explained. "We're sure it has some way of communicating directly with the mother ship."

The two men moved closer to examine the spacecraft. It was approximately thirty-five feet in diameter. The interior was shaped like a pearl, had an expandable ceiling, and contained three couches that resembled recliner chairs. The walls were covered with panels containing vibrating metal disks.

"There's a lot here we haven't been able to figure out yet," General Paxton admitted. "But what we've already learned is amazing." He pointed to an array of equipment in small panels. "There's an integrated wide-field-of-view optical system, what appears to be a life-scan system, a communication system with voice-synthesis capability, and a navigational system that, frankly, has us stumped. We think it works on some kind of electromagnetic pulse."

"Any weapons aboard?" Janus asked.

General Paxton spread out his hands in a gesture of defeat. "We're not sure. There's a lot of hardware here we don't begin to understand."

"What is its source of energy?"

"Our best guess is that it uses monoatomic hydrogen in a closed loop so that its waste product, water, can be continuously recycled into hydrogen for power. With all that perpetual energy, it has a free ride in interplanetary space. It may be years before we solve all the secrets here. And there's something else that's puzzling. The bodies of the two aliens were strapped into their couches. But the indentations in the third couch indicate that it was occupied."

"Are you saying," Janus asked slowly, "that one may be missing?"

"It certainly looks that way."

Janus stood there a moment frowning. "Let's have a look at our trespassers."

The two men walked over to the tables where the two aliens lay. Janus stood there staring at the strange figures. It was incredible that things so foreign to humanity could exist as sentient beings. The foreheads of the aliens were larger than he had expected. The creatures were completely bald, with no eyelids or eyebrows. The eyes resembled Ping-Pong balls.

The doctor performing the autopsy looked up as the men approached. "It's fascinating," he said. "A hand has been severed from one of the aliens. There's no sign of blood, but there are what appear to be veins that contain a green liquid. Most of it has drained out."

"A green liquid?" Janus asked.

"Yes." The doctor hesitated. "We believe these creatures are a form of vegetable life."

"A thinking vegetable? Are you serious?"

"Watch this." The doctor picked up a watering can and sprinkled water over the arm of the alien with a missing hand. For a moment, nothing happened. And then suddenly, at the end of the arm, green matter oozed out and slowly began to form a hand.

The two men stared, shocked. "Jesus! Are these things dead or not?"

"That's an interesting question. These two figures are not alive, in the human sense, but neither do they fit our definition of death. I would say they're dormant."

Janus was still staring at the newly formed hand.

"Many plants show various forms of intelligence."

"Intelligence?"

"Oh, yes. There are plants that disguise themselves, protect themselves. At this moment, we're doing some amazing experiments on plant life."

Janus said, "I would like to see those experiments."

"Certainly. I'll be happy to arrange it."

The huge greenhouse laboratory was in a complex of government buildings thirty miles outside of Washington, D.C. Hanging on the wall was an inscription that read:

> The maples and ferns are still uncorrupt,
> Yet, no doubt, when they come to consciousness,
> They too, will curse and swear.
>
> —Ralph Waldo Emerson
> *Nature,* 1836

Professor Rachman, who was in charge of the complex, was an earnest gnome of a man, filled with enthusiasm for his profession. "It was Charles Darwin who was the first to perceive the ability of plants to think. Luther Burbank followed up by communicating with them."

"You really believe that is possible?"

"We know it is. George Washington Carver communed with plants, and they gave him hundreds of new products. Carver said, 'When I touch a flower, I am touching Infinity. Flowers existed long before there were human beings on this earth, and they will continue to exist for millions of years after. Through the flower, I talk to Infinity . . .' "

Janus looked around the enormous greenhouse they were standing in. It was filled with plants and exotic flowers that rainbowed the room. The mixture of perfumes was overpowering.

"Everything in this room is alive," Professor Rachman said. "These plants can feel love, hate, pain, excitement . . . just as animals do. Sir Jagadis Chandra Bose proved that they respond to a tone of voice."

"How does one prove something like that?" Janus asked.

"I will be happy to demonstrate." Rachman walked over to a table covered with plants. Beside the table was a polygraph machine. Rachman lifted one of the electrodes and attached it to a plant. The needle on the dial of the polygraph was at rest. "Watch," he said.

He leaned closer to the plant and whispered, "I think you are very beautiful. You are more beautiful than all the other plants here. . . ."

Janus watched the needle move ever so slightly.

Suddenly, Professor Rachman screamed at the plant, "You are ugly! You are going to die! Do you hear me? You are going to die!"

The needle began to quiver, then it moved sharply upward.

"My God," Janus said. "I can't believe it."

"What you see," Rachman said, "is the equivalent of a human being screaming. National magazines have published articles about these experiments. One of the most interesting was a blind experiment conducted by six students. One of them, unknown to the others, was chosen to walk into a room with two plants, one of them wired to a polygraph. He completely destroyed the other plant. Later, one by one, the students were sent into the room to pass by the plants. When the innocent students walked in, the polygraph registered nothing. But the moment the guilty one appeared, the needle on the polygraph shot up."

"That's incredible."

"But true. We've also learned that plants respond to different kinds of music."

"*Different* kinds?"

"Yes. They did an experiment at Temple Buell College in Denver where healthy flowers were put in three separate glass cases. Acid rock was piped into one, soft East Indian sitar music was piped into the second, and the third had no music. A CBS camera crew recorded the experiment using time-lapse photography. At the end of two weeks, the flowers exposed to the rock music were dead, the group with no music was growing normally, and the ones that heard the sitar music had turned into beautiful blooms, with flowers and stems reaching toward the source of the sound. Walter Cronkite ran the film on his news show. If you wish to check it, it was on October 26, 1970."

"Are you saying plants have an intelligence?"

"They breathe, and eat, and reproduce. They can feel pain, and they can utilize defenses against their enemies. For example, terpenes are used by certain plants to poison the soil around them and to discourage competitors. Other plants exude alkaloids to make them unpalatable to insects. We've proved that plants communicate with one another by pheromones."

"Yes. I've heard of that," Janus said.

"Some plants are meat eaters. The venus flytrap, for example. Certain orchids look and smell like female bees, to decoy male bees. Others resemble female wasps to attract the males to visit them and pick up pollen. Another type of orchid has an aroma like rotting meat to coax carrion flies in the neighborhood to come to them."

Janus was listening to every word.

"The pink lady's-slipper has a hinged upper lip that closes when a bee lands, and traps it. The only escape is through a narrow passageway out the rear, and as the bee fights its way to freedom, it picks up a cap of pollen. There are five thousand flowering plants that grow in the Northeast, and each species has its own characteristics. There is no doubt about it. It's been proven over and over that living plants have an intelligence."

Janus was thinking: *And the missing alien is at large somewhere.*

Chapter Eleven

Day Three
Bern, Switzerland
Wednesday, October 17

Bern was one of Robert's favorite cities. It was an elegant town, filled with lovely monuments and beautiful old stone buildings dating back to the eighteenth century. It was the capital of Switzerland and one of its most prosperous cities, and Robert wondered whether the fact that the streetcars were green had anything to do with the color of money. He had found that the Berners were more easygoing than the citizens from other parts of Switzerland. They moved more deliberately, spoke more slowly, and were generally calmer. He had worked in Bern several times in the past with the Swiss Secret Service, operating out of their headquarters at Waisenhausplatz. He had friends there who could have been helpful, but his instructions were clear. Puzzling, but clear.

It took fifteen phone calls for Robert to locate the garage that towed the photographer's car. It was a small garage located on Friboursgstrasse, and the mechanic, Fritz Mandel, was also the owner. Mandel appeared to be in his late forties, with a gaunt, acne-pitted face, a thin body, and an enormous beer belly. He was working down in the pit of the grease rack when Robert arrived.

"Good afternoon," Robert called.

Mandel looked up. "*Guten Tag*. What can I do for you?"

"I'm interested in a car you towed in Sunday."

"Just a minute till I finish this up."

Ten minutes later, Mandel climbed out of the pit and wiped his oily hands on a filthy cloth.

"You're the one who called this morning. Was there some complaint about that tow job?" Mandel asked. "I'm not responsible for—"

"No," Robert reassured him. "Not at all. I'm conducting a survey, and I'm interested in the driver of the car."

"Come into the office."

The two men went into the small office, and Mandel opened a file cabinet. "Last Sunday, you said?"

"That's right."

Mandel took out a card. "*Ja*. That was the *Arschficker* who took our picture in front of that UFO."

Robert's palms felt suddenly moist. "You saw the UFO?"

"*Ja*. I almost *brachte aus*."

"Can you describe it?"

Mandel shuddered. "It—it seemed alive."

"I beg your pardon?"

"I mean . . . there was a kind of light around it. It kept changing colors. It looked blue . . . then green . . . I don't know. It's hard to describe. And there were these little creatures inside. Not human, but—" He broke off.

"How many?"

"Two."

"Were they alive?"

"They looked dead to me." He mopped his brow. "I'm glad you believe me. I tried to tell my friends, and they laughed at me. Even my wife thought I had been drinking. But I know what I saw."

"About the car you towed . . ." Robert said.

"*Ja*. The Renault. It had an oil leak, and the bearings burned out. The tow job cost a hundred and twenty-five francs. I charge double on Sundays."

"Did the driver pay by check or credit card?"

"I don't take checks, and I don't take no credit cards. He paid in cash."

"Swiss francs?"

"Pounds."

"Are you sure?"

"Yes. I remember I had to check the rate of exchange."

"Mr. Mandel, do you happen to have a record of the license number of the car?"

"Of course." Mandel said. He glanced down at the card. "It was a rental. Avis. He rented it in Geneva."

"Would you mind giving me that license number?"

"Sure, why not?" He wrote the number down on a piece of paper and handed it to Robert. "What is this all about, anyway? The UFO thing?"

"No," Robert said, in his sincerest voice. He took out his wallet and pulled out an identification card. "I'm with the IAC, the International Auto Club. My company is doing a survey on tow trucks."

"Oh."

Robert walked out of the garage and thought dazedly, *It looks like we have a fucking UFO with two dead aliens on our hands.* Then why had General Hilliard lied to him when he knew Robert would discover that it was a flying saucer that had crashed?

There could only be one explanation, and Robert felt a sudden, cold chill.

Chapter Twelve

The huge mothership floated noiselessly through dark space, seemingly motionless, traveling at twenty-two thousand miles an hour in exact synchronization with the orbit of the earth. The six aliens aboard were studying the three-dimensional field-of-view optical screen that covered one wall of the spaceship. On the monitor, as the planet Earth rotated, they watched holographic pictures of what lay below while an electronic spectrograph analyzed the chemical components of the images that appeared. The atmosphere of the land masses they overflew was heavily polluted. Huge factories befouled the air with thick, black, poisonous gases while unbiodegradable refuse was dumped into landfills and into the seas.

The aliens looked down at the oceans, once pristine and blue, now black with oil and brown with scum. The coral of the Great Barrier Reef was turning bleach-white, and fish were dying by the billions. Where trees had been stripped in the Amazon rain forest, there was a huge, barren crater. The instruments on the spaceship indicated that the earth's temperature had risen since their last exploration three years earlier. They could see wars being waged on the planet below, which spewed new poisons into the atmosphere.

The aliens communicated by mental telepathy.

Nothing has changed with the earthlings.

It is a pity. They have learned nothing.

We will teach them.

Have you tried to reach the others?

Yes. Something is wrong. There is no reply.

You must keep trying. We must find the ship.

On earth, thousands of feet below the spaceship's orbit, Robert placed a call from a secure phone to General Hilliard. He came on the line almost immediately.

"Good afternoon, Commander. Do you have anything to report?"

Yes. I would like to report that you are a lying sonofabitch. "About that weather balloon, General . . . it seems to have turned out to be a UFO." He waited.

"Yes, I know. There were important security reasons why I couldn't tell you everything earlier."

Bureaucratic double-talk. There was a short silence.

General Hilliard said, "I'm going to tell you something in the strictest confidence, Commander. Our government had an encounter with extraterrestrials three years ago. They landed at one of our NATO air bases. We were able to communicate with them."

Robert felt his heart begin to beat faster. "What—what did they say?"

"That they intended to destroy us."

He felt a shock go through him. *"Destroy us?"*

"Exactly. They said they were coming back to take over this planet and make slaves of us, and that there is nothing we can do to prevent them. Not yet. But we're working on ways to stop them. That's why it's imperative that we avoid a public panic so we can buy time. I think you can understand now why it's so important that the witnesses are warned not to discuss what they saw. If word of the Idents, as we refer to them, leaked out, it would be a worldwide disaster."

"You don't think it would be better to prepare people and—?"

"Commander, in 1938, a young actor named Orson Welles broadcast a radio play called 'War of the Worlds' about aliens invading the earth. Within minutes there was panic in cities all over America. A hysterical population tried to flee from the imaginary invaders. The telephone lines were jammed, the highways were clogged. People were killed. There was total chaos. No, we have to be prepared for the aliens before we go public with this. We want you to find those witnesses for their own protection, so we can keep this under control."

Robert found that he was perspiring. "Yes. I—I understand."

"Good. I gather you've talked to one of the witnesses?"

"I've found two of them."

"Their names?"

"Hans Beckerman—he was the driver of the tour bus. He lives in Kappel. . . ."

"And the second?"

"Fritz Mandel. He owns his own garage in Bern. He was the mechanic who towed the car of a third witness."

"The name of that witness?"

"I don't have it yet. I'm working on it. Would you like me to speak with them about not discussing this UFO business with anyone?"

"Negative. Your assignment is simply to locate the witnesses. After that we'll let their respective governments deal with them. Have you learned how many witnesses there are?"

"Yes. Seven passengers plus the driver, the mechanic, and a passing motorist."

"You must locate them all. Each and every one of the ten witnesses who saw the crash. Understood?"

"Yes, General."

Robert replaced the receiver, his mind in a whirl. UFOs were real. The aliens were enemies. It was a horrifying thought.

Suddenly, the uneasy feeling Robert had had earlier returned in full force. General Hilliard had given him this assignment, but they had not told him everything. What else were they holding back?

The Avis rental-car company is located at 44 Rue de Lausanne in the heart of Geneva. Robert stormed into the office and approached a woman behind the desk.

"May I help you?"

Robert slammed down the piece of paper with the license number of the Renault written on it. "You rented this car out last week. I want the name of the person who rented it." His voice was angry.

The clerk drew back. "I'm sorry, we are not permitted to give out that information."

"Well, that's just too bad," Robert retorted, "because in that case, I'm going to have to sue your company for a great deal of money."

"I do not understand. What is the problem?"

"I'll tell you what the problem is, lady. Last Sunday this car ran into mine on the highway and did a hell of a lot of damage. I managed to get his license number, but the man drove away before I could stop him."

"I see." The clerk studied Robert a moment. "Excuse me, please." She disappeared into a back room. In a few minutes when she returned, she was carrying a file. "According to our records, there was a problem with the engine of the car, but there was no report of any accident."

"Well, I'm reporting it now. And I'm holding your company responsible for this. You're going to have to pay to have my car repaired. It's a brand-new Porsche, and it's going to cost you a fortune. . . ."

"I'm very sorry, sir, but since the accident was not reported, we cannot take any responsibility for it."

"Look," Robert said in a more reasonable tone of voice, "I want to be fair. I don't want to hold your company responsible. All I want to do is have that man pay for the damage he did to my car. It was a hit-and-run. I may even have to bring the police into this. If you give me the man's name and address, I can talk directly to him, and we can settle it between us and leave your company out of it. Is that fair enough?"

The clerk stood there, making up her mind. "Yes. We would much prefer that." She looked down at the file in her hand. "The name of the person who rented the car is Leslie Mothershed."

"And his address?"

"Two thirteen A Grove Road, Whitechapel, London, East Three." She looked up. "You are certain our company will not be involved in any litigation?"

"You have my word on it," Robert assured her. "This is a private matter between Leslie Mothershed and me."

Commander Robert Bellamy was on the next Swissair flight to London.

He sat in the dark alone, concentrating, meticulously going over every phase of the plan, making certain that there were no loopholes, that nothing could go wrong. His thoughts were interrupted by the soft buzz of the telephone.

"Janus here."

"Janus. General Hilliard."

"Proceed."

"Commander Bellamy has located the first two witnesses."

"Very good. Have it attended to immediately."

"Yes, sir."

"Where is the commander now?"

"On his way to London. He should have number three confirmed shortly."

"I will alert the committee as to his progress. Continue to keep me informed. The condition of this operation must remain Nova Red."

"Understood, sir. I would suggest—"

The line was dead.

FLASH MESSAGE

TOP SECRET ULTRA

NSA TO DEPUTY DIRECTOR BUNDESANWALTSCHAFT

EYES ONLY

COPY ONE OF (ONE) COPIES

SUBJECT: OPERATION DOOMSDAY

1. HANS BECKERMAN—KAPPEL

2. FRITZ MANDEL—BERN

END OF MESSAGE

Chapter Thirteen

At midnight in a small farmhouse fifteen miles from Uetendorf, the Lagenfeld family was disturbed by a series of strange events. The older child was awakened by a shimmering yellow light shining through his bedroom window. When he got up to investigate, the light had disappeared.

In the yard, Tozzi, their German shepherd, began barking furiously, awakening old man Lagenfeld. Reluctantly, the farmer got out of bed to quiet the animal, and when he stepped outside he heard the sound of frightened sheep crashing against their pen, trying to escape. As Lagenfeld passed the trough, which had been filled to the brim by the recent rainfall, he noticed that it was bone dry.

Tozzi came running to his side, whimpering. Lagenfeld absently patted the animal on the head. "It's all right, boy. It's all right."

And at that moment, every light in the house went

out. When the farmer returned to the house and picked up the telephone to call the power company, the phone was dead.

If the lights had remained on a moment longer, the farmer might have seen a strangely beautiful woman walk out of his barnyard and into the field beyond.

Chapter Fourteen

The Bundesanwaltschaft—Geneva
1300 Hours

The government minister seated in the inner sanctum of the headquarters of the Swiss intelligence agency watched the deputy director finish reading the message. He put the message in a folder marked Top Secret, placed the folder in the desk drawer, and locked the drawer.

"Hans Beckerman *und* Fritz Mandel."

"Ja."

"No problem, *Herr* Minister. It shall be taken care of."

"Gut."

"Wann?"

"*Sofort.* Immediately."

The following morning on his way to work, Hans Beckerman's ulcers were bothering him. *I should have pushed that reporter fellow to pay me for that thing I found on the ground. These magazines are all rich. I probably could have gotten a few hundred marks. Then I could have gone to a decent doctor and had my ulcers taken care of.*

He was driving past Turler Lake, when ahead of him, at the side of the highway, he saw a woman waving, trying to get a lift. Beckerman slowed down to get a better look at her. She was young and attractive. Hans pulled over to the side of the road. The woman approached the car.

"Guten Tag," Beckerman said. "Can I help you?" She was even prettier close up.

"Danke." She had a Swiss accent. "I had a fight with my boyfriend, and he dropped me here in the middle of nowhere."

"Tsk, tsk. That's terrible."

"Would you mind giving me a lift into Zurich?"

"Not at all. Get in, get in."

The hitchhiker opened the door and climbed in beside him. "This is very kind of you," she said. "My name is Karen."

"Hans." He started driving.

"I don't know what I would have done if you hadn't come along, Hans."

"Oh, I'm sure someone else would have picked up a pretty woman like you."

She moved closer to him. "But I'll bet he wouldn't have been as good looking as you."

He glanced over at her. *"Ja?"*

"I think you are very handsome."

He smiled. "You should tell that to my wife."

"Oh, you're married." She sounded disappointed. "Why is it all the wonderful men are married? You look very intelligent, too."

He sat up straighter.

"To tell you the truth, I'm sorry I ever got involved with my boyfriend." She shifted around in her seat, and her skirt climbed up her thigh. He tried not to look. "I like older, mature men, Hans. I think they're much more sexy than young men." She snuggled up against him. "Do you like sex, Hans?"

He cleared his throat. "Do *I*—? Well, you know . . . I'm a man. . . ."

"I can see that," she said. She stroked his thigh. "Can I tell you something? That fight with my boyfriend made me very horny. Would you like me to make love to you?"

He could not believe his luck. She was a beauty, and from what he could see, she had a great body. He swallowed. "I would, but I'm on my way to work and—"

"It will only take a few minutes." She smiled. "There's a side road up ahead that leads into the woods. Why don't we stop there?"

He could feel himself getting excited. *Sicher. Wait until I tell the boys at the office about this! They'll never believe it.*

"Sure. Why not?" Hans turned the car off the highway and took the little dirt road that led into a grove where they could not be seen by passing motorists.

She slowly ran her hand up his thigh. "*Mein Gott,* you have strong legs."

"I was a runner when I was younger," Beckerman boasted.

"Let's get your trousers off." She undid his belt and helped him slide his pants down. He was already tumescent.

"Ach! Ein grosser!" She began to stroke him.

He moaned, *"Leck mich doch am Schwanz."*

"You like to be kissed down there?"

"Ja." His wife never did that for him.

"*Gut*. Now just relax."

Beckerman sighed and closed his eyes. Her soft hands were caressing his balls. He felt the sharp sting of a needle in his thigh, and his eyes flew open. *"Wie—?"*

His body stiffened, and his eyes bulged out. He was choking, unable to breathe. The woman watched as Beckerman slumped over the steering wheel. She got out of the car and slid his body into the passenger seat, then got behind the wheel of the car and drove back down the dirt road onto the highway. At the edge of the steep mountain road, she waited until the road was clear, then opened the door, stepped on the gas pedal, and as the car started to move, she jumped. She stood there watching the car tumble down the steep cliff. Five minutes later, a black limousine pulled up beside her.

"Irgendwelche Problem?"

"Keins."

Fritz Mandel was in his office ready to close the garage when two men approached.

"I'm sorry," he said, "I'm closing. I can't—"

One of the men interrupted. "Our car is stuck down the highway. *Kaputt!* We need a tow."

"My wife is waiting for me. We are having company tonight. I can give you the name of another—"

"It's worth two hundred dollars to us. We're in a hurry."

"Two hundred dollars?"

"Yes. And our car is in pretty bad shape. We'd like you to do some work on it. That would probably come to another two, three hundred."

Mandel was becoming interested. *"Ja?"*

"It's a Rolls," one of the men said. "Let's see the kind

of equipment you have here." They walked into the service area and stood at the edge of the pit. "That's pretty good equipment."

"Yes, sir," Mandel said proudly. "The very best."

The stranger took out a wallet. "Here. I can give you some money in advance." He removed some bills and handed them to Mandel. As he did so, the wallet slipped out of his hands and fell down into the pit. *"Verflucht!"*

"Don't worry," Mandel said. "I'll get it."

He climbed down into the pit. As he did so, one of the men walked over to the control button that operated the raised hydraulic lift and pressed it. The lift started to descend.

Mandel looked up. *"Be careful! What are you doing?"*

He started to scramble up the side. As his fingers touched the ledge, the second man slammed his foot down on Mandel's hand, smashing it, and Mandel dropped back down into the pit, shrieking. The heavy hydraulic lift was inexorably descending on him.

"Let me out of here!" he cried. *"Hilfe!"*

The lift caught him on his shoulder and began pressing him down into the cement floor. A few minutes later, when the terrible screams had stopped, one of the men pressed the button that raised the lift. His companion went down into the pit and retrieved his wallet, careful not to get blood on his clothes. The two men returned to their car and drove off into the quiet night.

FLASH MESSAGE

TOP SECRET ULTRA

ESPIONAGE ABTEILUNG TO DEPUTY DIRECTOR NSA

EYES ONLY

COPY ONE OF (ONE) COPIES

SUBJECT: OPERATION DOOMSDAY

1. HANS BECKERMAN—TERMINATED

2. FRITZ MANDEL—TERMINATED

END OF MESSAGE

Ottawa, Canada
2400 Hours

Janus was addressing the group of twelve.

"Satisfactory progress is being made. Two of the witnesses have already been silenced. Commander Bellamy is on the trail of a third."

"Has there been a breakthrough yet on SDI?" The Italian. *Impetuous. Volatile.*

"Not yet, but we're confident that the Star Wars technology will be up and functioning very soon."

"We must do everything possible to hurry it. If it is a question of money—" The Saudi. *Enigmatic. Withdrawn.*

"No. There's just a bit more testing to do."

"When is the next test taking place?" The Australian. *Hearty. Clever.*

"In one week. We will meet here again in forty-eight hours."

Chapter Fifteen

Day Four—London
Thursday, October 18

Leslie Mothershed's role model was Robin Leach. An avid viewer of "Lifestyles of the Rich and Famous," Mothershed carefully studied the way Robin Leach's guests walked and talked and dressed because he knew that one day he would appear on that program. From the time he was a small boy, he had felt that he was destined to be *somebody,* to be rich and famous.

"You're very special," his mother would tell him. "My baby is going to be known all over the world."

The young boy would go to sleep with that sentence ringing in his ears until he truly believed it. As Mothershed grew older, he became aware that he had a problem: He had no idea exactly *how* he was going to become rich and famous. For a period of time, he toyed with the notion of being a movie star, but he was inordinately shy. He briefly contemplated becoming a soccer star, but he was not athletic. He thought about being a famous scientist, or a great lawyer, commanding tremendous fees. His school grades, unfortunately, were mediocre, and he dropped out of school without being any closer to fame. Life was simply not fair. He was physically unprepossessing, thin, with a pale, sickly complexion, and he was short, exactly five feet five and a half inches. Mothershed always stressed the extra half inch. He consoled himself with the fact that many famous men were short: Dudley Moore, Dustin Hoffman, Peter Falk. . . .

The only profession that really interested Leslie Mothershed was photography. Taking photographs was so ridiculously simple. Anyone could do it. One simply pressed a button. His mother had bought him a camera for his sixth birthday and had been wildly extravagant in her praise of the pictures he had taken. By the time he was in his teens, Mothershed had become convinced that he was a brilliant photographer. He told himself that he was every bit as good as Ansel Adams, Richard Avedon, or Margaret Bourke-White. With a loan from his mother, Leslie Mothershed set up his own photography business in his Whitechapel flat.

"Start small," his mother told him, "but think big," and that is exactly what Leslie Mothershed did. He started very small and thought very big, but unfortunately, he had no talent for photography. He photographed parades and animals and flowers, and confidently sent his pictures off to newspapers and magazines, and they were always returned. Mothershed consoled himself with the thought of all the geniuses who had been rejected before their ability was recognized. He considered himself a martyr to philistinism.

And then, out of the blue, his big opportunity had come. His mother's cousin, who worked for the British publishing firm of HarperCollins, had confided to Mothershed that they were planning to commission a coffee-table book on Switzerland.

"They haven't selected the photographer yet, Leslie, so if you get yourself over to Switzerland right away and bring back some great pictures, the book could be yours."

Leslie Mothershed hurriedly packed up his cameras and headed for Switzerland. He knew—he really knew—that this was the break he had been looking for. At last the idiots were going to recognize his talents. He rented a car in Geneva and traveled around the country taking pictures of Swiss chalets, waterfalls, and snow-capped peaks. He photographed sunrises and sunsets and farmers working in the fields. And then, in the middle of all that, fate had stepped in and changed his life. He was on his way to Bern when his motor failed. He pulled over to the side of the highway, furious. *Why me?* Mothershed moaned. *Why do these things always happen to me?* He sat there fuming, thinking about the precious time lost and how expensive it would be to have his car towed. Fifteen kilometers behind him was the village of Thun. *I'll get a tow from there,* Mothershed thought. *That shouldn't cost too much.*

He flagged down a passing gasoline truck. "I need a tow truck," Mothershed explained. "Could you stop at a garage in Thun and have them come and get me?"

The truck driver shook his head. "It's Sunday, mister. The closest garage that's open will be in Bern."

"Bern? That's fifty kilometers from here. It will cost me a fortune."

The truck driver grinned. "*Ja*. There they get you by the Sundays." He started to drive on.

"Wait." It was difficult to get the words out. "I'll—I'll pay for a tow truck from Bern."

"*Gut.* I will have them send someone out."

Leslie Mothershed sat cursing in his disabled car. *All I needed was this,* he thought bitterly. He had already spent much too much money on film, and now he would have to pay some bloody thief to tow him to a garage. It took almost two interminable hours for the tow truck to arrive. As the mechanic started to attach the cable from his truck to the car, there was a flash of light from across the highway, followed by a loud explosion, and Mothershed looked up to see what appeared to be a bright object falling out of the sky. The only other traffic on the highway was a tour bus that had pulled to a stop in back of his car. The passengers from the bus were hurrying toward the scene of the crash. Mothershed hesitated, torn between his curiosity and his desire to move on. He turned and followed the bus passengers across the highway. When he reached the scene of the accident, he stood there transfixed. *Holy God,* he thought. *It's unreal.* He was staring at a flying saucer. Leslie Mothershed had heard about flying saucers and had read about them, but he had never believed they existed. He gaped at it, awed by the eerie spectacle. The shell had ripped open, and he could see two bodies inside, small, with large skulls, sunken eyes, no ears and almost no chins, and they seemed to be wearing some kind of silver metallic suits.

The group from the tour bus was standing around him staring in horrified silence. The man next to him fainted. Another man turned away and vomited. An elderly priest was clutching his beads and mumbling incoherently.

"My God," someone said. "It's a flying saucer!"

And that was when Mothershed had his epiphany. A miracle had fallen into his lap. He—Leslie Mothershed—was on the spot with his cameras to photograph the story of the century! There was not a magazine or newspaper in the world that would reject the photographs he was about to take. A coffee-table book about Switzerland? He almost laughed aloud at the idea. He was about to astonish the whole world. All the television talk shows would be begging from him, but he would do Robin Leach's show first. He would sell his photographs to the *London Times,* the *Sun,* the *Mail,* the *Mirror*—to all the English newspapers, and to the foreign papers and magazines—*Le Figaro* and *Paris-Match, Oggi* and *Der Tag. Time* and *USA Today*. The press everywhere would be pleading with him for his photographs. Japan and South America and Russia and China and—there was no end to it. Mothershed's heart was fluttering with excitement. *I won't give anyone an exclusive. Each one will have to pay me individually. I'll start at a hundred thousand pounds a picture, maybe two hundred thousand. And I'll sell them over and over again.* He began feverishly adding up the money he was going to make.

Leslie Mothershed was so busy adding up his fortune that he almost forgot to take the pictures. "Oh, my God! Excuse me," he said, to no one in particular, and raced back across the highway to get his camera equipment.

The mechanic had finished hoisting the front end of the disabled vehicle in the air, ready to tow it away.

"What's going on over there?" he asked.

Mothershed was busy grabbing his camera equipment. "Come and see for yourself."

The two men moved across the highway to the wooded area, and Mothershed pushed his way through the circle of tourists.

"Excuse me," he said. "Excuse me."

He adjusted the focus on his camera and started snapping pictures of the UFO and its eerie passengers. He took pictures in black and white and in color. As the shutter clicked each time, Mothershed thought, *A million pounds . . . another million pounds . . . another million pounds.*

The priest was crossing himself and saying, "It's the face of Satan."

Satan, hell, Mothershed thought exultantly. *It's the face of money. These will be the first pictures that prove that flying saucers really exist.* And then, suddenly, a terrifying thought occurred to him. *What if the magazines think these pictures are fake? There have been a lot of faked photographs of UFOs.* His euphoria vanished. *What if they don't believe me?* And that was when Leslie Mothershed had his second inspiration.

There were nine witnesses gathered around him. Without knowing it, they were about to lend authenticity to his discovery.

Mothershed turned to face the group. "Ladies and gentlemen," he called out. "If you would all like to have your photographs taken here, just line up and I'll be happy to send each of you a print, free."

There were excited exclamations. Within moments the passengers from the tour bus, except for the priest, were standing beside the remains of the UFO.

He was reluctant. "I can't," he said. "It's evil!"

Mothershed needed the priest. He would make the most convincing witness of them all.

"That's just the point," Mothershed said persuasively. "Don't you see? This will be your testimony about the existence of evil spirits."

And the priest was finally persuaded.

"Spread out a little," Mothershed ordered, "so we can see the flying saucer."

The witnesses shifted their positions.

"That's it. Very good. Excellent. Hold still, now."

He snapped half a dozen more pictures and took out a pencil and paper.

"If you'll write down your names and addresses, I'll see to it that each of you gets a print."

He had no intention of sending any prints. All he wanted was corroborating witnesses. *Let the bloody newspapers and magazines try to get around that!*

And then, suddenly, he noticed that several people in the group had cameras. He couldn't allow any other photographs but his! Only photos that had the credit "Photograph by Leslie Mothershed" could exist.

"Excuse me," he said to the group. "Those of you who have cameras, if you'll pass them to me, I'll take a few pictures of you so that you'll have some taken with your own cameras."

The cameras were quickly handed to Leslie Mothershed. As he knelt to frame the first shot, no one noticed that Mothershed clicked open the film compartment with his thumb and held it ajar. *There, a little bit of nice bright sunlight will help these photographs no end. Too bad, my friends, but only professionals are allowed to capture historic moments.*

Ten minutes later, Mothershed had all their names and addresses. He took one last look at the flying saucer and thought exultantly, *Mother was right. I am going to be rich and famous.*

He couldn't wait to return to England to develop his precious photographs.

"What the hell is going on?"

The police stations in the Uetendorf area had been inundated with telephone calls all evening.

"Someone is prowling around my house. . . ."

"There are strange lights outside. . . ."

"My livestock is going crazy. There must be wolves around. . . ."

"Someone drained my watering trough. . . ."

And the most inexplicable telephone call of all: "Chief, you'd better send a lot of tow trucks out to the main highway right away. It's a nightmare. All traffic has stopped."

"What? Why?"

"No one knows. The car engines just suddenly went dead."

It was a night they would never forget.

Chapter Sixteen

How long is this assignment going to take? Robert wondered, as he strapped himself into his first-class seat on the Swissair flight. As the plane rushed down the runway, its huge Rolls-Royce engines hungrily swallowing the night air, Robert relaxed and closed his eyes. *Was it really just a few years ago that I took this same flight with Susan to London? No. It was more like a lifetime ago.*

The plane touched down at Heathrow at 6:29 P.M., on schedule. Robert made his way out of the maze and took a taxi into the sprawling city. He passed a hundred familiar landmarks, and he could hear Susan's voice commenting excitedly on them. In those golden days, it had never mattered where they were. It was simply enough that they were together. They brought their own happiness with them, their own special excitement in each other. Theirs was the marriage that would have a happy ending.

Almost.

Their problems had started innocently enough with an overseas call from Admiral Whittaker while Robert and Susan were traveling in Thailand. It had been six months since Robert had been discharged from the Navy, and he had not talked to the admiral in all that time. The call, reaching them at the Oriental Hotel in Bangkok, was a surprise.

"Robert? Admiral Whittaker."

"Admiral! It's good to hear your voice."

"It hasn't been easy tracking you down. What have you been up to?"

"Not very much. Just taking it easy. Having a long honeymoon."

"How is Susan? It *is* Susan, isn't it?"

"Yes. She's fine, thank you."

"How soon can you get back to Washington?"

"I beg your pardon?"

"It hasn't been announced yet, but I've been given a new assignment, Robert. They've made me deputy director of 17th District Naval Intelligence. I'd like you to come aboard."

Robert was taken aback. "Naval Intelligence? Admiral, I don't know anything about—"

"You can learn. You would be doing an important service for your country, Robert. Will you come and discuss it with me?"

"Well—"

"Good. I'll expect you in my office Monday at oh nine hundred. Say hello to Susan for me."

Robert repeated the conversation to Susan.

"Naval Intelligence? That sounds so exciting."

"Maybe," Robert said doubtfully. "I have no idea what's involved."

"You must find out."

He studied her for a moment. "You want me to take it, don't you?"

She put her arms around him. "I want you to do whatever you want to do. I think you're ready to go back to work. I've noticed in the last few weeks how restless you've become."

"I think you're trying to get rid of me," Robert teased. "The honeymoon is over."

Susan put her lips close to his. "Never. Did I ever tell you how crazy I am about you, sailor? Let me show you. . . ."

Thinking about it later—too late—Robert decided that that was the beginning of the end of their marriage. The offer had seemed wonderful at the time, and he had gone back to Washington to meet with Admiral Whittaker.

"This job requires brains, courage, and initiative, Robert. You have all three. Our country has become a target for every little tinhorn dictatorship that can breed a terrorist group or build a chemical-weapons factory. A number of these countries are working on atomic bombs at this moment so that they can hold us at ransom. My job is to build an intelligence network to find out exactly what they're up to and to try to stop them. I want you to help me."

In the end, Robert had accepted the job with Naval Intelligence, and to his surprise, he found that he enjoyed it and had an aptitude for it. Susan found an attractive apartment in Rosslyn, Virginia, not far from where Robert worked, and busied herself furnishing it. Robert was sent to the Farm, the CIA training ground for Secret Service agents.

* * *

Located in a heavily guarded compound in the Virginia countryside, the Farm occupies twenty square miles, most of it covered in tall pine forest, with the central buildings in a ten-acre clearing two miles from the front gate. Dirt roads branch off through the woods, with locked swinging barricades, and No Entry signs posted. At a small airfield, unmarked aircraft arrive and depart several times a day. The Farm has a deceptively bucolic setting, with leafy trees, deer running in the fields, and small buildings innocently scattered around the extensive grounds. Inside the compound, however, it is a different world.

Robert had expected to train with other Navy personnel, but to his surprise, the students were a mixture of CIA inductees, marines, and Army, Navy, and Air Force personnel. Each student was assigned a number and housed in a dormitorylike room in one of several Spartan two-story brick buildings. At the Bachelor Officer Quarters, where Robert stayed, each man had his own room, and shared the bathroom with another. The mess hall was across the road from the BOQ cluster.

On the day Robert arrived, he was escorted to an auditorium with thirty other newcomers. A tall, powerfully built black colonel in Air Force uniform addressed the group. He appeared to be in his middle fifties, and he gave the impression of quick, cold intelligence. He spoke clearly and crisply with no wasted words.

"I'm Colonel Frank Johnson. I want to welcome you here. During your stay you will use only your first names. From this moment on, your lives will be a closed book. You've all been sworn to secrecy. I would advise you to take that oath very, very seriously. You are *never* to discuss your work with anyone—your wives, your family, your friends. You've been selected to come here because you have special qualifications. There's a lot of hard work ahead of you to develop those qualifications, and not all of you are going to make it. You're going to be involved in things you have never even heard of before. I cannot stress enough the importance of the work you will be doing when you finish here. It has become fashionable in certain liberal circles to attack our intelligence services, whether it's the CIA, the Army, the Navy or the Air Force, but I can assure you, gentlemen, that without dedicated people like yourselves, this country would be in one hell of a lot of trouble. It's going to be your job to help prevent that. Those of you who do pass will become case officers. To put it bluntly, a case officer is a spy. He works under cover.

"While you're here, you're going to get the best training in the world. You'll be trained in surveillance and countersurveillance. You'll have courses in radio communications, encoding, and weaponry and map reading.

"You'll attend a class in interpersonal relations. You'll be taught how to build a rapport, how to draw out an individual's motivations, how to make your target feel at ease."

The class was hanging on every word.

"You'll learn how to meet and recruit an agent. You'll be trained in how to make sure meeting places are secure.

"You'll learn about 'dead drops,' how to covertly communicate with your contacts. If you're successful at what you do, you will carry out your assignments unnoticed and undetected."

Robert could feel the excitement that charged the air.

"Some of you will work under official cover. It could

be diplomatic or military. Others will work under unofficial cover as private individuals—as businessmen, archaeologists, or novelists—any profession that will give you access to the areas and types of people likely to have the information you're looking for. And now I'm going to turn you over to your instructors. Good luck."

Robert found the training fascinating. The instructors were men who had worked in the field and were experienced professionals. Robert absorbed the technical information easily. In addition to the courses Colonel Johnson had mentioned, there was a brushup course on languages and one on cryptic codes.

Colonel Johnson was an enigma to Robert. The rumor circulating about him was that he had strong connections at the White House and was involved in high-level covert activities. He would disappear from the Farm for days at a time and suddenly reappear.

An agent named Ron was conducting a class.

"There are six phases to the clandestine operational process. The first is spotting. When you know what information you need, your first challenge is to identify and target individuals who have access to that information. The second phase is assessment. Once you have spotted your target, you have to decide if he really has the information you need, and if he might be susceptible to recruitment. What motivates him? Is he happy in his job? Does he have a grudge against his boss? Is he over his head financially? If the prospect is accessible and there's a motivation that can be exploited, you move along to phase three.

"Phase three is development. You build up a relationship with a prospect. You manage to run into him as often as possible and build a rapport. The next phase is recruitment. When you think he is ready, you go to work on him psychologically. You use whatever psychological weapons you've got—revenge against his boss, money, the thrill of it. If a case officer has done his job well, the prospect usually says yes.

"So far so good. You have a spy working for you. The next step is handling him. You must protect not only yourself, but him too. You will arrange surreptitious meetings and train him in the use of microfilm and, where appropriate, clandestine radio. You will teach him how to detect surveillance, what to say if questioned, and so on.

"The last phase is disconnecting. After some period of time, perhaps your recruit will be transferred to a different job and no longer have access to the information, or maybe we will no longer need the information to which he does have access. In any case, the relationship is ended, but it's important to end it in such a way that the recruit doesn't feel he has been used and is looking for vengeance. . . ."

Colonel Johnson had been right. Not every one made it through the course. Familiar faces kept disappearing. Washed out. No one knew why. No one asked.

One day, as a group was preparing to go into Richmond for a surveillance exercise, Robert's instructor said, "We're going to see how good you are, Robert. I'm going to send someone to tail you. I want you to lose him. Do you think you can do that?"

"Yes, sir."

"Good luck."

* * *

Robert took the bus into Richmond and began strolling the streets. Within five minutes, he identified his trackers. There were two of them. One was on foot and one was in an automobile. Robert tried ducking into restaurants and shops and hurrying out back doors, but he was unable to shake them. They were too well trained. Finally, it was almost time to return to the Farm, and Robert still had not been able to get away from them. They were watching him too closely. Robert walked into a department store, and the two men took up positions where they could cover the entrances and exits. Robert took the escalator up to the Men's Clothing Department. Thirty minutes later when he came down, he was wearing a different suit, a coat and hat, and was talking to a woman and carrying a baby in his arms. He walked past his pursuers without being recognized.

He was the only one that day who had successfully eluded surveillance.

The jargon taught at the Farm was a language unto itself.

"You probably won't use all these terms," the instructor told the class, "but you had better know them. There are two different kinds of agents: an 'agent of influence' and an 'agent provocateur.' The agent of influence tries to change opinion in the country where he operates. An agent provocateur is sent to stir up trouble and create chaos. 'Biographic leverage' is CIA code for blackmail. There are also 'black-bag jobs,' which can range from bribes to burglary. Watergate was a black-bag job."

He looked around to make sure that the class was paying attention. They were spellbound.

"From time to time some of you may need a 'cobbler'—that's a man who forges passports."

Robert wondered whether he would ever use a cobbler.

"The phrase *to demote maximally* is a nasty one. It means to purge by killing. So does the word *terminate*. If you hear someone talking about the Firm, it's the nickname we use to refer to the British Secret Service. If you're asked to 'fumigate' an office, you won't be looking for termites, you'll be looking for listening devices."

The arcane expressions fascinated Robert.

" 'Ladies' is a euphemism for females sent to compromise the opposition. A 'legend' is a biography of a spy that is faked to provide him with a cover. 'Going private' means leaving the service."

The instructor scanned the class. "Any of you know what a 'lion tamer' is?"

He waited for an answer. Silence.

"When an agent is sacked, he sometimes gets upset and may make threats to reveal what he knows. A muscleman, or lion tamer, is called in to soften him up. I'm sure none of you will ever have to deal with one."

That drew nervous laughter.

"Then, there's the term *measles*. If a target dies of measles, it means he was murdered so efficiently that death appeared to be accidental or due to natural causes. One method of inducing measles is to use 'Tabun.' That's a colorless or brownish liquid compound that causes nerve paralysis when absorbed through the skin. If someone offers you a 'music box,' they're offering you a wireless transmitter. The transmitter operator is called a musician. In the future, some of you will be operating 'naked.' Don't rush to take off your clothes; it simply means that you're alone and without any assistance.

"There's one more thing I want to discuss today. Coincidence. In our work, there is no such animal. It usually spells danger. If you keep running into the same person again and again, or you keep spotting the same automobile when you're on the move, cover your ass. You're probably in trouble.

"I think that's enough for today, gentlemen. We will take up where we left off, tomorrow."

From time to time, Colonel Johnson called Robert into his office "to have a chat," as he put it. The conversations were deceptively casual, but Robert was aware of an underlying probing being carried on.

"I understand you're happily married, Robert."

"That's right."

They spent the next half hour talking about marriage, fidelity, and trust.

Another time: "Admiral Whittaker thinks of you as a son, Robert. Did you know that?"

"Yes." The pain of Edward's death was something that would never go away.

They talked about loyalty and duty and death.

"You've faced death more than once, Robert. Are you afraid to die?"

"No." *But to die for a good reason,* Robert thought. *Not senselessly.*

The meetings were frustrating to Robert because they were like looking into a trick mirror. Colonel Johnson could see him clearly, but the colonel remained invisible, an enigma cloaked in secrecy.

The course lasted sixteen weeks, and during that

time, none of the men was permitted to communicate with the outside world. Robert missed Susan desperately. It was the longest they had ever been apart. When the four months were up, Colonel Johnson called Robert into his office.

"This is goodbye. You've done an excellent job, Commander. I think you're going to find your future very interesting."

"Thank you, sir. I hope so."

"Good luck."

Colonel Johnson watched Robert leave. He sat there for five minutes without moving, then reached a decision. He walked over to the door and locked it. Then he picked up the telephone and made a call.

Susan was waiting for him. She opened the door of their apartment, wearing a sheer negligee that concealed nothing. She flew into his arms and held him close. "Hi, sailor. Want to have a good time?"

"I'm having one," Robert said happily, "just holding you."

"God, I missed you so much!" Susan drew back and said fiercely, "If anything ever happened to you, I think I would die."

"Nothing is ever going to happen to me."

"Promise?"

"Promise."

She studied him a moment, concerned. "You look so tired."

"It was a pretty intensive course," Robert admitted. He was understating it. With all the texts and manuals to study, in addition to the practical, hands-on lessons, none of the recruits had been able to sleep more than a few hours a night. There was little grumbling for a very simple reason: They were well aware that what they were learning could one day save their lives.

"I know exactly what you need," Susan decided.

Robert grinned. "I'll say." He reached for her.

"Wait. Give me five minutes. Get undressed."

He watched her walk away and thought, *How damned lucky can a man get?* He began to get undressed.

Susan returned a few minutes later. She said softly, "Umm. I like you naked."

He heard his instructor's voice, saying, *"Some of you will be operating naked. It means you're alone and without any assistance." What have I gotten into? What have I gotten Susan into?*

She led him into the bathroom. The tub was filled with warm scented water, and the room was dark except for four candles flickering on the sink.

"Welcome home, darling." She slipped out of her negligee and stepped into the bathtub. He followed her.

"Susan—"

"Don't talk. Lean back against me."

He felt her hands gently caressing his back and shoulders, and he felt the soft curves of her body against him, and he forgot how tired he was. They made love in the warm water, and when they had dried themselves, Susan said, "So much for the foreplay. Now, let's get serious."

They made love again, and later, as Robert fell asleep, holding Susan in his arms, he thought, *It will always be like this. Forever.*

Chapter Seventeen

The following Monday morning, Robert reported for his first day of duty at the 17th District Office of Naval Intelligence at the Pentagon.

Admiral Whittaker said warmly, "Welcome home, Robert. Apparently you impressed the hell out of Colonel Johnson."

Robert smiled. "He's quite impressive himself."

Over coffee, the admiral asked, "Are you ready to go to work?"

"Eager."

"Good. We have a situation in Rhodesia . . ."

Working in the Office of Naval Intelligence was even more exciting than Robert had anticipated. Each assignment was different, and Robert was given the ones classified extremely sensitive. He brought in a defector who revealed Noriega's drug-smuggling operation in Panama, exposed a mole working for Marcos in the American Consulate in Manila, and helped set up a secret listening post in Morocco. He was sent on missions to South America and to the East Indies. The only thing that disturbed him was the long separations from Susan. He hated to be away from her, and he missed her terribly. He had the excitement of his job to occupy him, but Susan had nothing. Robert's caseload kept increasing. He spent less and less time at home, and that was when the problem with Susan became serious.

Whenever Robert came home, he and Susan would run hungrily into each other's arms and make passionate love. But those times began to be further and further apart. It seemed to Susan that no sooner did Robert return from one assignment than was he sent away on another.

To make matters worse, Robert could not discuss his work with her. Susan had no idea where he went or what he was doing. She knew only that whatever he was involved in was dangerous, and she was terrified that one day he would leave and never return. She dared not ask him questions. She felt like a stranger, completely shut out of an important part of his life. Of *their* life. *I can't go on like this,* Susan decided.

When Robert returned from a four-week assignment in Central America, Susan said, "Robert, I think we had better have a talk."

"What's the problem?" Robert asked. He knew what the problem was.

"I'm frightened. We're slipping away from each other, and I don't want to lose us. I couldn't stand it."

"Susan—"

"Wait. Let me finish. Do you know how much time

we've spent together in the last four months? Less than two weeks. Whenever you come home, I feel as though you're a visitor instead of my husband."

He took Susan in his arms and held her tightly. "You know how much I love you."

She laid her head on his shoulder. "Please don't let anything happen to us."

"I won't," he promised. "I'll have a talk with Admiral Whittaker."

"When?"

"Immediately."

"The admiral will see you now, Commander."

"Thank you."

Admiral Whittaker was seated behind his desk signing papers. He looked up as Robert entered and smiled. "Welcome home, Robert, and congratulations. That was an excellent job in El Salvador."

"Thank you, sir."

"Sit down. Can I offer you some coffee?"

"No, thank you, Admiral."

"You wanted to talk to me? My secretary said it was urgent. What can I do for you?"

It was difficult to begin. "Well, sir, this is personal. I've been married less than two years, and—"

"You made a wonderful choice, Robert. Susan's a fine woman."

"Yes, I agree. The problem is that I'm away most of the time, and she's unhappy about it." He added quickly, "And she has every right to be. It isn't a normal situation."

Admiral Whittaker leaned back in his chair and said thoughtfully, "Of course what you're doing isn't a normal situation. Sometimes sacrifices have to be made."

"I know," Robert said stubbornly, "but I'm not prepared to sacrifice my marriage. It means too much to me."

The admiral studied him reflectively. "I see. What is it you're asking?"

"I was hoping that you could find some assignments for me where I'm not away from home so much. This is such a large operation, there must be a hundred things I could do closer to home."

"Closer to home."

"Yes."

The admiral said slowly, "You've certainly earned that. I don't see why something like that can't be arranged."

Robert smiled in relief. "That's very good of you, Admiral. I would certainly appreciate it."

"Yes, I think we can definitely arrange that. Tell Susan for me that the problem is solved."

Robert stood up, beaming. "I don't know how to thank you."

Admiral Whittaker waved a hand of dismissal. "You're too valuable a piece of manpower for me to let anything happen to you. Now go home to your bride."

When Robert told Susan the news, she was thrilled. She threw her arms around him. "Oh, darling, that's wonderful."

"I'm going to ask him for a couple of weeks off so we can take a trip somewhere. It will be a second honeymoon."

"I've forgotten what a honeymoon is like," Susan murmured. "Show me."

Robert showed her.

* * *

Admiral Whittaker sent for Robert the following morning. "I just wanted you to know I'm making some arrangements about the matter we discussed yesterday."

"Thank you, Admiral." Now was the time to mention taking a leave. "Sir—"

Admiral Whittaker said, "Something has come up, Robert." The admiral began to pace. When he spoke, there was a note of deep concern in his voice. "I've just been informed that the CIA has been infiltrated. It seems that there has been a steady leak of top secret information. All they know about the spy is that his code name is the Fox. He's in Argentina right now. They need someone outside the agency to handle the operation. The director of the CIA has asked for you. They would like you to track the man down and bring him back. I told them the decision is up to you. Do you want to undertake it?"

Robert hesitated. "I'm afraid I'll have to pass on it, sir."

"I respect your decision, Robert. You've been traveling constantly and have never turned down an assignment. I know it hasn't been easy on your marriage."

"I'd like to take on this job, sir. It's just that—"

"You don't have to say it, Robert. My opinion of your work and dedication will always remain the same. I just have one favor to ask of you."

"What's that, Admiral?"

"The deputy director of the CIA asked to meet with you, regardless of your decision. As a courtesy. You don't mind do you?"

"Of course not, sir."

The next day Robert drove to Langley for his meeting with the deputy director.

"Sit down, Commander," the deputy director said after Robert entered the large corner office. "I've heard a lot about you. All good things, of course."

"Thank you, sir."

The deputy director was a man in his early sixties, reed thin with fine white hair and a small brush mustache that moved up and down as he drew on his pipe. A Yale graduate, he had joined the OSS during World War II and then moved into the CIA when it was formed after the conflict. He rose steadily up the ranks to his present position in one of the largest and most powerful intelligence agencies in the world.

"I want you to know, Commander, that I respect your decision."

Bellamy nodded toward the deputy director.

"There is one fact, however, that I feel I should bring to your attention."

"What's that, sir?"

"The President is personally involved in the operation to unmask the Fox."

"I didn't know that, sir."

"He regards it—as I do, too—as one of the most important assignments this agency has had since its inception. I know of your situation at home, and I'm sure the President is sympathetic too. He's a real family man. But your not taking on this assignment might throw—how should I say it—a cloud on the ONI *and* Admiral Whittaker."

"The admiral had nothing to do with my decision, sir," Robert said.

"I understand that, Commander, but will the President understand that?"

The honeymoon will have to be postponed, Robert thought.

* * *

When Robert broke the news to Susan, he said gently, "This is my last overseas assignment. After this I'll be home so much you'll get sick of me."

She smiled up at him. "There isn't that much time in the world. We're going to be together forever."

The chase after the Fox was the most frustrating thing Robert had ever experienced. He picked up his trail in Argentina but missed his quarry by one day. The trail led to Tokyo and China and then Malaysia. Whoever the Fox was, he left just enough of a trail to lead to where he had been but never to where he was.

The days turned into weeks, and the weeks turned into months, and always Robert was just behind the Fox. He called Susan almost every day. In the beginning, it was "I'll be home in a few days, darling." And then, "I might be home next week." And then, finally, "I'm not sure when I'll be back." In the end, Robert had to give up. He had been on the Fox's trail for two and a half months with no success.

When he returned to Susan, she seemed changed. A little cooler.

"I'm sorry, darling," Robert apologized. "I had no idea it would take so long. It was just—"

"They'll never let you go, will they, Robert?"

"What? Of course, they will."

She shook her head. "I don't think so. I've taken a job at Washington Memorial Hospital."

He was taken aback. "You've what?"

"I'm going to be a nurse again. I can't sit around waiting for you to come home to me, wondering where you are and what you're doing, wondering whether you're dead or alive."

"Susan, I—"

"It's all right, my sweetheart. At least I'll be doing something useful while you're gone. It will make the waiting easier."

And Robert had no answer to that.

He reported his failure to Admiral Whittaker. The admiral was sympathetic.

"It's my fault for agreeing to let you do it. From now on, we'll let the CIA handle their own damned problems. I'm sorry, Robert."

Robert told him about Susan taking a job as a nurse.

"That's probably a good idea," the Admiral said thoughtfully. "It will take the pressure off your marriage. If you took on some overseas caseloads now and then, I'm sure it won't matter as much."

Now and then turned out to be almost constantly. That was when the marriage really began to disintegrate.

Susan worked at Washington Memorial Hospital as an operating room nurse, and whenever Robert was home, she tried to take time off to be with him, but she was caught up more and more in her work.

"I'm really enjoying it, darling. I feel I'm doing something useful."

She would talk to Robert about her patients, and he remembered how caring she had been with him, how she had nurtured him back to health, back to life. He was pleased that she was doing important work that she loved, but the fact was, they were seeing less and less of each other. The emotional distance between them was widening. There was an awkwardness now that had not existed before. They were like two strangers trying desperately hard to make conversation.

When Robert returned to Washington from a six-week assignment in Turkey, he took Susan out to dinner at Sans Souci.

Susan said, "We have a new patient at the hospital. He was in a bad plane crash, and the doctors didn't think he was going to live, but I'm going to see to it that he does." Her eyes were glowing.

She was like that with me, Robert thought. And he wondered if she had leaned over the new patient and said, "Get well. I'm waiting for you." He rejected the thought.

"He's so nice, Robert. All the nurses are crazy about him."

All the nurses? he wondered.

There was a small, nagging doubt at the back of his mind, but he managed to get rid of it.

They ordered dinner.

The following Saturday, Robert left for Portugal, and when he returned three weeks later, Susan greeted him excitedly.

"Monte walked today for the first time!" Her kiss was perfunctory.

"Monte?"

"Monte Banks. That's his name. He's going to be fine. The doctors couldn't believe it, but we wouldn't give up."

We. "Tell me about him."

"He's really darling. He's always giving us gifts. He's very wealthy. He flies his own plane, and he was in a bad crash, and—"

"What kind of gifts?"

"Oh, you know, just little things—candies and flowers and books and records. He tried to give all of us expensive watches but of course we had to refuse."

"Of course."

"He has a yacht, polo ponies . . ."

That was the day Robert began calling him Moneybags.

Susan talked about him every time she came home from the hospital.

"He's really dear, Robert."

Dear is dangerous.

"And he's so thoughtful. Do you know what he did today? He had lunch sent from the Jockey Club for all the nurses on the floor."

The man is sickening. Ridiculously, Robert found himself getting angry. "Is this wonderful patient of yours married?"

"No, darling. Why?"

"I just wondered."

She laughed. "For heaven's sake, you're not jealous, are you?"

"Of some old man who's just learning to walk? Of course not." *Like hell I'm not.* But he wouldn't give Susan the satisfaction of saying so.

When Robert was at home, Susan tried not to talk about her patient, but if she did not bring up the subject, Robert would.

"How is old Moneybags doing?"

"His name is not Moneybags," she chided. "It's Monte Banks."

"Whatever." *It's too bad the sonofabitch couldn't have died in the plane crash.*

The following day was Susan's birthday.

"I'll tell you what," Robert said, enthusiastically, "we'll celebrate. We'll go out and have a wonderful dinner somewhere and—"

"I have to work at the hospital until eight."

"All right. I'll pick you up there."

"Fine. Monte is dying to meet you. I've told him all about you."

"I look forward to meeting the old man," Robert assured her.

When Robert arrived at the hospital, the receptionist said, "Good evening, Commander. Susan is working in the orthopedic ward on the third floor. She's expecting you." She picked up the telephone.

When Robert got off the elevator, Susan was waiting for him, wearing her white starched uniform, and his heart skipped a beat. She was, oh, so damned beautiful.

"Hello, gorgeous."

Susan smiled, strangely ill at ease. "Hello, Robert. I'll be off duty in a few minutes. Come on. I'll introduce you to Monte."

I can't wait.

She led him into a large private room filled with books and flowers and baskets of fruit, and said, "Monte, this is my husband, Robert."

Robert stood there staring at the man in the bed. He was three or four years older than Robert and resembled Paul Newman. Robert despised him on sight.

"I'm certainly pleased to meet you, Commander. Susan has been telling me all about you."

Is that what they talk about when she is at his bedside in the middle of the night?

"She's very proud of you."

That's it, buddy, throw me a few crumbs.

Susan was looking at Robert, willing him to be polite. He made an effort.

"I understand you'll be getting out of here soon."

"Yes, thanks mostly to your wife. She's a miracle worker."

"Come on, sailor. Do you think I'm going to let some other nurse have that great body?" "Yes, that's her specialty." Robert could not keep the bitterness out of his voice.

The birthday dinner was a fiasco. All Susan wanted to talk about was her patient.

"Did he remind you of anyone, darling?"

"Boris Karloff."

"Why did you have to be so rude to him?"

He said coldly, "I thought I was very civil. I don't happen to like the man."

Susan stared at him. "You don't even know him. What don't you like about him?"

I don't like the way he looks at you. I don't like the way you look at him. I don't like the way our marriage is going to hell. God, I don't want to lose you. "Sorry. I guess I'm just tired."

They finished their dinner in silence.

The next morning, as Robert was getting ready to go to the office, Susan said, "Robert, I have something to say to you. . . ."

And it was as if he had been struck in the pit of his stomach. He could not bear to have her put what was happening into words.

"Susan—"

"You know I love you. I'll always love you. You're the dearest, most wonderful man I've ever known."

"Please—"

"No, let me finish. This is very hard for me. In the last year, we've only spent minutes together. We don't have a marriage anymore. We've drifted apart."

Every word was a knife stabbing into him.

"You're right," he said desperately. "I'll change. I'll quit the agency. Now. Today. We'll go away somewhere and—"

She shook her head. "No, Robert. We both know that wouldn't work. You're doing what you want to do. If you stopped doing it because of me, you would always resent it. This isn't anybody's fault. It just—happened. I want a divorce."

It was as though the world had caved in on him. He felt suddenly sick to his stomach.

"You don't mean that, Susan. We'll find a way to—"

"It's too late. I've been thinking about this for a long time. All the while you were away and I sat home alone and waited for you to come back, I thought about it. We've been living separate lives. I need more than that. I need something you can't give me anymore."

He stood there, fighting to control his emotions. "Does this—does this have anything to do with Moneybags?"

Susan hesitated. "Monte has asked me to marry him."

He could feel his bowels turning to water. "And you're going to?"

"Yes."

It was some kind of crazy nightmare. *This isn't happening,* he thought. *It can't be.* His eyes filled with tears.

Susan put her arms around him and held him close. "I will never again feel about any man the way I felt about you. I loved you with all my heart and soul. I will always love you. You are my dearest friend." She pulled back and looked into his eyes. "But that isn't enough. Do you understand?"

All he understood was that she was tearing him apart. "We could try again. We'll start over and—"

"I'm sorry, Robert." Her voice was choked. "I'm so sorry, but it's finished."

Susan flew to Reno for a divorce, and Commander Robert Bellamy went on a two-week drunk.

Old habits die hard. Robert telephoned a friend at the FBI. Al Traynor had crossed Robert's path half a dozen times in the past, and Robert trusted him.

"Tray, I need a favor."

"A favor? You need a psychiatrist. How the hell could you let Susan get away?"

The news was probably all over town.

"It's a long, sad story."

"I'm really sorry, Robert. She was a great lady. I—never mind. What can I do for you?"

"I'd like you to run a computer check on someone."

"You've got it. Give me a name."

"Monte Banks. It's just a routine inquiry."

"Right. What do you want to know?"

"He's probably not even in your files, Tray, but if he is—did he ever get a parking ticket, beat his dog, run a red light? The usual."

"Sure."

"And I'm curious about where he got his money. I'd like a fix on his background."

"So, just routine, huh?"

"And Tray, let's keep this between us. It's personal. Okay?"

"No problem. I'll call you in the morning."

"Thanks. I owe you a lunch."

"Dinner."

"You've got it."

Robert replaced the receiver and thought: *Portrait of a man clutching at straws. What am I hoping for, that he's*

Jack the Ripper and Susan will come flying back into my arms?

Early the following morning, Dustin Thornton sent for Robert. "What are you working on, Commander?"

He knows perfectly well what I'm working on, Robert thought. "I'm winding up my file on the diplomat from Singapore, and—"

"It doesn't seem to be occupying enough of your time."

"I beg your pardon?"

"In case you've forgotten, Commander, the Office of Naval Intelligence is not mandated to investigate American citizens."

Robert was watching him, puzzled. "What are you—?"

"I've been notified by the FBI that you have been trying to obtain information that is completely out of the jurisdiction of this agency."

Robert felt a sudden rush of anger. That sonofabitch Traynor had betrayed him. So much for friendship. "It was a personal matter," Robert said. "I—"

"The computers of the FBI are not there for your convenience, nor to help you harass private citizens. Do I make myself clear?"

"Very."

"That's all."

Robert raced back to his office. His fingers trembled as he dialed 202-324-3000. A voice answered, "FBI."

"Al Traynor."

"Just a moment, please."

A minute later, a man's voice came on the line. "Hello. May I help you?"

"Yes. I'm calling Al Traynor."

"I'm sorry, Agent Traynor is no longer with this office."

Robert felt a shock go through him. "What?"

"Agent Traynor has been transferred."

"Transferred?"

"Yes."

"To where?"

"Boise. But he won't be up there for a while. A long while, I'm afraid."

"What do you mean?"

"He was struck by a hit and run driver last night while jogging in Rock Creek Park. Can you believe it? Some creep must have been drunk out of his mind. He ran his car right up on the jogging path. Traynor's body was thrown more than forty feet. He may not make it."

Robert replaced the receiver. His mind was spinning. What the hell was going on? Monte Banks, the blue-eyed all-American boy was being protected. From what? By whom? *Jesus,* Robert thought, *what is Susan getting herself into?*

He went to visit her that afternoon.

She was in her new apartment, a beautiful duplex on M Street. He wondered whether Moneybags had paid for it. It had been weeks since he had seen Susan, and the sight of her took his breath away.

"Forgive me for barging in like this, Susan. I know I promised not to."

"You said it was something serious."

"It is." Now that he was here, he didn't know how to begin. *Susan, I came here to save you?* She would laugh in his face.

"What's happened?"

"It's about Monte."

She frowned. "What about him?"

This was the difficult part. How could he tell her what he himself didn't know? All he knew was that something was terribly wrong. Monte Banks was in the FBI computer all right, with a tickler: *No information to be given out without proper authorization.* And the inquiry had been kicked right back on ONI. *Why?*

"I don't think he's—he's not what he seems to be."

"I don't understand."

"Susan—where does he get his money?"

She looked surprised at the question. "Monte has a very successful import-export business."

The oldest cover in the world.

He should have known better than to have come charging in with his half-baked theory. He felt like a fool. Susan was waiting for an answer, and he had none.

"Why are you asking?"

"I was—I just wanted to make sure he's right for you," Robert said lamely.

"Oh, Robert." Her voice was filled with disappointment.

"I guess I shouldn't have come." *You got that right, buddy.* "I'm sorry."

Susan walked up to him and gave him a hug. "I understand, "she said softly.

But she didn't understand. She didn't understand that an innocent inquiry about Monte Banks had been stonewalled, referred to the Office of Naval Intelligence, and that the man who had tried to get that information had been transferred to the boondocks.

There were other ways of obtaining information, and Robert went about them circumspectly. He telephoned a friend who worked for *Forbes* magazine.

"Robert! Long time no see. What can I do for you?"

Robert told him.

"Monte Banks? Interesting you should mention him. We think he should be on our Forbes Four Hundred wealthiest list, but we can't get any hard information on him. Do you have anything for us?"

A zero.

Robert went to the public library and looked up Monte Banks in *Who's Who.* He was not listed.

He turned to the microfiche and looked up back issues of the *Washington Post* around the time that Monte Banks had had his plane accident. There was a brief item about the plane crash. It mentioned Banks as an entrepreneur.

It all sounded innocent enough. *Maybe I'm wrong,* Robert thought. *Maybe Monte Banks is a guy in a white hat. Our government wouldn't have protected him if he were a spy, a criminal, into drugs. . . . The truth is that I'm still trying to hold on to Susan.*

Being a bachelor again was a loneliness, an emptiness, a round of busy days and sleepless nights. A tide of despair would sweep over him without warning, and he would weep. He wept for himself and for Susan and for everything that they had lost. Susan's presence was everywhere. The apartment was alive with reminders of her. Robert was cursed with total recall, and each room tormented him with memories of Susan's voice, her laughter, her warmth. He remembered the soft hills and valleys of her body as she lay in bed naked, waiting for him, and the ache inside him was unbearable.

His friends were concerned.

"You shouldn't be alone, Robert."

And their rallying cry became "Have I got a girl for you!"

They were tall and beautiful, and small and sexy. They were models and secretaries and advertising executives and divorcées and lawyers. But none of them was Susan. He had nothing in common with any of them, and trying to make small talk with strangers in whom he had no interest only made him feel more lonely. Robert had no desire to go to bed with any of them. He wanted to be alone. He wanted to rewind the film back to the beginning, to rewrite the script. With hindsight it was so easy to see his mistakes, to see how the scene with Admiral Whittaker should have played.

The CIA has been infiltrated by a man called the Fox. The deputy director has asked for you to track him down.

No, Admiral. Sorry. I'm taking my wife on a second honeymoon.

He wanted to reedit his life, to give it a happy ending. Too late. Life did not give second chances. He was alone.

He did his own shopping, cooked his meals for himself, and went to the neighborhood laundromat once a week when he was home.

It was a lonely, miserable time in Robert's life. But the worst was yet to come. A beautiful designer he had met in Washington telephoned him several times to invite him to dinner. Robert had been reluctant, but he had finally accepted. She prepared a delicious candlelight dinner for the two of them.

"You're a very good cook," Robert said.

"I'm very good at everything." And there was no mistaking her meaning. She moved closer to him. "Let me prove it to you." She put her hands on his thighs and ran her tongue around his lips.

It's been a long time, Robert thought. *Maybe too long.*

They went to bed, and to Robert's consternation, it

was a disaster. For the first time in his life, Robert was impotent. He was humiliated.

"Don't worry, darling," she said. "It will be all right."

She was wrong.

Robert went home feeling embarrassed, crippled. He knew that in some crazy, convoluted way, he had felt that making love to another woman was a betrayal of Susan. *How stupid can I get?*

He tried to make love again several weeks later with a bright secretary at ONI. She had been wildly passionate in bed, stroking his body and taking him inside her hot mouth. But it was no use. He wanted only Susan. After that, he stopped trying. He thought about consulting a doctor, but he was too ashamed. He knew the answer to his problem, and it had nothing to do with medical advice. He poured all his energy into work.

Susan called him at least once a week. "Don't forget to pick up your shirts at the laundry," she would say. Or: "I'm sending over a maid to clean up the apartment. I'll bet it's a mess."

Each call made the loneliness more intolerable.

She had called him the night before her wedding.

"Robert, I want you to know I'm getting married tomorrow."

It was difficult for him to breathe. He began to hyperventilate.

"Susan—"

"I love Monte," she said, "but I love you, too. I'll love you until the day I die. I don't want you ever to forget that."

What was there to say to that?

"Robert, are you all right?"

Sure. I'm great. Except that I'm a fucking eunuch. Scratch the adjective.

"Robert?"

He could not bear to punish her with his problem. "I'm fine. Just do me a favor, will you, baby?"

"Anything I can."

"Don't—don't let him take you on your honeymoon to any of the places we went to."

He hung up and went out and got drunk again.

That had been a year earlier. That was the past. He had been forced to face the reality that Susan now belonged to someone else. He had to live in the present. He had work to do. It was time to have a chat with Leslie Mothershed, the photographer who had the photographs and names of the witnesses Robert had been assigned to track down on what was going to be his last assignment.

Chapter Eighteen

Leslie Mothershed was in a state beyond euphoria. The moment he had returned to London, clutching his precious film, he had hurried into the small pantry he had converted into a darkroom and checked to make sure he had everything on hand: film-processing tank, thermometer, spring-type clothespins, four large beakers, a timer, and developer, stop-bath solutions, and fixer. He turned out the light and switched on a small red overhead lamp. His hands were trembling as he opened the cartridges and removed the film. He took deep breaths to control himself. *Nothing must go wrong this time,* he thought. *Nothing. This is for you, Mother.*

Carefully, he rolled the film into reels. He placed the reels in the tank and filled it with developer, the first of the liquids he would use. It would require a constant temperature of 68°F and periodic agitation. After eleven minutes, he emptied the contents and poured the fixer over the reels.

He was getting nervous again, terrified of making a mistake. He poured off the fixer for the first wash and then let the film sit in a tankful of water for ten minutes. This was followed by two minutes of constant agitation in a hypocleansing agent and twelve more minutes in water. Thirty seconds in photo-flo solution ensured there would be no streaks or flaws in the negatives. Finally, very, very carefully, he removed the film, hung it up with clothespins, and used a squeegee to remove the last drips from the film. He waited impatiently for the negatives to dry.

It was time to have a look. Holding his breath, heart pounding, Mothershed picked up the first strip of negatives and held it up to the light. *Perfect. Absolutely perfect!*

Each one was a gem, a picture that any photographer in the world would be proud to have taken. Every detail of the strange spacecraft was outlined, including the bodies of the two alien forms lying inside.

Two things he had not noticed before caught Mothershed's eye, and he took a closer look. Where the spaceship had cracked open he could see three narrow couches inside the ship—and yet there were only two aliens. The other thing that was strange was that one of the aliens' hands had been severed. It was nowhere to be seen in the photograph. *Maybe the creature had only one hand,* Mothershed thought. *My God, these pictures are masterpieces! Mother was right. I'm a genius.* He looked around the tiny room and thought, *The next time I develop my film, it will be in a big, beautiful darkroom in my mansion in Eaton Square.*

He stood there fingering his treasures like a miser fingering his gold. There wasn't a magazine or newspaper in the world that wouldn't kill to get these pictures. All these years the bastards had rejected his photographs with their insulting little notes. "Thank you for submitting the photos that we are herewith returning. They do not fit our present needs." And: "Thank you for your submission. They are too similar to pictures we have already printed." Or simply: "We are returning the photographs you sent us."

For years he had gone begging to the creeps for jobs, and now they were going to crawl to him, and he was going to make them pay through the nose.

He could not wait. He had to start immediately. Since bloody British Telecom had shut off his phone merely because he happened to be a few weeks late making his last quarterly payment, Mothershed had to go outside to find a phone. On an impulse, he decided to go to Langan's, the celebrity hangout, and treat himself to a much-deserved lunch. Langan's was well beyond his means, but if there was ever a time to celebrate, this was it. Wasn't he on the verge of becoming rich and famous?

A maître d' seated Mothershed at a table in a corner of the restaurant, and there, at a booth not ten feet away, he saw two familiar faces. He suddenly realized who they were, and a little thrill ran through him. Michael Caine and Roger Moore, in person! He wished his mother were still alive so he could tell her about it. She had loved reading about movie stars. The two men were laughing and having a good time, not a care in the world, and Mothershed could not help staring. Their glances moved past him. *Smug bastards,* Leslie Mothershed thought angrily. *I suppose they expect me to come over and ask for their autographs. Well, in a few days they're going to be asking for mine. They'll be falling all over themselves to introduce me to their friends. "Leslie, I want you to meet Charles and Di, and this is Fergie and Andrew. Leslie, you know, is the chap who took those famous photos of the UFO."*

When Mothershed finished his lunch, he walked past the two stars and went upstairs to the phone booth. Director Inquiries gave him the number of the *Sun*.

"I'd like to speak to your Picture editor."

A male voice came on the line. "Chapman."

"What would it be worth to you to have photographs of a UFO with the bodies of two aliens in it?"

The voice at the other end of the phone said, "If the pictures are good enough, we might run them as an example of a clever hoax, and—"

Mothershed said waspishly, "It so happens that this is no hoax. I have the names of nine reputable witnesses who will testify that it's real, including a priest."

The man's tone changed. "Oh? And where were these pictures taken?"

"Never mind," Mothershed said cagily. He was not going to let them trick him into giving away any information. "Are you interested?"

The voice said cautiously, "If you can prove that the pictures are authentic, yes, we would be very interested."

Damn right you would, Mothershed thought gleefully. "I'll get back to you." He hung up.

The other two phone calls were just as satisfactory. Mothershed had to admit to himself that getting the names and addresses of the witnesses had been a stroke of pure genius. There was no way now that anyone could accuse him of trying to perpetrate a fraud. These pictures were going to appear on the front pages of every important newspaper and magazine in the world. *With my credit: Photographs by Leslie Mothershed.*

As Mothershed left the restaurant, he could not resist walking up to the booth where the two stars were seated. "Excuse me, I'm sorry to bother you, but would you give me your autographs?"

Roger Moore and Michael Caine smiled up at him pleasantly. They scribbled their names on pieces of paper and handed them to the photographer.

"Thank you."

When Leslie Mothershed got outside, he savagely tore up the autographs and threw them away.

Screw them! he thought. *I'm more important than they are.*

Chapter Nineteen

Robert took a taxi to Whitechapel. They drove through the City, the business section of London, heading east until they reached the Whitechapel Road, the area made infamous a century earlier by Jack the Ripper. Along the Whitechapel Road were dozens of outside stalls selling everything from clothing to fresh vegetables to carpets.

As the taxi neared Mothershed's address, the neighborhood became more and more dilapidated. Graffiti was scrawled all over the peeling, brownstone buildings. They passed the Weaver's Arms Pub. *That would be Mothershed's local,* Robert thought. Another sign read: Walter Bookmaker. . . . *Mothershed probably places his bets on horses there.*

They finally reached 213A Grove Road. Robert dismissed the taxi and studied the building in front of him. It was an ugly two-story building that had been divided into small flats. Inside was the man who had a complete list of the witnesses Robert had been sent to find.

Leslie Mothershed was in the living room poring over his windfall when the doorbell rang. He looked up, startled, filled with a sudden inexplicable fear. The ring was repeated. Mothershed scooped up his precious photographs and hurried into the converted darkroom. He slipped the pictures into a pile of old prints, then walked back into the living room and opened the front door. He stared at the stranger who stood there.

"Yes?"

"Leslie Mothershed?"

"That's right. What can I do for you?"

"May I come in?"

"I don't know. What is this about?"

Robert pulled out a Defence Ministry identification card and flashed it. "I'm here on official business, Mr. Mothershed. We can either talk here or at the ministry." It was a bluff. But he could see the sudden fear on the photographer's face.

Leslie Mothershed swallowed. "I don't know what you're talking about, but—come in."

Robert entered the drab room. It was shabby-genteel, dreary, not a place where anyone would live by choice.

"Would you kindly explain what you're doing here?" Mothershed put the proper note of innocent exasperation in his voice.

"I'm here to question you about some photographs you took."

He knew it! He had known it from the moment he heard the bell. *The bastards are going to try to take my fortune away from me. Well, I'm not going to let them do it.* "What photographs are you talking about?"

Robert said patiently, "The ones you took at the site of the UFO crash."

Mothershed stared at Robert a moment, as though caught by surprise, and then forced a laugh. "Oh, *those*! I wish I had them to give to you."

"You *did* take those pictures?"

"I tried."

"What do you mean . . . you tried?"

"The bloody things never came out." Mothershed gave a nervous cough. "My camera fogged. That's the second time that's happened to me." He was babbling now. "I even threw out the negatives. They were no good. It was a complete waste of film. And you know how expensive film is these days."

He's a bad liar, Robert thought. *He's on the edge of panic.* Robert said sympathetically, "Too bad. Those photographs would have been very helpful." He said nothing about the list of passengers. If Mothershed lied about the photographs, he would lie about the list. Robert glanced around. The photographs and the list had to be hidden here somewhere. *They shouldn't be difficult to find.* The flat consisted of a small living room, a bedroom, a bathroom, and what looked like a door to a utility closet. There was no way he could force the man to hand over the material. He had no real authority. But he wanted those photographs and the list of witnesses before the SIS came and took them away. He needed that list for himself.

"Yes." Mothershed sighed. "Those pictures would have been worth a fortune."

"Tell me about the spaceship," Robert said.

Mothershed gave an involuntary shudder. The eerie scene was fixed in his mind forever. "I'll never forget it," he said. "The ship seemed to—to pulsate, like it was alive. There was something evil about it. And then there were these two dead aliens inside."

"Can you tell me anything about the passengers on the bus?"

Sure I can, Mothershed gloated to himself. *I have all their names and addresses.* "No, I'm afraid I can't." Mothershed went on, talking to conceal his nervousness. "The reason I can't help you with the passengers is that I wasn't on that bus. They were all strangers."

"I see. Well, thank you for your cooperation, Mr. Mothershed. I appreciate it. Sorry about your pictures."

"So am I," Mothershed said. He watched the door close behind the stranger and thought happily, *I've done it! I've outsmarted the sonsofbitches.*

Outside in the hall, Robert was examining the lock on the door. A Chubb. And an old model. It would take him seconds to open it. He would start surveillance in the middle of the night and wait for the photographer to leave the flat in the morning. *Once I have the list of passengers in my possession, the rest of the assignment will be simple.*

Robert checked into a small hotel near Mothershed's flat and telephoned General Hilliard.

"I have the name of the English witness, General."

"Just a moment. All right. Go ahead, Commander."

"Leslie Mothershed. He lives in Whitechapel, at 213A Grove Road."

"Excellent. I'll arrange for the British authorities to speak to him."

Robert did not mention the passenger list or the photographs. Those were his aces in the hole.

* * *

Reggie's Fish and Chip Shop was located in a little cul-de-sac off the Brompton Road. It was a small establishment with a clientele made up mainly of clerks and secretaries who worked in the neighborhood. Its walls were covered with football posters, and the parts that were exposed had not seen fresh paint since the Suez conflict.

The phone behind the counter rang twice before it was answered by a large man dressed in a greasy wool sweater. The man looked like a typical East Ender except for a gold-rimmed monocle fixed tightly in the socket of his left eye. The reason for the monocle was apparent to anyone who looked closely at the man: His other eye was made of glass and of a color blue that was generally seen on travel posters.

"Reggie here."

"This is the Bishop."

"Yes, sir," said Reggie, his voice dropping to a whisper.

"Our client's name is Mothershed. Christian tag, Leslie. Resides at 213A Grove Road. We need this order filled quickly. Understood?"

"It's already done, sir."

Chapter Twenty

Leslie Mothershed was lost in a golden daydream. He was being interviewed by members of the world press. They were asking him about the huge castle he had just bought in Scotland, his château in the South of France, his enormous yacht. *"And is it true that the Queen has invited you to become the official royal photographer?" "Yes. I said I would let her know. And now, ladies and gentlemen, if you will all excuse me, I'm late for my show at the BBC. . . ."*

His reverie was interrupted by the sound of the doorbell. He looked at his watch. Eleven o'clock. *Has that man returned?* He walked over to the door and cautiously opened it. In the doorway stood a man shorter than Mothershed (that was the first thing he noticed about him), with thick glasses and a thin, sallow face.

"Excuse me," the man said diffidently. "I apologize for disturbing you at this hour. I live just down the block. The sign outside says you're a photographer."

"So?"

"Do you do passport photos?"

Leslie Mothershed do passport photos? The man who is about to own the world? That is like asking Michelangelo to paint the bathroom.

"No," he said rudely. He started to close the door.

"I really hate to bother you, but I'm in a terrible jam. My plane leaves for Tokyo at eight o'clock in the morning, and a little while ago when I took out my passport, I saw that somehow my photograph had been torn loose. It's missing. I've looked everywhere. They won't let me on the plane without a passport photo." The little man was near tears.

"I'm sorry," Mothershed said. "I can't help you."

"I'd be willing to pay you a hundred pounds."

A hundred pounds? To a man with a castle and a château and a yacht? It's an insult.

The pathetic little man was going on. "I could go even higher. Two hundred or three hundred. You see, I really must be on that plane or I'll lose my job."

Three hundred pounds to take a passport picture? Not including the developing, it would take about 10 seconds. Mothershed began to calculate. That came to 1,800 pounds a minute. Eighteen hundred pounds a minute was 10,800 pounds an hour. If he worked an eight-hour day, that would be 94,400 pounds a day. In one week, that would come to—

"Will you do it?"

Mothershed's ego jockeyed with his greed, and greed won out. *I can use a bit of pocket money.*

"Come in," Mothershed said. "Stand against that wall."

"Thank you. I really appreciate this."

Mothershed wished he had a Polaroid camera. That

would have made it so simple. He picked up his Vivitar and said, "Hold still."

Ten seconds later it was done.

"It will take a while to develop it," Mothershed said. "If you come back in—"

"If you don't mind, I'll wait."

"Suit yourself."

Mothershed took the camera into the darkroom, put it into the black bag, turned off the overhead light, switched on the red light, and removed the film. He would do this in a hurry. Passport pictures always looked terrible anyway. Fifteen minutes later, as Mothershed was timing the film in the developer tanks, he began to smell smoke. He paused. Was it his imagination? No. The smell was getting stronger. He turned to open the door. It seemed to be stuck. Mothershed pushed against it. It held fast.

"Hello," he called out. "What's happening out there?"

There was no response.

"Hello?" He pressed his shoulder against the door, but there seemed to be something heavy on the other side of it keeping it closed. "Mister?"

There was no answer. The only sound he could hear was a loud crackling noise. The smell of smoke was becoming overpowering. The flat was on fire. *That's probably why he left. He must have gone to get help.* Leslie Mothershed slammed his shoulder against the door, but it would not budge. "Help!" he screamed. "Get me out of here!"

Smoke was starting to pour under the door, and Mothershed could feel the heat of the flames beginning to lick at it. It was getting difficult to breathe. He was starting to choke. He tore at his collar, gasping for air. His lungs were burning. He was beginning to lose consciousness. He sank down on his knees. "Oh, God, please don't let me die now. Not now that I'm going to be rich and famous. . . ."

"Reggie here."

"Was the order filled?"

"Yes, sir. A bit overcooked but delivered on time."

"Excellent."

When Robert arrived at Grove Road at two o'clock in the morning to begin his surveillance, he was confronted with an enormous traffic jam. The street was filled with official vehicles, a fire engine, ambulances, and three police cars. Robert pushed his way through the crowd of bystanders and hurried over to the center of activity. The whole building had been engulfed by the fire. From the outside he could see that the first-floor flat occupied by the photographer had been completely gutted.

"How did it happen?" Robert asked a fireman.

"We don't know yet. Stand back, please."

"My cousin lives in that flat. Is he all right?"

"I'm afraid not." His tone became sympathetic. "They're just taking him out of the building now."

Robert watched as two ambulance attendants pushed a gurney carrying a body into the ambulance.

"I was staying with him," Robert said. "All my clothes are in there. I'd like to go in and—"

The fireman shook his head. "It wouldn't do you any good, sir. There's nothing left of the flat but ashes."

Nothing left but ashes. Including the photographs and the precious list of passengers with their names and addresses.

So much for fucking serendipity, Robert thought bitterly.

In Washington Dustin Thornton was having lunch with his father-in-law in the lavish private dining room in Willard Stone's offices. Dustin Thornton was nervous. He was always nervous in the presence of his powerful father-in-law.

Willard Stone was in a good mood. "I had dinner with the President last evening. He told me that he's very pleased with your work, Dustin."

"I'm very gratified."

"You're doing a fine job. You're helping to protect us against the hordes."

"The hordes?"

"Those who would try to bring this great country to its knees. But it is not just the enemy outside the walls we have to beware of. It is those who pretend to be serving our country, who fail to do their duty. Those who do not carry out their orders."

"The mavericks."

"That's right, Dustin. The mavericks. They must be punished. If—"

A man walked into the room. "Excuse me, Mr. Stone. The gentlemen have arrived. They're waiting for you."

"Yes." Stone turned to his son-in-law. "Finish your lunch, Dustin. I have something important to take care of. One day I may be able to tell you about it."

Chapter Twenty-one

The streets of Zurich were filled with weird-looking creatures with odd shapes, misshapen giants with large, grotesque bodies and tiny eyes, and with skin the color of boiled fish. They were meat eaters, and she hated the fetid smells they exuded from their bodies. Some of the females wore animal skins, the remains of the creatures they had murdered. She was still stunned by the terrible accident that had taken away the life essence of her companions.

She had been on earth for four cycles of what these strange-looking beings called *luna,* and she had not eaten in all that time. She was faint from thirst. The only water she had been able to drink was the fresh rainwater in the farmer's trough, and it had not rained since the night she arrived. The rest of the water on earth was undrinkable. She had gone into an alien feeding place, but she had been unable to stand the stench. She had tried to eat their raw vegetables and fruit, but they were tasteless, not like the succulent food at home.

She was called the Graceful One, and she was tall and stately and beautiful with luminous green eyes. She had adopted the appearance of an earthling after she left the site of the crash, and she walked through the crowds unnoticed.

She was seated at a table in a hard, uncomfortable chair that had been built for the human body, and she read the minds of the creatures around her.

Two of the beings were seated at a table near her. One was speaking aloud. "It's the chance of a lifetime, Franz! For fifty thousand francs you can get in at the start. You've got fifty thousand francs, haven't you?" She read the loud thoughts in his head. *Come on, you swine. I need the commission.*

"Sure, but I don't know—" *I'll have to borrow it from my wife.*

"Have I ever given you bad investment advice?" *Make up your mind.*

"It's a lot of money." *She'll never give it to me.*

"What about the potential? There's a chance to make millions." *Say yes.*

"All right. I'm in." *Maybe I can sell some of her jewelry.*

I have him! "You'll never regret it, Franz." *He can always take a tax loss.*

The Graceful One had no idea what the conversation meant.

At the far end of the restaurant, a man and woman were seated at a table. They were talking in low voices. She stretched her mind to hear them.

"Jesus Christ!" the man said. "How the hell could you get pregnant?" *You stupid bitch!*

"How do you think I got pregnant?" *Your cock did it!*

Pregnant was how these beings gestated, procreating clumsily with their genitals, like their animals in the fields.

"What are you going to do about it, Tina?" *You've got to get an abortion.*

"What do you expect me to do? You said you were going to tell your wife about me." *You lying bastard.*

"Look, honey, I am, but this is a bad time." *I was crazy to ever get involved with you. I should have known you were trouble.*

"It's a bad time for me, too, Paul. I don't even think you love me." *Please tell me you do.*

"Of course I love you. It's just that my wife is going through a rough period right now." *I don't intend to lose her.*

"I'm going through a rough period right now too. Don't you understand? I'm having your baby." *And you're damn well going to marry me.* Water was coming from her eyes.

"Calm down, honey. I tell you, everything is going to be fine. I want the baby as much as you do." *I'll have to talk her into an abortion.*

At a table next to them, a male creature was seated alone.

They promised me. They said the race was fixed, that I couldn't lose, and like a fool, I turned all my money over to them. I've got to find a way to put it back before the auditors come. I couldn't stand it if they put me in jail. I'll kill myself first. I swear to God, I'll kill myself.

At another table, a male and female were in the middle of a discussion.

". . . it's nothing like that. It's just that I've got this beautiful chalet in the mountains, and I thought it would be good for you to get away for a weekend and relax." *We'll spend a lot of time relaxing in my bed, chérie.*

"I don't know, Claude. I've never gone away with a man before." *I wonder if he believes that.*

"*Oui,* but this is not a sex thing. I just thought of the chalet because you said you needed a rest. You can think of me as your brother." *And we will try some good, old-fashioned incest.*

The Graceful One was unaware that the various people were speaking in different languages, for she was able to filter them all through her consciousness and understand what they were saying.

I must find a way to get in touch with the mothership, she thought. She took out the small, hand-held silver-colored transmitter. It was a divided neuronet system, half of it consisting of living organic material and the other half of a metallic compound from another galaxy. The organic material was composed of thousands of single cells, so that as they died off, others would multiply, keeping the connections constant. Unfortunately, the dilitheum crystal that activated the transmitter had broken off and was lost. She had tried to communicate with her ship, but the transmitter was useless without it.

She tried to eat another leaf of lettuce, but she could no longer stand the stench. She rose and started toward the door. The cashier called out after her, "Just a minute, miss. You haven't paid for your meal."

"I'm sorry. I do not have your medium of exchange."

"You can tell that to the police."

The Graceful One stared into the cashier's eyes and watched her go limp. She turned and walked out of the feeding place.

I must find the crystal. They are waiting to hear from me. She had to concentrate to focus her senses. But everything seemed blurred and distorted. Without water, she knew, she was going to die soon.

Chapter Twenty-two

Day Five
Bern, Switzerland

Robert had come to a dead end. He had not realized how much he had counted on obtaining Mothershed's list of names. *Up in smoke,* Robert thought. *Literally.* The trail was cold now. *I should have gotten the list when I was in Mothershed's flat. That will teach me to—teach.* Of course! A thought that had been in the back of his mind suddenly came into focus. Hans Beckerman had said, *"Affenarsch! All the other passengers were excited about seeing the UFO and those dead creatures in it, but this old man kept complaining about how we had to hurry up to get to Bern because he had to prepare some lecture for the university."* It was a long shot, but it was all Robert had.

He rented a car at the Bern airport and headed for the university. He turned off Rathausgasse, the main street of Bern, and drove to Länggassestrasse, where the University of Bern was located. The university is composed of several buildings, the main one a large four-story stone building with two wings and large stone gargoyles adorning the roof. At each end of the courtyard in front of the building are glass skylights over classrooms, and at the rear of the university is a large park overlooking the Aare River.

Robert walked up the front steps of the administration building and entered the reception hall. The only information Beckerman had given him was that the passenger was German and that he was preparing his lecture for Monday.

A student directed him to the Office of the Administration. The woman seated behind the desk was a formidable figure. She had on a severely tailored suit, black-framed spectacles, and she wore her hair in a bun. She looked up as Robert entered her office.

"Bitte?"

Robert pulled out an identification card. "Interpol. I'm conducting an investigation, and I would appreciate your cooperation, Miss—"

"Frau. Frau Schreiber. What kind of investigation?"

"I'm looking for a professor."

She frowned. "His name?"

"I don't know."

"You do not know his name?"

"No. He's a visiting professor. He gave a lecture here a few days ago. *Montag*."

"Many visiting professors come here every day to give lectures. What is his discipline?"

"I beg your pardon?"

"What does he teach?" Her tone was growing impatient. "What subject did he lecture on?"

"I don't know."

She let her exasperation show. "*Tut mir leid.* I can't

help you. And I am too busy for frivolous questions like this—" She started to turn away.

"Oh, it's not frivolous," Robert assured her. *"Es ist sehr dringend."* He leaned forward and said in a low voice, "I'm going to have to take you into my confidence. The professor we're looking for is involved in a prostitution ring."

Frau Schreiber's mouth made a small "o" of surprise.

"Interpol has been on his trail for months. The current information we have on him is that he is German and that he gave a lecture here on the fifteenth of this month." He straightened up. "If you don't want to help, we can conduct an official investigation of the university. Of course, the publicity—"

"Nein, nein!" she said. "The university must not be involved in anything like this." She looked worried. "You say he lectured here on—what day?"

"The fifteenth. Monday."

Frau Schreiber rose and walked over to a filing cabinet. She pulled it open and scanned some papers. She extracted several sheets from a folder. "Here we are. There were three guest professors who gave lectures here on the fifteenth."

"The man I want is German."

"They are all German," Frau Schreiber said stiffly. She shuffled the papers in her hand. "One of the lectures was on economics, one on chemistry, and one on psychology."

"May I see those?"

Reluctantly, she handed the reports to Robert.

He studied the sheets. Each one had a name written down with a home address and a telephone number.

"I can make a copy of these for you, if you wish."

"No, thank you." He had already memorized the

names and numbers. "None of these is the man I'm looking for."

Frau Schreiber gave a sigh of relief. "Well, thank God for that. Prostitution! We would never be involved in such a thing."

"I'm sorry I troubled you for nothing." Robert left and headed for a telephone booth in town.

The first telephone call was to Berlin. "Professor Streubel?"

"Ja."

"This is the Sunshine Tours Bus Company. You left a pair of glasses on our bus last Sunday when you were touring with us in Switzerland and—"

"I do not know what you are speaking about." He sounded annoyed.

"You were in Switzerland on the fourteenth, were you not, Professor?"

"No. On the fifteenth. To give a lecture at the University of Bern."

"And you did not take our bus tour?"

"I have no time for such foolishness. I'm a busy man." And the professor hung up.

The second call was to Hamburg. "Professor Heinrich?"

"This is Professor Heinrich."

"This is the Sunshine Tours Bus Company. You were in Switzerland on the fourteenth of this month?"

"Why do you wish to know?"

"Because we found a briefcase of yours on one of our buses, Professor, and . . ."

"You have the wrong person. I have been on no tour buses."

"You did not take a tour of ours to the Jungfrau?"

"I just told you, no."

"I'm sorry to have bothered you."

The third call was to Munich. "Professor Otto Schmidt?"

"Yes."

"Professor Schmidt, this is the Sunshine Tours Bus Company. We have a pair of your glasses that you left on our bus a few days ago, and—"

"There must be some mistake."

Robert's heart sank. He had struck out. There was nowhere left to go.

The voice went on. "I have my glasses here. I have not lost them."

Robert's spirits soared. "Are you sure, Professor? You *were* on the Jungfrau trip on the fourteenth, were you not?"

"Yes, yes, but I told you, I have not lost anything."

"Thank you very much, Professor." Robert replaced the receiver. *Jackpot!*

Robert dialed another number, and within two minutes he was speaking with General Hilliard.

"I have two things to report," Robert said. "The witness in London I told you about?"

"Yes?"

"He died in a fire last night."

"Really? Too bad."

"Yes, sir. But I believe I've located another witness. I'll let you know as soon as I check him out."

"I'll wait to hear from you, Commander."

General Hilliard was reporting to Janus.

"Commander Bellamy has located another witness."

"Good. The group is getting restless. Everyone is worried that this story will surface before SDI is operational."

"I'll have more information for you soon."

"I don't want information, I want results."

"Yes, Janus."

Plattenstrasse, in Munich, is a quiet residential street with drab brownstone buildings huddled together as though for protection. Number 5 was identical to its neighbors. Inside the vestibule was a row of mailboxes. A small card below one of them read, "Professor Otto Schmidt." Robert rang the bell.

The apartment door was opened by a tall, thin man with an untidy mop of white hair. He was wearing a tattered sweater and smoking a pipe. Robert wondered whether he had created the image of an archetypical college professor, or whether the image had created him.

"Professor Schmidt?"

"Yes?"

"I wonder if I might talk to you a moment. I'm with—"

"We have already talked," Professor Schmidt said. "You are the man who telephoned me this morning. I am an expert at recognizing voices. Come in."

"Thank you." Robert entered a living room crowded with books. Against the walls, rising from floor to ceiling were bookcases filled with hundreds of volumes. Books were stacked everywhere: on tables, on the floor, on chairs. The sparse furniture in the room seemed to be an afterthought.

"You're not with any Swiss tour bus company, are you?"

"Well, I—"

"You are American."

"Yes."

"And this visit has nothing to do with my lost glasses that were not lost."

"Well—no, sir."

"You are interested in the UFO I saw. It was a very upsetting experience. I always believed they might exist, but I never thought I would see one."

"It must have been a terrible shock."

"It was."

"Can you tell me anything about it?"

"It was—it was almost alive. There was a kind of shimmering light around it. Blue. No, maybe more of a gray. I—I'm not sure."

He remembered Mandel's description: *"It kept changing colors. It looked blue . . . then green."*

"It had broken open, and I could see two bodies inside. Small . . . big eyes. They were wearing some kind of silver suit."

"Is there anything you can tell me about your fellow passengers?"

"My fellow passengers on the bus?"

"Yes."

The professor shrugged. "I know nothing of them. They were all strangers. I was concentrating on a lecture I was going to give the next morning, and I paid very little attention to the other passengers."

Robert watched his face, waiting.

"If it will help you any," the professor said, "I can tell you what countries some of them came from. I teach chemistry, but the study of phonetics is my hobby."

"Anything you can remember would be appreciated."

"There was an Italian priest, a Hungarian, an American with a Texas accent, an Englishman, a Russian girl—"

"Russian?"

"Yes. But she was not from Moscow. From her accent, I would say Kiev, or very near there."

Robert waited, but there was only silence. "You didn't

hear any of them mention their names or talk about their professions?"

"I'm sorry. I told you, I was thinking about my lecture: It was difficult to concentrate. The Texan and the priest sat together. The Texan never stopped talking. It was very distracting. I don't know how much the priest even understood."

"The priest—"

"He had a Roman accent."

"Can you tell me anything more about any of them?"

The professor shrugged. "I'm afraid not." He took another puff on his pipe. "I'm sorry I can't be of any help to you."

A sudden thought came to Robert. "You said you're a chemist?"

"Yes."

"I wonder if you would mind taking a look at something, Professor." Robert reached in his pocket and pulled out the piece of metal Beckerman had given him. "Can you tell me what this is?"

Professor Schmidt took the object in his hand, and as he examined it, his expression changed. "Where—where did you get this?"

"I'm afraid I can't say. Do you know what it is?"

"It appears to be part of a transmitting device."

"Are you sure?"

He turned it over in his hand. "The crystal is dilithium. It's very rare. See these notches here? They suggest that this fits into a larger unit. The metal itself is . . . My God, I've never seen anything like it!" His voice was charged with excitement. "Can you let me have this for a few days? I would like to do some spectrographic studies on it."

"I'm afraid that's impossible," Robert said.

"But—"

"Sorry." Robert took back the piece of metal.

The professor tried to conceal his disappointment. "Perhaps you can bring it back. Why don't you give me your card? If I think of anything more, I'll call you."

Robert fumbled in his pockets for a moment. "I don't seem to have any of my cards with me."

Professor Schmidt said slowly, "Yes, I thought not."

"Commander Bellamy is on the line."

General Hilliard picked up the telephone. "Yes, Commander?"

"The latest witness's name is Professor Schmidt. He lives at Plattenstrasse 5 in Munich."

"Thank you, Commander. I'll notify the German authorities immediately."

Robert was on the verge of saying "I'm afraid that's the last witness I'll be able to find," but something held him back. He hated to admit failure. And yet, the trail had become cold. A Texan and a priest. The priest was from Rome. Period. Along with a million other priests. And there was no way to identify him. *I have a choice,* Robert thought. *I can give up and go back to Washington, or I can go to Rome and give it one last try. . . .*

Bundesverfassungsschutzamt, the headquarters of the Office for the Protection of the Constitution, is located in central Berlin on Neumarkterstrasse. It is a large, gray, nondescript building, indistinguishable from the buildings around it. Inside on the second floor, in the conference room, the chief of the department, Inspector Otto Joachim, was studying a message. He read it twice, then reached for the red telephone on his desk.

Day Six
Munich, Germany

The following morning, as Otto Schmidt headed for his chemistry lab, he was thinking about the conversation he had had with the American the evening before. Where could that piece of metal have come from? It was astonishing, beyond anything in his experience. And the American puzzled him. *He said he was interested in the passengers on the bus. Why? Because they've all been witnesses to the flying saucer? Are they going to be warned not to talk? If so, why didn't the American warn him? There's something strange going on,* the professor decided. He entered the laboratory and took off his jacket and hung it up. He put on an apron to keep his clothes from getting soiled and walked over to the table where he had been working for many weeks on a chemical experiment. *If this works,* he thought, *it could mean a Nobel prize.* He lifted the beaker of sterile water and started to pour it into a container filled with a yellow liquid. *That's strange. I don't remember it being such a bright yellow.*

The roar of the explosion was tremendous. The laboratory erupted in a gigantic blast, and pieces of glass and human flesh spattered the walls.

FLASH MESSAGE

TOP SECRET ULTRA

BFV TO DEPUTY DIRECTOR NSA

EYES ONLY

COPY ONE OF (ONE) COPIES

SUBJECT: OPERATION DOOMSDAY

4. OTTO SCHMIDT—TERMINATED

END OF MESSAGE

Robert missed the news of the professor's death. He was aboard an Alitalia plane, on his way to Rome.

Chapter Twenty-three

Dustin Thornton was getting restless. He had power now, and it was like a drug. He wanted more. His father-in-law, Willard Stone, kept promising to bring him into some mysterious inner circle, but so far he had failed to fulfill that promise.

It was by pure chance that Thornton learned that his father-in-law disappeared every Friday. Thorton had called to have lunch with him.

"I'm sorry," Willard Stone's personal secretary said, "but Mr. Stone is away for the day."

"Oh, too bad. What about lunch next Friday?"

"I'm sorry, Mr. Thornton. Mr. Stone will be away next Friday also."

Strange. And it became even stranger, because when Thornton called two weeks later, he received the same reply. *Where does the old man disappear to every Friday?* He was not a golfer or a man to indulge in any hobbies.

The obvious answer was a woman. Willard Stone's wife was very social and very rich. She was an imperious woman, almost as strong in her way as her husband. She was not the sort of woman who would tolerate her husband having an affair. *If he is having an affair,* Thornton thought, *I've got him by the balls.* He knew he had to find out.

With all the facilities at his command, Dustin Thornton could have found out very quickly what his father-in-law was up to, but Thornton was no fool. He was well aware that if he made one misstep, he would be in big trouble. Willard Stone was not the kind of man to brook any interference in his life. Thornton decided to investigate the matter himself.

At five A.M. on the following Friday, Dustin Thornton was slumped behind the wheel of an inconspicuous Ford Taurus, half a block from Willard Stone's imposing mansion. It was a cold, miserable dawn, and Thornton kept asking himself what he was doing there. There was probably some perfectly reasonable explanation for Stone's odd behavior. *I'm wasting my time,* Thornton thought. But something kept him there.

At seven o'clock, the driveway gates opened, and a car appeared. Willard Stone was at the wheel. Instead of his usual limousine, he was in a small, black van used by the household staff. A feeling of exultation spread through Thornton. He knew he was onto something. People lived according to their pattern, and Stone was breaking the pattern. It *had* to be another woman.

Driving carefully and staying well behind the van, Thornton followed his father-in-law through the streets of Washington to the road that led to Arlington.

I'll have to handle this very delicately, Thornton

thought. *I don't want to push him too hard. I'll get all the information I can about his mistress, and then I'll confront him with it. I'll tell him my only interest is in protecting him. He'll get the message. The last thing he wants is a public scandal.*

Dustin Thornton was so wrapped up in his own thoughts that he almost missed the turn that Willard Stone had taken. They were in an exclusive residential district. The black van abruptly disappeared up a long, tree-shaded driveway.

Dustin Thornton stopped the car, deciding on the best way to proceed. Should he face Willard Stone with his infidelity now? Or should he wait until Stone left and then talk to the woman first? Or should he quietly gather all the information he needed and then have a talk with his father-in-law? He decided to reconnoiter.

Thornton parked his car on a side street and walked around to the alley at the back of the two-story house. A wooden fence blocked off the back of the yard, but that was no problem. Thornton opened the gate and stepped inside. He was facing huge, beautiful, manicured grounds with the house at the rear.

He moved quietly in the shadow of the trees that lined the lawn and stood at the back door, deciding what his next move should be. He needed proof of what was going on. Without it the old man would laugh at him. Whatever was happening inside at this moment could be the key to his future. He had to find out.

Very gently, Thornton tried the back door. It was unlocked. He slipped inside and found himself in a large, old-fashioned kitchen. There was no one around. Thornton moved toward the service door and pushed it open slightly. He was facing a large reception hall. At the far end was a closed door that could have led to a library. Thornton walked toward it, moving quietly. He stood there listening. There was no sign of life in the house. *The old man is probably upstairs in the bedroom.*

Thornton walked toward the closed door and opened it. He stood in the doorway, staring. There were a dozen men seated in the room around a large table.

"Come in, Dustin," Willard Stone said. "We've been expecting you."

Chapter Twenty-four

Rome proved to be difficult for Robert, an emotional ordeal that drained him. He had honeymooned there with Susan, and the memories were overpowering. Rome was Roberto, who managed the Hassler Hotel for his mother, and who was partially deaf but could lip-read in five languages. Rome was the gardens of Villa d'Este in Tivoli, and the Ristorante Sibilla and Susan's delight at the one hundred fountains created by the son of Lucretia Borgia. Rome was Otello, at the foot of the Spanish Steps, and the Vatican, and the Colosseum and the Forum and Michelangelo's Moses. Rome was sharing a *tartufo* at Tre Scalini and the sound of Susan's laughter, and her voice saying, "Please promise me we'll always be this happy, Robert."

What the hell am I doing here? Robert wondered. *I don't have any idea who the priest is, or whether he's even in Rome. It's time to retire, to go home and forget all this.*

But something inside him, some stubborn streak inherited from a long-dead ancestor, would not let him. *I'll give it one day,* Robert decided. *Just one more day.*

The Leonardo da Vinci Airport was crowded, and it seemed to Robert that every other person was a priest. He was looking for one priest in a city of—what? Fifty thousand priests? A hundred thousand? In the taxi on the way to the Hassler Hotel, he noticed crowds of robed priests on the streets. *This is impossible,* Robert thought. *I must be out of my mind.*

He was greeted in the lobby of the Hassler Hotel by the assistant manager.

"Commander Bellamy! What a pleasure to see you again."

"Thank you, Pietro. Do you have a room for me for one night?"

"For you—of course. Always!"

Robert was escorted to a room he had occupied before.

"If there's anything you need, Commander, please . . ."

I need a bloody miracle, Robert thought. He sat down on the bed and lay back, trying to clear his mind.

Why would a priest from Rome travel to Switzerland? There were several possibilities. He might have gone on vacation, or there might have been a convocation of priests. He was the only priest on the tour bus. What did that signify? Nothing. Except, perhaps, that he was not traveling with a group. So it could have been a trip to visit his friends or family. Or maybe he *was* with a group, and they had other plans that day. Robert's thoughts were going around in a futile circle.

Back to the beginning. How did the priest get to Switzerland? The chances are pretty good that he doesn't own a car. Someone could have given him a lift, but more probably he traveled by plane or train or took a bus. If he were on vacation, he wouldn't have a lot of time. So let's assume he took a plane. That line of reasoning led nowhere. Airlines did not list the occupations of their passengers. The priest would be yet another name on the passenger manifest. But if he were part of a group . . .

The Vatican, the official residence of the pope, rises majestically on Vatican Hill, on the west bank of the Tiber, in the northwest end of Rome. The dome of St. Peter's Basilica, designed by Michelangelo, towers over the huge piazza, filled day and night with avid sightseers of all faiths.

The piazza is surrounded by two semicircular colonnades completed in 1667 by Bernini, with 284 columns of travertine marble placed in 4 rows and surmounted by a balustrade on which stand 140 statues. Robert had visited there a dozen times, but each time the sight took his breath away.

The interior of the Vatican, of course, was even more spectacular. The Sistine Chapel and the museum and the Sala Rotonda were indescribably beautiful.

But on this day, Robert had not come here to sightsee.

He found the Office of Public Relations for the Vatican in the wing of the building devoted to secular affairs. The young man behind the desk was polite.

"May I help you?"

Robert flashed an identification card. "I'm with *Time* magazine. I'm doing an article on some priests who attended a convocation in Switzerland in the past week or two. I'm looking for background information."

The man studied him for a moment, then frowned.

"We had some priests attend a convocation in Venice last month. None of our priests was in Switzerland recently. I'm sorry, I'm afraid I can't help you."

"It's really very important," Robert said earnestly. "How would I go about getting that information?"

"The group you are looking for—what branch of the church do they represent?"

"I beg your pardon?"

"There are many Roman Catholic orders. There are Franciscans, Marists, Benedictines, Trappists, Jesuits, Dominicans, and several others. I suggest you go to the order they belong to and inquire there."

Where the hell is "there"? Robert wondered. "Do you have any other suggestions?"

"I'm afraid not."

Neither have I, Robert thought. *I found the haystack. I can't find the needle.*

He left the Vatican and wandered through the streets of Rome, heedless of the people around him, concentrating on his problem. At the Piazza del Popolo, he sat down at an outdoor café and ordered a Cinzano. It sat in front of him, untouched.

For all he knew, the priest could still be in Switzerland. *What order does he belong to? I don't know. And I have only the professor's word that he was Roman.*

He took a sip of his drink.

There was a late-afternoon plane to Washington. *I'm going to be on it,* Robert decided. *I give up.* The thought galled him. *Out, not with a bang, but with a whimper.* It was time to leave.

"Il conto, per favore."

"Si, signore."

Robert's eyes swept idly around the piazza. Across from the café, a bus was loading passengers. In the line were two priests. Robert watched as the passengers paid their fares and moved toward the back of the bus. When the priests reached the conductor, they smiled at him and took their seats without paying.

"Your check, *signore,*" the waiter said.

Robert didn't even hear him. His mind was racing. Here, in the heart of the Catholic church, priests had certain privileges. It was possible, just possible . . .

The offices of Swissair are located at 10 Via Po, five minutes from the Via Veneto. Robert was greeted by a man behind the counter.

"May I see the manager, please?"

"I am the manager. Can I help you?"

Robert flashed an identification card. "Michael Hudson. Interpol."

"What can I do for you, Mr. Hudson?"

"Some international carriers are complaining about illegal price discounting in Europe—in Rome, particularly. According to international convention—"

"Excuse me, Mr. Hudson, but Swissair does not give discounts. Everyone pays the posted fares."

"Everyone?"

"With the exception of employees of the airline, of course."

"Don't you have a discount for priests?"

"No. On this airline, they pay full fare."

On this airline. "Thank you for your time." And Robert was gone.

His next stop—and his last hope—was Alitalia. "Illegal discounts?" The manager was staring at Robert, puzzled. "We give discounts only to our employees."

"Don't you give discounts to priests?"

The manager's face brightened. "Ah, that, yes. But

that is not illegal. We have arrangements with the Catholic church."

Robert's heart soared. "So, if a priest wanted to fly from Rome, say, to Switzerland, he would use this airline?"

"Well, it would be cheaper for him. Yes."

Robert said, "In order to bring our computers up-to-date, it would be helpful if you could tell me how many priests have flown to Switzerland in the past two weeks. You would have a record of that, wouldn't you?"

"Yes, of course. For tax purposes."

"I would really appreciate that information."

"You wish to know how many priests have flown to Switzerland in the past two weeks?"

"Yes. Zurich or Geneva."

"Just a moment. I will talk to our computers."

Five minutes later, the manager returned with a computer printout. "There was only one priest who flew Alitalia to Switzerland in the past two weeks." He consulted the printout. "He left Rome on the seventh and flew to Zurich. His return flight was booked for two days ago."

Robert took a deep breath. "His name?"

"Father Romero Patrini."

"His address?"

He looked down at the paper again. "He lives in Orvieto. If you need any further—" He looked up.

Robert was gone.

Chapter Twenty-five

Day Seven
Orvieto, Italy

He stopped the car on a hairpin bend on route S-71, and there across the valley, high on a rise of volcanic rock, was a breathtaking view of the city. It was an ancient Etruscan center with a world-famous cathedral, half a dozen churches, and a priest who had witnessed the crash of a UFO.

The town was untouched by time, with cobblestone streets and lovely old buildings, and an open-air market where farmers came to sell their fresh vegetables and chickens.

Robert found a parking place in the Piazza del Duomo. He crossed to the cathedral and went inside. The enormous interior was deserted, except for an elderly priest who was just leaving the altar.

"Excuse me, Father," Robert said. "I'm looking for a priest from this town who was in Switzerland last week. Perhaps you—"

The priest drew back, his face hostile. "I cannot discuss this."

Robert looked at him in surprise. "I don't understand. I just want to find—"

"He is not of this church. He is from the Church of San Giovenale." And the priest hurried past Robert. *Why is he so unfriendly?*

The Church of San Giovenale was in the Quartiere Vecchio, a colorful area with medieval towers and churches. A young priest was tending the garden next to it. He looked up as Robert approached.

"Buon giorno, signore."

"Good morning. I'm looking for one of the priests who was in Switzerland last week. He—"

"Yes, yes. Poor Father Patrini. It was a terrible, terrible thing that happened to him."

"I don't understand. What terrible thing?"

"Seeing the devil's chariot. It was more than he could stand. The poor man had a nervous breakdown."

"I'm sorry to hear that," Robert said. "Where is he now? I would like to talk to him."

"He's in the hospital near the Piazza di San Patrizio, but I doubt if the doctors will allow anyone to see him."

Robert stood there, troubled. A man suffering a nervous breakdown was not going to be much help. "I see. Thank you very much."

The hospital was an unpretentious one-story building near the outskirts of the city. He parked the car and walked into the small lobby. There was a nurse behind the reception desk.

"Good morning," Robert said. "I would like to see Father Patrini."

"*Mi scusi, ma*—that is impossible. He cannot speak with anyone."

Robert was determined not to be stopped now. He had to follow up the lead Professor Schmidt had given him. "You don't understand," Robert said smoothly. "Father Patrini *asked* to see me. I've come to Orvieto at his request."

"He *asked* to see you?"

"Yes. He wrote to me in America. I've come all this way just to see him."

The nurse hesitated. "I do not know what to say. He is very ill. *Molto.*"

"I'm sure it would cheer him up to see me."

"The doctor is not here—" She made a decision. "Very well. You may go into his room, *signore,* but you may only stay a few minutes."

"That's all I'll need," Robert said.

"This way, *per piacere.*"

They walked down a short corridor with small, neat rooms on either side. The nurse led Robert to one of the doors.

"Only a few minutes, *signore.*"

"Grazie."

Robert entered the little room. The man in the bed looked like a pale shadow lying on the white sheets. Robert approached him and said softly, "Father—"

The priest turned to look up at him, and Robert had never seen such agony in a man's eyes.

"Father, my name is—"

He grabbed Robert's arm. "Help me," the priest mumbled. "You must help me. My faith is gone. All my life I have preached of God and the Holy Spirit, and now I know that there is no God. There is only the devil, and he has come for us—"

"Father, if you—"

"I saw it with my own eyes. There were two of them in the devil's chariot, but, oh, there will be more! Others will come! Wait and see. We are all doomed to hell."

"Father—listen to me. What you saw was not the devil. It was a space vehicle that—"

The priest let go of Robert and looked at him with sudden clarity. "Who are you? What do you want?"

Robert said, "I'm a friend. I came here to ask you about the bus trip you took in Switzerland."

"The bus. I wish I had never gone near it." The priest was becoming agitated again.

Robert hated to press him, but he had no choice.

"You sat next to a man on that bus. A Texan. You had a long conversation with him, remember?"

"A conversation. The Texan. Yes, I remember."

"Did he mention where he lived in Texas?"

"Yes, I remember him. He was from America."

"Yes. From Texas. Did he tell you where his home was?"

"Yes, yes. He told me."

"Where, Father? Where is his home?"

"Texas. He talked of Texas."

Robert nodded encouragingly. "That's right."

"I saw them with my own eyes. I wish God had blinded me. I—"

"Father—the man from Texas. Did he say where he was from? Did he mention a name?"

"Texas, yes. The Ponderosa."

Robert tried again. "That's on television. This was a real man. He sat next to you on—"

The priest was becoming delirious again. "They're coming! Armageddon is here. The Bible lies! It is the devil who will invade the earth." He was shouting loudly now. "Look out! Look out! I can see them!"

The nurse came hurrying in. She looked at Robert reprovingly. "You will have to leave, *signore.*"

"I need just one more minute—"

"No, signore. Adesso!"

Robert took one last look at the priest. He was raving incoherently. Robert turned to go. There was nothing further he could do. He had gambled on the priest giving him a lead to the Texan, and he had lost.

Robert returned to his car and headed back toward Rome. It was finally over. The only clues he had left—if they could be called clues—were the mention of a Russian woman, a Texan, and a Hungarian. But there was no way to pursue them any farther. *Check and checkmate.* It was frustrating to have come this far and then to be stopped. If only the priest had remained coherent long enough to give him the information he needed! He had been so close. What was it the priest had said? *The Ponderosa. The old priest has been watching too much television and, in his delirium, he obviously associated Texas with the once-popular TV show, "Bonanza."* The Ponderosa, where the mythical Cartwright family lived. *The Ponderosa.* Robert slowed the car and pulled over to the side of the road, his mind racing. He made a U-turn and sped back toward Orvieto.

Half an hour later, Robert was talking to the bartender in a small trattoria in the Piazza della Repubblica. "You have a beautiful town here," Robert said. "It's very peaceful."

"Oh, *si, signore,* we are quite content here. Have you visited Italy before?"

"I spent part of my honeymoon in Rome." *"You make all my dreams come true, Robert. I've wanted to see Rome ever since I was a little girl."*

"Ah, Rome. Too big. Too noisy."

"I agree."

"We live simple lives here, but we are happy."

Robert said casually, "I noticed television antennas on many of the roofs here."

"Oh, yes, indeed. We are quite up-to-date in that respect."

"One can see that. How many television channels does the town receive?"

"Only one."

"I suppose you get a good many American shows?"

"*No, no.* This is a government channel. Here we receive only shows made in Italy."

Bingo! "Thank you."

Robert placed a call to Admiral Whittaker. A secretary answered the phone. "Admiral Whittaker's office."

Robert could visualize the office. It would be the kind of anonymous cubbyhole they kept for nonpersons the government no longer had any use for.

"Could I speak to the admiral, please? Commander Robert Bellamy calling."

"Just a moment, Commander."

Robert wondered whether anybody bothered to keep in touch with the admiral now that the once-powerful figure was part of the mothball fleet. Probably not.

"Robert, it's very good to hear from you." The old man's voice sounded tired. "Where are you?"

"I can't say, sir."

There was a pause. "I understand. Is there something I can do for you?"

"Yes, sir. This is rather awkward because I've been ordered not to communicate with anyone. But I need some outside help. I wonder if you could check on something for me?"

"I can certainly try. What would you like to know?"

"I need to know whether there's a ranch anywhere in Texas called The Ponderosa."

"As in *Bonanza*?"

"Yes, sir."

"I can find out. How will I reach you?"

"I think it would be better if I called you, Admiral."

"Right. Give me an hour or two. I'll keep this just between ourselves."

"Thank you."

It seemed to Robert that the tiredness had gone out of the old man's voice. He had, at last, been asked to do something, even if it was as trivial as locating a ranch.

Two hours later, Robert telephoned Admiral Whittaker again.

"I've been waiting for your call," the admiral said. There was a satisfied note in his voice. "I have the information you wanted."

"And?" Robert held his breath.

"There *is* a Ponderosa ranch in Texas. It's located just outside of Waco. It's owned by a Dan Wayne."

Robert heaved a deep sigh of relief. "Thank you very much, Admiral," Robert said. "I owe you a dinner when I get back."

"I'll be looking forward to that, Robert."

Robert's next call was to General Hilliard. "I located another witness in Italy. Father Patrini."

"A priest?"

"Yes. In Orvieto. He's in the hospital, very ill. I'm

afraid the Italian authorities won't be able to communicate with him."

"I'll pass that on. Thank you, Commander."

Two minutes later, General Hilliard was on the line to Janus.

"I've heard from Commander Bellamy again. The latest witness is a priest. A Father Patrini in Orvieto."

"Take care of it."

FLASH MESSAGE

TOP SECRET ULTRA

NSA TO DEPUTY DIRECTOR SIFAR

EYES ONLY

COPY ONE OF (ONE) COPIES

SUBJECT: OPERATION DOOMSDAY

5. FATHER PATRINI—ORVIETO

END OF MESSAGE

The headquarters of SIFAR is on Via della Pineta, on the southernmost outskirts of Rome, in an area surrounded by farmhouses. The only thing that would cause a passerby to give a second glance at the innocent, industrial-looking stone buildings occupying two square blocks would be the high wall surrounding the complex, topped by barbed wire, with security posts at each corner. Hidden in a military compound, it is one of the most secretive security agencies in the world, and one of the least known. There are signs outside the compound reading: *Vietate Passare Oltre i Limiti.*

Inside a Spartan office on the first floor of the main building, Colonel Francesco Cesar was studying the flash message he had just received. The colonel was a man in his early fifties with a muscular body, topped by a pitted, bulldog face. He read the message for the third time.

So, Operation Doomsday is finally happening. E una bella fregatura. It is good that we have prepared for this, Cesar thought. He looked down at the cable again. A priest.

It was after midnight when the nun walked past the desk of the night-duty nurses at the little hospital in Orvieto.

"I guess she's going to see Signora Fillipi," said Nurse Tomasino.

"Either her or old man Rigano. They're both on their last legs." The nun glided silently round the corner and walked directly into the priest's room. He was sleeping peacefully, his hands gathered almost as if in prayer, on his chest. A wedge of moonlight sliced through the blinds, casting a golden band across the priest's face.

The nun removed a small box from beneath her habit. Carefully, she took out a beautiful cut-glass rosary and placed it in the old priest's hands. As she adjusted the beads, she drew one of them quickly across his thumb. A thin line of blood appeared. The nun took a tiny bottle from the box and, with an eye dropper, delicately squeezed three drops into the open cut.

It took only a few minutes for the deadly, fast-acting poison to work. The nun sighed as she made the sign of the cross over the dead man. She left as silently as she had come in.

FLASH MESSAGE

TOP SECRET ULTRA

SIFAR TO DEPUTY DIRECTOR NSA

EYES ONLY

COPY ONE OF (ONE) COPIES

SUBJECT: OPERATION DOOMSDAY

5. FATHER PATRINI—ORVIETO—TERMINATED

END OF MESSAGE

Chapter Twenty-six

Frank Johnson was recruited because he had been a Green Beret in Vietnam and was known among his comrades as the Killing Machine. He loved to kill. He was motivated and highly intelligent.

"He's perfect for us," Janus said. "Approach him carefully. I don't want to lose him."

The first meeting took place in an army barracks. A captain was talking to Frank Johnson.

"Don't you worry about our government?" the captain asked. "It's being run by a bunch of bleeding hearts who are giving the store away. This country needs nuclear power, but the damned politicians are stopping us from building new plants. We depend on the damn Arabs for oil, but will the government let us do our own offshore drilling? Oh, no. They're more worried about the fish than they are about us. Does that make sense to you?"

"I see your point," Frank Johnson said.

"I knew you would, because you're intelligent." He was watching Johnson's face as he spoke. "If Congress won't do anything to save our country, then it's up to some of us to do something."

Frank Johnson looked puzzled. "Some of *us*?"

"Yeah." *Enough for now,* the captain thought. "We'll talk about it later."

The next conversation was more specific. "There's a group of patriots, Frank, who are interested in protecting our world. They're pretty high-powered gentlemen. They've formed a committee. The committee may have to bend a few laws to get its work done, but in the end, it will be worth it. Are you interested?"

Frank Johnson grinned. "I'm very interested."

That was the beginning. The next meeting took place in Ottawa, Canada, and Frank Johnson met some of the members of the committee. They represented powerful interests from a dozen countries.

"We're well organized," a member explained to Frank Johnson. "We have a strict chain of command. There's a Propaganda Division, Recruiting, Tactics, Liaison . . . and a Death Squad." He went on. "Almost every intelligence organization in the world is part of this."

"You mean the heads of—?"

"No, not the heads. The deputies. The hands-on people who know what's going on, who know what danger our countries are in."

The meetings took place all over the world—Switzerland, Morocco, China—and Johnson attended all of them.

* * *

It was six months before Colonel Johnson met Janus. Janus had sent for him.

"I've been given excellent reports about you, Colonel."

Frank Johnson grinned. "I enjoy my work."

"So I've heard. You're in an advantageous position to help us."

Frank Johnson sat up straighter. "I'll do anything I can."

"Good. At the Farm, you're in charge of supervising the training of secret agents in the various services."

"That's right."

"And you get to know them and their capabilities."

"Intimately."

"What I would like you to do," Janus said, "is to recruit those whom you feel would be most helpful to our organization. We're interested only in the best."

"That's easy," Colonel Johnson said. "No problem." He hesitated a moment. "I wonder—"

"Yes?"

"I can do that with my left hand. I'd really like to do something more, something bigger." He leaned forward. "I've heard about Operation Doomsday. Doomsday is right up my alley. I'd like to be a part of that, sir."

Janus sat there, studying him a moment. Then he nodded. "Very well, you're in."

Johnson smiled. "Thank you. You won't be sorry." Colonel Frank Johnson left the meeting a very happy man. Now he would have a chance to show them what he could do.

Chapter Twenty-seven

Day Eight
Waco, Texas

Dan Wayne was not having a good day. As a matter of fact, he was having a dreadful day. He had just returned from the Waco county courthouse, where he was facing bankruptcy proceedings. His wife, who had been having an affair with her young doctor, was divorcing him, intent on getting half of everything he had (which could be half of nothing, he had assured her lawyer). And one of his prize bulls had to be destroyed. Dan Wayne felt that fate was kicking him in the balls. He had done nothing to deserve all this. He had been a good husband and a good rancher. He sat in his study contemplating the gloomy future.

Dan Wayne was a proud man. He was well aware of all the jokes about Texans being loudmouthed, larger-than-life braggarts, but he honestly felt he had something to brag about. He had been born in Waco, in the rich agricultural region of the Brazos River valley. Waco was modern, but it still retained a flavor of the past, when the five C's had been its support: cattle, cotton, corn, collegians, and culture. Wayne loved Waco with all his heart and soul, and when he had met the Italian priest on the Swiss tour bus, he had spent almost five hours going on about his hometown. The priest had told him he wanted to practice his English, but actually, as he thought back on it, Dan had done almost all the talking.

"Waco has everything," he had confided to the priest. "Our climate's great. We don't allow it to get too hot or too cold. We have twenty-three schools in the school district and Baylor University. We have four newspapers, ten radio stations, and five television stations. We have a Texas Ranger Hall of Fame that will knock you out. I mean, we're talking *history*. If you like fishing, Father, the Brazos River is an experience you'll never forget. Then, we have a safari ranch and a big art center. I tell you, Waco is one of the unique cities of the world. You must come and pay us a visit."

And the little old priest had smiled and nodded, and Wayne wondered how much English he really understood.

Dan Wayne's father had left him a thousand acres of ranchland, and the son had built up his cattle herd from two thousand to ten thousand. There was also a prize stallion that was going to be worth a fortune. And now the bastards were trying to take it all away from him. It wasn't his fault that the cattle market had gone to hell, or that he had gotten behind with his mortgage payments. The banks were closing in for the kill, and his only chance to save himself was to find someone who would buy the ranch, pay off his creditors, and leave him with a little profit.

Wayne had heard about a rich Swiss who was looking for a ranch in Texas, and he had flown over to Zurich to meet him. In the end, it had turned out to be a wild-goose chase. The dude's idea of a ranch was an acre or two with a nice little vegetable garden. *She-eet!*

That was how Dan Wayne had happened to be on the tour bus when that extraordinary thing occurred. He had read about flying saucers, but he had never believed in them. Now, by God, he certainly did. As soon as he returned home, he had called the editor of the local newspaper.

"Johnny, I just saw an honest-to-God flying saucer with some dead, funny-looking people in it."

"Yeah? Did you get any pictures, Dan?"

"No. I took some, but they didn't come out."

"Never mind. We'll send a photographer out there. Is it on your ranch?"

"Well, no. As a matter of fact, it was in Switzerland."

There was a silence.

"Oh. Well, if you happen to come across one on your ranch, Dan, give me another call."

"Wait! I'm being sent a picture by some fellow who saw the thing." But Johnny had already hung up.

And that was that.

Wayne almost wished that there *would* be an invasion of aliens. Maybe they would kill off his damned creditors. He heard the sound of a car coming up the drive and rose and walked over to the window. Looked like an easterner. *Probably another creditor*. These days they were coming out of the woodwork.

Dan Wayne opened the front door.

"Howdy."

"Daniel Wayne?"

"My friends call me Dan. What can I do for you?"

Dan Wayne was not at all what Robert had expected. He had envisioned a stereotype of a burly Texan. Dan

Wayne was slight and aristocratic-looking, with an almost shy manner. The only thing that gave away his heritage was his accent.

"I wonder if I might have a few minutes of your time?"

"That's about all I've got left," Wayne said. "By the way, you're not a creditor, are you?"

"A creditor? No."

"Good. Come on in."

The two men walked into the living room. It was large and comfortably furnished with western-style furniture.

"This is a nice place you have here," Robert said.

"Yeah. I was born in this house. Can I offer you anything? A cold drink, maybe?"

"No, thanks. I'm fine."

"Have a seat."

Robert sat down on a soft, leather couch.

"What did you want to see me about?"

"I believe you took a bus tour in Switzerland last week?"

"That's right. Is my ex-wife having me followed? You don't work for her, do you?"

"No, sir."

"Oh." He suddenly understood. "You're interested in that UFO thing. Damndest thing I ever saw. It kept changing colors. And those dead aliens!" He shuddered. "I keep dreaming about it."

"Mr. Wayne, can you tell me anything about the other passengers who were on that bus?"

"Sorry, I can't help you out there. I was traveling alone."

"I know, but you spoke to some of the other passengers, didn't you?"

"To tell you the truth, I had a lot on my mind. I wasn't paying much attention to anyone else."

"Do you remember anything about any of them?"

Dan Wayne was silent for a moment. "Well, there was an Italian priest. I talked to him quite a bit. He seemed like a nice fellow. I want to tell you something, that flying saucer thing really shook him up. He kept talking about the devil."

"Did you speak to anyone else?"

Dan Wayne shrugged. "Not really. . . . Wait a minute. I talked a little bit to some fellow who owns a bank in Canada." He ran his tongue across his lips. "To tell you the truth, I'm having a little financial problem here with the ranch. It looks as though I might lose it. I hate goddamn bankers. They're all bloodsuckers. Anyway, I thought this fellow might be different. When I found out he was a banker, I talked to him about trying to work out some kind of loan arrangement here. But he was just like all the rest of them. He couldn't have been less interested."

"You said he was from Canada?"

"Yeah, Fort Smith, up in the Northwest Territories. I'm afraid that's about all I can tell you."

Robert tried to conceal his excitement. "Thank you, Mr. Wayne, you've been very helpful." Robert rose.

"That's it?"

"That's it."

"Would you like to stay for supper?"

"No, thanks. I have to be on my way. Good luck with the ranch."

"Thanks."

Fort Smith, Canada
Northwest Territories

Robert waited until General Hilliard came on the line.

"Yes, Commander?"

"I found another witness. Dan Wayne. He owns The Ponderosa, a ranch outside of Waco, Texas."

"Very good. I'll have our office in Dallas speak to him."

FLASH MESSAGE

TOP SECRET ULTRA

NSA TO DEPUTY DIRECTOR DCI

EYES ONLY

COPY ONE OF (ONE) COPIES

SUBJECT: OPERATION DOOMSDAY

6. DANIEL WAYNE—WACO

END OF MESSAGE

In Langley, Virginia, the deputy director of the Central Intelligence Agency studied the transmission thoughtfully. *Number six.* Things were going well. Commander Bellamy was doing an extraordinary job. The decision to select him had been a wise one. Janus had been right. The man was always right. And he had the power to have his wishes carried out. So much power. . . . The director looked at the message again. *Make it look like an accident,* he thought. *That shouldn't be difficult.* He pressed a buzzer.

The two men arrived at the ranch in a dark blue van. They parked in the courtyard and got out of the car, carefully looking around. Dan Wayne's first thought was that they had come to take possession of the ranch. He opened the door for them.

"Dan Wayne?"

"Yes. What can I—?"

That was as far as he got.

The second man had stepped behind him and hit him hard across the skull with a blackjack.

The larger of the two men slung the unconscious rancher over his shoulder and carried him outside to the barn. There were eight horses in the barn. The men ignored them and walked to the last stall in back. Inside was a beautiful black stallion.

The large man said, "This is the one." He put Wayne's body down.

The second man picked up a cattle prod from the ground, stepped up to the stall door, and hit the stallion with the electric prod. The stallion whinnied and reared up. The man hit him hard again across the nose. The stallion was bucking wildly now, confined in the small space, smashing against the walls of the stall, his teeth bared and the whites of his eyes flashing.

"Now," the smaller man said. His companion lifted the body of Dan Wayne and tossed it over the half door into the stall. They watched the bloody scene for several moments, then, satisfied, turned and left.

FLASH MESSAGE

TOP SECRET ULTRA

DCI TO DEPUTY DIRECTOR NSA

EYES ONLY

COPY ONE OF (ONE) COPIES

SUBJECT: OPERATION DOOMSDAY

6. DANIEL WAYNE—WACO—TERMINATED

END OF MESSAGE

Chapter Twenty-eight

Day Nine
Fort Smith, Canada

Fort Smith, in the Northwest Territories, is a prosperous town of two thousand people, most of them farmers and cattle ranchers, with a sprinkling of merchants. The climate is demanding, with long and rigorous winters, and the town is living proof of Darwin's theory of the survival of the fittest.

William Mann was one of the fit ones, a survivor. He had been born in Michigan, but in his early thirties, he had passed through Fort Smith on a fishing trip and had decided that the community needed another good bank. He had seized the opportunity. There was only one other bank there, and it took William Mann less than two years to put his competitor out of business. Mann ran his bank the way a bank should be run. His god was mathematics, and he saw to it that the numbers always came out to his benefit. His favorite story was the joke about the man who went to a banker pleading for a loan so that his young son could have an immediate operation to save his life. When the applicant said he had no security, the banker told him to get out of his office.

"I'll go," the man said, "but I want to tell you that in all my years, I've never met anyone as coldhearted as you are."

"Wait a minute," the banker replied. "I'll make you a sporting proposition. One of my eyes is a glass eye. If you can tell me which one it is, I'll give you the loan."

Instantly, the man said, "Your left one."

The banker was amazed. "No one knows that. How could you tell?"

The man said, "That's easy. For a moment, I thought I detected a gleam of sympathy in your left eye, so I knew it must be your glass eye."

That, to William Mann, was a good businessman's story. One did not conduct business based on sympathy. You had to look at the bottom line. While other banks in Canada and the United States were toppling like tenpins, William Mann's bank was stronger than ever. His philosophy was simple: No loans to start up businesses. No investments in junk bonds. No loans to neighbors whose children might desperately need an operation.

Mann had a respect that bordered on awe for the Swiss banking system. The gnomes of Zurich were bankers' bankers. So, one day, William Mann decided to go to Switzerland to speak to some of the bankers there to learn if there was anything he was missing, any way he could squeeze more cents out of the Canadian dollar. He had been received graciously, but in the end he had learned nothing new. His own banking methods were admirable, and the Swiss bankers had not hesitated to tell him so.

On the day he was to leave for home, Mann decided to treat himself to a tour of the Alps. He had found the tour boring. The scenery was interesting, but no prettier than the scenery around Fort Smith. One of the passengers, a Texan, had dared try to persuade him to make a loan on a ranch that was going into bankruptcy. He had laughed in the man's face. The only thing about the tour that was of any interest was the crash of the so-called flying saucer. Mann had not believed in the reality of that for an instant. He was sure it had been staged by the Swiss government to impress tourists. He had been to Walt Disney World, and he had seen similar things that looked real but were faked. *It's Switzerland's glass eye,* he thought sardonically.

William Mann was happy to return home.

Every minute of the banker's day was meticulously scheduled, and when his secretary came in and said that a stranger wished to see him, Mann's first instinct was to dismiss him. "What is it he wants?"

"He says he wants to do an interview with you. He's writing an article about bankers."

That was a different matter entirely. Publicity of the right kind was good for business. William Mann straightened his jacket, smoothed down his hair, and said, "Send him in."

His visitor was an American. He was well-dressed, which indicated that he worked for one of the better magazines or newspapers.

"Mr. Mann?"

"Yes."

"Robert Bellamy."

"My secretary tells me you want to do an article about me."

"Well, not entirely about you," Robert said. "But you'll

certainly be prominent in it. My newspaper—"

"Which newspaper is that?"

"The *Wall Street Journal.*"

Ah, yes. This is going to be excellent.

"The *Journal* feels that most bankers are too isolated from what's going on in the rest of the world. They seldom travel, they don't go to other countries. You, on the other hand, Mr. Mann, have the reputation of being very well traveled."

"I suppose I am," Mann said modestly. "As a matter of fact, I came back from a trip to Switzerland just last week."

"Really? Did you enjoy it?"

"Yes. I met with several other bankers there. We discussed world economics."

Robert had pulled out a notebook and was making notes. "Did you have any time for pleasure?"

"Not really. Oh, I took a little tour on one of those buses. I had never seen the Alps before."

Robert made another note. "A tour. Now that's exactly the kind of thing we're looking for," Robert said encouragingly. "I imagine you met a lot of interesting people on the bus."

"Interesting?" He thought about the Texan who had tried to borrow money. "Not really."

"Oh?"

Mann looked at him. The reporter obviously expected him to say more. *"You'll certainly be prominent in it."* "There was this Russian girl."

Robert made a note. "Really? Tell me about her."

"Well, we got to talking, and I explained to her how backward Russia was and what terrible trouble they were heading for unless they changed."

"She must have been very impressed," Robert said.

"Oh, she was. Seemed like a bright girl. For a Russian, that is. They're all pretty insulated, you know."

"Did she mention her name?"

"No—wait. It was Olga something."

"Did she happen to say where she was from?"

"Yes. She works as a librarian at the main branch in Kiev. It was her first trip abroad, I guess because of *glasnost.* If you want my opinion . . ." He stopped to make sure Robert was writing it down. "Gorbachev sent Russia to hell in a handbasket. East Germany was handed to Bonn on a plate. On the political front, Gorbachev moved too fast, and on the economic front he moved too slowly."

"That's fascinating," Robert murmured. He spent another half hour with the banker, listening to his opinionated comments on everything from the Common Market to arms control. He was able to get no further information about other passengers.

When Robert returned to his hotel, he telephoned General Hilliard's office.

"Just a moment, Commander Bellamy."

He heard a series of clicks, and then General Hilliard was on the line.

"Yes, Commander?"

"I've traced another passenger, General."

"The name?"

"William Mann. He owns a bank in Fort Smith, Canada."

"Thank you. I'll have the Canadian authorities speak to him right away."

"By the way, he gave me another lead. I'll be flying to Russia this evening. I'll need a visa from Intourist."

"Where are you calling from?"

"Fort Smith."

"Stop at the Visigoth Hotel in Stockholm. There will be an envelope for you at the desk."

"Thank you."

FLASH MESSAGE

TOP SECRET ULTRA

NSA TO DEPUTY DIRECTOR CGHQ

EYES ONLY

COPY ONE OF (ONE) COPIES

SUBJECT: OPERATION DOOMSDAY

7. WILLIAM MANN—FORT SMITH

END OF MESSAGE

At eleven o'clock that evening, William Mann's doorbell rang. He was not expecting anyone, and he disliked unannounced callers. His housekeeper had retired, and his wife was asleep in her room upstairs. Annoyed, Mann opened the front door. Two men dressed in black suits stood in the doorway.

"William Mann?"

"Yes."

One of the men pulled out an identification card. "We're from the Bank of Canada. May we come in?"

Mann frowned. "What's this about?"

"We would prefer to discuss this inside, if you don't mind."

"Very well." He led the men into the living room.

"You were recently in Switzerland, were you not?"

The question threw him off guard. "What? Yes, but what on earth—?"

"While you were gone we had your books audited, Mr.

Mann. Are you aware that there is a shortage in your bank of one million dollars?"

William Mann looked at the two men, aghast. "What are you talking about? I check those books every week myself. There has never been one penny missing!"

"One million dollars, Mr. Mann. We think you're responsible for embezzling it."

His face was turning red. He found himself sputtering. "How—how dare you! Get out of here before I call the police."

"That won't do you any good. What we want you to do is repent."

He was staring at them now, confused. "Repent? Repent *what*? You're crazy!"

"No, sir."

One of the men pulled out a gun. "Sit down, Mr. Mann."

Oh, my God! I'm being robbed. "Look," Mann said, "take whatever you want. There's no need for violence and—"

"Sit down, please."

The second man walked over to the liquor cabinet. It was locked. He smashed the glass and opened the cabinet. He picked up a large water glass, filled it with scotch, and carried it over to where Mann was seated.

"Drink this. It will relax you."

"I—I never drink after dinner. My doctor—"

The other man put the gun to William Mann's temple. "Drink it, or the glass is going to be full of your brains."

Mann understood now that he was in the hands of two maniacs. He took the glass in his shaking hand and took a sip.

"Drink it down."

He took a larger swallow. "What—what is it you

want?" He raised his voice, hoping that his wife might hear and come downstairs, but it was a vain hope. He knew what a sound sleeper she was. The men were obviously here to rob the house. *Why don't they just get on with it?*

"Take anything," he said. "I won't stop you."

"Finish up what's in the glass."

"This isn't necessary. I—"

The man punched him hard above his ear. Mann gasped with pain. "Finish it."

He swallowed the rest of the whiskey in one gulp and felt it burning as it went down. He was beginning to feel giddy. "My safe is upstairs in the bedroom," he said. His words were beginning to slur. "I'll open it for you." Maybe that would wake his wife and she would call the police.

"There's no hurry," the man with the gun said. "You have plenty of time for another drink."

The second man went back to the cabinet and filled the glass to the brim again. "Here."

"No, really," William Mann protested. "I don't want it."

The glass was shoved into his hand. "Drink it down."

"I really don't—"

A fist slammed into the same spot above his ear. Mann almost fainted from the pain.

"Drink it."

Well, if that's what they want, why not? The quicker this nightmare is over with, the better. He took a big swallow and gagged.

"If I drink any more, I'm gonna be sick."

The man said quietly, "If you get sick, I'll kill you."

Mann looked up at him and then at his partner. There seemed to be two of everybody.

"What do all of you want?" he mumbled.

"We told you, Mr. Mann. We want you to repent."

William Mann nodded drunkenly. "Okay, I repent."

The man smiled. "You see, that's all we ask. Now . . ." He put a piece of paper in Mann's hand. "All you have to do is write 'I'm sorry. Forgive me.' "

William Mann looked up blearily. "Tha's all?"

"That's all. And then we'll leave."

He felt a sudden sense of elation. *So this is what it's all about. They're religious fanatics.* As soon as they left, he would call the police and have them arrested. *I'll see to it that the bastards are hanged.*

"Write, Mr. Mann."

It was difficult for him to focus. "What did you say you want me to write?"

"Just write 'I'm sorry. Forgive me.' "

"Right." He had difficulty holding the pen. He concentrated very hard and began to write. "I'm sorry. Forgive me."

The man took the paper from Mann's hand, holding it by the edges. "That's very good, Mr. Mann. See how easy that was?"

The room was beginning to spin around. "Yeah. Thank you. I've repented. Now would you leave?"

"I see that you're left-handed."

"What?"

"You're left-handed."

"Yes."

"There's been a lot of crime around here lately, Mr. Mann. We're going to give you this gun to keep."

He felt a gun being placed in his left hand.

"Do you know how to use a gun?"

"No."

"It's very simple. You use it like this. . . ." The man lifted the gun to William Mann's temple and squeezed the banker's finger on the trigger. There was a muffled roar. The bloodstained note dropped to the floor.

"That's all there is to it," one of the men said. "Good night, Mr. Mann."

FLASH MESSAGE

TOP SECRET ULTRA

CGHQ TO DEPUTY DIRECTOR NSA

EYES ONLY

COPY ONE OF (ONE) COPIES

SUBJECT: OPERATION DOOMSDAY

7. WILLIAM MANN—FORT SMITH—TERMINATED

END OF MESSAGE

Day Ten
Fort Smith, Canada

The following morning, bank examiners reported a million dollars missing from Mann's bank. The police listed Mann's death as a suicide.

The missing money was never found.

Chapter Twenty-nine

Day Eleven
Brussels, 0300 Hours

General Shipley, the commandant at NATO headquarters, was awakened by his adjutant.

"I'm sorry to wake you up, General, but we seem to have a situation on our hands."

General Shipley sat up, rubbing the sleep from his eyes. He had had a late night entertaining a group of visiting senators from the United States. "What's the problem, Billy?"

"I just received a call from the radar tower, sir. Either all our equipment has gone crazy or we're having some strange visitors."

General Shipley pushed himself out of bed. "Tell them I'll be there in five minutes."

* * *

The darkened radar room was filled with enlisted men and officers gathered around the lighted radar screens in the center of the room. They turned and sprang to attention as the general entered.

"At ease." He walked over to the officer in charge, Captain Muller. "What's going on here, Lewis?"

Captain Muller scratched his head. "It beats me. Do you know any plane that can travel twenty-two thousand miles per hour, stop on a dime, and go into reverse?"

General Shipley was staring at him. "What are you talking about?"

"According to our radar screens, that's what's been going on for the last half hour. At first we thought it might be some kind of electronic device that's being tested, but we checked with the Russians, the British, and the French, and they're picking up the same thing on their radar screens."

"So, it couldn't be something in the equipment," General Shipley said heavily.

"No, sir. Not unless you want to assume that all the radar in the world has suddenly gone crazy."

"How many of these have appeared on the screen?"

"Over a dozen. They move so fast that it's hard to even keep track of them. We pick them up, and they disappear again. We've eliminated atmospheric conditions, meteors, fireballs, weather balloons, and any kind of flying machine known to man. I was going to scramble some planes, but these objects—whatever they are—are flying so damned high that we'd never be able to get near them."

General Shipley walked over to one of the radar screens. "Is anything coming in on your screens now?"

"No, sir. They're gone." He hesitated a moment. "But General, I have a terrible feeling they'll be coming back."

Chapter Thirty

Ottawa, 0500 Hours

When Janus finished reading General Shipley's report aloud, the Italian stood up and said excitedly, "They are getting ready to invade us!"

"They have already invaded us." The Frenchman.

"We are too late. It is a catastrophe." The Russian. "There is no way—"

Janus interrupted. "Gentlemen, it is a catastrophe we can prevent."

"How? You know their demands." The Englishman.

"Their demands are out of the question." The Brazilian. "It's no business of theirs what we do with our trees. The so-called greenhouse effect is scientific garbage, totally unproven."

"And what about us?" The German. "If they forced us to clean up the air over our cities, we would have to shut down our factories. We would have no industries left."

"And we would have to stop manufacturing cars," the Japanese said. "And then where would the civilized world be?"

"We are all in the same position." The Russian. "If we have to stop all pollution, as they insist, it would destroy the world's economies. We must buy more time until Star Wars is ready to take them on."

Janus said crisply, "We are agreed on that. Our immediate problem is to keep our people calm and to avoid the spread of panic."

"How is Commander Bellamy progressing?" The Canadian.

"He's making excellent progress. He should be finished in the next day or two."

Chapter Thirty-one

Kiev, the Soviet Union

Like most of her countrywomen, Olga Romanchanko had become disenchanted with *perestroika.* In the beginning, all the promised changes that were going to happen in Mother Russia sounded so exciting. The winds of freedom were blowing through the streets, and the air was filled with hope. There were promises of fresh meat and vegetables in the shops, pretty dresses and real leather shoes, and a hundred other wonderful things. But now, six years after it had all begun, bitter disillusion had set in. Goods were scarcer than ever. It was impossible to survive without the black market. There was a shortage of virtually everything, and prices had soared. The main streets were still filled with *rytvina*—huge potholes. There were protest marches in the streets, and crime was on the increase. Restrictions were more severe than ever. *Perestroika* and *glasnost* had begun to seem as empty as the promises of the politicians who promoted them.

Olga had worked at the library in Lenkomsomol Square, in the center of Kiev, for seven years. She was thirty-two years old and had never been outside the Soviet Union. Olga was reasonably attractive, a bit overweight, but in Russia that was not considered a disadvantage. She had been engaged twice to men who had moved away and deserted her: Dmitri, who had left for Leningrad; and Ivan, who had moved to Moscow. Olga had tried to move to Moscow to be with Ivan, but without a *propiska,* a Moscow residence permit, it was not possible.

As her thirty-third birthday approached, Olga was determined that she was going to see something of the world before the Iron Curtain closed around her once again. She went to the head librarian, who happened to be her aunt.

"I would like to take my vacation, now," Olga said.

"When do you want to leave?"

"Next week."

"Enjoy yourself."

It was as simple as that. In the days before *perestroika,* taking a vacation would have meant going to the Black Sea or Samarkand or Tbilisi, or any one of a dozen other places inside the Soviet Union. But now, if she were quick about it, the whole world was open to her. Olga took an atlas from the library shelf and pored over it. There was such a big world out there! There was Africa and Asia, and North and South America. . . . She was afraid to venture that far. Olga turned to the map of Europe. *Switzerland,* she thought. *That's where I'll go.*

She would never have admitted it to anyone in the world, but the main reason Switzerland appealed to her was that she had once tasted Swiss chocolate, and she had never forgotten it. She loved sweets. The candy in Russia—when one could get it—was sugarless and tasted terrible.

Her taste for chocolate was to cost Olga her life.

The journey on Aeroflot to Zurich was an exciting beginning. She had never flown before. She landed at the international airport in Zurich filled with anticipation. There was something in the air that was different. *Maybe it is the smell of real freedom,* Olga thought. Her finances were strictly limited, and she had made reservations at a small, inexpensive hotel, the Leonhare, at Limmatquai 136.

Olga checked in at the reception desk. "This is my first time in Switzerland," she confided to the clerk, in halting English. "Could you suggest some things for me to do?"

"Certainly. There is much to do here," he told her. "Perhaps you should start with a tour of the city. I will arrange it."

"Thank you."

Olga found Zurich extraordinary. She was awed by the sights and sounds of the city. The people on the street were dressed in such fine clothes and drove such expensive automobiles. It seemed to Olga that everyone in Zurich must be a millionaire. And the stores! She window shopped along Bahnhofstrasse, the main shopping street of Zurich, and she marveled at the incredible cornucopia of goods in the windows: There were dresses and coats and shoes and lingerie and jewelry and dishes and furniture and automobiles and books and television sets and radios and toys and pianos. There seemed to be no end to the goods for sale. And then Olga stumbled across Sprüngli's, famous for their confections and chocolates. And what chocolates! Four large storefront windows were filled with a dazzling array of them. There were huge boxes of mixed chocolates, chocolate bunnies, chocolate loaves, chocolate-covered nuts. There were chocolate-covered bananas and chocolate beans filled with liqueurs. It was a feast just to look at the display in the windows. Olga wanted to buy everything, but when she learned the prices, she settled for a small box of assorted chocolates and a large candy bar.

Over the next week, Olga visited the Zurichhorn Gardens and the Rietberg Museum and the Grossmünster, the church erected in the eleventh century, and a dozen other wonderful tourist attractions. Finally, her time was running out.

The hotel clerk at the Leonhare said to her, "The Sunshine Tours Bus Company has a fine tour of the Alps. I think you might enjoy that before you leave."

"Thank you," Olga said. "I will try it."

When Olga left the hotel, her first stop was to visit Sprüngli's again, and the next stop was at the office of the Sunshine Tours Bus Company, where she arranged to go on a tour. It had proved to be most exciting. The scenery was breathtaking, and in the middle of the tour, they had seen the explosion of what she thought was a flying saucer, but the Canadian banker she was seated next to explained that it was merely a spectacle arranged by the Swiss government for tourists, that there were no such things as flying saucers. Olga was not completely convinced. When she returned home to Kiev, she discussed it with her aunt.

"Of course there are flying saucers," her aunt said.

"They fly over Russia all the time. You should sell your story to a newspaper."

Olga had considered doing it, but she was afraid that she would be laughed at. The Communist party did not like its members to get publicity, especially the kind that might subject them to ridicule. All in all, Olga decided that, Dmitri and Ivan aside, her vacation had been the highlight of her life. It was going to be difficult to settle down to work again.

The ride along the newly built highway from the airport into the center of Kiev took the Intourist bus one hour. It was Robert's first time in Kiev, and he was impressed by the ubiquitous construction along the road and the large apartment buildings that seemed to be springing up everywhere. The bus pulled up in front of the Dnieper Hotel and disgorged its two dozen passengers. Robert looked at his watch. Eight P.M. The library would be closed. His business would have to wait until morning. He checked into the huge hotel, where a reservation had been made for him, had a drink at the bar, and went into the austere whitewashed dining room for a dinner of caviar, cucumbers, and tomatoes, followed by a potato casserole flavored with tiny bits of meat and covered with heavy dough, all accompanied by vodka and mineral water.

His visa had been waiting for him at the hotel in Stockholm, as General Hilliard had promised. *That was a quick bit of international cooperation,* Robert thought. *But no cooperation for me. "Naked" is the operational word.*

After dinner Robert made a few inquiries at the desk and meandered over to Lenkomsomol Square. Kiev was a surprise to him. One of the oldest cities in Russia, it was an attractive, European-looking city, situated on the Dnieper River, with green parks and tree-lined streets. Churches were everywhere, and they were spectacular examples of religious architecture: There were the churches of St. Vladimir and St. Andrew, and St. Sophia, the last completed in 1037, pure white with its soaring blue bell tower, and the Pechersk Monastery, the tallest structure in the city. *Susan would have loved all this,* Robert thought. She had never been to Russia. He wondered if she had returned from Brazil yet. On an impulse, when he returned to his hotel room, he telephoned her, and to his surprise the call was put through almost immediately.

"Hello?" *That throaty, sexy voice.*

"Hi. How was Brazil?"

"Robert! I tried to telephone you several times. There was no answer."

"I'm not home."

"Oh." She had been trained too well to ask where he was. "Are you feeling well?"

For a eunuch, I'm in wonderful shape. "Sure. Great. How's Money—Monte?"

"He's fine. Robert, we're leaving for Gibraltar tomorrow." *On Moneybags's fucking yacht, of course. What was the name of it? Ah, yes. The Halcyon.* "The yacht?"

"Yes. You can call me on it. Do you remember the call letters?"

He remembered. *WS 337. What did the WS stand for? Wonderful Susan? . . . Why separate? . . . Wife stealer?*

"Robert?"

"Yes, I remember. Whiskey Sugar 337."

"Will you call? Just to let me know you're all right."

"Sure. I miss you, baby."

A long, painful silence. He waited. What did he expect her to say? *Come rescue me from this charming man who looks like Paul Newman and forces me to go on his two-hundred-and-fifty-foot yacht and live in our squalid little palaces in Monte Carlo and Morocco and Paris and London and God alone knew where else.* Like an idiot, he found himself half hoping she would say it.

"I miss you, too, Robert. Take care of yourself." And the connection was broken. He was in Russia, alone.

Day Twelve
Kiev, the Soviet Union

Early the following morning, ten minutes after the library opened, Robert walked into the huge, gloomy building and approached the reception desk.

"Good morning," Robert said.

The woman behind the desk looked up. "Good morning. Can I help you?"

"Yes. I'm looking for a woman whom I believe works here, Olga—"

"Olga? Yes, yes." She pointed to another room. "She will be in there."

"Thank you."

It had been as easy as that. Robert walked into the other room past groups of students solemnly studying at long tables. *Preparing for what kind of future?* Robert wondered. He reached a smaller reading room and walked inside. A woman was busily stacking books.

"Excuse me," Robert said.

She turned. "Yes?"

"Olga?"

"I am Olga. What do you wish with me?"

Robert smiled disarmingly. "I'm writing a newspaper article on *perestroika* and how it affects the average Russian. Has it made much difference in your life?"

The woman shrugged. "Before Gorbachev we were afraid to open our mouths. Now we can open our mouths, but we have nothing to put in them."

Robert tried another tactic. "Surely there are some changes for the better. For instance, you are able to travel now."

"You must be joking. With a husband and six children, who can afford to travel?"

Robert plowed on. "Still, you went to Switzerland, and—"

"Switzerland? I have never been to Switzerland in my life."

Robert said slowly, "You've never been to Switzerland?"

"I just told you." She nodded toward a dark-haired woman who was collecting books from the table. "She's the lucky one who got to go to Switzerland."

Robert took a quick look. "What's her name?"

"Olga. The same as mine."

He sighed. "Thank you."

A minute later, Robert was in a conversation with the second Olga.

"Excuse me," Robert said. "I'm writing a newspaper article on *perestroika* and the effect that it's had on Russian lives."

She looked at him warily. "Yes?"

"What's your name?"

"Olga. Olga Romanchanko."

"Tell me, Olga, has *perestroika* made any difference to you?"

Six years earlier, Olga Romanchanko would have

been afraid to speak to a foreigner, but now it was allowed. "Not really," she said carefully. "Everything is much the same."

The stranger was persistent. "Nothing at all has changed in your life?"

She shook her head. "No." And then added patriotically, "Of course, we can travel outside the country now."

He seemed interested. "And have you traveled outside the country?"

"Oh, yes," she said proudly. "I have just returned from Switzerland. Is very beautiful country."

"I agree," he said. "Did you get a chance to meet anyone on the trip?"

"I met many people. I took bus, and we went through high mountains. The Alps." Suddenly, Olga realized she shouldn't have said that because the stranger might ask her about the spaceship, and she did not want to talk about that. It could only get her into trouble.

"Really?" asked Robert. "Tell me about the people on the bus."

Relieved, Olga responded, "Very friendly. They were dressed so—" She gestured. "Very rich. I even met man from your capital city, Washington, D.C."

"You did?"

"Yes. Very nice. He gave me card."

Robert's heart skipped a beat. "Do you still have it?"

"No. I threw it away." She looked around. "Is better not keep things like that."

Damn!

And then she added, "I remember his name. Parker, like your American pen. Kevin Parker. Very important in politics. He tells senators how vote."

Robert was taken aback. "Is that what he told you?"

"Yes. He takes them on trips and gives gifts, and then

they vote for things his clients need. That is the way democracy works in America."

A lobbyist. Robert let Olga talk for the next fifteen minutes, but he got no further useful information about the other passengers.

Robert telephoned General Hilliard from his hotel room.

"I found the Russian witness. Her name is Olga Romanchanko. She works in the main library in Kiev."

"I'll have a Russian official speak to her."

FLASH MESSAGE

TOP SECRET ULTRA

NSA TO DEPUTY DIRECTOR GRU

EYES ONLY

COPY ONE OF (ONE) COPIES

SUBJECT: OPERATION DOOMSDAY

8. OLGA ROMANCHANKO—KIEV

END OF MESSAGE

That afternoon Robert was on an Aeroflot Tupolev Tu-154 jet to Paris. When he arrived three hours and twenty-five minutes later, he transferred to an Air France flight to Washington, D.C.

At two A.M. Olga Romanchanko heard the squeal of brakes as a car pulled up in front of the apartment building where she lived, on Vertryk Street. The walls of the apartment were so thin that she could hear voices outside on the street. She got out of bed and looked out the window. Two men in civilian clothes were getting out of a black Chaika, the model used by government officials. They were approaching the entrance to her apartment building. The sight of them sent a shiver through her. Over the years, some of her neighbors had disappeared, never to be seen again. Some of them had been sent to the Gulags in Siberia. Olga wondered whom the secret police were after this time, and even as she was thinking it, there was a knock on her door, startling her. *What do they want with me?* she wondered. *It must be some mistake.*

When she opened the door, the two men were standing there.

"Comrade Olga Romanchanko?"

"Yes."

"Glavnoye Razvedyvatelnoye Upravleniye."

The dreaded GRU.

They pushed their way past her into the room.

"What—what is it you want?"

"We will ask the questions. I am Sergeant Yuri Gromkov. This is Sergeant Vladimir Zemsky."

She felt a sudden sense of terror. "What's—what's wrong? What have I done?"

Zemsky pounced on it. "Oh, so you know you have done something wrong!"

"No, of course not," Olga said, flustered. "I do not know why you are here."

"Sit down," Gromkov shouted. Olga sat.

"You have just returned from a trip to Switzerland, *nyet*?"

"Y—yes," she stuttered, "but it—it was. . . . I got permission from—"

"Espionage is not legal, Olga Romanchanko."

"Espionage?" She was horrified. "I don't know what you are talking about."

The larger man was staring at her body, and Olga

suddenly realized she was wearing only a thin nightgown.

"Let's go. You are coming with us."

"But there is some terrible mistake. I'm a librarian. Ask anybody here who—"

He pulled her to her feet. "Come."

"Where are you taking me?"

"To headquarters. They want to question you."

They allowed her to put on a coat over her nightgown. She was shoved down the stairs and into the Chaika. Olga thought of all the people who had ridden in cars like this before and had never returned, and she was numb with fear.

The larger man, Gromkov, was driving. Olga was seated in the back with Zemsky. He somehow seemed less frightening to her, but she was petrified by who they were and what was going to happen to her.

"Please believe me," Olga said earnestly. "I would never betray my—"

"Shut up," Gromkov barked.

Vladimir Zemsky said, "Look, there's no reason to be rough with her. As a matter of fact, I believe her."

Olga felt her heart leap with hope.

"Times have changed," Comrade Zemsky went on. "Comrade Gorbachev doesn't like us to go around bothering innocent people. Those days are past."

"Who said she's innocent?" Gromkov growled. "Maybe she is, maybe she isn't. They'll find out soon enough at headquarters."

Olga sat there listening to the two men discussing her as if she were not there.

Zemsky said, "Come now, Yuri, you know that at headquarters she will confess, whether she's guilty or not. I don't like this."

"That's too bad. There's nothing we can do about it."

"Yes, there is."

"What?"

The man next to Olga was silent for a moment. "Listen," he said, "why don't we just let her go? We could tell them she was not at home. We'll put them off for a day or two, and they will forget all about her because they have so many people to question."

Olga tried to say something, but her throat was too dry. She desperately wanted the man beside her to win the argument.

Gromkov grumbled. "Why should we risk our necks for her? What do we get out of it? What is she going to do for us?"

Zemsky turned and looked at Olga questioningly. Olga found her voice. "I have no money," she said.

"Who needs your money? We have plenty of money."

Gromkov said, "She has something else."

Before Olga could reply, Zemsky said, "Wait a minute, Yuri Ivanovich, you can't expect her to do that."

"That's up to her. She can either be nice to us or go down to headquarters and get beaten up for a week or two. Maybe they'll keep her in a nice *shizo*."

Olga had heard about *shizos*. Unheated four-by-eight-foot cells with wooden-plank bed and no blankets. *"Be nice to us."* What did that mean?

"It's up to her."

Zemsky turned to Olga. "What do you want to do?"

"I—I don't understand."

"What my partner is saying is that if you're nice to us, we could just drop this whole thing. In a little while, they'll probably forget about you."

"What—what would I have to do?"

Gromkov grinned at her in the rearview mirror. "Just give us a few minutes of your time." He remembered something he had once read. "Just lie there and think of the czar." He giggled.

Olga suddenly understood what they were getting at. She shook her head. "No, I could not do that."

"Right." Gromkov started speeding up. "They'll have a good time with you at headquarters."

"Wait!" She was in a panic, not knowing what to do. She had heard horror stories of what had happened to people who had been arrested and become *zeks*. She had thought that that was all finished, but now she could see that it was not. *Perestroika* was still just a fantasy. They would not allow her to have an attorney or talk to anyone. In the past, friends of hers had been raped and murdered by the GRU. She was trapped. If she went to jail, they could keep her for weeks, beating her and raping her, maybe worse. With these two men, at least it would be over in a few minutes and then they would let her go. Olga made her decision.

"All right," she said miserably. "Do you wish to go back to my apartment?"

Gromkov said, "I know a better place." He turned the car around.

Zemsky whispered, "I'm sorry about this, but he's in charge. I can't stop him."

Olga said nothing.

They drove past the bright red Shevchenko Opera House and headed for a large park bordered by trees. It was completely deserted at this hour. Gromkov drove the car under the trees and turned off the lights and engine.

"Let's get out," he said.

The three of them got out of the car.

Gromkov looked at Olga. "You're lucky. We're letting you off easy. I hope you appreciate it."

Olga nodded, too frightened to speak.

Gromkov led them to a small cleared area. "Get undressed."

"It's cold," Olga said. "Couldn't we—?"

Gromkov slapped her hard across the face. "Do as you're told before I change my mind."

Olga hesitated an instant, and as his arm drew back to hit her again, she started unbuttoning her coat.

"Take it off."

She let it drop to the ground.

"Now the nightgown."

Slowly, Olga lifted the nightgown over her head and pulled it off, shivering in the cold night air, standing naked in the moonlight.

"Nice body," Gromkov said. He squeezed her nipples.

"Please—"

"You make one sound, and we take you to headquarters." He pushed her to the ground.

I won't think about this. I'll pretend I'm in Switzerland on the bus tour, looking at all the beautiful scenery.

Gromkov had dropped his pants and was spreading Olga's legs apart.

I can see the Alps covered with snow. There is a sleigh going by with a young boy and girl in it.

She felt him place his hands under her hips, and he shoved his maleness into her, hurting her.

There are beautiful cars along the highway. More cars than I have ever seen in my life. In Switzerland everybody has a car.

He was plunging into her harder now, pinching her, making wild, animal noises.

I will have a little home in the mountains. What do the Swiss call them? Chalets. And I will have chocolates every day. Boxes of them.

Gromkov was withdrawing now, breathing heavily. He stood up and turned to Zemsky. "Your turn."

I will get married and have children, and we will all go skiing in the Alps in winter.

Zemsky had zipped open his pants and was climbing on top of her.

It will be such a wonderful life. I will never return to Russia. Never. Never. Never.

He was inside her now, hurting her more than the other man had, squeezing her buttocks and pushing her body into the cold ground until the pain was almost unbearable.

We will live on a farm where it's quiet and peaceful all the time, and we will have a garden with beautiful flowers.

Zemsky finished with her and looked up at his companion. "I bet she enjoyed it." He grinned.

He reached down for Olga's neck and broke it.

The following day there was an item in the local paper about a librarian who had been raped and strangled in the park. There was a stern warning from the authorities that it was dangerous for young women to go to the park alone at night.

FLASH MESSAGE

TOP SECRET ULTRA

DEPUTY DIRECTOR GRU TO DEPUTY DIRECTOR NSA

EYES ONLY

COPY ONE OF (ONE) COPIES

SUBJECT: OPERATION DOOMSDAY

8. OLGA ROMANCHANKO—KIEV—TERMINATED

END OF MESSAGE

Chapter Thirty-two

Willard Stone and Monte Banks were natural enemies. They were both ruthless predators, and the jungle they prowled was the stone canyons of Wall Street, with its high-powered takeovers, leveraged buyouts, and stock deals.

The first time the two men clashed was during the attempted takeover of a huge utility company. Willard Stone made the first bid and anticipated no problem. He was so powerful and his reputation so fearsome that very few people dared challenge him. It was a great surprise then when he learned that a young upstart named Monte Banks was contesting his bid. Stone was forced to raise his own bid, and the ante kept going up. Willard Stone finally acquired control of the company, but at a much higher price than he had anticipated paying.

Six months later, in a takeover bid for a large electronics firm, Stone was confronted again by Monte Banks. The bidding kept escalating, and this time Banks won.

When Willard Stone learned that Monte Banks intended to compete with him for control of a computer company, he decided it was time to meet with his competitor. The two men met on neutral ground in Paradise Island, in the Bahamas. Willard Stone had made a thorough investigation into the background of his competitor, learning that Monte Banks came from a wealthy oil family and had brilliantly managed to parlay his inheritance into an international conglomerate.

The two men sat down to lunch. Willard Stone, old and wise; Monte Banks, young and eager.

Willard Stone opened the conversation. "You're becoming a pain in the ass."

Monte Banks grinned. "Coming from you, that's a big compliment."

"What is it you want?" Stone asked.

"The same as you. I want to own the world."

Willard Stone said thoughtfully, "Well, it's a big enough world."

"Meaning?"

"There's room enough for both of us."

That was the day they became partners. Each ran his own business separately, but when it came to new projects—timber and oil and real estate—they went into deals together, instead of competing with each other. Several times the Antitrust Division of the Justice Department tried to stop their deals, but Willard Stone's connections always prevailed. Monte Banks owned chemical companies responsible for massive pollution of lakes and rivers, but when he was indicted, the indictment was mysteriously dropped.

The two men had a perfect symbiotic relationship.

Operation Doomsday was a natural for them, and they were heavily involved in it. They were on the verge of closing a deal to purchase ten million acres of lush, tree-rich land in the Amazon rain forest. It was going to be one of the most profitable deals they had ever gone into.

They could not afford to let anything stand in their way.

Chapter Thirty-three

Day Thirteen
Washington, D.C.

The Senate of the United States was in plenary session. The junior senator from Utah had the floor.

". . . and what is happening to our ecology is a national disgrace. It is time that this great body realized that it is its sworn duty to preserve the precious heritage that our forefathers entrusted to us. It is not only our sworn duty but our privilege to protect the land, the air, and the seas from those vested interests that are selfishly destroying it. And are we doing this? Are we in all conscience doing our best? Or are we allowing the voice of mammon to influence us . . . ?"

Kevin Parker, seated in the visitors' gallery, glanced at his watch for the third time in five minutes. He wondered how much longer the speech was going to last. He was sitting through this only because he was having lunch with the senator and he needed a favor from him. Kevin

Parker enjoyed walking through the corridors of power, hobnobbing with congressmen and senators, dispensing largess in return for political favors.

He had grown up poor in Eugene, Oregon. His father was an alcoholic who had owned a small lumberyard. An inept businessman, he had turned what should have been a thriving business into a disaster. The young boy had to work from the age of fourteen, and because his mother had run away with another man years earlier, he had no home life at all. He could easily have become a drifter and ended up like his father, but his saving grace was that he was extraordinarily handsome and personable. He had wavy blond hair and fine aristocratic features that he must have inherited from some long-forgotten ancestor. A few affluent townspeople took pity on the boy, giving him jobs and encouragement, going out of their way to assist him. The wealthiest man in town, Jeb Goodspell, was particularly eager to help Kevin and gave him a part-time job with one of his companies. A bachelor, Goodspell often invited young Parker to join him for dinner at his home.

"You can *be* somebody in this life," Goodspell told him, "but you can't make it without friends."

"I know that, sir. And I certainly appreciate your friendship. Working for you is a real lifesaver."

"I could do a lot more for you," Goodspell said. They were seated on the couch in the living room, after dinner. He put his arm around the young boy. "A *lot* more." He squeezed the boy's shoulder. "You have a good body, do you know that?"

"Thank you, sir."

"Do you ever get lonely?"

He was lonely all the time. "Yes, sir."

"Well, you don't have to be lonely anymore." He stroked the boy's arm. "I get lonely, too, you know. You need someone to hold you close and comfort you."

"Yes, sir."

"Have you ever had any girls?"

"Well, I went with Sue Ellen for a while."

"Did you sleep with her?"

The boy blushed. "No, sir."

"How old are you, Kevin?"

"Sixteen, sir."

"It's a great age. It's an age when you should be beginning to start a career." He studied the boy a moment. "I'll bet you'd be darn good in politics."

"Politics? I don't know anything about that, sir."

"That's why you're going to school, to learn things. And I'm going to help you."

"Thank you."

"There are plenty of ways of thanking people," Goodspell said. He rubbed his hand along the boy's thigh. "Many ways." He looked into Parker's eyes. "You know what I mean?"

"Yes, Jeb."

That was the beginning.

When Kevin Parker was graduated from Churchill High School, Goodspell sent him to the University of Oregon. The boy studied political science, and Goodspell saw to it that his protégé met everybody. They were all impressed with the attractive young man. With his connections, Parker found that he was able to do favors for important people and to bring people together. Becoming a lobbyist in Washington was a natural step, and Parker was good at the job.

Goodspell had died two years earlier, but Parker had by then acquired a talent and a taste for what his mentor had taught him. He liked to pick up young boys and take them to out-of-the-way hotels where he would not be recognized.

The senator from Utah was finally finishing. ". . . and I say to you now that we must pass this bill if we want to save what is left of our ecology. At this time, I would like to ask for a roll-call vote."

Thank God, the endless session was almost over. Kevin Parker thought about the evening that lay ahead of him, and he began to get an erection. The night before, he had met a young man at Danny's P Street Station, a well-known gay bar. Unfortunately, the young man had been with a companion. But they had eyed each other during the evening, and before he left, Parker had written a note and slipped it into the young man's hand. It said simply, "Tomorrow night." The young man had smiled and nodded.

Kevin Parker was hurriedly getting dressed to go out. He wanted to be at the bar when the boy arrived. The young man was much too attractive, and Parker did not want him picked up by someone else. The front doorbell rang. *Damn.* Parker opened the door.

A stranger stood there. "Kevin Parker?"

"Yes—"

"My name is Bellamy. I'd like to talk to you for a minute."

Parker said impatiently, "You'll have to make an appointment with my secretary. I don't discuss business after office hours."

"This isn't exactly business, Mr. Parker. It concerns your trip to Switzerland a couple of weeks ago."

"My trip to Switzerland? What about it?"

"My agency is interested in some of the people you

might have met over there." Robert flashed his false CIA identification.

Kevin Parker studied the man more carefully. What could the CIA want with him? They were so goddamned nosy. *Have I covered my ass?*

There was no point in antagonizing the man. He smiled. "Come in. I'm late for an appointment, but you said this won't take more than a minute?"

"No, sir. I believe you took a bus tour out of Zurich?"

So that's what this is all about. That flying saucer business. It had been the goddamndest thing he had ever seen. "You want to know about the UFO, don't you? Well, I want to tell you, it was a weird experience."

"It must have been, but frankly, we at the agency don't believe in flying saucers. I'm here to find out what you can tell me about your fellow passengers on the bus."

Parker was taken aback. "Oh. Well, I'm afraid I can't help you there. They were all strangers."

"I understand that, Mr. Parker," Robert said patiently, "but you must remember *something* about them."

Parker shrugged. "Well, a few things. . . . I remember exchanging a few words with an Englishman who took our pictures."

Leslie Mothershed. "Who else?"

"Oh, yes. I talked a little to a Russian girl. She seemed very pleasant. I think she said she was a librarian somewhere."

Olga Romanchanko. "That's excellent. Can you think of anyone else, Mr. Parker?"

"No, I guess that's about—oh, there were two other men. One was an American, a Texan."

Dan Wayne. "And the other one?"

"He was a Hungarian. He owned a carnival or circus

or something like that in Hungary." He remembered. "It was a carnival."

"Are you sure about that, Mr. Parker?"

"Oh, yes. He was telling me some stories about the carnival business. He was certainly excited seeing that UFO. I think if he could have, he would have put it in his carnival as a sideshow. I must admit, it was a pretty awesome sight. I would have reported it, but I can't afford to get mixed up with all the weirdos who claim they saw flying saucers."

"Did he happen to mention his name?"

"Yes, but it was one of these unpronounceable foreign names. I'm afraid I don't remember it."

"Do you remember anything else about him?"

"Only that he was in a hurry to get back to his carnival." He glanced at his watch. "Is there anything else I can do for you? I'm running a little late."

"No, thank you, Mr. Parker. You've been very helpful."

"My pleasure." He flashed Robert a beautiful smile. "You must drop by my office and see me sometime. We'll have a nice chat."

"I'll do that."

So it's nearly over, Robert thought. *They can take my job and shove it. It's time to pick up the pieces of my life and start over.*

Robert placed a call to General Hilliard. "I've just about wrapped it up, General. I found Kevin Parker. He's a lobbyist in Washington, D.C. I'm on my way to check out the last passenger."

"I'm very pleased," General Hilliard said. "You've

done an excellent job, Commander. Get back to me as quickly as you can."

"Yes, sir."

FLASH MESSAGE

TOP SECRET ULTRA

NSA TO DEPUTY DIRECTOR CIA

EYES ONLY

COPY ONE OF (ONE) COPIES

SUBJECT: OPERATION DOOMSDAY

9. KEVIN PARKER—WASHINGTON, D.C.

END OF MESSAGE

When Kevin Parker arrived at Danny's P Street Station, he found it even more crowded than it had been the evening before. The older men were dressed in conservative suits, while most of the younger men were in Levi's, blazers, and boots. There were a few who looked out of place, in black-leather outfits, and Parker thought that that element was disgusting. Rough trade was dangerous, and he had never gone in for that sort of bizarre behavior. *Discretion,* that had always been his motto. *Discretion.* The handsome young boy was not there yet, but Parker had not expected him to be. He would make his entrance later, beautiful and fresh, when the others in the bar would be tired and sweaty. Kevin Parker walked up to the bar, ordered a drink, and looked around. Television sets on the walls were playing the MTV station. Danny's was an S-and-M—stand and model—bar. The younger men would assume poses that made them appear as attractive as possible, while the older men—the buyers—would look them over and make their selections. The S-and-M bars were the classiest. There were never any fights in them, for most of the customers had capped teeth, and they could not afford to chance having them knocked out.

Kevin Parker noticed that many of the patrons had already selected their partners. He listened to the familiar conversations going on around him. It fascinated him that the conversations were always the same, whether they took place in leather bars, dance bars, video bars, or underground clubs that changed their locations every week. There was an indigenous argot. "That queen is nobody. She thinks she's Miss Thing. . . ." "He went off on me for no reason. He gets so terribly upset. Talk about sensitive. . . ."

"Are you a top or a bottom?"

"A top. I have to give the orders, girl," snapping his fingers.

"Good. I like taking them. . . ."

"He read me for filth. . . . Just stood there criticizing me . . . my weight, my complexion, my attitude. I said, 'Mary, it's over between us.' But it hurt. That's why I'm here tonight . . . trying to forget him. Could I have another drink? . . ."

At one A.M., the young boy walked in. He looked around, saw Parker, and walked over to him. The boy was even more beautiful than Parker had remembered.

"Good evening."

"Good evening. Sorry I'm late."

"That's all right. I didn't mind waiting."

The young man took out a cigarette and waited while the older man lit it for him.

"I've been thinking about you," Parker said.

"Have you?"

The boy's eyelashes were incredible.

"Yes. Can I buy you a drink?"

"If it will make you happy."

Parker smiled. "Are you interested in making me happy?"

The boy looked him in the eyes and said softly, "I think so."

"I saw the man you were here with last night. He's wrong for you."

"And you're right for me?"

"I could be. Why don't we find out? Would you like to go for a little walk?"

"Sounds good."

Parker felt a tingle of excitement. "I know a cozy place where we can be alone."

"Fine. I'll skip the drink."

As they started toward the front door, it suddenly opened and two large young men entered the bar. They stepped in front of the boy, blocking his way. "There you are, you sonofabitch. Where's the money you owe me?"

The young man looked up at him, bewildered. "I don't know what you're talking about. I've never seen you be—"

"Don't give me that shit." The man grabbed him by the shoulder and started marching him out to the street.

Parker stood there, furious. He was tempted to interfere, but he could not afford to get involved in anything that might turn into a scandal. He stayed where he was, watching the boy disappear into the night.

The second man smiled at Kevin Parker sympathetically. "You should choose your company more carefully. He's bad news."

Parker took a closer look at the speaker. He was blond and attractive, with almost perfect features. Parker had a feeling that the evening might not be a total loss, after all. "You could be right," he said.

"We never know what fate has in store for us, do we?" He was looking into Parker's eyes.

"No, we don't. My name's Tom. What's your name?"

"Paul."

"Why don't you let me buy you a drink, Paul?"

"Thank you."

"Do you have any special plans for tonight?"

"That's up to you."

"How would you like to spend the night with me?"

"That sounds like fun."

"How much money are we talking about?"

"I like you. For you, two hundred."

"That seems reasonable."

"It is. You won't be sorry."

Thirty minutes later, Paul was leading Kevin Parker into an old apartment building on Jefferson Street. They walked upstairs to the third floor and entered a small room. Parker looked around. "It's not much, is it? A hotel would have been nicer."

Paul grinned. "It's more private here. Besides, all we need is the bed."

"You're right. Why don't you get undressed? I want to see what I'm buying."

"Sure." Paul started stripping. He had a great body.

Parker watched him, and he felt the old familiar urge beginning to build.

"Now, you get undressed," Paul whispered. "Hurry, I want you."

"I want you too, Mary." Parker began to take off his clothes.

"What do you like?" Paul asked. "Lips or hips?"

"Let's make it a cocktail. Excuse the pun. We've got all night."

"Sure. I'm going into the bathroom," Paul said. "I'll be right back."

Parker lay on the bed naked, anticipating the exquisite pleasures that were about to happen. He heard his companion come out of the bathroom and approach the bed.

He held out his arms. "Come to me, Paul," he said.

"I'm coming."

And Parker felt a burst of agony as a knife slashed into his chest. His eyes flew open. He looked up, gasping. "My God, what—?"

Paul was getting dressed. "Don't worry about the money," he said. "It's on the house."

FLASH MESSAGE

TOP SECRET ULTRA

CIA TO DEPUTY DIRECTOR NSA

EYES ONLY

COPY ONE OF (ONE) COPIES

SUBJECT: OPERATION DOOMSDAY

9. KEVIN PARKER—WASHINGTON, D.C.—TERMINATED

END OF MESSAGE

Robert Bellamy missed the late news bulletin because he was on a plane to Hungary to find a man who owned a carnival.

Chapter Thirty-four

Day Fourteen
Budapest

The flight from Paris to Budapest on Malév Airlines took two hours and five minutes. Robert knew very little about Hungary except that during World War II, it had been a partner in the Axis, and had later become a Russian satellite. Robert took the airport bus to the center of Budapest, impressed by what he saw. The buildings were old and the architecture classic. Parliament House on the Rudolph Quay was a huge, Neo-Gothic structure that dominated the city, and high above the city on Castle Hill was the Royal Palace. The streets were crowded with automobiles and shoppers.

The bus stopped in front of the Hotel Duna Intercontinental. Robert walked into the lobby and approached the concierge.

"Excuse me," Robert said, "do you speak English?"

"*Igan.* Yes. What may I do for you?"

"A friend of mine was in Budapest a few days ago, and he told me he saw a wonderful carnival. I thought as long as I was in town, I might take a look at it. Can you tell me where I might find it?"

The concierge frowned. "Carnival?" He pulled out a sheet of paper and scanned it. "Let's see. In Budapest at the present time, we have an opera, several theater productions, ballet, night and day tours of the city, excursions in the country . . ." He looked up. "I'm sorry. There are no carnivals."

"Are you sure?"

The concierge handed the list to Robert. "See for yourself." It was written in Hungarian.

Robert handed it back. "Right. Is there anyone else I might talk to about this?"

The concierge said, "The Ministry of Culture might be able to help you."

Thirty minutes later, Robert was speaking to a clerk in the office of the Culture Ministry.

"There is no carnival in Budapest. Are you sure your friend saw it in Hungary?"

"Yes."

"But he did not say where?"

"No."

"I am sorry. I cannot help you." The clerk was impatient. "If there is nothing else—"

"No." Robert rose to his feet. "Thank you." He hesitated. "I do have one more question. If I wanted to bring a circus or a carnival into Hungary, would I have to get a permit?"

"Certainly."

"Where would I go for that?"

"To the Budapest Administration of Licenses."

* * *

The licenses building was located in Buda near the medieval city wall. Robert waited for thirty minutes before he was ushered into the office of a formal, pompous official.

"Can I help you?"

Robert smiled. "I hope so. I hate to take up your time with something as trivial as this, but I'm here with my young son, and he heard about a carnival playing somewhere in Hungary, and I promised to take him to see it. You know how kids are when they get an idea in their heads."

The official stared at Robert, puzzled. "What is it you wanted to see me about?"

"Well, to tell you the truth, no one seems to know where the carnival is, and Hungary is such a big and beautiful country—well, I was told that if anyone knew what was going on in Hungary, it would be you."

The official nodded. "Yes. Nothing like that is permitted to open without being issued a license." He pressed the buzzer, and a secretary came in. There was a rapid exchange in Hungarian. The secretary left and came back two minutes later with some papers. She handed them to the official. He looked at them and said to Robert, "In the past three months, we have issued two permits for carnivals. One closed a month ago."

"And the other?"

"The other is currently playing in Sopron. A little town near the German frontier."

"Do you have the owner's name?"

The official consulted the paper again. "Bushfekete. Laslo Bushfekete."

* * *

Laslo Bushfekete was having one of the best days of his life. Few people are lucky enough to spend their lives doing exactly what they want to do, and Laslo Bushfekete was one of those fortunate few. At six foot four and three hundred pounds, Bushfekete was a big man. He sported a diamond wristwatch, diamond rings, and a large gold bracelet. His father had owned a small carnival, and when he died, the son had taken it over. It was the only life he had ever known.

Laslo Bushfekete had grandiose dreams. He intended to expand his little carnival into the biggest and best in Europe. He wanted to be known as the P. T. Barnum of carnivals. At the moment, however, he could only afford the usual sideshow attractions: the Fat Lady and the Tattooed Man, the Siamese Twins and the Thousand-Year-Old Mummy, "dug up from the bowels of tombs in ancient Egypt." Then there was the Sword Swallower and the Flame Eater, and the cute little Snake Charmer, Marika. But in the end, all they really added up to was just another traveling carnival.

Now, overnight, all that was going to change. Laslo Bushfekete's dream was about to come true.

He had gone to Switzerland to audition an escape artist he had heard about. The *pièce de résistance* of the act was a routine where the performer was blindfolded, handcuffed, locked in a small trunk, then locked in a larger trunk, and finally lowered into a tank of water. It had sounded fantastic over the telephone, but when Bushfekete flew to Switzerland to see it, he found that there was one insurmountable problem: It took the escape artist thirty minutes to escape. No audience in the world was going to stay around staring at a trunk in a tank of water for thirty minutes.

It had looked as though the trip had been a complete waste of time. Laslo Bushfekete had decided to take a tour to kill the day until it was time to catch his plane. As it turned out, that ride changed his life.

Like his fellow passengers, Bushfekete had seen the explosion and raced across the field to try to help any survivors in what they all thought was a plane crash. But the sight that had confronted him was incredible. There was no question but that it was a flying saucer, and in it were two strange-looking little bodies. The other passengers stood there gaping at it. Laslo Bushfekete had walked around to see what the back of the UFO looked like, and then he had stopped, staring. About ten feet in back of the wreck, lying on the ground out of sight of the other tourists, was a tiny severed hand with six fingers and two opposing thumbs. Without even thinking, Bushfekete had taken out his handkerchief, scooped up the hand, and slipped it into his carryall. His heart was beating wildly. He had in his possession the hand of a genuine extraterrestrial! *From now on you can forget all your fat ladies, tattooed men, sword swallowers and flame eaters,* he thought. *"Step right up, ladies and gentlemen, for the thrill of a lifetime. What you're about to see is a sight that no mortal has ever seen before. You are looking at one of the most incredible objects in the universe. It's not an animal. It's not a vegetable. It's not a mineral. What is it? It's part of the remains of an extraterrestrial . . . a creature from outer space. . . . This is not science fiction, ladies and gentlemen, this is the real thing. . . . For five hundred forints, you can have your photograph taken with the . . ."*

And that reminded him. He hoped that the photographer who had been at the crash site would remember to send the photograph he had promised. He would have it blown up and put next to the exhibit. That would be a neat touch. *Showmanship. That's what life is all about. Showmanship.*

He could not wait to return to Hungary and start to fulfill his grandiose dream.

When he arrived home and unwrapped the handkerchief, he noticed that the hand had shriveled. But when Bushfekete rinsed off the dirt, amazingly, it regained its original firmness.

Bushfekete had hidden the hand safely away and had ordered an impressive glass case with a special humidifier built for it. When he was through exhibiting it in his carnival, he planned to travel with it all over Europe. All over the world. He would set up exhibits in museums. He would have private showings for scientists; perhaps, even for heads of state. And he would charge them all. There was no end to the fabulous fortune that lay ahead.

He had told no one about his good luck, not even his sweetheart, Marika, the sexy little dancer who worked with cobras and puff adders, two of the most dangerous ophidians. Of course, their poison sacs had been removed, but the audience did not know that because Bushfekete also kept a cobra with its poison sac intact. He displayed the snake free of charge to the public, which watched it kill rats. It wasn't surprising that people got a thrill out of watching the beautiful Marika let her pet snakes slither across her sensuous, half-naked body. Two or three nights a week, Marika came into Laslo Bushfekete's tent and crawled across his body, her tongue flicking in and out like her pets. They had made love the night before, and Bushfekete was still exhausted from Marika's incredible gymnastics. His reminiscences were interrupted by a visitor.

"Mr. Bushfekete?"

"You're talking to him. What can I do for you?"

"I understand you were in Switzerland last week."

Bushfekete was instantly wary. *Did someone see me pick up the hand?* "What—what about it?"

"You went on a bus tour last Sunday?"

Bushfekete said cautiously, "Yes."

Robert Bellamy relaxed. It was finally over. This was the last witness. He had taken on an impossible assignment, and he had done a good job. *A damned good job, if I say so myself. "We have no idea where they are. Or who they are."* And he had found them all. He felt as if a tremendous burden had been lifted from his shoulders. He was free now. Free to return home and to begin a new life.

"What about my trip, mister?"

"It's not important," Robert Bellamy assured him. And it wasn't, not any longer. "I was interested in your fellow passengers, Mr. Bushfekete, but now I think I have all the information I need, so—"

"Oh, hell, I can tell you all about them," Laslo Bushfekete said. "There was an Italian priest from Orvieto, Italy; a German—I think he was a chemistry professor from Munich; some Russian girl who worked in the library in Kiev; a rancher from Waco, Texas; a Canadian banker from the Territories; and some lobbyist named Parker from Washington, D.C."

My God, Robert thought. *If I had gotten to him first, I could have saved a lot of time. The man is amazing. He recalled them all.* "You have quite a memory," Robert said.

"Yeah." Bushfekete smiled. "Oh, and there was that other woman."

"The Russian woman."

"No, no, the *other* woman. The tall, thin one who was dressed in white."

Robert thought for a moment. None of the others had

mentioned a second woman. "I think you must be mistaken."

"No, I'm not." Bushfekete was insistent. "There were two women there."

Robert made a mental count. It simply did not add up. "There couldn't have been."

Bushfekete was insulted. "When that photographer fellow took the pictures of all of us in front of that UFO, she was standing right next to me. She was a real beauty." He paused. "The funny part is I don't recall seeing her on the bus. She was probably in the back somewhere. I remember she seemed kind of pale. I was a little worried about her."

Robert frowned. "When all of you returned to the bus, was she with you?"

"Come to think of it, I don't remember seeing her after that. But I was so excited by that UFO thing, I wasn't paying much attention."

There was something here that did not fit. *Could there have been eleven witnesses instead of ten? I'll have to check that out,* Robert thought. "Thank you, Mr. Bushfekete," he said.

"My pleasure."

"Good luck."

Bushfekete grinned. "Thanks." He didn't need luck. Not anymore. Not with the hand of a real genuine alien in his possession.

That night Robert Bellamy made his final report to General Hilliard. "I have his name. It's Laslo Bushfekete. He runs a carnival outside of Sopron, Hungary."

"That's the last of the witnesses?"

Robert hesitated an instant. "Yes, sir." He had started

to mention the eighth passenger, but he decided to wait until he had verified it. It seemed too improbable.

"Thank you, Commander. Well done."

FLASH MESSAGE

TOP SECRET ULTRA

NSA TO DEPUTY DIRECTOR HRQ

EYES ONLY

COPY ONE OF (ONE) COPIES

SUBJECT: OPERATION DOOMSDAY

10. LASLO BUSHFEKETE—SOPRON

END OF MESSAGE

They arrived in the middle of the night, when the carnival was shut down. They left fifteen minutes later, as silently as they had come.

Laslo Bushfekete dreamed he was standing at the entrance to the large white tent, watching the huge crowd lined up at the box office to buy their five-hundred-forint tickets.

"Come right this way, folks. See the genuine body part of an alien from outer space. Not a drawing, not a photograph, but an actual part of an actual ET. Only five hundred forints for the thrill of a lifetime, a sight you will never forget."

And then he was in bed with Marika, and they were both naked, and he could feel her nipples pressing against his chest and her tongue slithering across his body and she was crawling all over him, and he got an erection, and he reached for her and his hands closed over something cold and slimy, and he woke up and opened his eyes and screamed, and that was when the cobra struck.

They found his body in the morning. The cage for the poisonous snake was empty.

FLASH MESSAGE

TOP SECRET ULTRA

HRQ TO DEPUTY DIRECTOR NSA

EYES ONLY

COPY ONE OF (ONE) COPIES

SUBJECT: OPERATION DOOMSDAY

10. LASLO BUSHFEKETE—SOPRON—TERMINATED

END OF MESSAGE

General Hilliard made a call on the red phone. "Janus, I've received the final report from Commander Bellamy. He's found the last of the witnesses. They've all been taken care of."

"Excellent. I'll inform the others. I want you to proceed at once with the rest of our plan."

"Immediately."

FLASH MESSAGE

TOP SECRET ULTRA

NSA TO DEPUTY DIRECTORS:

SIFAR, MI6, GRU, CIA, COMSEC, DCI, CGHQ, BFV

EYES ONLY

COPY ONE OF (ONE) COPIES

SUBJECT: OPERATION DOOMSDAY

11. COMMANDER ROBERT BELLAMY—TERMINATE

END OF MESSAGE

BOOK TWO

THE HUNTED

Chapter Thirty-five

Day Fifteen

Robert Bellamy was in a dilemma. *Could there be an eleventh witness? And if there was, why didn't any of the others mention her before?* The clerk who sold the bus tickets had told him there were only seven passengers. Robert was convinced that the Hungarian carnival owner had made a mistake. It would have been easy to ignore it, to assume that it was untrue, but Robert's training would not permit it. He had been too well disciplined. Bushfekete's story had to be checked out. *How?* Robert thought about it. *Hans Beckerman. The bus driver will know.*

He placed a call to Sunshine Tours. The office was closed. There was no listing in Kappel for a Hans Beckerman. *I'm going to have to go back to Switzerland and settle this,* Robert thought. *I can't leave any loose ends.*

It was late at night when Robert arrived in Zurich. The air was cold and crisp, and there was a full moon. Robert rented a car and took the now-familiar drive to the little village of Kappel. He drove past the church and pulled up in front of Hans Beckerman's home, convinced that he was on a wild-goose chase. The house was dark. Robert knocked on the door and waited. He knocked again, shivering in the cold night air.

Mrs. Beckerman finally answered the door. She was wearing a faded flannel robe. *"Bitte?"*

"Mrs. Beckerman, I wonder if you remember me? I'm the reporter who's writing an article on Hans. I'm sorry to bother you so late, but it's important that I speak to your husband."

His words were greeted with silence. "Mrs. Beckerman?"

"Hans is dead."

Robert felt a small shock go through him. "What?"

"My husband is dead."

"I—I'm sorry. How?"

"His car went over the side of the mountain." Her voice was filled with bitterness. "The *Dummkopf Polizei* said it was because he was full of drugs."

"Drugs?" *"Ulcers. The doctors cannot even give me drugs to relieve the pain. I am allergic to all of them."*

"The police said it was an accident?"

"Ja."

"Did they perform an autopsy?"

"They did, and they found drugs. It makes no sense."

He had no answer. "I'm terribly sorry, Mrs. Beckerman. I—"

The door closed, and Robert stood there alone in the cold night.

One witness was gone. No—two. Leslie Mothershed had died in a fire. Robert stood thinking for a long time. Two witnesses dead. He could hear the voice of his instructor at the Farm: *"There's one more thing I want to discuss today. Coincidence. In our work, there is no such animal. It usually spells danger. If you keep running into the same person again and again, or you keep spotting the same automobile when you're on the move, cover your ass. You're probably in trouble."*

"Probably in trouble." Robert was caught up in a series of conflicting emotions. What had happened *had* to be coincidence, and yet . . . *I've got to check out the mystery passenger.*

His first call was to Fort Smith, Canada. A distraught woman's voice answered the telephone. "Yes?"

"William Mann, please."

The voice said tearfully, "I'm sorry. My husband is—is no longer with us."

"I don't understand."

"He committed suicide."

Suicide? That hardheaded banker? What the hell is going on? Robert wondered. What he was thinking was inconceivable, and yet . . . He began making one phone call after another.

"Professor Schmidt, please."

"*Ach!* The professor died in an explosion in his laboratory. . . ."

"I'd like to speak to Dan Wayne."

"Poor devil. His prize stallion kicked him to death last . . ."

* * *

"Laslo Bushfekete, please."
"The carnival's closed. Laslo is dead. . . ."

"Fritz Mandel, please."
"Fritz was killed in a freak accident. . . ."
The alarms were going full blast now.

"Olga Romanchanko."
"The poor girl. And she was so young. . . ."

"I'm calling to check on Father Patrini."
"The poor soul passed away in his sleep."

"I have to speak to Kevin Parker."
"Kevin was murdered. . . ."

Dead. Every one of the witnesses dead. And he was the one who had found and identified them. Why had he not known what was going on? Because the bastards had waited until he was out of each country before executing their victims. The only one he had reported to was General Hilliard. *"We must not involve anyone else in this mission. . . . I want you to report your progress to me every day."*

They had used him to finger the witnesses. *What is behind all this?* Otto Schmidt had been killed in Germany, Hans Beckerman and Fritz Mandel in Switzerland, Olga Romanchanko in Russia, Dan Wayne and Kevin Parker in America, William Mann in Canada, Leslie Mothershed

America, William Mann in Canada, Leslie Mothershed in England, Father Patrini in Italy, and Laslo Bushfekete in Hungary. That meant that the security agencies in more than half a dozen countries were engaged in the biggest cover-up in history. Someone at a very high level had decided that all the witnesses to the UFO crash must die. *But who? And why?*

It's an international conspiracy, and I'm in the middle of it.

Priority: Get under cover. It was hard for Robert to believe that they intended to kill him too. He was one of them. But until he knew for certain, he could not take any chances. The first thing he had to do was to get a phony passport. That meant Ricco in Rome.

Robert caught the next plane out and found himself fighting to stay awake. He had not realized how exhausted he was. The pressure of the last fifteen days, in addition to all the jet lag, had left him drained.

He landed at Leonardo da Vinci Airport, and when he walked into the terminal, the first person he saw was Susan. He stopped, in shock. Her back was to him, and for a moment, he thought he might be mistaken. And then he heard her voice.

"Thank you. I have a car picking me up."

Robert moved to her side. "Susan—"

She turned, startled. "Robert! What—what a coincidence! But what a lovely surprise."

"I thought you were in Gibraltar," Robert said.

She smiled uneasily. "Yes. We're on our way there. Monte had some business here to take care of first. We're leaving tonight. What are you doing in Rome?"

Running for my life. "I'm finishing up on a job." *It's*

my last. I've quit, darling. We can be together from now on, and nothing will ever separate us again. Leave Monte and come back to me. But he could not bring himself to say the words. He had done enough to her. She was happy in her new life. *Leave it alone,* Robert thought.

She was watching him. "You look tired."

He smiled. "I've been running around a little."

They looked into each other's eyes, and the magic was still there. The burning desire, and the memories, and the laughter, and the yearning.

Susan took his hand in hers and said softly, "Robert. Oh, Robert. I wish we—"

"Susan—"

And at that moment, a burly man in a chauffeur's uniform walked up to Susan. "The car is ready, Mrs. Banks." And the spell was broken.

"Thank you." She turned to Robert. "I'm sorry. I have to go now. Please take care of yourself."

"Sure." He watched her leave. There were so many things he wanted to say to her. *Life has a lousy sense of timing.* It had been wonderful seeing Susan again, but what was it that was troubling him? Of course! *Coincidence. Another coincidence.*

He took a taxi to the Hassler Hotel.

"Welcome back, Commander."

"Thank you."

"I'll have a bellman take up your bags."

"Wait." Robert looked at his watch. Ten P.M. He was tempted to go upstairs and get some sleep, but he had to arrange his passport first.

"I won't be going to my room right away," Robert said. "I would appreciate it if you would have my bags sent up."

"Of course, Commander."

As Robert turned to leave, the elevator door opened, and a group of Shriners came pouring out, laughing and chattering. They had obviously had a few drinks. One of them, a stout, red-faced man, waved to Robert.

"Hi there, buddy . . . having a good time?"

"Wonderful," Robert said. "Just wonderful."

Robert walked through the lobby to the taxi stand outside. As he started to get into the taxi, he noticed an inconspicuous gray Opel parked across the street. It was too inconspicuous. It stood out among the large, luxurious automobiles around it.

"Via Monte Grappa," Robert told the taxi driver. During the drive, Robert looked out the rear window. No gray Opel. *I'm getting jumpy,* Robert thought. When they arrived at Via Monte Grappa, Robert got out at the corner. As he started to pay the driver, he saw, out of the corner of his eye, the gray Opel half a block down the street, yet he could have sworn it had not followed him. He paid his fare and started walking, moving away from the car, strolling slowly, stopping to look in shop windows. In the reflection of a store window, he saw the Opel, moving slowly behind him. When Robert reached the next corner, he noticed that it was a one-way street. He turned into it, going against the heavy traffic. The Opel hesitated at the corner, then sped away to beat Robert to the other end. Robert reversed direction and walked back to the Via Monte Grappa. The Opel was nowhere in sight.

Robert hailed a taxi. "Via Monticelli."

The building was old and unprepossessing, a relic of better days. Robert had visited it many times before on various missions. He walked down three basement steps and knocked on the door. An eye appeared at the peephole, and a moment later the door was flung open.

"Roberto!" a man exclaimed. He threw his arms around Robert. "How are you, *mi amico*?"

The speaker was a fat man in his sixties with white, unshaven stubble, thick eyebrows, yellowed teeth, and several chins. He closed the door behind him and locked it.

"I'm fine, Ricco."

Ricco had no second name. *"For a man like me," he liked to boast, "one name is enough. Like Garbo."* "What can I do for you today, my friend?"

"I'm working on a case," Robert said, "and I'm in a hurry. Can you fix me up with a passport?"

Ricco smiled. "Is the pope Catholic?" He waddled over to a cabinet in the corner and unlocked it. "What country would you like to be from?" He pulled out a handful of passports with different colored covers and sorted through them. "We have a Greek passport, Turkish, Yugoslavian, English—"

"American," Robert said.

Ricco pulled out a passport with a blue cover. "Here we are. Does the name Arthur Butterfield appeal to you?"

"Perfect," Robert said.

"If you'll stand over by the wall, I will take your picture."

Robert moved over to the wall. Ricco opened a drawer and took out a Polaroid camera. A minute later, Robert was looking at a picture of himself.

"I wasn't smiling," Robert said.

Ricco looked at him, puzzled. "What?"

"I wasn't smiling. Take another one."

Ricco shrugged. "Sure. Whatever you say."

Robert smiled while the second passport picture was

taken. He looked at it and said, "That's better." He casually slipped the first picture into his pocket.

"Now comes the high-tech part," Ricco announced. Robert watched as Ricco walked over to a workbench where there was a laminating machine. He placed the picture on the inside of the passport.

Robert moved to a table covered with pens, ink, and other paraphernalia and slipped a razor blade and a small bottle of glue into his jacket pocket.

Ricco was studying his handiwork. "Not bad," he said. He handed the passport to Robert. "That will be five thousand dollars."

"And well worth it," Robert assured him, as he peeled off 10 five-hundred-dollar bills.

"It's always a pleasure doing business with you people. You know how I feel about you."

Robert knew exactly how he felt. Ricco was an expert cobbler who worked for half a dozen different governments—and was loyal to none. He put the passport in his coat pocket.

"Good luck, Mr. Butterfield." Ricco smiled.

"Thanks."

The moment the door closed behind Robert, Ricco reached for the telephone. Information was always worth money to someone.

Outside, twenty yards down the street, Robert took the new passport out of his pocket and buried it in a trash can. *Chaff.* The technique he had used as a pilot to lay false trails for enemy missiles. *Let them look for Arthur Butterfield.*

The gray Opel was parked half a block away. Waiting. *Impossible.* Robert was sure that the car was the only tail they had. He was certain the Opel had not followed him, and yet it kept finding him. They had to have some way of keeping track of his location. There was only one answer: They were using some kind of homing device. And he had to be carrying it. Attached to his clothes? No. They had had no opportunity. Captain Dougherty had stayed with him while he packed, but he would not have known what clothes Robert would take. Robert made a mental inventory of what he was carrying—cash, keys, a wallet, handkerchief, credit card. *The credit card! "I doubt if I'll need that, General." "Take it. And keep it with you at all times."*

The sneaky sonofabitch. No wonder they had been able to find him so easily.

The gray Opel was no longer in sight. Robert took out the card and examined it. It was slightly thicker than an ordinary credit card. By squeezing it, he could feel an inner layer. They would have a remote control to activate the card. *Good,* Robert thought. *Let's keep the bastards busy.*

There were several trucks parked along the street loading and unloading goods. Robert examined the license plates. When he came to a red truck with French plates, he looked around to make sure he was not observed and tossed the card in the back of the truck.

He flagged down a taxi. "Hassler, *per favore*."

In the lobby, Robert approached the concierge. "See if there's a flight out of here tonight to Paris, please."

"Certainly, Commander. Do you prefer any particular airline?"

"It doesn't matter. The first flight out."

"I will be happy to arrange it."

"Thank you." Robert walked over to the hotel clerk. "My key, please. Room 314. And I'll be checking out in a few minutes."

"Very good, Commander Bellamy." The clerk reached

in a pigeonhole and pulled out a key and an envelope. "There's a letter here for you."

Robert stiffened. The envelope was sealed and addressed simply: "Commander Robert Bellamy." He fingered it, feeling for plastique or any metal inside. He opened it carefully. Inside was a printed card advertising an Italian restaurant. It was innocent enough. Except, of course, for his name on the envelope.

"Do you happen to remember who gave you this?"

"I'm sorry," the clerk said apologetically, "but we have been so busy this evening. . . ."

It was not important. The man would have been faceless. He would have picked up the card somewhere, slipped it into the envelope, and stood by the desk, watching to see the room number of the slot that the envelope was placed in. He would be waiting upstairs now in Robert's room. It was time to see the face of the enemy.

Robert became aware of raised voices and turned to watch the Shriners he had seen earlier, entering the lobby, laughing and singing. They had obviously had a few more drinks. The portly man said, "Hi there, pal. You missed a great party."

Robert's mind was racing. "You like parties?"

"Hoo hoo!"

"There's a real live one going on upstairs," Robert said. "Booze, girls—anything you want. Just follow me, fellows."

"That's the American spirit, pal." The man clapped Robert on the back. "You hear that, boys? Our friend here is throwing a party!"

They crowded into the elevator together and rode up to the third floor.

The Shriner said, "These Italians sure know how to live it up. I guess they invented orgies, huh?"

"I'm going to show you a *real* orgy," Robert promised.

They followed him down the hall to his room. Robert put the key in the lock and turned to the group. "Are you all ready to have some fun?"

There was a chorus of yeses . . .

Robert turned the key, pushed the door open, and stepped to one side. The room was dark. He snapped on the light. A tall, thin stranger was standing in the middle of the room with a Mauser equipped with a silencer, half drawn. The man looked at the group with a startled expression and quickly shoved the gun back in his jacket.

"Hey! Where's the booze?" one of the Shriners demanded.

Robert pointed to the stranger. "He has it. Go get it."

The group surged toward the man. "Where's the liquor, buddy?" . . . "Where are the girls?" . . . "Let's get this party on the road. . . ."

The thin man was trying to get through to Robert, but the crowd was blocking his way. He watched helplessly as Robert bolted out the door. He took the stairs two at a time.

Downstairs in the lobby, Robert was moving toward the exit when the concierge called out, "Oh, Commander Bellamy, I made your reservation for you. You are on Air France flight 312 to Paris. It leaves at one A.M."

"Thanks," Robert said hurriedly.

He was out the door, into the small square overlooking the Spanish Steps. A taxi was discharging a passenger. Robert stepped into it. "Via Monte Grappa."

He had his answer now. They intended to kill him. *They're not going to find it easy.* He was the hunted now instead of the hunter, but he had one big advantage. They had trained him well. He knew all their techniques, their strengths, and their weaknesses, and he intended to use that knowledge to stop them. First, he had to find a way to throw them off his trail. The men after him would have been given a story of some kind. They would have been told he was wanted for smuggling drugs, or for murder, or espionage. They would have been warned: *He's dangerous. Take no chances. Shoot to kill.*

Robert said to the taxi driver, "Roma Termini." They were hunting for him, but they would not have had enough time to disseminate his photograph. So far, he was faceless.

The taxi pulled up at Via Giovanni Giolitti 36, and the driver announced, "Stazione Termini, *signore*."

"Let's just wait here a minute." Robert sat in the taxi, studying the front of the railway station. There seemed to be only the usual activity. Everything appeared to be normal. Taxis and limousines were arriving and departing, discharging and picking up passengers. Porters were loading and unloading luggage. A policeman was busily ordering cars to move out of the restricted parking zone. But something was disturbing Robert. He suddenly realized what was wrong with the picture. Parked directly in front of the station, in a no-parking zone, were three unmarked sedans, with no one inside. The policeman ignored them.

"I've changed my mind," Robert said to the driver. "Via Veneto 110/A." It was the last place anyone would look for him.

The American Embassy and Consulate are located in a pink stucco building facing the Via Veneto, with a black wrought-iron fence in front of it. The embassy was closed at this hour, but the passport division of the consulate was open on a twenty-four-hour basis to handle emergencies. In the foyer on the first floor, a marine sat behind a desk.

The marine looked up as Robert approached. "May I help you, sir?"

"Yes," Robert said. "I want to inquire about getting a new passport. I lost mine."

"Are you an American citizen?"

"Yes."

The marine indicated an office at the far end. "They'll take care of you in there, sir. Last door."

"Thank you."

There were half a dozen people in the room applying for passports, reporting lost ones, and getting renewals and visas.

"Do I need a visa to visit Albania? I have relatives there. . . ."

"I need this passport renewed by tonight. I have a plane to catch. . . ."

"I don't know what happened to it. I must have left it in Milan. . . ."

"They grabbed my passport right out of my purse. . . ."

Robert stood there listening. Stealing passports was a thriving cottage industry in Italy. Someone here would be getting a new passport. At the head of the line was a well-dressed, middle-aged man being handed an American passport.

"Here is your new passport, Mr. Cowan. I'm sorry you had such a bad experience. I'm afraid there are a lot of pickpockets in Rome."

"I'll sure see to it that they don't get hold of this one," Cowan said.

"You do that, sir."

Robert watched Cowan put the passport in his jacket pocket and turn to leave. Robert stepped ahead of him. As a woman brushed by, Robert lunged into Cowan, as if he had been pushed, almost knocking him down.

"I'm terribly sorry," Robert apologized. He leaned over and straightened the man's jacket for him.

"No problem," Cowan said.

Robert turned and walked into the public men's room down the hall, the stranger's passport in his pocket. He looked around to make sure he was alone, then went into one of the booths. He took out the razor blade and bottle of glue he had stolen from Ricco. Very carefully, he slit the top of the plastic and removed Cowan's photograph. Next, he inserted the picture of himself that Ricco had taken. He glued the top of the plastic slot closed and examined his handiwork. Perfect. He was now Henry Cowan. Five minutes later, he was out in the Via Veneto, getting into a taxi. "Leonardo da Vinci."

It was twelve-thirty when Robert arrived at the airport. He stood outside, looking for anything unusual. On the surface, everything appeared to be normal. No police cars, no suspicious-looking men. Robert entered the terminal and stopped just inside the door. There were various airline counters scattered around the large terminal. There seemed to be no one loitering or hiding behind posts. He stayed where he was, wary. He could not explain it, even to himself, but somehow everything seemed *too* normal.

Across the room was an Air France counter. *"You are on Air France flight 312 to Paris. . . . It leaves at one* A.M." Robert walked past the counter and approached a woman in uniform behind the Alitalia counter. "Good evening."

"Good evening. Can I help you, *signore*?"

"Yes," Robert said. "Would you please page Commander Robert Bellamy to come to the courtesy telephone?"

"Certainly," she said. She picked up a microphone.

A few feet away, a fat middle-aged woman was checking a number of suitcases, heatedly arguing with an airline attendant about overweight fees. "In America, they never charged me for overweight."

"I'm sorry, madam. But if you wish all these bags to go on, you must pay for excess baggage."

Robert moved closer. He heard the attendant's voice over the loudspeaker. "Will Commander Robert Bellamy please come to the white courtesy telephone. Commander Robert Bellamy, please come to the white courtesy telephone." The announcement echoed throughout the airport.

A man holding a carry-on bag was walking past Robert. "Excuse me," Robert said.

The man turned. "Yes?"

"I hear my wife paging me, but"—he indicated the woman's bags—"I can't leave my luggage." He pulled out a ten-dollar bill and handed it to the man. "Would you please go over to that white telephone and tell her I'll pick her up at our hotel in an hour? I'd really appreciate it."

The man looked at the ten-dollar bill in his hand. "Sure."

Robert watched him walk over to the courtesy telephone and pick it up. He held the receiver to his ear and said, "Hello? . . . Hello? . . ."

The next moment, four large men in black suits appeared from nowhere and closed in, pinning the hapless man to the wall.

"Hey! What is this?"

"Let's do this quietly," one of the men said.

"What do you think you're doing? Get your hands off me!"

"Don't make a fuss, Commander. There's no point—"

"*Commander?* You've got the wrong man! My name is Melvyn Davis. I'm from Omaha!"

"Let's not play games."

"Wait a minute! I've been set up. The man you want is over there!" He pointed to where Robert had been standing.

There was no one there.

Outside the terminal, an airport bus was getting ready to depart. Robert boarded it, mingling with the other passengers. He sat at the back of the bus, concentrating on his next move.

He was desperate to talk to Admiral Whittaker to try to get answers about what was going on, to learn who was responsible for killing innocent people because they had witnessed something they were not supposed to have seen. Was it General Hilliard? Dustin Thornton? Or Thornton's father-in-law, Willard Stone, the man of mystery. Could he be involved in this in some way? Was it Edward Sanderson, the director of NSA? Could they be working together? Did it go as high as the President? Robert needed answers.

The bus trip into Rome took an hour. When the bus stopped in front of the Eden Hotel, Robert disembarked.

I've got to get out of the country, Robert thought. There was only one man in Rome he could trust. Colonel Francesco Cesar, head of SIFAR, the Italian Secret Service. He was going to be Robert's escape from Italy.

Colonel Cesar was working late. Messages had been flashing back and forth among foreign security agencies, and they all involved Commander Robert Bellamy. Colonel Cesar had worked with Robert in the past, and he was very fond of him. Cesar sighed as he looked at the latest message in front of him. *Terminate.* And as he was reading it, his secretary came into the office.

"Commander Bellamy is on line one for you."

Colonel Cesar stared at her. "Bellamy? Himself? Never mind." He waited until the secretary left the room, then snatched up the telephone.

"Robert?"

"*Ciao,* Francesco. What the hell is going on?"

"You tell me, *amico*. I've been getting all kinds of urgent communiqués about you. What have you done?"

"It's a long story," Robert said. "And I haven't time. What have you heard?"

"That you've gone private. That you've been turned and are singing like a canary."

"What?"

"I heard you've made a deal with the Chinese and—"

"*Jesus Christ.* That's ridiculous!"

"Is it? Why?"

"Because an hour later they'd be hungry for more information."

"For God's sake, Robert, this is nothing to joke about."

"Tell me about it, Francesco. I've just sent ten innocent people to their deaths. I'm scheduled to be number eleven."

"Where are you?"

"I'm in Rome. I can't seem to get out of your fucking city."

"Cacatura!" There was a thoughtful silence. "What can I do to help?"

"Get me to a safe house where we can talk, and I can figure out how to get away. Can you arrange that?"

"Yes, but you must be careful. Very careful. I will pick you up myself."

Robert breathed a deep sigh of relief. "Thanks, Francesco. I really appreciate it."

"As you Americans say, you owe me one. Where are you?"

"The Lido bar in Trastevere."

"Wait right there. I'll see you in exactly one hour."

"Thanks, *amico*." Robert replaced the receiver. It was going to be a long hour.

Thirty minutes later, two unmarked cars coasted to a stop ten yards from the Lido bar. There were four men in each car, and they were all carrying automatic weapons.

Colonel Cesar got out of the first car. "Let's do this quickly. We don't want anyone else to get hurt. *Andate al dietro, subito.*"

Half the men silently went around to cover the back of the building.

Robert Bellamy watched from the rooftop of the building across the street as Cesar and his men raised their weapons and charged into the bar.

All right, you bastards, Robert thought grimly, *we'll play it your way.*

Chapter Thirty-six

Day Sixteen
Rome, Italy

Robert placed a call to Colonel Cesar from a phone booth in the Piazza del Duomo. "Whatever happened to friendship?" Robert asked.

"Don't be naive, my friend. I'm under orders, just as you are. I can assure you, there is no use in your running. You're at the head of every intelligence agency's most wanted list. Half the governments of the world are looking for you."

"Do you believe I'm a traitor?"

Cesar sighed. "It doesn't matter what I believe, Robert. This is nothing personal. I have my orders."

"To take me out."

"You can make it easier by turning yourself in."

"Thanks, *paesano*. If I need more advice, I'll call Dear Abby." He slammed down the receiver.

Robert was aware that the longer he was at large, the greater the danger he was in. There would be security agents closing in on him from half a dozen countries.

There has to be a tree, Robert thought. The line came from a legend about a hunter who was relating an experience he had on safari. "This huge lion was racing toward me, and all my gun bearers had fled. I had no gun, and there was nowhere to hide. Not a bush or a tree in sight. And the beast was charging straight at me, coming closer and closer." "How did you escape?" a listener asked. "I ran over to the nearest tree and climbed it." "But you said there were no trees." "You don't understand. There *has* to be a tree!" *And I have to find it,* Robert thought.

He looked around the piazza. It was almost deserted at this hour. He decided it was time to have a talk with the man who had started him on this nightmare, General Hilliard. But he would have to be careful. Modern electronic phone tracing was almost instantaneous. Robert observed that the two telephone booths next to the one he was in were both empty. *Perfect.* Ignoring the private number General Hilliard had given him, he dialed the switchboard of NSA. When an operator answered, Robert said, "General Hilliard's office, please."

A moment later, he heard a secretary's voice. "General Hilliard's office."

Robert said, "Please hold for an overseas call." He dropped the receiver and hurried into the next booth. He quickly redialed the number. A different secretary answered, "General Hilliard's office."

"Please hold for an overseas call," Robert said. He let the receiver hang, walked into the third booth, and dialed. When another secretary answered, Robert said, "This is Commander Bellamy. I want to speak to General Hilliard."

There was a gasp of surprise. "Just a moment, Commander." The secretary buzzed the intercom. "General, Commander Bellamy is on line three."

General Hilliard turned to Harrison Keller. "Bellamy is on line three. Start a trace, fast."

Harrison Keller hurried over to a telephone on a side table and dialed the Network Operations Center, manned and monitored twenty-four hours a day. The senior officer on duty answered. "NOC. Adams."

"How long will it take to do an emergency trace on an incoming call?" Keller whispered.

"Between one and two minutes."

"Start it. General Hilliard's office, line three. I'll hang on." He looked over at the general and nodded.

General Hilliard picked up the telephone.

"Commander—is that you?"

In the operations center, Adams punched a number into a computer. "Here we go," he said.

"I thought it was time you and I had a talk, General."

"I'm glad you called, Commander. Why don't you come in and we can discuss the situation? I'll arrange a plane for you, and you can be here in—"

"No thanks. Too many accidents happen in airplanes, General."

In the communications room, ESS, the electronic switching system had been activated. The computer screen began lighting up. *AX121-B* . . . *AX122-C* . . . *AX123-C* . . .

"What's happening?" Keller whispered into the phone.

"The Network Operations Center in New Jersey is searching the Washington, D.C., trunks, sir. Hold on."

The screen went blank. Then the words *Overseas Trunk Line One* flashed onto the screen.

"The call is coming from somewhere in Europe. We're tracing the country. . . ."

General Hilliard was saying, "Commander Bellamy, I think there's been a misunderstanding. I have a suggestion. . . ."

Robert replaced the receiver.

General Hilliard looked over at Keller. "Did you get it?"

Harrison Keller talked into the phone to Adams. "What happened?"

"We lost him."

Robert moved into the second booth and picked up the telephone.

General Hilliard's secretary said, "Commander Bellamy is calling on line two."

The two men looked at each other. General Hilliard pressed the button for line two.

"Commander?"

"Let *me* make a suggestion," Robert said.

General Hilliard put his hand over the mouthpiece. "Get the trace working again."

Harrison Keller picked up the telephone and said to Adams, "He's on again. Line two. Move fast."

"Right."

"My suggestion, General, is that you call off all your men. And I mean *now*."

"I think you misunderstand the situation, Commander. We can work this problem out if—"

"I'll tell you how we can work it out. There's a termination order out on me. I want you to cancel it."

In the Network Operations Center, the computer screen was flashing a new message: *AX155-C Subtrunk A21 verified. Circuit 301 to Rome. Atlantic Trunk 1.*

"We've got it," Adams said into the phone. "We've traced the trunk to Rome."

"Get me the number and location," Keller told him.

In Rome Robert was glancing at his watch. "You gave me an assignment. I carried it out."

"You did very well, Commander. Here is what I—"

The line went dead.

The general turned to Keller. "He hung up, again."

Keller spoke into the phone, "Did you get it?"

"Too quick, sir."

Robert moved into the next booth and picked up the telephone.

General Hilliard's secretary's voice came over the intercom. "Commander Bellamy is on line one, General."

The general snapped, "Find the bastard!" He picked up the telephone. "Commander?"

"I want you to listen, General, and listen closely. You've murdered a lot of innocent people. If you don't call off your men, I'm going to the media and tell them what's going on."

"I wouldn't advise you to do that, unless you want to start a worldwide panic. The aliens are real, and we're defenseless against them. They're getting ready to make their move. You have no idea what would happen if word of this leaked out."

"Neither have you," Bellamy retorted. "I'm not giving you a choice. Call off the contract on me. If there's one more attempt made on my life, I'm going public."

"All right," General Hilliard said. "You win. I'll call it off. Why don't we do this? We can—"

"Your trace should be working pretty good, now," Robert said. "Have a good day."

The connection was broken.

"Did you get it?" Keller barked into the phone.

Adams said, "Close, sir. He was calling from an area in central Rome. He kept switching numbers on us."

The general looked over at Keller. "Well?"

"I'm sorry, General. All we know is that he's somewhere in Rome. Do you believe his threat? Are we going to call off the contract on him?"

"No. We're going to eliminate him."

Robert went over his options again. They were pitifully few. They would be watching the airports, railroad stations, bus terminals, and rental-car agencies. He could not check into a hotel because SIFAR would be circulating red notices. Yet he had to get out of Rome. He needed a cover. A companion. They would not be looking for a man and a woman together. It was a beginning.

A taxi was standing at the corner. Robert mussed his hair, pulled down his tie, and staggered drunkenly toward the taxi. "Hey, there," he called. "You!"

The driver looked at him distastefully.

Robert pulled out a twenty-dollar bill and slapped it into the man's hand. "Hey, buddy, I'm lookin' a'get laid. You know what tha' means? D'you speak any goddamn English?"

The driver looked at the bill. "You wish a woman?"

"You got it, pal. I wish a woman."

"Andiamo," the driver said.

Robert lurched into the cab, and it took off. Robert looked back. He was not being followed. The adrenaline was pumping. *"Half the governments in the world are looking for you."* And there would be no appeal. Their orders were to assassinate him.

Twenty minutes later they had reached Tor di Ounto, Rome's red-light district, populated by whores and pimps. They drove down Passeggiata Archeologica, and the driver pulled to a stop at a corner.

"You will find a woman here," he said.

"Thanks, buddy." Robert paid the amount on the meter and stumbled out of the taxi. It pulled away with a squeal of tires.

Robert looked around, studying his surroundings. No police. A few cars and a handful of pedestrians. There were more than a dozen whores cruising the street. In the spirit of "Let's round up the usual suspects," the police had conducted their bimonthly sweep to satisfy the voices of morality and moved the city's prostitutes from the Via Veneto, with its high visibility, to this area, where they would not offend the dowagers taking tea at Doney's. For that reason, most of the ladies were attractive and well-dressed. There was one in particular who caught Robert's eye.

She appeared to be in her early twenties. She had long, dark hair and was dressed in a tasteful black skirt and white blouse, over which she wore a camel-hair coat. Robert guessed that she was a part-time actress or model. She was watching Robert.

Robert staggered up to her. "Hi, baby," he mumbled. "D'you speak English?"

"Yes."

"Good. Le's you an' me have a party."

She smiled uncertainly. Drunks could be trouble. "Maybe you should go sober up first." She had a soft Italian accent.

"Hey, I'm sober enough."

"It will cost you a hundred dollars."

"Tha's okay, honey."

She made her decision. "*Va bene*. Come. There is a hotel just around the corner."

"Great. What's your name, baby?"

"Pier."

"Mine's Henry." A police car appeared in the distance, headed their way. "Let's get outta here."

The other women cast envious glances as Pier and her American customer walked away.

The hotel was no Hassler, but the pimply faced boy at the desk downstairs did not ask for a passport. In fact, he barely glanced up as he handed Pier a key. "Fifty thousand lira."

Pier looked at Robert. He took the money from his pocket and gave it to the boy.

The room they entered contained a large bed in the corner, a small table, two wooden chairs, and a mirror over the sink. There was a clothes rack in back of the door.

"You must pay me in advance."

"Sure." Robert counted out one hundred dollars.

"Grazie."

Pier began to get undressed. Robert walked over to the window. He pushed aside a corner of the curtain and peered out. Everything appeared to be normal. He hoped that by now the police were following the red truck back to France. Robert dropped the curtain and turned around. Pier was naked. She had a surprisingly lovely body. Firm, young breasts, rounded hips, a small waist, and long, shapely legs.

She was watching Robert. "Aren't you going to get undressed, Henry?"

This was the tricky part. ". . . tell you the truth," Robert said, "I think I had a little too much to drink. I can't give you any action."

She was regarding him with wary eyes. "Then why did you—?"

"If I stay here and sleep it off, we can make love in the morning."

She shrugged. "I have to work. It would cost me money to—"

"Don't worry. I'll take care of that." He pulled out several hundred-dollar bills and handed them to her. "Will that cover it?"

Pier looked at the money, making up her mind. It was tempting. It was cold outside, and business was slow. On the other hand, there was something strange about this man. First of all, he did not really seem to be drunk. He was nicely dressed, and for this much money, he could have checked them into a fine hotel. *Well,* Pier thought, *what the hell? Questo cazzo se ne frega?* "All right. There's only this bed for the two of us."

"That's fine."

Pier watched as Robert walked over to the window again and moved the edge of the curtain aside.

"You are looking for something?"

"Is there a back door out of the hotel?"

What am I getting myself into? Pier wondered. Her best friend had been murdered hanging out with mobsters. Pier considered herself wise in the ways of men, but this one puzzled her. He did not seem like a criminal, but still . . . "Yes, there is," she said.

There was a sudden scream, and Robert whirled around.

"Dio! Dio! Sono venuta tre volte!" It was a woman's voice, coming from the next room through the paper-thin walls.

"What's that?" Robert's heart was pounding.

Pier grinned. "She's having fun. She said she just came for the third time."

Robert heard the creaking of bed springs.

"Are you going to bed?" Pier stood there naked, unembarrassed, watching him.

"Sure." Robert sat down on the bed.

"Aren't you going to get undressed?"

"No."

"Suit yourself." Pier moved over to the bed and lay down beside Robert. "I hope you don't snore," Pier said.

"You can tell me in the morning."

Robert had no intention of sleeping. He wanted to check the street during the night to make sure they did not come to the hotel. They would get around to these small, third-class hotels eventually, but it would take them time. They had too many other places to cover first. He lay there, feeling bone-tired, and closed his eyes for a moment to rest. He slept. He was back home, in his own bed, and he felt Susan's warm body next to his. *She's back,* he thought, happily. *She's come back to me. Baby, I've missed you so much.*

Day Seventeen
Rome, Italy

Robert was awakened by the sun hitting his face. He sat up abruptly, looking around for an instant in alarm, disoriented. When he saw Pier, memory flooded back. He relaxed. Pier was at the mirror, brushing her hair.

"Buon giorno," she said. "You do not snore."

Robert looked at his watch. Nine o'clock. He had wasted precious hours.

"Do you want to make love now? You have already paid for it."

"That's all right," Robert said.

Pier, naked and provocative, walked over to the bed. "Are you sure?"

I couldn't if I wanted to, lady. "I'm sure."

"Va bene." She began to dress. She asked casually, "Who is Susan?"

The question caught him off guard. "Susan? What made you ask?"

"You talk in your sleep."

He remembered his dream. Susan had come back to him. Maybe it was a sign. "She's a friend." *She's my wife. She's going to get tired of Moneybags and return to me some day. If I'm still alive, that is.*

Robert walked over to the window. He lifted the curtain and looked out. The street was crowded now with pedestrians and merchants opening up their shops. There were no signs of danger.

It was time to put his plan into motion. He turned to the girl. "Pier, how would you like to go on a little trip with me?"

She looked at him with suspicion. "A trip—where?"

"I have to go to Venice on business, and I hate traveling alone. Do you like Venice?"

"Yes. . . ."

"Good. I'll pay you for your time, and we'll have a little holiday together." He was staring out the window again. "I know a lovely hotel there. The Cipriani." Years ago he and Susan had stayed at the Royal Danieli, but he had been back since, and it had become sadly run down, and the beds were impossible. The only thing that remained of the hotel's former elegance was Luciano, at the reception desk.

"It will cost you a thousand dollars a day." She was ready to settle for five hundred.

"It's a deal." Robert said. He counted out two thousand dollars. "We'll start with this."

Pier hesitated. She had a premonition that something was wrong. But the start of the movie she had been promised a bit part in had been delayed, and she needed the money. "Very well," she said.

"Let's go."

Downstairs, Pier watched him scan the street carefully before stepping out to hail a taxi. *He's a target for somebody,* Pier thought. *I'm getting out of here.*

"Look," Pier said, "I'm not sure I should go to Venice with you. I—"

"We're going to have a great time," Robert told her.

Directly across the street he saw a jewelry store. He took Pier's hand. "Come on. I'm going to get you something pretty."

"But—"

He led her across the street to the jewelry store.

The clerk behind the counter said, "*Buon giorno, signore.* Can I help you?"

"Yes," Robert said. "We're looking for something lovely for the lady." He turned to Pier. "Do you like emeralds?"

"I—yes."

Robert said to the clerk, "Do you have an emerald bracelet?"

"*Si, signore.* I have a beautiful emerald bracelet." He walked over to a case and took out a bracelet. "This is our finest. It is fifteen thousand dollars."

Robert looked at Pier. "Do you like it?"

She was speechless. She nodded.

"We'll take it," Robert said. He handed the clerk his ONI credit card.

"One moment, please." The clerk disappeared into the back room. When he returned, he said, "Shall I wrap it for you, or—?"

"No. My friend will wear it." Robert put the bracelet on Pier's wrist. She was staring at it, stunned.

Robert said, "That will look pretty in Venice, won't it?"

Pier smiled up at him. "Very."

When they were out on the street, Pier said, "I—I don't know how to thank you."

"I just want you to have a good time," Robert told her. "Do you have a car?"

"No. I used to have an old one, but it was stolen."

"Do you still have your driver's license?"

She was watching him, puzzled. "Yes, but without a car, what good is a driver's license?"

"You'll see. Let's get out of here."

He hailed a taxi. "Via Po, please."

She sat in the taxi, studying him. Why was he so eager for her company? He had not even touched her. *Could he be—?*

"Qui!" Robert called to the driver. They were a hundred yards away from Maggiore's Car Rental Agency.

"We're getting out here," Robert told Pier. He paid the driver and waited until the taxi was out of sight. He handed Pier a large bundle of bank notes. "I want you to rent a car for us. Ask for a Fiat or an Alfa Romeo. Tell them we'll want it for four or five days. This money will cover the deposit. Rent it in your name. I'll wait for you in the bar across the street."

Less than eight blocks away, two detectives were questioning the hapless driver of a red truck with French license plates.

"*Vous me faites chier*. I have no idea how the fuck that

card got in the back of my truck," the driver screamed. "Some crazy Italian probably put it in there."

The two detectives looked at each other. One of them said, "I'll phone it in."

Francesco Cesar sat at his desk, thinking about the latest development. Earlier the assignment had seemed so simple. *"You won't have any trouble finding him. When the time comes, we will activate the homing device, and it will lead you right to him."* Someone had obviously underestimated Commander Bellamy.

Colonel Frank Johnson was seated in General Hilliard's office, his huge frame filling the chair.

"We have half the agents in Europe looking for him," General Hilliard said. "So far, they've had no luck."

"It's going to take more than luck," Colonel Johnson said. "Bellamy's good."

"We know he's in Rome. The sonofabitch just charged a bracelet for fifteen thousand dollars. We have him bottled up. There's no way he can get out of Italy. We know the name he's using on his passport—Arthur Butterfield."

Colonel Johnson shook his head. "If I know Bellamy, you haven't a clue about what name he's using. The only thing you can count on is that Bellamy won't do what you count on him to do. We're after a man who's as good as the best in the business. Maybe better. If there's any place to run, Bellamy will run there. If there's any place to hide, he'll hide there. I think our best bet is to bring him out in the open, to smoke him out. Right now, he's controlling all the moves. We have to take the initiative away from him."

"You mean, go public? Give it to the press?"

"Exactly."

General Hilliard pursed his lips. "That's going to be touchy. We can't afford to expose ourselves."

"We won't have to. We'll put out a release that he's wanted on a drug-smuggling charge. That way we can get Interpol and all the police departments in Europe involved without tipping our hand."

General Hilliard thought about it for a moment. "I like it."

"Good. I'm leaving for Rome," Colonel Johnson said. "I'm going to take charge of the hunt myself."

When Colonel Frank Johnson returned to his office, he was in a thoughtful mood. He was playing a dangerous game. There was no question about it. He had to find Commander Bellamy.

Chapter Thirty-seven

Robert listened to the phone ring again and again. It was six A.M. in Washington. *I'm always waking the old man up,* Robert thought.

The admiral answered on the sixth ring. "Hello—"

"Admiral, I—"

"Robert! What—?"

"Don't say anything. Your phone is probably bugged. I'm going to make this fast. I just wanted to tell you not to believe anything they're saying about me. I'd like you to try to find out what's going on. I may need your help later."

"Of course. Anything I can do, Robert."

"I know."

"I'll call you later."

Robert replaced the receiver. No time for a trace. He

saw a blue Fiat pull up outside the bar. Pier was at the wheel.

"Move over," Robert said. "I'll drive."

Pier made room for him as he slid in behind the wheel.

"Are we on our way to Venice?" Pier asked.

"Uh-huh. We have a couple of stops to make first." It was time to spread some more chaff around. He turned onto Viale Rossini. Ahead was the Rossini Travel Service. Robert pulled over to the curb. "I'll be back in a minute."

Pier watched him walk into the travel agency. *I could just drive away,* she thought, *and keep the money, and he would never find me. But the damn car is rented in my name. Cacchio!*

Inside the agency, Robert walked up to the woman behind the counter.

"Good day. May I help you?"

"Yes. I'm Commander Robert Bellamy. I'm going to do a bit of traveling," Robert told her. "I'd like to make some reservations."

She smiled. "That's what we are here for, *signore.* Where are you planning to go?"

"I'd like a first-class airline ticket to Beijing, one-way."

She made a note. "And when would you like to leave?"

"This Friday."

"Very good." She pressed some keys on a computer. "There's an Air China flight leaving at seven forty P.M. Friday night."

"That will do nicely."

She pressed some more keys. "There we are. Your reservation is confirmed. Will that be cash or—?"

"Oh, I'm not through yet. I want to reserve a train ticket to Budapest."

"And when would that be, Commander?"

"Next Monday."

"And in what name?"

"The same."

She looked at him strangely. "You are flying to Beijing on Friday and—"

"I'm not finished," Robert said pleasantly. "I want a one-way airline ticket to Miami, Florida, on Sunday."

Now she was openly staring at him. "*Signore,* if this is some kind of a —"

Robert pulled out his ONI credit card and handed it to her. "Just charge the tickets to this card."

She studied it a moment. "Excuse me." She went into the back office and came out a few minutes later. "That will be perfectly all right. We will be happy to make the arrangements. Do you wish all the reservations under one name?"

"Yes. Commander Robert Bellamy."

"Very good."

Robert watched as she pressed more buttons on the computer. A minute later, three tickets appeared. She tore them off the printer.

"Please put the tickets in separate envelopes," Robert said.

"Of course. Would you like me to send them to—?"

"I'll take them with me."

"Si, signore."

Robert signed the credit card slip, and she handed him his receipt.

"There you are. Have a nice trip—trips—er—"

Robert grinned. "Thanks." A minute later he was behind the wheel of the car.

"Are we going now?" Pier asked.

"We have just a few more stops to make," Robert said.

Pier watched him carefully scan the street again before pulling out.

"I want you to do something for me," Robert told her.

Now it's coming, Pier thought. *He's going to ask me to do something terrible.* "What is it?" she asked.

They had stopped in front of the Hotel Victoria. Robert handed Pier one of the envelopes. "I want you to go to the desk and reserve a suite in the name of Commander Robert Bellamy. Tell them you're his secretary and that he'll be arriving in an hour, but that you want to go up to the suite and approve it. When you get inside, leave this envelope on a table in the room."

She looked at him puzzled. "That's all?"

"That's all."

The man made no sense at all. *"Bene."* She wished she knew what the crazy American was up to. *And who is Commander Robert Bellamy?* Pier got out of the car and walked into the lobby of the hotel. She was a bit nervous. In the course of practicing her profession, she had been thrown out of a few first-class hotels. But the clerk behind the desk greeted her politely. "May I help you, *signora*?"

"I am the secretary to Commander Robert Bellamy. I wish to reserve a suite for him. He will be here in an hour."

The clerk consulted the room chart. "We do happen to have one very nice suite available."

"May I see it, please?" Pier asked.

"Certainly. I'll have someone show it to you."

An assistant manager escorted Pier upstairs. They

walked into the living room of the suite and Pier looked around. "Will this be satisfactory, *signora*?"

Pier had not the faintest idea. "Yes, this will be fine." She removed the envelope from her purse and laid it on a coffee table. "I will leave this here for the commander," she said.

"Bene."

Curiosity got the better of Pier. She opened the envelope. Inside was a one-way plane ticket to Beijing in the name of Robert Bellamy. Pier put the ticket back in the envelope, left it on the table, and went downstairs.

The blue Fiat was parked in front of the hotel.

"Any problem?" Robert asked.

"No."

"We have just two more stops to make, and then we're on our way," Robert said cheerfully.

The next stop was the Hotel Valadier. Robert handed Pier another envelope. "I want you to reserve a suite here in the name of Commander Robert Bellamy. Tell them he'll be checking in within an hour. Then—"

"I leave the envelope upstairs."

"Right."

This time Pier walked into the hotel with more confidence. *Just act like a lady,* she thought. *You've got to have dignity. That's the fucking secret.*

There was a suite available in the hotel.

"I would like to look at it," Pier said.

"Of course, *signora*."

An assistant manager escorted Pier upstairs. "This is one of our nicest suites." It was beautiful.

Pier said haughtily, "I suppose it might do. The commander is very particular, you know." She took the second envelope out of her purse, opened it, and glanced inside. It contained a train ticket to Budapest in the name of

Commander Robert Bellamy. Pier stared at it, confused. *What kind of game is this?* She left the ticket by the bed stand.

When Pier returned to the car, Robert asked, "How did it go?"

"Fine."

"Last stop."

This time it was the Hotel Leonardo da Vinci. Robert handed Pier the third envelope. "I would like you to—"

"I know."

Inside the hotel, a clerk said, "Yes, indeed, *signora,* we have a lovely suite. When did you say the commander will be arriving?"

"In an hour. I would like to examine the suite to see if it is satisfactory."

"Of course, *signora.*"

The suite was more lavish than the other two Pier had looked at. The assistant manager showed her the huge bedroom with a large canopied bed in the center. *What a waste,* Pier thought. *In one night, I could make a fortune here.* She took out the third envelope and looked inside. It contained an airplane ticket to Miami, Florida. Pier left the envelope on the bed.

The assistant manager escorted Pier back to the living room. "We have color TV," he said. He walked over to the television set and turned it on. A picture of Robert leaped onto the screen. The anchorman's voice was saying: ". . . and Interpol believes that he is presently in Rome. He is wanted for questioning in an international drug smuggling operation. This is Bernard Shaw for CNN News." Pier was staring at the screen, transfixed.

The assistant manager turned off the television set. "Is everything satisfactory?"

"Yes," Pier said slowly. *A drug smuggler!*

"We'll be looking forward to seeing the commander."

When Pier joined Robert in the car downstairs, she looked at him with different eyes.

"Now we're ready." Robert smiled.

At the Hotel Victoria, a man in a dark suit was studying the guest register. He looked up at the clerk. "What time did Commander Bellamy check in?"

"He has not been here yet. His secretary reserved the suite. She said he would be here within the hour."

The man turned to his companion. "Have the hotel staked out. Get reinforcements. I'll wait upstairs." He turned to the clerk. "Open the suite for me."

Three minutes later, the clerk was opening the door to the suite. The man in the dark suit moved in cautiously, gun in hand. The suite was empty. He saw the envelope on the table and picked it up. The front of it read: "Commander Robert Bellamy." He opened the envelope and glanced inside. A moment later he was dialing the headquarters of SIFAR.

Francesco Cesar was in the middle of a meeting with Colonel Frank Johnson. Colonel Johnson had landed at Leonardo da Vinci Airport two hours earlier, but he showed no signs of fatigue.

"As far as we know," Cesar was saying, "Bellamy is still in Rome. We've had more than thirty reports on his whereabouts."

"Any of them check out?"

"No."

The phone rang. "It's Luigi, Colonel," the voice on the telephone said. "We've got him. I'm in his hotel suite at the Hotel Victoria. I have his airline ticket to Beijing. He is planning to leave Friday."

Cesar's voice filled with excitement. "Good! Stay there. We will be right over." He hung up and turned to Colonel Johnson. "I'm afraid your journey was for nothing, Colonel. We've got him. He's registered at the Hotel Victoria. They found an airline ticket in his name for Beijing on Friday."

Colonel Johnson said mildly, "Bellamy registered at the hotel in his own name?"

"Yes."

"And the plane ticket is in his name?"

"Yes." Colonel Cesar rose. "Let's get on over there."

Colonel Johnson shook his head. "Don't waste your time."

"What?"

"Bellamy would never—"

The telephone rang again. Cesar snatched it up. A voice said, "Colonel? This is Mario. We've located Bellamy. He's at the Hotel Valadier. He's taking a train Monday to Budapest. What do you want us to do?"

"I'll get back to you," Colonel Cesar said. He turned to look at Colonel Johnson. "They found a train ticket to Budapest in Bellamy's name. I don't understand what—"

The telephone rang again.

"Yes?" His voice was pitched higher.

"It's Bruno. We've located Bellamy. He's registered at the Hotel Leonardo da Vinci. He's planning to leave Sunday for Miami. What shall I—?"

"Come back here," Cesar snapped. He slammed down the phone. "What the hell is his game?"

Colonel Johnson said grimly, "He's seeing to it that you're wasting a lot of manpower, isn't he?"

"What do we do now?"

"We trap the bastard."

They were driving on the Via Cassia, near Olgiata, headed north toward Venice. The police would be covering all the major exits from Italy, but they would be expecting him to go west, to head for France or Switzerland. *From Venice,* Robert thought, *I can take the hydrofoil to Trieste and make my way up to Austria. After that . . .*

Pier's voice interrupted his thoughts. "I'm hungry."

"What?"

"We haven't had any breakfast or lunch."

"I'm sorry," Robert said. He had been too preoccupied to think about eating. "We'll stop at the next restaurant."

Pier watched him as he drove. She was more puzzled than ever. She lived in a world of pimps and thieves—and drug smugglers. This man was no criminal.

They stopped at the next town in front of a small trattoria. Robert pulled into the parking lot, and he and Pier got out of the car.

The restaurant was crowded with patrons, and noisy with conversations and the clatter of dishes. Robert found a table against the wall and took a seat facing the door. A waiter approached and handed them menus.

Robert was thinking: *Susan should be on the boat by now. This may be my last chance to talk to her.* "Look over the menu." Robert rose. "I'll be right back."

Pier watched him walk over to the public telephone near their table. He put a coin in the slot.

"I would like to talk to the marine operator in Gibraltar. Thank you."

Who is he calling in Gibraltar? Pier wondered. *Is that his getaway?*

"Operator, I want to place a collect call to the American yacht, *Halcyon,* off Gibraltar. Whiskey Sugar 337. Thank you."

A few minutes passed while the operators talked to each other and his call was accepted.

Robert heard Susan's voice on the telephone.

"Susan—"

"Robert! Are you all right?"

"I'm fine. I just wanted to tell you—"

"I know what you want to tell me. It's all over the radio and television. Why is Interpol hunting you?"

"It's a long story."

"Take your time. I want to know."

He hesitated. "It's political, Susan. I have evidence that some governments are trying to suppress. That's why Interpol is after me."

Pier was listening intently to Robert's end of the conversation.

"What can I do to help?" Susan asked.

"Nothing, honey. I just called to hear your voice once more in case—in case I don't get out of this."

"Don't say that." There was panic in her voice. "Can you tell me what country you're in?"

"Italy."

There was a brief silence. "All right. We're not far from you. We're just off the coast of Gibraltar. We can pick you up at any place you say."

"No, I—"

"Listen to me. It's probably your only chance of escape."

"I can't let you do that, Susan. You'd be in jeopardy."

Monte had walked into the salon in time to hear part of the conversation. "Let me talk to him."

"Just a moment, Robert, Monte wants to speak to you."

"Susan, I haven't—"

Monte's voice came over the line. "Robert, I understand you're in serious trouble."

The understatement of the year. "You might say that."

"We'd like to help you out. They won't be looking for you on a yacht. Why don't you let us pick you up?"

"Thanks, Monte, I appreciate it. The answer is no."

"I think you're making a mistake. You'll be safe here."

Why is he so eager to help? "Thanks, anyway. I'll take my chances. I'd like to speak to Susan again."

"Of course." Monte Banks handed the phone to Susan. "Talk him into it," he urged.

Susan spoke into the phone. "Please let us help you."

"You have helped me, Susan." He had to stop for a moment. "You're the best part of my life. I just want you to know that I'll always love you." He gave a little laugh. "Although *always* may not be such a big deal anymore."

"Will you call me again?"

"If I can."

"Promise me."

"All right. I promise."

He slowly replaced the receiver. *Why did I do that to her? Why did I do that to myself? You're a sentimental idiot, Bellamy.* He walked back to the table.

"Let's eat," Robert said. They ordered.

"I heard your conversation. The police are looking for you, aren't they?"

Robert stiffened. *Careless. She was going to be trouble.* "It's just a little misunderstanding. I—"

"Don't treat me like a fool. I want to help you."

He was watching her warily. "Why should you help me?"

Pier leaned forward. "Because you've been generous to me. And I hate the police. You don't know what it's like to be out on the streets, hounded by them, treated like dirt. They arrest me for prostitution, but they take me to their back rooms and pass me around. They are animals. I would do anything to get even with them. Anything. I can help you."

"Pier, there's nothing you—"

"In Venice the police will catch you easily. If you stay at a hotel, they will find you. If you try to get on a ship, they will trap you. But I know a place where you will be safe from them. My mother and brother live in Naples. We can stay at their house. The police will never look for you there."

Robert was silent for a moment, thinking about it. What Pier said made a good deal of sense. A private house would be much safer than any other place, and Naples was a big port. It would be easy to get a ship out of there. He hesitated before he answered. He did not want to put Pier in danger.

"Pier, if the police find me, they have orders to kill me. You would be considered an accomplice. You could be letting yourself in for trouble."

"It's very simple." Pier smiled. "We won't let them find you."

Robert returned her smile. He made up his mind. "All right. Eat your lunch. We're going to Naples."

Colonel Frank Johnson said, "Your men have no idea where he is headed?"

Francesco Cesar sighed. "Not at the moment. But it is only a matter of time before—"

"We don't have time. Have you checked the whereabouts of his ex-wife?"

"His ex-wife? No. I don't see what—"

"Then you haven't done your homework," Colonel Johnson snapped. "She's married to a man named Monte Banks. I would suggest that you locate them. And fast."

Chapter Thirty-eight

She wandered down the broad boulevard, barely conscious of where she was going. How many days had it been since the terrible crash? She had lost count. She was so tired that it was difficult for her to concentrate. She desperately needed water; not the polluted water that the earthlings drank, but fresh, clear rainwater. She needed the pure fluid to revive her life essence, to gain the strength to find the crystal. She was dying.

She staggered and bumped into a man.

"Hey! Watch where—" The American salesman took a closer look at her and smiled. "Hi, there. Imagine bumping into you like this!" *What a doll.*

"Yes, I can imagine that."

"Where are you from, honey?"

"The seventh sun of the Pleiades."

He laughed. "I like a gal with a sense of humor. Where you headed?"

She shook her head. "I do not know. I am a stranger here."

Jesus, I think I'm on to something. "Have you had dinner?"

"No. I cannot eat your food."

I've got a real weirdo here. But a beauty. "Where are you staying?"

"I am not staying anywhere."

"You don't have a hotel?"

"A hotel?" She remembered. *Boxes for traveling strangers.* "No. I must find a place to sleep. I am very tired."

His smile broadened. "Well, Papa can take care of that. Why don't we go up to my hotel room? I've got a nice, big comfortable bed there. Would you like that?"

"Oh, yes, very much."

He could not believe his good luck. "Wonderful!" *I'll bet she's great in the hay.*

She looked at him, puzzled. "Your bed is made of hay?"

He was staring at her. "What? No, no. You like your little jokes, don't you?"

She could barely keep her eyes open. "Could we go to bed now?"

He rubbed his hands together. "You bet! My hotel is just around the corner."

He picked up his key at the desk, and they took the elevator to his floor. When they got to his room, the man asked, "Would you like a little drink?" *Let's loosen you up.*

She wanted one desperately, but not the liquids the earthlings had to offer. "No," she said. "Where is the bed?"

My God, she's a hot little thing. "In here, honey." He led her into the bedroom. "You're sure you wouldn't like a drink?"

"I am sure."

He licked his lips. "Then why don't you—er—get undressed?"

She nodded. It was an earthling custom. She removed the dress she was wearing. She was wearing nothing underneath. Her body was exquisite.

The man stared at her and said happily, "This is my lucky night, honey. Yours, too." *I'm going to fuck you like you've never been fucked before.* He tore off his clothes as fast as he could and jumped into bed beside her. "Now!" he said. "I'm going to show you some real action." He glanced up. "Damn! I left the light on." He started to get up.

"Never mind," she said sleepily. "I will turn it off."

And as he watched, her arm reached out, out, across the wide room, and her fingers became leafy green tendrils as they brushed against the light switch.

He was alone in the dark with her. He screamed.

Chapter Thirty-nine

They were traveling at high speed on the Autostrada del Sole, the freeway to Naples. They had been driving in silence for the last half hour, each preoccupied with his own thoughts.

Pier broke the silence. "How long would you like to stay at my mother's house?" she asked.

"Three or four days, if that's all right."

"That will be fine."

Robert had no intention of staying there for more than one night, two at the most. But he kept his plans to himself. As soon as he found a ship that was safe, he would be on his way out of Italy.

"I'm looking forward to seeing my family," Pier said.

"You have just one brother?"

"Yes. Carlo. He is younger than me."

"Tell me about your family, Pier."

She shrugged. "There is not much to tell. My father worked on the docks all his life. A crane fell on him and killed him when I was fifteen. My mother was ill, and I had to support her and Carlo. I had a friend at Cinecittà studios, and he got me bit parts. They paid very little, and I had to sleep with the assistant director. I decided I could make more money on the streets. Now I do a little of both." There was no self-pity in her voice.

"Pier, are you sure your mother won't object to your bringing a stranger home?"

"I am sure. We are very close. Mother will be happy to see me. Do you love her very much?"

Robert glanced over at her in surprise. "Your mother?"

"The woman you were talking to on the telephone in the restaurant—Susan."

"What makes you think I love her?"

"The tone of your voice. Who is she?"

"A friend."

"She is very lucky. I wish I had someone who cared for me like that. Is Robert Bellamy your real name?"

"Yes."

"And are you a commander?"

That was more difficult to answer. "I'm not sure, Pier," he said. "I used to be."

"Can you tell me why Interpol is after you?"

He said carefully, "It's better if I don't tell you anything. You could be in enough trouble just being with me. The less you know, the better."

"All right, Robert."

He thought about the strange circumstances that had brought the two of them together. "Let me ask you something. If you knew that there were aliens coming down to earth in spaceships, would you panic?"

Pier studied him a moment. "Are you serious?"

"Very."

She shook her head. "No. I think it would be exciting. Do you believe such things exist?"

"There's a possibility," he said cautiously.

Pier's face lit up "Really? Do they have real—I mean—are they built like men?"

Robert laughed. "I don't know."

"Does this have anything to do with why the police are after you?"

"No," Robert said quickly. "Nothing."

"If I tell you something, will you promise not to be angry with me?"

"I promise."

When she spoke, her voice was so low he could hardly hear her. "I think I am falling in love with you."

"Pier—"

"I know. I am being foolish. But I have never said that to anyone before. I wanted you to know."

"I'm flattered, Pier."

"You're not making fun of me?"

"No. I'm not." He looked at the gas gauge. "We'd better find a filling station soon."

They came to a service station fifteen minutes later. "We'll fill the tank here," Robert said.

"Fine." Pier smiled. "I can call my mother and let her know that I am bringing home a handsome stranger."

Robert drove up to the gas pump and said to the attendant, *"Il pieno, per favore."*

"Si, signore."

Pier leaned over and gave Robert a kiss on the cheek. "I will be right back."

Robert watched her walk into the office and get change for the telephone. *She's really very pretty,* Robert thought. *And intelligent. I must be careful not to hurt her.*

Inside the office, Pier was dialing. She turned to smile and wave at Robert. When the operator came on, Pier said, "Get me Interpol. *Subito!*"

Chapter Forty

From the moment Pier had seen the news broadcast about Robert Bellamy, she had known she was going to be rich. If Interpol, the international criminal police force, was looking for Robert, there had to be a huge reward out for him. And she was the only one who knew where he was! The reward would be all hers. Persuading him to go to Naples, where she could keep an eye on him, had been a stroke of genius.

A man's voice on the telephone said, "Interpol. May I help you?"

Pier's heart was pounding. She glanced out the window to make sure Robert was still at the gas pump. "Yes. You are looking for a man named Commander Robert Bellamy, yes?"

There was a moment of silence. "Who is calling, please?"

"Never mind. Are you after him or not?"

"I'll have to transfer you to someone else. Will you hold the line, please?" He turned to his assistant, "Put a trace on this. *Pronto!*"

Thirty seconds later, Pier was speaking with a senior official. "Yes, *signora.* Can I help you?"

No, you fool. I'm trying to help you. "I have Commander Robert Bellamy. Do you want him, or don't you?"

"But, yes, *signora,* we want him very much. And you say you have him?"

"That's right. He's with me now. How much is he worth to you?"

"Are you speaking of a reward?"

"Of course I'm speaking of a reward." She glanced out the window again. *What kind of idiots are these?*

The official signaled to his assistant to move faster.

"We have not yet set a price on him, *signora,* so—"

"Well, set one now. I'm in a hurry."

"How much of a reward are you expecting?"

"I don't know." Pier thought for a moment. "Would fifty thousand dollars be all right?"

"Fifty thousand dollars is a lot of money. If you tell me where you are, we could come to you and negotiate a deal that—"

He must think I'm pazza. "No. You either agree to pay me what I want now or—" Pier looked up and saw Robert approaching the office. "Hurry! Yes or no?"

"Very well, *signora.* Yes. We agree to pay you. . . ."

Robert came through the door, moving toward her.

Pier said into the telephone, "We should be there in time for dinner, Mama. You will like him. He is very nice. Good. We will see you later. *Ciao.*"

Pier replaced the receiver and turned to Robert. "Mother is dying to meet you."

* * *

At Interpol headquarters, the senior official said, "Did you trace the call?"

"Yes. It came from a filling station on the Autostrada del Sole. It looks like they're on their way to Naples."

Colonel Francesco Cesar and Colonel Frank Johnson were studying a map on the wall of Cesar's office.

"Naples is a big city," Colonel Cesar was saying. "There are a thousand places for him to hide there."

"What about the woman?"

"We have no idea who she is."

"Why don't we find out?" Johnson asked.

Cesar looked at him, puzzled. "How?"

"If Bellamy needed a woman companion in a hurry, as a cover, what would he do?"

"He would probably pick up a whore."

"Right. Where do we start?"

"Tor di Ounto."

They drove down the Passeggiata Archeologica and watched the streetwalkers peddling their wares. In the car with Colonel Cesar and Colonel Johnson was Captain Bellini, the police supervisor of the district.

"This is not going to be easy," Bellini said. "They're all in competition with one another, but when it comes to the police, they're like blood sisters. They won't talk."

"We'll see," Colonel Johnson said.

Bellini ordered the driver to pull over to the curb, and the three men got out of the car. The prostitutes were eyeing them warily. Bellini walked up to one of the women. "Good afternoon, Maria. How's business?"

"It will be better when you leave."

"We're not planning to stay. I just want to ask you a question. We're looking for an American who picked up one of the girls last night. We think they are traveling together. We want to know who she is. Can you help us?" He showed her a photograph of Robert.

Several other prostitutes had gathered around to listen to the conversation.

"I can't help you," Maria said, "but I know someone who can."

Bellini nodded approvingly. "Good. Who?"

Maria pointed to a storefront across the street. A sign in the window read: Fortune-teller—Palm Reader. "Madam Lucia might help you."

The girls laughed appreciatively.

Captain Bellini looked at them and said, "So you like jokes, do you? Well, we're going to play a little joke I think you're going to love. These two gentlemen are very eager to have the name of the girl who went off with the American. If you don't know who she is, I suggest you talk to your friends, find someone who does know, and when you have the answer, give me a call."

"Why should we?" one of them asked defiantly.

"You'll find out."

One hour later, the prostitutes of Rome found themselves under siege. Patrol wagons swept the city, picking up all the women working the streets and their pimps. There were screams of protest.

"You can't do this. . . . I pay police protection."

"This has been my beat for five years. . . ."

"I've been giving it to you and your friends for free. Where's your gratitude? . . ."

"What do I pay you protection for? . . ."

By the following day, the streets were virtually empty of prostitutes, and the jails were full.

Cesar and Colonel Johnson were sitting in Captain Bellini's office. "It's going to be difficult to keep them in jail," Captain Bellini warned. "I might also add that this is very bad for tourism."

"Don't worry," Colonel Johnson said, "someone will talk. Just keep the pressure on."

Their break came late in the afternoon. Captain Bellini's secretary said, "There's a Mr. Lorenzo to see you."

"Send him in."

Mr. Lorenzo was dressed in a very expensive suit and wore diamond rings on three fingers. Mr. Lorenzo was a pimp.

"What can I do for you?" Bellini asked.

Lorenzo smiled. "It's what I can do for *you,* gentlemen. Some of my associates inform me that you are looking for a particular working girl who left town with an American, and since we are always eager to cooperate with the authorities, I thought I would give you her name."

Colonel Johnson said, "Who is she?"

Lorenzo ignored the question. "Naturally, I'm sure you would want to express your appreciation by releasing my associates and their friends."

Colonel Cesar said, "We are not interested in any of your whores. All we want is the name of the girl."

"That is very gratifying news, sir. It's always a pleasure to deal with reasonable men. I know that—"

"Her name, Lorenzo."

"Yes, of course. Her name is Pier. Pier Valli. The American spent the night with her at the L'Incrocio Hotel, and the next morning they took off. She is not one of my girls. If I may say so—"

Bellini was already on the telephone. "Bring up the records on a Pier Valli. *Subito!*"

"I hope you gentlemen are going to show your gratitude by—"

Bellini looked up, and then said into the phone, "And cancel Operation Puttana."

Lorenzo beamed. *"Grazie."*

Pier Valli's records were on Bellini's desk five minutes later. "She started streetwalking when she was fifteen. She has been arrested a dozen times since then. She—"

"Where does she come from?" Colonel Johnson interrupted.

"Naples." The two men looked at each other. "She has a mother and brother living there."

"Can you find out where?"

"I can check it out."

"Do that. *Now.*"

Chapter Forty-one

They were approaching the suburbs of Naples. Old apartment houses lined the narrow streets, with laundry hanging out of almost every window, making the buildings look like concrete mountains flying colorful flags.

Pier asked, "Have you ever been to Naples?"

"Once." Robert's voice was tight. *Susan was sitting beside him, giggling. I heard Naples is a wicked city. Can we do a lot of wicked things here, darling?*

We're going to invent some new things, Robert promised.

Pier was watching him. "Are you all right?"

Robert brought his mind back to the present. "I'm fine."

They were driving along bay harbor, formed by the Castel dell'Ovo, the old abandoned castle near the water.

When they arrived at Via Toledo, Pier said, excitedly, "Turn here."

They were approaching Spaccanapoli, the old section of Naples.

Pier said, "It's just up ahead. Turn left onto Via Benedetto Croce."

Robert made the turn. The traffic here was heavier, and the noise of horns deafening. He had forgotten how noisy Naples could be. He slowed the car down to avoid hitting the pedestrians and dogs that ran in front of the car as if they were blessed with some kind of immortality.

"Turn right here," Pier directed, "into Piazza del Plebiscito." The traffic was even worse here, and the neighborhood more run down.

"Stop!" Pier cried out.

Robert pulled over to the curb. They had stopped in front of a row of seedy shops.

Robert glanced around. "This is where your mother lives?"

"No," Pier said. "Of course not." She leaned over and pressed the horn. A moment later, a young woman came out of one of the shops. Pier got out of the car and raced to greet her. They hugged each other.

"You look wonderful!" the woman exclaimed. "You must be doing very well."

"I am." Pier held out her wrist. "Look at my new bracelet!"

"Are those real emeralds?"

"Of course they are real."

The woman yelled at someone inside the store. "Anna! Come on out. Look who is here!"

Robert was watching the scene, unbelievingly. "Pier—"

"In a minute, darling," she said. "I have to say hello to my friends."

Within minutes half a dozen women were clustered

around Pier, admiring her bracelet, while Robert sat there helplessly, gritting his teeth.

"He is crazy about me," Pier announced. She turned to Robert. "Aren't you, *caro*?"

Robert wanted to strangle her, but there was nothing he could do. "Yes," he said. "Can we go now, Pier?"

"In a minute."

"Now!" Robert said.

"Oh, very well." Pier turned to the women. "We must leave now. We have an important appointment. *Ciao!*"

"Ciao!"

Pier got into the car beside Robert, and the women stood there watching them drive away.

Pier said happily, "They are all old friends."

"Wonderful. Where's your mother's house?"

"Oh, she doesn't live in the city."

"What?"

"She lives outside of town in a little farmhouse, half an hour from here."

The farmhouse was on the southern outskirts of Naples, an old stone building set off from the road.

"There it is!" Pier exclaimed. "Isn't it beautiful?"

"Yes." Robert liked the fact that the house was away from the center of town. There would be no reason for anyone to come looking for him here. *Pier was right. It's a perfect safe house.*

They walked up to the front door, and before they reached it, the door flew open and Pier's mother stood there smiling at them. She was an older version of her daughter, thin and gray-haired, with a lined, careworn face.

"Pier, *cara! Mi sei mancata!*"

"I've missed you too, Mama. This is the friend I telephoned you about that I was bringing home."

Mama did not miss a beat. "Ah? *Si,* you are welcome Mr.—?"

"Jones," Robert said.

"Come in, come in."

They entered the living room. It was a large room comfortable and homey, crammed with furniture.

A boy in his early twenties entered the room. He was short and dark, with a thin, sullen face and brooding brown eyes. He wore jeans and a jacket with the name Diavoli Rossi sewn on it. His face lit up when he saw his sister. "Pier!"

"Hello, Carlo." They hugged.

"What are you doing here?"

"We came to visit for a few days." She turned to Robert. "This is my brother, Carlo. Carlo, this is Mr. Jones."

"Hello, Carlo."

Carlo was sizing Robert up. "Hello."

Mama said, "I will fix a nice bedroom for you two lovebirds in the back."

Robert said, "If you don't mind—that is, if you have an extra bedroom, I'd prefer a room to myself."

There was an awkward pause. The three of them were staring at Robert.

Mama turned to Pier. *"Omosessuale?"*

Pier shrugged. *I don't know*. But she was sure he was *not* a homosexual.

Mama looked at Robert. "As you wish." She hugged Pier again. "I'm so happy to see you. Come into the kitchen. I will make some coffee for us."

In the kitchen, Mama exclaimed, "*Benissimo!* How did you meet him? He looks very rich. And that bracelet you are wearing. It must have cost a fortune. My goodness!

Tonight I will cook a big dinner. I will invite all the neighbors so they can meet your—"

"No, Mama. You must not do that."

"But *cara,* why should we not spread the news of your good luck? All our friends will be so pleased."

"Mama, Mr. Jones just wants to rest for a few days. No party. No neighbors."

Mama sighed. "All right. Whatever you wish."

I'll arrange for him to be picked up away from the house, so Mama will not be disturbed.

Carlo had noticed the bracelet, too. "That bracelet. Those are real emeralds, huh? Did you buy that for my sister?"

There was an attitude about the boy that Robert did not like. "Ask her."

Pier and Mama came out of the kitchen. Mama looked at Robert. "You are sure you do not want to sleep with Pier?"

Robert was embarrassed. "Thank you. No."

Pier said, "I'll show you your bedroom." She led him toward the back of the house to a large, comfortable bedroom with a double bed in the middle of the room.

"Robert, are you afraid of what Mama might think if we slept together? She knows what I do."

"It's not that," Robert said. "It's—" There was no way he could explain. "I'm sorry, I—"

Pier's voice was cold. "Never mind."

She felt unreasonably offended. Twice now he had refused to sleep with her. *It serves him right that I am turning him over to the police,* she thought. And yet she felt a small, nagging sense of guilt. He was really very nice. But fifty thousand dollars was fifty thousand dollars.

* * *

At dinner Mama was talkative, but Pier and Robert and Carlo were silent and preoccupied.

Robert was busily working out his plan of escape. *Tomorrow,* he thought, *I'll go down to the docks and find a ship out of here.*

Pier was thinking about the phone call she was planning to make. *I'll call from town, so the police cannot trace it here.*

Carlo was studying the stranger his sister had brought to the house. *He should be an easy make.*

When dinner was over, the two women went into the kitchen. Robert was alone with Carlo.

"You're the first man my sister has ever brought here," Carlo said. "She must like you a lot."

"I like her a lot."

"Do you? Are you going to take care of her?"

"I think your sister can take care of herself."

Carlo smirked. "Yeah. I know." The stranger seated across from him was well dressed and obviously rich. Why was he staying here when he could have stayed at some fancy hotel? The only reason Carlo could think of was that the man was in hiding. And that brought up an interesting point. When a rich man was in hiding, somehow, some way, there was money to be made from the situation.

"Where are you from?" Carlo asked.

"From no place in particular," Robert said pleasantly. "I travel a lot."

Carlo nodded. "I see." *I'll find out from Pier who he is. Somebody will probably be willing to pay a lot of money for him, and Pier and I can split it.*

"Are you in business?" Carlo asked.

"Retired."

It would not be hard to force this man to talk, Carlo decided. Lucca, the leader of the Diavoli Rossi, could crack him open in no time.

"How long will you be staying with us?"

"It's hard to say." The boy's curiosity was beginning to get on Robert's nerves.

Pier and her mother came out of the kitchen.

"Would you like some more coffee?" Mama asked.

"No, thank you. That was a delicious dinner."

Mama smiled. "That was nothing. Tomorrow I will prepare a feast for you."

"Good." He would be gone by then. He stood up. "If you don't mind, I'm rather tired. I'd like to turn in."

"Of course," Mama said. "Good night."

"Good night."

They watched Robert as he walked toward the bedroom.

Carlo grinned. "He doesn't think you're good enough to sleep with him, eh?"

The remark stung Pier, as it was meant to. She would not have minded it if Robert were a homosexual, but she had heard him talk to Susan, and she knew better. *I'll show the stronzo.*

Robert lay in bed thinking about his next move. Laying a false trail with the homing device that had been hidden in the credit card would give him a little time, but he was not depending too much on it. They probably would have caught up with the red truck by now. The men who were after him were ruthless and smart. Were heads of world governments involved in the massive cover-up? Robert wondered. Or was it an organization within an organization, a cabal in the intelligence community acting illegally on its own? The more

Robert thought about it, the more feasible it seemed that the heads of state might be unaware of what was going on. And a thought struck him. It had always seemed odd to him that Admiral Whittaker had suddenly been retired from ONI and relegated to some Siberia. But if someone had *forced* him out because they knew he would never be part of the conspiracy, then it began to make sense. *I have to contact the admiral,* Robert thought. He was the only one he could trust to get to the truth of what was happening. *Tomorrow,* he thought. *Tomorrow.* He closed his eyes and slept.

The creaking of the bedroom door awakened him. He sat up in bed, instantly alert. Someone was moving toward the bed. Robert tensed, ready to spring. He smelled her perfume then and felt her slide in bed beside him.

"Pier—What are you—?"

"Ssh." Her body pressed against his. She was naked. "I got lonely," she whispered. She snuggled closer to him.

"I'm sorry, Pier, I—I can't do anything for you."

Pier said, "No? Then let me do something for you." Her voice was soft.

"It's no use. You can't." Robert felt a deep frustration. He wanted to spare both of them the embarrassment of what was not going to happen.

"Don't you like me, Robert? Do you not think I have a beautiful body?"

"Yes." And she did. He could feel the warmth of her body pressing closer.

She was stroking him gently, rippling her fingers up and down his chest, moving lightly toward his groin.

He had to stop her before the humiliating fiasco was repeated. "Pier, I can't make love. I haven't been able to be with a woman since—for a long time."

"You don't have to do anything, Robert," she said. "I just want to play. Do you like being played with?"

He felt nothing. *Goddamn Susan!* She had taken more than herself away from him, she had taken a part of his manhood.

Pier was sliding down his body now. "Turn over," she said.

"It's no use, Pier. I—"

She rolled him over, and he lay there cursing Susan, cursing his impotence. He could feel Pier's tongue moving along his back, making tiny, delicate circles, moving lower and lower. Her fingers were gently flicking over his skin.

"Pier—"

"Ssh."

He felt her tongue spiraling down deeper and deeper, and he began to feel aroused. He started to move.

"Ssh. Lie still."

Her tongue was soft and warm, and he could feel her breasts trailing along his skin. His pulse began to quicken. *Yes,* he thought. *Yes! Oh, yes!* His tumescence grew until he became rock hard, and when he could stand it no longer, he grabbed Pier and turned her over.

She felt him and gasped, "My God, you're enormous. I want you inside me."

And a moment later Robert plunged into her, and then again and again, and it was as if he had been reborn. Pier was skillful and wild, and Robert reveled in the dark cave of her velvety softness. They made love three times that night. Finally, they slept.

Day Eighteen
Naples, Italy

In the morning, as the pale light was coming through the window, Robert awakened. He held Pier close in his arms and whispered, "Thank you."

Pier smiled mischievously. "How do you feel?"

"Wonderful," Robert said. And he did.

Pier snuggled against him. "You are an animal!"

Robert grinned. "You're good for my ego," he said.

Pier sat up and said seriously, "You are not a drug smuggler, are you?"

It was a naive question. "No."

"But Interpol is after you."

That hit closer to home. "Yes."

Her face lit up. "I know! You're a spy!" She was as excited as a child.

Robert had to laugh. "Am I?" And he thought, *Out of the mouths of babes . . .*

"Admit it," Pier insisted. "You're a spy, aren't you?"

"Yes," Robert said gravely. "I'm a spy."

"I knew it!" Pier's eyes were glowing. "Can you tell me some secrets?"

"What kind of secrets?"

"You know, spy secrets—codes and things like that. I love to read spy novels. I read them all the time."

"Do you?"

"Oh, yes! But they're just made-up stories. You know all the real things, don't you? Like the signals that spies use. Are you allowed to tell me one?"

Robert said seriously, "Well, I really shouldn't, but I suppose *one* would be all right." *What can I tell her that she'll believe?* "There's the old window-shade trick."

She was wide-eyed. "The old window-shade trick?"

"Yes." Robert pointed to a window in the bedroom. "If everything is under control, you leave the shades up. But if there's trouble, you pull one shade down. That's the signal to warn your fellow agent away."

Pier said excitedly, "That's wonderful! I've never read that in a book."

"You won't," Robert said. "It's very secret."

"I won't tell anyone," Pier promised. "What else?"

What else? Robert thought for a moment. "Well, there's the telephone trick."

Pier snuggled closer to him. "Tell me about that."

"Er—let's say a fellow spy telephones you to find out if everything is all right. He'll ask for Pier. If everything is fine, you say, 'This is Pier.' But if there is any problem, you say, 'You have the wrong number.'"

"That's wonderful!" Pier exclaimed.

My instructors at the Farm would have a heart attack if they heard me talking this nonsense.

"Can you tell me anything else?" Pier asked.

Robert laughed. "I think those are enough secrets for one morning."

"All right." She rubbed her body along his body.

"Would you like to take a shower?" Pier asked.

"Love to."

They soaped each other under the warm water, and as Pier spread Robert's legs and began to wash him, he became tumescent again.

They made love in the shower.

While Robert was getting dressed, Pier put on a robe and said, "I'll see about breakfast."

Carlo was waiting for her in the dining room.

"Tell me about your friend," he said.

"What about him?"

"Where did you meet him?"

"In Rome."

"He must be very rich to have bought you that emerald bracelet."

She shrugged. "He likes me."

Carlo said, "Do you know what I think? I think your friend is running away from something. If we told the right party, there could be a big reward in it."

Pier moved over to her brother, her eyes blazing. "Stay out of this, Carlo."

"So, he *is* running away."

"Listen you little *piscialetto,* I'm warning you—mind your own business." She had no intention of sharing the reward with anyone.

Carlo said reproachfully, "Little sister, you want it all for yourself."

"No. You don't understand, Carlo."

"No?"

Pier said earnestly, "I'll tell you the truth. Mr. Jones is running away from his wife. She has hired a detective to find him. That's all there is to it."

Carlo smiled. "Why didn't you tell me this before? Then it's no big deal, I'll forget about it."

"Good," Pier said.

And Carlo thought, *I've got to find out who he really is.*

Janus was on the telephone. "Have you any news yet?"

"We know that Commander Bellamy is in Naples."

"Do you have any assets there?"

"Yes. They're looking for him now. We have a lead. He's traveling with a prostitute who has a family in Naples. We think they may have gone there. We're following through on it."

"Keep me informed."

* * *

In Naples the Bureau of Municipal Housing was busily trying to track down the whereabouts of Pier Valli's mother.

A dozen security agents and the Naples police force were scouring the city for Robert.

Carlo was busily making his own plans for Robert.

Pier was getting ready to telephone Interpol again.

Chapter Forty-two

The danger in the air was almost palpable, and Robert felt as if he could reach out and touch it. The waterfront was a beehive of activity, with cargo ships busily loading and unloading. But another element had been added: There were police cars cruising up and down the quai, and uniformed policemen and obvious-looking detectives questioning dockworkers and sailors. The concentrated manhunt took Robert by complete surprise. It was almost as if they had known he was in Naples, for it would have been impossible for them to be conducting this intense a search for him in every major city in Italy. He did not even bother to get out of the car. He turned around and headed away from the docks. What he had thought would be an easy plan—to board a cargo ship bound for France—had now become too dangerous. Somehow they had managed to track him here. He went over his options again. Traveling any distance by car was too risky. There would be roadblocks around the city by now. The docks were guarded. That meant the railroad station and airport would be covered as well. He was in a vise, and it was closing in on him.

Robert thought about Susan's offer. *"We're just off the coast of Gibraltar. We can turn around and pick you up, anyplace you say. It's probably your only chance of escape."* He was reluctant to involve Susan in his danger, and yet he could think of no other alternative. It was the only way out of the trap he was in. They would not be looking for him on a private yacht. *If I can find a way to get to the Halcyon,* he thought, *they could drop me off near the coast of Marseilles, and I can get ashore by myself. That way, they won't be in danger.*

He parked the car in front of a small trattoria on a side street and went inside to make the call. In five minutes, he was connected with the *Halcyon.*

"Mrs. Banks, please."

"Who shall I say is calling?"

Monte has a fucking butler to answer his phone on the yacht. "Just tell her an old friend."

A minute later he heard Susan's voice. "Robert—is that you?"

"The bad penny."

"They—they haven't arrested you, have they?"

"No. Susan." It was difficult for him to ask the question. "Is your offer still open?"

"Of course it is. When—?"

"Can you reach Naples by tonight?"

Susan hesitated. "I don't know. Hold on a moment." Robert heard talking in the background. Susan came on the line again. "Monte says we have an engine problem, but we can reach Naples in two days."

Damn. Every day here increased the chances of his getting caught. "All right. That will be fine."

"How will we find you?"

"I'll contact you."

"Robert, please take care of yourself."

"I'm trying. I really am."

"You won't let anything happen to you?"

"No, I won't let anything happen to me." *Or to you.*

When Susan replaced the receiver, she turned to her husband and smiled. "He's coming aboard."

One hour later, in Rome, Francesco Cesar handed a cable to Colonel Frank Johnson. It was from the *Halcyon.* It read: BELLAMY COMING ABOARD HALCYON. WILL KEEP YOU INFORMED. It was unsigned.

"I've made arrangements to monitor all communication to and from the *Halcyon,*" Cesar said. "As soon as Bellamy steps aboard, we've got him."

Chapter Forty-three

The more Carlo Valli thought about it, the more certain he was that he was about to make a big score. Pier's fairy tale about the American running away from his wife was a joke. Mr. Jones was on the run, all right, but he was running from the police. There was probably a reward out for the man. Maybe a big reward. This had to be handled very delicately. Carlo decided to discuss it with Mario Lucca, the leader of the Diavoli Rossi.

Early in the morning, Carlo got on his Vespa motor scooter and headed for Via Sorcella, behind the Piazza Garibaldi. He stopped in front of a run-down apartment building, and pressed the bell on a broken mailbox marked "Lucca."

A minute later a voice yelled out, "Who the fuck is it?"

"Carlo. I have to talk to you, Mario."

"It better be good at this hour of the morning. Come on up."

The door buzzer sounded, and Carlo went upstairs.

Mario Lucca was standing at an open door, naked. At the end of the room Carlo could see a girl in his bed.

"*Che cosa?* What the hell are you doing up so early?"

"I couldn't sleep, Mario. I'm too excited. I think I'm onto something big."

"Yeah? Come in."

Carlo entered the small, messy apartment. "Last night my sister brought home a mark."

"So what? Pier's a whore. She—"

"Yeah, but this one is rich. And he's in hiding."

"Who is he hiding from?"

"I don't know. But I'm going to find out. I think there might be a reward out for him."

"Why don't you ask your sister?"

Carlo frowned. "Pier wants to keep it all for herself. You should see the bracelet he bought her—emeralds."

"A bracelet? Yeah? How much is it worth?"

"I'll let you know. I'm going to sell it this morning."

Lucca stood there, thoughtful. "I'll tell you what, Carlo. Why don't we have a talk with your sister's friend? Let's pick him up and take him over to the club this morning." The club was an empty warehouse in Quartiere Sanità that had a room that was soundproof.

Carlo smiled. "*Bene.* I can get him down there easy enough."

"We'll be waiting for him," Lucca said. "We'll have a little talk with him. I hope he has a nice voice, because he's going to sing for us."

When Carlo returned to the house, Mr. Jones was gone. Carlo panicked.

"Where did your friend go?" he asked Pier.

"He said he had to go into town for a little while. He'll be back. Why?"

He forced a smile. "Just curious."

Carlo waited until his mother and Pier were in the kitchen preparing lunch, then hurried into Pier's room. He found the bracelet hidden under some lingerie in a dresser drawer. He swiftly pocketed it and was on his way out when his mother came out of the kitchen.

"Carlo, aren't you staying for lunch?"

"No. I have an appointment, Mama. I'll be back later."

He got on his Vespa and headed toward the Quartiere Spagnolo. *Maybe the bracelet is phony,* he thought. *It could be paste. I hope I don't make a fool of myself with Lucca.* He parked the motorbike in front of a small jewelry store that had a sign in front that read: Orologia. The owner, Gambino, was an elderly, wizened man, with an ill-fitting black wig and a mouthful of false teeth. He looked up as Carlo entered.

"Good morning, Carlo. You're out early."

"Yeah."

"What have you got for me today?"

Carlo took out the bracelet and laid it on the counter. "This."

Gambino picked it up. As he studied it, his eyes widened. "Where did you get this?"

"A rich aunt died and left it to me. Is it worth anything?"

"It could be," Gambino said cautiously.

"Don't fuck around with me."

Gambino looked hurt. "Have I ever cheated you?"

"All the time."

"You boys are always kidding around. I'll tell you

what I will do, Carlo. I'm not sure I can handle this by myself. It's very valuable."

Carlo's heart skipped a beat. "Really?"

"I'll have to see if I can lay it off somewhere. I'll give you a call tonight."

"Okay," Carlo said. He snatched up the bracelet. "I'll keep this until I hear from you."

Carlo left the shop walking on air. So, he had been right! The sucker was rich, and he was also crazy. *Why else would someone give an expensive bracelet to a whore?*

In the store, Gambino watched Carlo leave. He thought, *What the hell have those idiots gotten themselves into?* From under the counter, he picked up a circular that had been sent to all pawn shops. It had a description of the bracelet he had just seen, but at the bottom, instead of the usual police number to call, there was a special notice: "Notify SIFAR immediately." Gambino would have ignored an ordinary police circular, as he had hundreds of times in the past, but he knew enough about SIFAR to know that one never crossed them. He hated to lose the profit on the bracelet, but he did not intend to put his neck in a noose. Reluctantly, he picked up the telephone and dialed the number on the circular.

Chapter Forty-four

It was the season of fear, of swirling, deadly shadows. Years earlier Robert had been sent on a mission to Borneo and had gone into the deep jungle after a traitor. It had been in October, during *musim takoot,* the traditional head-hunting season, when the jungle natives lived in terror of *Balli Salang,* the spirit that sought out humans for their blood. It was a season of murders, and now for Robert, Naples had suddenly become the jungles of Borneo. Death was in the air. *Do not go gentle into the fucking night,* Robert thought. *They'll have to catch me first.* How had they traced him here? *Pier.* They must have tracked him down through Pier. *I have to get back to the house and warn her,* Robert thought. *But first I have to find a way out of here.*

He drove toward the outskirts of the city, to where the autostrada began, hoping that by some miracle it might be clear. Five hundred yards before he reached the entrance, he saw the police roadblock. He turned around and headed back toward the center of the city.

Robert drove slowly, concentrating, putting himself into the minds of his pursuers. They would have all avenues of escape out of Italy blocked. Every ship leaving the country would be searched. A plan suddenly came to him. They would have no reason to search ships *not* leaving Italy. *It's a chance,* Robert thought. He headed for the harbor again.

The little bell over the door of the jewelry shop rang, and Gambino looked up. Two men in dark suits walked in. They were not customers.

"Can I help you?"

"Mr. Gambino?"

He exposed his false teeth. "Yes."

"You called about an emerald bracelet."

SIFAR. He had been expecting them. But this time he was on the side of the angels. "That's right. As a patriotic citizen, I felt it was my duty—"

"Cut the bullshit. Who brought it in?"

"A young boy named Carlo."

"Did he leave the bracelet?"

"No, he took it with him."

"What's Carlo's last name?"

Gambino lifted a shoulder. "I don't know his last name. He's one of the boys in the Diavoli Rossi. That's one of our local gangs. It's run by a kid named Lucca."

"Do you know where we can find this Lucca?"

Gambino hesitated. If Lucca found out that he had talked, he would have his tongue cut out. If he did *not* tell these men what they wanted to know, he would have his brains bashed in. "He lives on Via Sorcella, behind the Piazza Garibaldi."

"Thank you, Mr. Gambino. You've been very helpful."

"I'm always happy to cooperate with—"

The men were gone.

Lucca was in bed with his girlfriend when the two men shoved open the door to his apartment.

Lucca leapt out of bed. "What the hell is this? Who are you?"

One of the men pulled out his identification.

SIFAR! Lucca swallowed. "Hey, I haven't done anything wrong. I'm a law abiding citizen who—"

"We know that, Lucca. We're not interested in you. We're interested in a boy named Carlo."

Carlo. So that's what this is about. That fucking bracelet! What the hell had Carlo gotten himself into? SIFAR did not send men around looking for stolen jewelry.

"Well—do you know him or don't you?"

"I might."

"If you aren't sure, we'll refresh your memory down at headquarters."

"Wait! I do remember, now," Lucca said. "You must mean Carlo Valli. What about him?"

"We'd like to have a talk with him. Where does he live?"

Every member of the Diavoli Rossi had to swear a blood oath of loyalty, an oath that they would die before they would betray a fellow member. That was what made the Diavoli Rossi such a great club. They stuck together. One for all and all for one.

"Do you want to take that trip downtown?"

"What for?" Lucca shrugged. He gave them Carlo's address.

Thirty minutes later, Pier opened the door to find two strangers standing there.

"Signorina Valli?"

Trouble. "Yes."

"May we come in?"

She wanted to say no, but she did not dare. "Who are you?"

One of the men pulled out a wallet and flashed an identification card. *SIFAR*. These were not the people she had made her deal with. Pier felt a sense of panic that they were going to try to cheat her out of her reward. "What do you want with me?"

"We'd like to ask you a few questions."

"Go ahead. I have nothing to hide." *Thank God,* Pier thought, *Robert is out. I can still negotiate.*

"You drove down from Rome yesterday, didn't you." It was a statement.

"Yes. Is that against the law? Was I speeding?"

The man smiled. It did nothing to change the expression on his face. "You had a companion with you?"

Pier answered carefully. "Yes."

"Who was he, *signorina*?"

She shrugged. "Some man I picked up on the road. He wanted a ride to Naples."

The second man asked, "Is he here with you now?"

"I don't know where he is. I dropped him off when we got into town, and he disappeared."

"Was your passenger's name Robert Bellamy?"

She knitted her brow in concentration. "Bellamy? I don't know. I don't think he told me his name."

"Oh, we think he did. He picked you up on the Tor di

Ounto, you spent the night with him at the L'Incrocio Hotel, and the next morning he bought you an emerald bracelet. He sent you to some hotels with airline and train tickets, and you rented a car and came down to Naples, right?"

They know everything. Pier nodded, her eyes filled with fear.

"Is your friend coming back, or has he left Naples?"

She hesitated, deciding which was the best answer. If she told them that Robert had left town, they would not believe her anyway. They would wait here at the house, and when he turned up, they could accuse her of lying for him and hold her as an accomplice. She decided that the truth would serve her better. "He's coming back," Pier said.

"Soon?"

"I'm not sure."

"Well, we'll just make ourselves comfortable. You don't mind if we look around, do you?" They opened their jackets, exposing their guns.

"N—no."

They fanned out, moving through the house.

Mama walked in from the kitchen. "Who are these men?"

"They are friends of Mr. Jones," Pier said. "They have come to see him."

Mama beamed. "Such a nice man. Would you like some lunch?"

"Sure, Mama," one of the men said. "What are we having?"

Pier's mind was in a turmoil. *I have to call Interpol again,* she thought. *They said they would pay fifty thousand dollars.* Meanwhile, she had to keep Robert away from the house until she could make arrangements to turn him in. But how? She suddenly remembered their conversation that morning. *"If there's trouble you pull one shade down . . . to warn someone away."* The two men were seated at the dining room table eating a bowl of capellini.

"It's too bright in here," Pier said. She rose and walked into the living room and pulled down the window shade. Then she went back to the table. *I hope Robert remembers about the warning.*

Robert was driving toward the house, reviewing his plan of escape. *It's not perfect,* he thought, *but at least it should get them off the trail long enough to buy me some time.* He was approaching the house. As he neared it, he slowed down and looked around. Everything appeared to be normal. He would warn Pier to get out and then take off. As Robert started to park in front of the house, something struck him as odd. One of the front shades was down. The others were up. It was probably a coincidence, but still . . . An alarm bell sounded. Could Pier have taken his little game seriously? Was it meant to be a warning of some kind? Robert stepped on the accelerator and kept driving. He could not afford to take any chances, no matter how remote. He drove to a bar a mile away and went inside to use the telephone.

They were seated at the dining-room table when the telephone rang. The men tensed. One of them started to rise.

"Would Bellamy be calling here?"

Pier gave him a scornful look. "Of course not. Why should he?" She rose and walked over to the telephone. She picked up the receiver. "Hello?"

"Pier? I saw the window shade and—"

All she had to do was say that everything was all right, and he would come back to the house. The men would arrest him, and she could demand her reward. But would they merely arrest him? She could hear Robert's voice, saying, *"If the police find me, they have orders to kill me."*

The men at the table were watching her. There was so much she could do with fifty thousand dollars. There were beautiful clothes to buy, cruises to take, a pretty little apartment in Rome. . . . And Robert would be dead. Besides, she hated the goddamned police. Pier said into the telephone, "You have the wrong number."

Robert heard the click of the receiver and stood there, stunned. She had believed the tall tales he had told her, and it had probably saved his life. *Bless her.*

Robert turned the car around and headed away from the house toward the docks, but instead of going to the main part of the port that serviced the freighters and ocean liners leaving Italy, he drove to the other side, past Santa Lucia, to a small pier where the sign over a kiosk read: "Capri and Ischia." Robert parked the car where it could easily be spotted, and walked up to the ticket seller.

"When does the next hydrofoil leave for Ischia?"

"In thirty minutes."

"And for Capri?"

"Five minutes."

"Give me a one-way ticket to Capri."

"Si, signore."

"What's this *'si signore'* crap?" Robert said in a loud voice. "Why don't you people speak English like everybody else?"

The man's eyes widened in shock.

"You goddamn guineas are all alike. Stupid! Or, as you people would say, *stupido.*" Robert shoved some money at the man, grabbed the ticket, and walked toward the hydrofoil.

Three minutes later he was on his way to the island of Capri. The boat started out slowly, making its way cautiously through the channel. When it reached the outer limits, it surged forward, rising out of the water like a graceful porpoise. The ferry was full of tourists from a variety of countries, happily chattering away in different tongues. No one was paying any attention to Robert. He made his way to the small bar where they served drinks. He said to the bartender, "Give me a vodka and tonic."

"Yes, sir."

He watched the bartender mix the drink. "There you are, *signore*."

Robert picked up the glass and took a swallow. He slammed the glass back down on the bar. "You call this a drink for Christ's sakes?" he said. "It tastes like horse piss. What's the matter with you goddamn Italians?"

People around him were turning to stare.

The bartender said, stiffly, "I'm sorry, *signore,* we use the best—"

"Don't give me that shit!"

An Englishman nearby said stiffly, "There are women here. Why don't you watch your language?"

"I don't have to watch my language," Robert yelled. "Do you know who I am? I'm Commander Robert Bellamy. And they call this a boat? It's a piece of junk!"

He made his way to the bow and sat down. He could feel the eyes of the other passengers on him. His heart was hammering, but the charade was not over yet.

When the hydrofoil docked at Capri, Robert walked over to the ticket booth at the entrance to the *funicolare*. An elderly man was in the booth selling tickets.

"One ticket," Robert yelled. "And hurry up! I don't

have all day. You're too old to be selling tickets, anyway. You should stay home. Your wife is probably screwing all your neighbors."

The old man started to rise in anger. Passersby were giving Robert furious glances. Robert grabbed the ticket and stepped into the crowded *funicolare. They'll remember me,* he thought grimly. He was leaving a trail that no one could miss.

When the *funicolare* came to a stop, Robert shoved his way through the crowd. He walked up the winding Via Vittorio Emanuele, to the Quisisana Hotel.

"I need a room," Robert told the clerk behind the desk.

"I'm sorry," the clerk apologized, "but we are fully booked. There is—"

Robert handed him sixty thousand lire. "Any room will do."

"Well, in that case, I think we can accommodate you, *signore.* Would you register, please?"

Robert signed his name: Commander Robert Bellamy.

"How long will you be staying with us, Commander?"

"One week."

"That will be fine. May I have your passport?"

"It's in my luggage. It'll be here in a few minutes."

"I will have a bellboy show you to your room."

"Not now. I have to go out for a few minutes. I'll be right back."

Robert stepped out of the lobby, into the street. Memories hit him like a blast of cold air. He had walked here with Susan, exploring the little side streets, and strolled down Via Ignazio Cerio and Via Li Campo. It had been a magic time. They visited the Grotta Azzurra, and had morning coffee at the Piazza Umberto. They took the *funicolare* up to Anacapri, and rode donkeys to Villa Jovis, Tiberius's villa, and swam in the emerald green waters at the Marina Piccola. They shopped along Via Vittorio Emanuele and took the chair lift to the top of Monte Solaro, their feet skimming over the vine leaves and leafy trees. Off to the right, they could see the houses sprinkled down the hillside toward the sea, flowering yellow broom covering the ground, an eleven-minute ride through a colorful fairyland of green trees, white houses and, in the distance, the blue sea. At the top, they had coffee at the Barbarossa Ristorante, and then went into the little church in Anacapri to thank God for all their blessings, and for each other. Robert had thought then that the magic was Capri. He had been wrong. The magic was Susan, and the magician had left the stage.

Robert went back to the *funicolare* station at the Piazza Umberto, and took the tram down, quietly mingling with the other passengers. When the *funicolare* arrived at the bottom, he walked out, carefully avoiding the ticket seller. He went over to the kiosk at the boat landing. In a heavy Spanish accent, Robert asked, *"¿A qué hora sale el barco a Ischia?"*

"Sale en treinta minutos."

"Gracias." Robert bought a ticket.

He walked into a bar at the waterfront and took a seat in the back, where he nursed a scotch. By now they would have undoubtedly found the car, and the hunt for him would narrow. He spread out the map of Europe in his mind. The logical thing for him to do would be to head for England and find a way to get back to the States. It would make no sense for him to return to France. *So, France it is,* Robert thought. A busy seaport to leave Italy from. Civitavecchia. *I have to get to Civitavecchia. The Halcyon.*

He got change from the owner of the bar and used the telephone. It took the marine operator ten minutes to put his call through. Susan was on the line almost immediately.

"We've been waiting to hear from you." *We*. He found that interesting. "The engine is fixed. We can be in Naples early in the morning. Where shall we pick you up?"

It was too risky for the *Halcyon* to come here. Robert said, "Do you remember the palindrome? We went there on our honeymoon."

"The what?"

"I made a joke about it because I was so exhausted."

There was a silence on the other end of the line. Then Susan said softly, "I remember."

"Can the *Halcyon* meet me there tomorrow?"

"Hold on a moment."

He waited.

Susan returned to the telephone. "Yes, we can be there."

"Good." Robert hesitated. He thought of all the innocent people who had already died. "I'm asking a lot of you. If they ever found out you helped me, you could be in terrible danger."

"Don't worry. We'll meet you there. Be careful."

"Thanks."

The connection was broken.

Susan turned to Monte Banks. "He's coming."

At SIFAR headquarters in Rome, they were listening to the conversation in the communications room. There were four men in the room. The radio operator said, "We've recorded it if you would like to hear it again, sir."

Colonel Cesar looked at Frank Johnson questioningly.

"Yes. I'm interested in hearing the part about where

they're going to meet. It sounded like he said Palindrome. Is that somewhere in Italy?"

Colonel Cesar shook his head. "I never heard of it. We'll check it out." He turned to his aide. "Look it up on the map. And keep monitoring all transmissions to and from the *Halcyon.*"

"Yes, sir."

At the farmhouse in Naples, the phone rang. Pier started to get up to answer it.

"Hold it," one of the men said. He walked over to the phone and picked it up. "Hello?" He listened for a moment, then threw the phone down and turned to his companion. "Bellamy took the hydrofoil to Capri. Let's go!"

Pier watched the two men hurry out the door and thought: *God never meant me to have so much money, anyway. I hope he gets away.*

When the ferryboat to Ischia arrived, Robert mingled with the crowd boarding it. He kept to himself, avoiding eye contact. Thirty minutes later, when the boat docked at Ischia, Robert disembarked and walked over to the ticket booth on the pier. A sign announced that the ferry to Sorrento was due in ten minutes.

"A round-trip ticket to Sorrento," Robert said.

Ten minutes later he was on his way to Sorrento, back to the mainland. *With a little luck, the search will have shifted to Capri,* Robert thought. *With a little luck.*

The food market at Sorrento was crowded. Farmers had come in from the countryside bringing fresh fruit and vegetables and sides of beef that lined the meat stalls. The street was thronged with vendors and shoppers.

Robert approached a husky man in a stained apron loading a truck. *"Pardon, monsieur,"* Robert said, speaking with a perfect French accent, "I'm looking for transportation to Civitavecchia. Would you happen to be going that way?"

"No. Salerno." He pointed to a man loading another truck nearby. "Giuseppe might be able to help you."

"Merci."

Robert moved over to the next truck. *"Monsieur,"* would you be going to Civitavecchia by any chance?"

The man said noncommittally, "I might be."

"I would be glad to pay you for the ride."

"How much?"

Robert handed the man a hundred thousand lire.

"You could buy yourself a plane ticket to Rome for that much money, couldn't you?"

Robert instantly realized his mistake. He looked around nervously. "The truth is, I have some creditors watching the airport. I'd prefer to go by truck."

The man nodded. "Ah. I understand. All right, get in. We're ready to leave."

Robert yawned. "I am *très fatigué*. How do you say? Tired? Would you mind if I slept in the back?"

"It's going to be a bumpy ride, but suit yourself."

"Merci."

The back of the truck was filled with empty crates and boxes. Giuseppe watched Robert climb in, and he closed up the tailgate. Inside, Robert concealed himself behind some crates. He suddenly realized how exhausted he really was. The chase was beginning to wear him down. How long had it been since he had slept? He thought of Pier and how she had come to him in the night and had made him feel whole again, a man again. He hoped she was all right. Robert slept.

In the cab of the truck, Giuseppe was thinking about his passenger. The word was out about an American the authorities were looking for. His passenger had a French accent, but he looked like an American, and he dressed like an American. It would be worth checking out. There might be a nice reward.

One hour later, at a truck stop along the highway, Giuseppe pulled up in front of a gas pump. "Fill it up," he said. He walked around to the back of the truck and peered inside. His passenger was asleep.

Giuseppe went inside the restaurant and made a telephone call to the local police.

Chapter Forty-five

The call had been routed to Colonel Cesar. "Yes," he said to Giuseppe, "that sounds very much like our man. Listen carefully. He is dangerous, so I want you to do exactly as I tell you. Do you understand?"

"Yes, sir."

"Where are you now?"

"At the AGIP truck stop on the way to Civitavecchia."

"And he's in the back of your truck now?"

"Yes." The conversation was making him nervous. *Maybe I should have minded my own business.*

"Don't do anything to make him suspicious. Get back in your truck and keep driving. Give me your license number and a description of your truck."

Giuseppe gave it to him.

"Fine. We will take care of everything. Now get moving."

Colonel Cesar turned to Colonel Johnson and nodded. "We have him. I'll have a roadblock set up. We can be there by helicopter in thirty minutes."

"Let's go."

When Giuseppe replaced the receiver, he wiped his sweaty palms on his shirt and headed for the truck. *I hope there won't be a shoot-out. Maria would kill me. On the other hand, if the reward is large enough . . .* He climbed into the cab of the truck and headed for Civitavecchia.

Thirty-five minutes later, Giuseppe heard the sound of a helicopter overhead. He looked up. It had the markings of the state police. Ahead of him on the highway, he saw two police cars lined up next to each other, forming a roadblock. Behind the cars were policemen with automatic weapons. The helicopter landed at the side of the road, and Cesar and Colonel Frank Johnson stepped out.

As he neared the roadblock, Giuseppe slowed the truck down. He shut off the ignition and jumped out, running toward the officers. "He's in back!" he shouted.

The truck rolled to a stop. Cesar shouted, "Close in."

The policemen converged on the truck, weapons ready.

"Don't shoot," Colonel Johnson yelled. "I'll take him." He moved toward the back of the truck. "Come on out, Robert," Colonel Johnson called, "it's over."

There was no response.

"Robert, you have five seconds."

Silence. They waited.

Cesar turned to his men and nodded.

"No!" Colonel Johnson yelled. But it was too late.

The police began firing into the back of the truck. The noise of the automatic fire was deafening. Splinters of crates began flying into the air. After ten seconds, the firing ceased. Colonel Frank Johnson jumped into the back of the truck and moved the crates and boxes out of his way.

He turned to Cesar. "He's not here."

Day Nineteen
Civitavecchia, Italy

Civitavecchia is the ancient seaport for Rome, guarded by a massive fort completed by Michelangelo in 1537. The port is one of the busiest in Europe, servicing all seagoing traffic to and from Rome and Sardinia. It was early in the morning, but the port was already alive with noisy activity. Robert made his way past the railroad yards and stepped into a small trattoria filled with pungent cooking odors and ordered breakfast.

The *Halcyon* would be waiting for him at the appointed place, Elba. He was grateful that Susan had remembered it. On their honeymoon, they had stayed in their room there making love for three days and nights. Susan had said, "Would you like to go for a swim, darling?"

Robert had shaken his head. "No. I can't move. 'Able was I, ere I saw Elba.' " And Susan had laughed, and they had made love again. *And bless her, she has remembered the palindrome.*

Now all he had to do was to find a boat to take him to Elba. He walked down the streets leading to the harbor. It was bustling with maritime activity, crowded with freighters, motor boats and private yachts. There was a landing for a ferryboat. Robert's eyes lit up when he saw it. *That would be the safest way to get over to Elba.* He would be able to lose himself in the crowds.

As Robert started toward the ferry landing, he noticed

a dark, unmarked sedan parked half a block away, and he stopped. It had official license plates. There were two men seated inside the car watching the docks. Robert turned and walked in the other direction.

Scattered among the dockworkers and tourists, he spotted plainclothes detectives trying to look unobtrusive. They stood out like beacons. Robert's heart began to pound. How could they possibly have tracked him here? And then he realized what had happened. *My God, I told the truck driver where I was going! Stupid! I must be very tired.*

He had fallen asleep in the truck, and the absence of movement had awakened him. He had gotten up to look out and had seen Giuseppe go into the gas station and make a phone call. Robert had slipped out of the truck and climbed into the back of another truck headed north toward Civitavecchia.

He had trapped himself. They were looking for him here. A few hundred yards away were dozens of boats that could have afforded him an escape. Not any longer.

Robert turned away from the harbor and walked toward town. He passed a building with a huge colorful poster on the wall. It read: Come to the Fairgrounds. Fun for All! Food! Games! Rides! See the Big Race! He stopped and stared.

He had found his escape.

Chapter Forty-six

At the fairgrounds, five miles outside the town, were a number of large, colorful balloons spread across the field, looking like round rainbows. They were moored to trucks while ground crews were busily filling their envelopes with cold air. Half a dozen chase cars stood by, ready to track the balloons, two men in each car, the driver and the spotter.

Robert walked up to a man who seemed to be in charge. "It looks like you're getting ready for the big race," Robert said.

"That's right. Ever been in a balloon?"

"No."

They were skimming over Lake Como and he dropped the balloon down until it touched the water. "We're going to crash," Susan screamed. He smiled. "No, we're not." The bottom of the balloon was dancing on the waves. He threw out a sandbag, and the balloon began to lift again. Susan laughed and hugged him and said . . .

The man was speaking. "You should try it sometime. It's a great sport."

"Yeah. Where is the race heading?"

"Yugoslavia. We have a nice easterly wind. We'll be taking off in a few minutes. It's better to fly early in the morning when the wind is cool."

"Really?" Robert said politely. He had a quick flash of a summer day in Yugoslavia. *"We have four people to smuggle out of here, Commander. We must wait until the air is cooler. A balloon that can lift four people in the winter air can only lift two people in the summer air."*

Robert noticed that the crews were almost finished filling the balloons with air and had started to light the large propane burners, pointing the flame into the envelope opening, to warm the air inside. The balloons, which were lying on their sides, began to rise until the baskets stood upright.

"Mind if I look around?" Robert asked.

"Go ahead. Just stay out of everyone's way."

"Right." Robert walked over to a yellow and red balloon that was filled with propane gas. The only thing holding it to the ground was a rope attached to one of the trucks.

The crewman who had been working on it had wandered off to talk to someone. There was no one else near.

Robert climbed into the basket of the balloon, and the huge envelope seemed to fill the sky above him. He checked the rigging and equipment, the altimeter, charts, a pyrometer to monitor the temperature of the envelope, a rate-of-climb indicator, and a tool kit. Everything was in order. Robert reached into the tool kit and pulled out a knife. He sliced into the mooring rope, and a moment later, the balloon started to ascend.

"Hey!" Robert yelled. "What's going on here? Get me down!"

The man he had spoken to was gaping up at the runaway balloon. "*Figlio d'una mignotta!* Don't panic," he shouted. "There's an altimeter on board. Use your ballast and stay at one thousand feet. We'll meet you in Yugoslavia. Can you hear me?"

"I hear you."

The balloon was rising higher and higher, carrying him east, away from Elba, which was to the west. But Robert was not concerned. The wind changed direction at varying altitudes. None of the other balloons had taken off yet. Robert spotted one of the chase cars start up, moving to track him. He dropped ballast and watched the altimeter climb. Six hundred feet . . . seven hundred feet . . . nine hundred feet . . . eleven hundred feet . . .

At fifteen hundred feet, the wind began to weaken. The balloon was almost stationary now. Robert dropped more ballast. He used the stair-step technique, stopping at different altitudes to check the wind direction.

At two thousand feet, Robert could feel the wind begin to shift. It swayed in the turbulent air for a moment, then slowly began to reverse direction and move west.

In the distance, far below, Robert could see the other balloons rising and moving east toward Yugoslavia. There was no sound at all except for the soft whispering of the wind. *"It's so quiet, Robert. It's like flying on a cloud. I wish we could stay up here forever."* She had held him close. *"Have you ever made love in a balloon?" she murmured. "Let's try it."*

And later, *"I'll bet we're the only people in the world who have made love in a balloon, darling."*

Robert was over the Tyrrhenian Sea now, heading northwest toward the coast of Tuscany. Below, a string of islands stretched in a circle off the coast, with Elba the largest.

Napoleon had been exiled here, and he had probably chosen it because on a clear day, Robert thought, *he could see his beloved island of Corsica, where he had been born. In exile Napoleon's one thought was how to escape and get to France. Mine, too. Only Napoleon didn't have Susan and the Halcyon to rescue him.*

In the distance, Monte Capanne suddenly loomed up, rising more than three thousand feet into the sky. Robert pulled the safety line that opened the valve at the top of the balloon to allow the hot air to escape, and the balloon began to descend. Below him, Robert could see the lush pink and green of Elba, the pink that came from the granite outcrops and Tuscan houses, and the green of the heavy forests. Below, pristine white beaches were scattered around the edges of the island.

He landed the balloon at the base of the mountain, away from the city, to attract as little attention to himself as possible. There was a road not far from where he had landed, and he walked over to it and waited until a car came by.

"Could you give me a lift into town?" Robert called.

"Certainly. Jump in."

The driver appeared to be somewhere in his eighties, with an old, wrinkled face.

"I could have swore I saw a balloon in the sky a little while ago. Did you see it, mister?"

"No," Robert said.

"Visiting?"

"Just passing through. I'm on my way to Rome."

The driver nodded. "I was there once."

The rest of the ride was made in silence.

When they reached Portoferraio, the capital and only city of Elba, Robert stepped down from the car.

"Have a nice day," the driver said in English.

My God, Robert thought, *Californians have been here.*

Robert walked along Via Garibaldi, the main street,

crowded with tourists, mostly families, and it was as though time had stood still. Nothing had changed; *except that I've lost Susan, and half the governments in the world are trying to assassinate me. Otherwise,* Robert thought wryly, *everything is exactly the same.*

He bought binoculars in a gift shop, walked to the waterfront, and sat at a table outside the Stella Mariner Restaurant, where he had a clear view of the harbor. There were no suspicious cars, no police boats, and no policemen in sight. They still thought they had him bottled up on the mainland. It would be safe for him to board the *Halcyon.* All he had to do now was wait for it to arrive.

He sat there sipping *procanico,* the delicate native white wine, watching for the *Halcyon.* He went over his plan again. The yacht would drop him off near the coast of Marseilles, and he would make his way to Paris where he had a friend, Li Po, who would help him. It was ironic. He heard Francesco Cesar's voice saying: *"I've heard you've made a deal with the Chinese."*

He knew that Li Po would help him because Li had once saved Robert's life, and according to ancient Chinese tradition, he had become responsible for Robert. It was a matter of *win yu*—"honor."

Li Po was with the Guojia Anquanbu, the Chinese Ministry of State Security, which dealt with espionage. Years earlier Robert had been caught while trying to smuggle a dissident out of China. He had been sent to Qincheng, the top security prison in Beijing. Li Po was a double agent who had worked with Robert before. He managed to arrange for Robert to escape.

At the Chinese border, Robert had said, "You should

get out of this while you're still alive, Li. Your luck won't last forever."

Li Po had smiled. "I have *ren*—the ability to endure, to survive."

One year later, Li Po had been transferred to the Chinese Embassy in Paris.

Robert decided that it was time to make his first move. He left the restaurant and wandered down to the waterfront. It was crowded with large and small boats leaving from Portoferraio.

Robert approached a man polishing the hull of a sleek motorboat. It was a Donzi, powered by a V-8 351 horsepower inboard engine.

"Nice boat," Robert said.

The man nodded. *"Merci."*

"I wonder if I could rent it to take a little cruise around the harbor?"

The man stopped what he was doing and studied Robert. "That might be possible. Are you familiar with boats?"

"Yes. I have a Donzi back home."

The man nodded approvingly. "Where are you from?"

"Oregon," Robert said.

"It will cost you four hundred francs an hour."

Robert smiled. "That's fine."

"And a deposit, of course."

"Of course."

"She's ready to go. Would you like to take her out now?"

"No, I have some errands to run. I thought tomorrow morning."

"What time?"

"I'll let you know," Robert said.

He handed the man some money. "Here's a partial deposit. I'll see you tomorrow."

He had decided it would be dangerous to let the *Halcyon* come into port. There were formalities. The *capitaniera di porto*—the "harbormaster"—issued each yacht an *autorizzazione* and recorded its stay. Robert intended for the *Halcyon* to be as little involved with him as possible. He would meet it at sea.

In the office of the French Marine Ministry, Colonel Cesar and Colonel Johnson were talking to the marine operator. "Are you sure there has been no further communication with the *Halcyon*?"

"No, sir, not since the last conversation I reported to you."

"Keep listening." Colonel Cesar turned to Colonel Johnson and smiled. "Don't worry. We'll know the moment Commander Bellamy boards the *Halcyon*."

"But I want to get him before he's aboard."

The marine operator said, "Colonel Cesar, there is no Palindrome listed on the map of Italy. But I think we've pinned it down."

"Where is it?"

"It's not a place, sir. It's a word."

"What?"

"Yes, sir. A palindrome is a word or sentence that is spelled the same forward or backward. For example, 'Madam I'm Adam.' We've run some through our computers." He handed him a long list of words.

Colonel Cesar and Colonel Johnson scanned the list. "Kook . . . deed . . . bib . . . bob . . . boob . . . dad . . . dud . . . eve . . . gag . . . mom . . . non . . . noon . . . Otto . . . pop . . . sees . . . tot . . . toot . . ." Cesar looked up. "It's not much help, is it?"

"It might be, sir. They were obviously using some

kind of code. And one of the most famous palindromes was supposedly said by Napoleon: 'Able was I, ere I saw Elba.'"

Colonel Cesar and Colonel Johnson looked at each other. "*Elba!* Jesus Christ! That's where he is!"

Day Twenty
The Island of Elba

It first appeared as a faint speck on the horizon, rapidly looming larger in the early morning light. Through the binoculars, Robert watched it materialize into the *Halcyon.* There was no mistaking the ship. There were not many at sea like it.

Robert hurried down to the beach where he had arranged to rent the motorboat.

"Good morning."

The owner of the boat looked up. "*Bonjour, monsieur.* Are you ready to take it out?"

Robert nodded. "Yes."

"How long will you want it for?"

"No more than an hour or two."

Robert gave the man the rest of the deposit and stepped down into the boat.

"Take good care of it," the man said.

"Don't worry," Robert assured him, "I will."

The owner untied the painter, and moments later the boat was headed out to sea, racing toward the *Halcyon.* It took Robert ten minutes to reach the yacht. As he approached it, he saw Susan and Monte Banks standing on the deck. Susan waved to him, and he could see the anxiety in her face. Robert maneuvered the small boat next to the yacht and tossed a line to a deckhand.

"Do you want to bring it aboard, sir?" the man called.

"No, let it go." The owner would find it soon enough.

Robert walked up the ladder to the spotless teak deck. Susan had once described the *Halcyon* to Robert, and he had been impressed, but seen in person it was even more impressive. The *Halcyon* was two hundred and eighty feet long, with a luxurious owner's cabin, eight double suites for guests, and cabins for a crew of sixteen. It had a drawing room, a dining room, a study, a salon, and a swimming pool.

The ship was propelled by two twelve-hundred-and-fifty horsepower sixteen-cylinder turbocharged Caterpillar D399 diesel engines, and carried six small tenders for going ashore. The interior design had been done in Italy by Luigi Sturchio. It was a floating palace.

"I'm glad you made it," Susan said.

And Robert had the impression that she was ill at ease, that something was wrong. Or was it just his nerves?

She looked absolutely beautiful, yet somehow, he was disappointed. *What the hell had I expected? That she would look pale and miserable?*

He turned to Monte. "I want you to know how much I appreciate this."

Monte shrugged. "Glad to help you out."

The man was a saint.

"What's your plan?"

"I'd like you to turn and head due west to Marseilles. You can drop me off the coast and . . ."

A man in a crisp white uniform approached. He was in his fifties, heavy-set, with a neatly trimmed beard.

"This is Captain Simpson. This is . . ." Monte Banks looked at Robert for help.

"Smith. Tom Smith."

Monte said, "We'll be heading for Marseilles, Captain."

"We're not going into Elba?"

"No."

Captain Simpson said, "Very well." He sounded surprised.

Robert scanned the horizon. All clear.

"I'd suggest we go below," Monte Banks said.

When the three of them were seated in the salon, Monte asked, "Don't you think you owe us an explanation?"

"Yes, I do," Robert said, "but I'm not going to give you one. The less you know about this whole affair, the better. I can only tell you that I'm innocent. I'm involved in a political situation. I know too much, and I'm being hunted. If they find me, they'll kill me."

Susan and Monte exchanged a look.

"They have no reason to connect me with the *Halcyon*," Robert went on. "Believe me, Monte, if there were any other way for me to escape, I would have taken it."

Robert thought of all the people who had been killed because he had tracked them down. He could not bear to have anything happen to Susan. He tried to keep his voice light. "I would appreciate it for your own sake if you didn't mention that I was ever aboard this ship."

"Of course not," Monte said.

The yacht had slowly swung around and was heading west.

"If you'll excuse me, I have to have a word with the captain."

Dinner was an awkward affair. There were strange undercurrents that Robert did not understand, a tension that was almost tangible. Was it because of his presence? Or was it something else? Something between the two of them? *The sooner I get away from here, the better,* Robert thought.

They were in the salon having an after-dinner drink when Captain Simpson came into the room.

"When will we reach Marseilles?" Robert asked.

"If the weather holds, we should be there tomorrow afternoon, Mr. Smith."

There was something about Captain Simpson's manner that irritated Robert. The captain was gruff, almost to the point of being rude. *But he must be good,* Robert thought, *or Monte would not have hired him. Susan deserves this yacht. She deserves the best of everything.*

At eleven o'clock, Monte looked at his watch and said to Susan, "I think we had better turn in, darling."

Susan glanced at Robert. "Yes."

The three of them rose.

Monte said, "You'll find a change of clothes in your cabin. We're about the same size."

"Thank you."

"Good night, Robert."

"Good night, Susan."

Robert stood there, watching the woman he loved going off to bed with his rival. *Rival? Who the hell am I kidding? He's the winner. I'm the loser.*

Sleep was an elusive shadow dancing just out of reach. Lying in his bed, Robert was thinking that on the other side of the wall, only a few feet away, was the woman he loved more than anyone in the world. He thought of Susan lying in her bed, naked—*she never wore a nightgown*—and he felt himself beginning to get an erection. *Was Monte making love to her at this moment or was she alone? . . . And was she thinking of him and remembering all the great times they had had together? Probably not. Well, he would be out of her life soon. He would probably never see her again.*

It was dawn before he closed his eyes.

In the communications room at SIFAR, radar was tracking the *Halcyon*. Colonel Cesar turned to Colonel Johnson and said, "Too bad we couldn't intercept him at Elba, but we've got him now! We have a cruiser standing by. We're just awaiting word from the *Halcyon* to board her."

Day Twenty-one

Early in the morning, Robert was on deck looking out over the calm sea. Captain Simpson approached him. "Good morning. It looks like the weather is going to hold, Mr. Smith."

"Yes."

"We'll be in Marseilles by three o'clock. Will we be staying there long?"

"I don't know," Robert said pleasantly. "We'll see."

"Yes, sir."

Robert watched Simpson stride off. *What is it about the man?*

Robert walked back to the stern of the yacht and scanned the horizon. He could see nothing, and yet— In the past, his instincts had saved his life more than once. He had long ago learned to rely on them. Something was wrong.

* * *

Out of sight beyond the horizon, the Italian navy cruiser *Stromboli* was stalking the *Halcyon.*

When Susan appeared for breakfast, she looked pale and drawn.

"Did you sleep well, darling?" Monte asked.

"Fine," Susan said.

So they didn't share the same cabin! Robert felt an unreasonable sense of pleasure from that knowledge. He and Susan had always slept in the same bed, her naked, nubile body spooning into his. *Jesus, I've got to stop thinking like this.*

Ahead of the *Halcyon,* on the starboard bow was a fishing boat from the Marseilles fleet bringing in a fresh catch.

"Would you like some fish for lunch?" Susan asked.

Both men nodded. "Fine."

They were almost abreast of the fishing boat.

As Captain Simpson walked by, Robert asked, "What is our ETA to Marseilles?"

"We'll be there in two hours, Mr. Smith. Marseilles is an interesting port. Have you ever been there?"

"It *is* an interesting port," Robert said.

In the communications room at SIFAR, the two colonels were reading the message that had just come in from the *Halcyon.* It read simply: "Now."

"What's the *Halcyon*'s position?" barked Colonel Cesar.

"They're two hours out of Marseilles, heading for port."

"Order the *Stromboli* to overtake and board her immediately."

Thirty minutes later, the Italian navy cruiser *Stromboli* was closing in on the *Halcyon*. Susan and Monte were at the fantail of the yacht watching the warship racing toward them.

A voice came over the cruiser's loudspeaker. "Ahoy, *Halcyon*. Heave to. We're coming aboard."

Susan and Monte exchanged a look. Captain Simpson came hurrying toward them.

"Mr. Banks—"

"I heard it. Do as they say. Stop the engines."

"Yes, sir."

A minute later, the pulse of the engines stopped, and the yacht lay still in the water. Susan and her husband watched as armed sailors from the Navy cruiser were lowered into a dinghy.

Ten minutes later, a dozen sailors were swarming up the ladder of the *Halcyon*.

The naval officer in charge, a lieutenant commander, said, "I'm sorry to trouble you, Mr. Banks. The Italian government has reason to believe that you are harboring a fugitive. We have orders to search your ship."

Susan stood there watching as the sailors started spreading out, moving along the deck and going below to search the cabins.

"Don't say anything."

"But—"

"Not a word."

They stood on the deck in silence, watching the search go on.

Thirty minutes later, they were assembled again on the main deck.

"There's no sign of him, Commander," a sailor reported.

"You're certain of that?"

"Absolutely, sir. There are no passengers aboard, and we have identified each member of the crew."

The commander stood there a moment, frustrated. His superiors had made a serious mistake.

He turned to Monte and Susan and Captain Simpson. "I owe you an apology," he said. "I'm terribly sorry to have inconvenienced you. We'll leave now." He turned to go.

"Commander—"

"Yes?"

"The man you're looking for got away on a fishing boat half an hour ago. You should have no trouble picking him up."

Five minutes later, the *Stromboli* was speeding toward Marseilles. The lieutenant commander had every reason to be pleased with himself. The governments of the world had been pursuing Commander Robert Bellamy, and he was the one who had found him. *There could be a nice promotion in this,* he thought.

From the bridge, the navigation officer called out, "Commander, could you come up here, please?"

Had they spotted the fishing boat already? The lieutenant commander hurried up to the bridge.

"Look, sir!"

The commander took one look, and his heart sank. In the distance ahead, covering the horizon, was the entire Marseilles fishing fleet, a hundred identical boats returning to port. There was no way in the world to identify the one Commander Bellamy was on.

Chapter Forty-seven

He stole a car in Marseilles. It was a Fiat 1800 Spider convertible, parked on a dimly lit side street. It was locked, and there was no key in the ignition. No problem. Looking around to make sure he was not observed, Robert made a rip in the canvas top and shoved his hand inside to unlock the door. He slid inside the car and reached under the dashboard and pulled out all the wires of the ignition switch. He held the thick red wire in one hand while, one by one, he touched the other wires to it until he found one that lit up the dashboard. He then hooked those two wires together and touched the remaining ones to the two wires hooked together until the engine began to turn over. He pulled out the choke, and the engine roared into life. A moment later, Robert was on his way to Paris.

His first priority was to get hold of Li Po. When he reached the Paris suburbs, he stopped at a phone booth.

He telephoned Li's apartment and heard the familiar voice on the answering machine: *"Zao, mes amis. . . . Je regrette que je ne sois pas chez moi, mais il n'y a pas du danger que je réponde pas à votre coup de téléphone. Prenez garde que vous attendiez le signal de l'appareil."*

"Good morning. I regret that I am not at home, but there is no danger of my not returning your call. Be careful to wait for the tone." Robert counted out the words in their private code. The key words were: *Regret . . . danger . . . careful.*

The phone was tapped, of course. Li had been expecting his call, and this was his way of warning Robert. He had to get to him as quickly as possible. He would use another code they had employed in the past.

Robert walked along the Rue du Faubourg St. Honoré. He had walked this street with Susan. She had stopped in front of a shop window and posed like a mannequin. *"Would you like to see me in that dress, Robert?" "No, I'd prefer to see you out of it."* And they had visited the Louvre, and Susan had stood transfixed in front of the Mona Lisa, her eyes brimming with tears. . . .

Robert headed for the offices of *Le Matin*. Just down the block from the entryway, he stopped a teenager on the street.

"Would you like to make fifty francs?"

The boy looked at him suspiciously. "Doing what?"

Robert scribbled something on a piece of paper and handed it to the boy with a fifty-franc note.

"Just take this into *Le Matin* to the want-ads desk."

"Bon, d'accord."

Robert watched the boy go into the building. The ad would get in in time to make next morning's edition. It read: *"Tilly. Dad very ill. Needs you. Please meet with him soon. Mother."*

There was nothing to do now but wait. He dared not check into a hotel because they would all have been alerted. Paris was a ticking time bomb.

Robert boarded a crowded tour bus and sat in back, keeping a low, silent profile. The tour group visited the Luxembourg Gardens, the Louvre, Napoleon's tomb in Les Invalides, and a dozen other monuments. And always Robert managed to lose himself in the middle of the crowd.

Day Twenty-two
Paris, France

He bought a ticket for the midnight show at the Moulin Rouge as part of another tour group. The show started at two A.M. When it was over, he filled in the rest of the night moving around Montmartre, going from small bar to small bar.

The morning papers would not be out on the streets until five A.M. A few minutes before five, Robert was standing near a newspaper stand waiting. A red truck drove up, and a boy threw a bundle of papers onto the pavement. Robert picked up the first one. He turned to the want ads. His ad was there. Now there was nothing to do but wait.

At noon Robert wandered into a small tobacconist shop, where dozens of personal messages were tacked to a board. There were help wanted ads, advertisements for apartments to let, students seeking roommates, bicycles for sale. In the middle of the board, Robert found the message he was looking for. *"Tilly eager to see you. Call her at 50 41 26 45."*

Li Po answered on the first ring. "Robert?"

"*Zao,* Li."

"My God, man, what is happening?"

"I was hoping you could tell me."

"My friend, you're getting more attention than the president of France. The cables are burning up about you. What have you done? No, don't tell me. Whatever it is, you're in serious trouble. They've tapped the phone at the Chinese Embassy, my phone at home is tapped, and they're watching my flat. They've been asking me a lot of questions about you."

"Li, do you have any idea what this is all—?"

"Not over the phone. Do you remember where Sung's apartment is?"

Li's girlfriend. "Yes."

"I'll meet you there in half an hour."

"Thanks." Robert was keenly aware of what jeopardy Li Po was putting himself in. He remembered what had happened to Al Traynor, his friend at the FBI. *I'm a fucking Jonah. Everyone I come near, dies.*

The apartment was on Rue Bénouville in a quiet arrondissement of Paris. When Robert reached the building, the sky was heavy with rain clouds, and he could hear the distant rumble of thunder. He walked into the lobby and rang the doorbell of the apartment. Li Po opened the door at once.

"Come inside," he said. "Quickly." He closed the door behind Robert and locked it. Li Po had not changed since the last time Robert had seen him. He was tall and thin and ageless.

The two men clasped hands.

"Li, do you know what the hell is going on?"

"Sit down, Robert."

Robert sat.

Li studied him for a moment. "Have you ever heard of Operation Doomsday?"

Robert frowned. "No. Does it have anything to do with UFOs?"

"It has everything to do with UFOs. The world is facing disaster, Robert."

Li Po began to pace. "Aliens are coming to earth to destroy us. Three years ago, they landed here and met with government officials to demand that all the industrial powers close down their nuclear plants and stop burning fossil fuel."

Robert was listening, puzzled.

"They demanded a stop to the manufacturing of petroleum, chemicals, rubber, plastics. That would mean the closing down of thousands of factories all over the world. Automobile and steel plants would be forced to shut down. The world economy would be a shambles."

"Why would they—?"

"They claim we're polluting the universe, destroying the earth and the seas. . . . They want us to stop making weapons, to stop waging war."

"Li—"

"A group of powerful men from twelve countries got together—top industrialists from the United States, Japan, Russia, China. . . . A man with the code name of Janus organized intelligence agencies around the world to collaborate in Operation Doomsday to stop the aliens." He turned to Robert. "You've heard of SDI?"

"Star Wars. The satellite system to shoot down Soviet intercontinental ballistic missiles."

Li shook his head. "No. That was a cover. SDI was not created to fight the Russians. It is being designed for the specific purpose of knocking down UFOs. It's the only chance there is of stopping them."

Robert sat there in stunned silence, trying to absorb what Li Po was saying, while the rumble of thunder grew louder. "You mean, the governments are behind—?"

"Let's say there are cabals within each government. Operation Doomsday is being run privately. Do you understand now?"

"My God! The governments aren't aware that . . ." He looked up at Li. "Li—how did you learn all this?"

"It's very simple, Robert," Li said quietly. "I'm the Chinese connection." There was a Beretta in his hand.

Robert stared at the gun. "Li—!"

Li squeezed the trigger, and the sound of the shot mingled with a sudden deafening crack of thunder and a flash of lightning outside the window.

Chapter Forty-eight

The first few drops of clean rainwater awakened her. She was lying on a park bench, too exhausted to move. For the last two days, she had felt her life energy flowing out of her. *I am going to die here on this planet.* She drifted into what she thought would be her last sleep. And then the rain came. The blessed rain. She could hardly believe it. She lifted her head to the sky and felt the cool drops running down her face. It began to rain harder and harder. Fresh, pure liquid. She stood up then and raised her hands high, letting the water pour over her, giving her new strength, bringing her back to life. She let the rainwater fill her body, absorbing it into her very essence until she began to feel her tiredness vanish. She felt herself growing stronger and stronger until finally, she thought, *I am ready. I can think clearly. I know who can help me find my way back.* She took out the small transmitter, closed her eyes, and began to concentrate.

Chapter Forty-nine

It was the lightning streak that saved Robert's life. At the instant that Li Po started to squeeze the trigger, the sudden flash of light outside the window distracted him for a moment. Robert moved, and the bullet hit him in his right shoulder instead of his chest.

As Li raised the gun to fire again, Robert gave a side thrust kick, knocking the gun out of Li's hand. Li spun forward and punched Robert hard in his wounded shoulder. The pain was excruciating. Robert's jacket was covered with blood. He lashed out with a forward elbow smash. Li grunted with pain. He riposted with a deadly *shuto* chop to the neck, and Robert evaded it. The two men circled each other, both of them breathing hard, looking for an opening. They fought silently in a deadly ritual older than time, and each knew that only one of them would come out of this alive. Robert was weakening. The pain in his shoulder was increasing, and he could see his blood dripping to the floor.

Time was on Li Po's side. *I've got to end this quickly,* Robert thought. He moved in with a front snap kick. Instead of evading it, Li took the full force of it, and was close enough to Robert to drive his elbow into Robert's shoulder. Robert staggered. Li moved in with a spin and back kick, and Robert faltered. Li was on top of him in an instant, pummeling him, pounding his shoulder again and again, backing him across the room. Robert was too weak to stop the rain of punishing blows. His eyes began to dim. He fell against Li, grabbing him, and the two men went down, smashing a glass table, shattering it. Robert lay on the floor, powerless to move. *It's over,* he thought. *They've won.*

He lay there, half-conscious, waiting for Li to finish him off. Nothing happened. Slowly, painfully, Robert lifted his head. Li lay next to him on the floor, his eyes opened wide, staring at the ceiling. A large shard of glass protruded from his chest like a transparent dagger.

Robert struggled to sit up. He was weak from the loss of blood. His shoulder was an ocean of pain. *I have to get to a doctor,* he thought. *There was a name—someone that the agency used in Paris—someone at the American Hospital. Hilsinger. That was it. Leon Hilsinger.*

Dr. Hilsinger was ready to leave his office for the day when the telephone call came in. His nurse had already gone home, so he picked up the phone. The voice at the other end of the phone was slurred.

"Dr. Hilsinger?"

"Yes."

"This is Robert Bellamy . . . Need your help. I've been badly hurt. Will you help me?"

"Of course. Where are you?"

"Never mind that. I'll meet you at the American Hospital in half an hour."

"I'll be there. Go right to the emergency room."

"Doctor—don't mention this call to anyone."

"You have my word." The line went dead.

Dr. Hilsinger dialed a number. "I just heard from Commander Bellamy. I'm meeting him at the American Hospital in half an hour. . . ."

"Thank you, Doctor."

Dr. Hilsinger replaced the receiver. He heard the reception door open and looked up. Robert Bellamy was standing there with a gun in his hand.

"On second thought," Robert said, "it might be better if you treated me here."

The doctor tried to conceal his surprise. "You—you should be in a hospital."

"Too close to the morgue. Patch me up and make it fast." It was difficult to talk.

He started to protest, then thought better of it. "Yes. Whatever you say. I'd better give you an anesthetic. It will—"

"Don't even think about it," Robert said. "No tricks." He was holding the gun in his left hand. "If I don't get out of here alive, neither do you. Any questions?" He felt faint.

Dr. Hilsinger swallowed. "No."

"Then get to work. . . ."

Dr. Hilsinger led Robert into the next room, an examining room filled with medical equipment. Slowly and carefully, Robert slipped out of his jacket. Holding the gun in his hand, he sat down on the table. Dr. Hilsinger had a scalpel in his hand. Robert's fingers tightened on the trigger.

"Relax," Dr. Hilsinger said nervously. "I'm just going to cut your shirt."

The wound was raw and red and seeping blood. "The bullet is still in there," Dr. Hilsinger said. "You won't be able to stand the pain unless I give you—"

"No!" He was not going to let himself be drugged. "Just take it out."

"Whatever you say."

Robert watched the doctor walk over to a sterilizing unit and put in a pair of forceps. Robert sat on the edge of the table, fighting off the dizziness that threatened to engulf him. He closed his eyes for a moment, and Dr. Hilsinger was standing in front of him, the forceps in his hand.

"Here we go." He pushed the forceps into the raw wound, and Robert screamed aloud with the pain. Bright lights flashed in front of his eyes. He started to lose consciousness.

"It's out," Dr. Hilsinger said.

Robert sat there for a moment trembling, taking deep breaths, fighting to regain control of himself.

Dr. Hilsinger was watching him closely. "Are you all right?"

It took Robert a moment to find his voice. "Yes.... Patch it up."

The doctor poured peroxide into the wound, and Robert started to pass out again. He gritted his teeth. *Hang on. We're almost there.* And finally, blessedly, the worst was over. The doctor was strapping a heavy bandage across Robert's shoulder.

"Give me my jacket," Robert said.

Dr. Hilsinger stared at him. "You can't go out now. You can't even walk."

"Bring me my jacket." His voice was so weak he could hardly talk. He watched the doctor walk across the room to get his jacket, and there seemed to be two of him.

"You've lost a lot of blood," Dr. Hilsinger cautioned. "It would be dangerous for you to leave."

And more dangerous for me to stay, Robert thought. Carefully, he slipped his jacket on and tried to stand. His legs began to buckle. He grabbed the side of the table.

"You'll never make it," Dr. Hilsinger warned.

Robert looked up at the blurry figure in front of him. "I'll make it."

But he knew that the moment he left, Dr. Hilsinger would be on the phone again. Robert's eyes fell on the spool of heavy surgical tape Dr. Hilsinger had used.

"Sit in the chair." His words were slurred.

"Why? What are you—?"

Robert raised the gun. "Sit down."

Dr. Hilsinger sat. Robert picked up the roll of tape. It was awkward because he only had the use of one hand. He pulled the end of the wide tape loose and began to unroll it. He moved over to Dr. Hilsinger. "Just sit quietly and you won't get hurt."

He fastened the end of the tape to the arm of the chair, and then started winding it around the doctor's hands.

"This really isn't necessary," Dr. Hilsinger said. "I won't—"

"Shut up." Robert continued to bind the doctor to the chair. The effort had started the rivers of pain flowing again. He looked at the doctor and said quietly, "I'm not going to faint."

He fainted.

* * *

He was floating in space, drifting weightlessly through white clouds, at peace. *Wake up.* He did not want to wake up. He wanted this wonderful feeling to go on forever. *Wake up.* Something hard was pressing against his side. Something in his jacket pocket. With his eyes still closed, he reached in and held it in his hand. It was the crystal. He drifted back to sleep.

Robert. It was a woman's voice, soft and soothing. He was in a lovely green meadow, and the air was filled with music, and there were bright lights in the sky overhead. A woman was moving toward him. She was tall and beautiful with a gentle, oval face and a soft, almost translucent complexion. She was dressed in a snow white gown. Her voice was gentle and hushed.

"No one's going to hurt you anymore, Robert. Come to me. I'm waiting here for you."

Slowly, Robert opened his eyes. He lay there for a long moment, then sat up, filled with a sudden sense of excitement. He knew now who the eleventh witness was, and he knew where he was to meet her.

Chapter Fifty

Day Twenty-three
Paris, France

He telephoned Admiral Whittaker from the doctor's office.

"Admiral? Robert."

"Robert! What's going on? They told me—"

"Never mind that now. I need your help, Admiral. Have you ever heard the name Janus?"

Admiral Whittaker said slowly, "Janus? No. I never heard of him."

Robert said, "I've found out he's heading some kind of secret organization that's killing innocent people, and now he's trying to kill me. We have to stop him."

"How can I help?"

"I need to get to the President. Can you arrange a meeting?"

There was a moment of silence. "I'm certain I can."

"There's more. General Hilliard is involved."

"What? How?"

"And there are others. Most of the intelligence agencies in Europe are in it, too. I can't explain anymore now. I want you to call Hilliard. Tell him I've found an eleventh witness."

"I don't understand. An eleventh witness to what?"

"I'm sorry, Admiral, but I can't tell you. Hilliard will know. I want him to meet me in Switzerland."

"Switzerland?"

"Tell him I'm the only one who knows where the eleventh witness is. If he makes one wrong move, the deal is off. Tell him to go to the Dolder Grand in Zurich. There will be a note waiting for him at the desk. Tell him I also want Janus in Switzerland—in person."

"Robert, are you certain you know what you're doing?"

"No, sir, I'm not. But this is the only chance I've got. I want you to tell him my conditions are not negotiable. Number one, I want safe passage to Switzerland. Number two, I want General Hilliard and Janus to meet me there. Number three, after that, I want a meeting with the President of the United States."

"I will do everything I can, Robert. How will I get in touch with you?"

"I'll call you back. How much time will you need?"

"Give me one hour."

"Right."

"And Robert—"

He could hear the pain in the old man's voice. "Yes, sir?"

"Be careful."

"Don't worry, sir. I'm a survivor. Remember?"

* * *

One hour later, Robert was speaking to Admiral Whittaker again.

"You have a deal. General Hilliard seemed shaken by the news of another witness. He's given me his word you will not be harmed. Your conditions will be met. He's flying to Zurich and will be there tomorrow morning."

"And Janus?"

"Janus will be on the plane with him."

Robert felt a surge of relief. "Thank you, Admiral. And the President?"

"I spoke to him myself. His aides will arrange a meeting for you whenever you're ready."

Thank God!

"General Hilliard has a plane to fly you to—"

"No way." He was not going to let them get him into a plane. "I'm in Paris. I want a car and I'll drive it myself. I want it left in front of the Hotel Littré in Montparnasse within half an hour."

"I'll see to it."

"Admiral?"

"Yes, Robert?"

It was difficult to keep his voice steady. "Thank you."

He walked down Rue Littré, moving slowly because of the pain. He approached the hotel cautiously. Parked directly in front of the building was a black Mercedes sedan. There was no one inside. Across the street was a blue and white police car with a uniformed policeman behind the wheel. On the sidewalk, two men in civilian clothes stood watching Robert approach. *French Secret Service.*

Robert found that he was having trouble breathing.

His heart was pounding. Was he stepping into a trap? The only insurance he had was the eleventh witness. Did Hilliard believe him? Was it enough?

He walked toward the sedan, waiting for the men to make a move. They stood there, silently watching him.

Robert moved toward the driver's side of the Mercedes and looked inside. The keys were in the ignition. He could feel the eyes of the men fastened on him as he opened the door and slid into the driver's seat. He sat there a moment, staring at the ignition. *If General Hilliard had double-crossed Admiral Whittaker, this was the moment when everything would end in a violent explosion.*

Here goes. Robert took a deep breath, reached down with his left hand, and turned the key. The motor purred into life. The secret servicemen stood there watching him drive away. As Robert approached the intersection, a police car pulled in front of his car, and for a moment, Robert thought he was going to be stopped. Instead, the police turned on their red flashing light, and the traffic seemed to melt away. *They're giving me a fucking escort!*

Overhead Robert heard the sound of a helicopter. He glanced up. The side of the helicopter was marked with the insignia of the French national police. General Hilliard was doing everything possible to see that he arrived in Switzerland safely. *And after I show him the last witness,* Robert thought grimly, *he thinks he's going to kill me. But the general is in for a surprise.*

Robert reached the Swiss border at four o'clock in the afternoon. At the border, the French police car turned back, and a Swiss police car became his escort. For the first time since the affair had started, Robert began to relax. *Thank God Admiral Whittaker had friends in high places.* With the President expecting a meeting with Robert, General Hilliard would not dare to harm him. His mind turned to the woman in white, and at that instant, he heard her voice. The sound of it reverberated through the car.

"Hurry, Robert. We are all waiting for you."

All? Is there more than one? I'll find out soon enough, Robert thought.

In Zurich Robert stopped at the Dolder Grand Hotel and wrote a note at the desk for the general.

"General Hilliard will ask for me," Robert told the clerk. "Please give this to him."

"Yes, sir."

Outside, Robert walked over to the police car that had been escorting him. He leaned down to talk to the driver. "From here on in, I want to be on my own."

The driver hesitated. "Very well, Commander."

Robert got back in his car and started driving toward Uetendorf and the scene of the UFO crash. As he drove, he thought of all the tragedies that had occurred because of it and all the lives that had been taken. *Hans Beckerman and Father Patrini; Leslie Mothershed and William Mann; Daniel Wayne and Otto Schmidt; Laslo Bushfekete and Fritz Mandel; Olga Romanchanko and Kevin Parker. Dead. All of them dead.*

I want to see the face of Janus, Robert thought, *and look into his eyes.*

The villages seemed to race by, and the pristine beauty of the Alps belied all the bloodshed and terror that had started here. The car approached Thun, and Robert's adrenaline began to flow. Ahead was the field where he and Beckerman had found the weather balloon, where the nightmare had begun. Robert pulled the car over to the side of the road and switched off the engine. He said a silent prayer. Then he got out of the car and crossed the highway and went into the field.

A thousand memories flashed through Robert's mind. The phone call at four in the morning. *"You are ordered to report to General Hilliard at National Security Agency Headquarters at Fort Meade at oh six hundred this morning. Is this message understood, Commander?"*

How little he had understood it then. He recalled General Hilliard's words: *"You must find those witnesses. All of them."* And the search had led from Zurich to Bern, London, Munich, Rome, and Orvieto; from Waco to Fort Smith; from Kiev to Washington, and Budapest. Well, the bloody trail had finally come to an end, here where it had all begun.

She was waiting for him, as Robert had known she would be, and she looked exactly as she had appeared in his dream. They moved toward each other, and she seemed to be floating toward him, a radiant smile on her face.

"Thank you for coming, Robert."

Had he actually heard her speak, or was he hearing her thoughts? How did one talk to an alien being?

"I had to come," he said simply. There was a totally unreal quality to the scene. *I'm standing here speaking with someone from another world! I should be terrified, but in my whole life, I've never felt more at peace.* "I have to warn you," Robert said. "Some men are coming here who want to harm you. It would be better if you left before they arrive."

"I cannot leave."

And Robert understood. He reached in his pocket with his left hand and pulled out the small piece of metal containing the crystal.

Her face lit up. *"Thank you, Robert."*

He handed it to her and watched her fit it into the piece she held in her hand.

"What happens now?" Robert asked.

"Now I can communicate with my friends. They will be coming for me."

Was there something ominous in that sentence? Robert recalled General Hilliard's words: *"They intend to take over this planet and make slaves of us."* What if General Hilliard was right? What if the aliens did intend to take over the earth? Who was going to stop them? Robert looked at his watch. It was almost time for General Hilliard and Janus to arrive, and even as Robert thought it, he heard the sound of a giant Huey helicopter approaching from the north.

"Your friends are here."

Friends. They were his mortal enemies, and he was determined to expose them as murderers, to destroy them.

The grass and flowers in the field began to flutter wildly as the helicopter came to a landing.

He was about to come face to face with Janus. The thought of it filled him with a murderous rage. The door of the helicopter opened.

Susan stepped out.

Chapter Fifty-one

In the mothership, floating high above earth, there was great joy. All the lights on the panels were flashing green.

"We have found her!"

"We must hurry."

The huge ship started to hurl itself toward the planet far below.

Chapter Fifty-two

For a single instant, time was frozen, and then it shattered into a thousand pieces. Robert watched, stunned, as Susan stepped out of the helicopter. She stood there for a second, and then started toward Robert, but Monte Banks, who was right behind her, grabbed her and held her back.

"Run, Robert! Run! They're going to kill you!"

Robert took a step toward her, and at that moment General Hilliard and Colonel Frank Johnson stepped out of the helicopter.

General Hilliard said, "I'm here, Commander. I've kept my part of the bargain." He walked over to Robert and the woman in white. "I assume this is the eleventh witness. The missing alien. I'm sure we'll find her very interesting. So it's finally finished."

"Not yet. You said you would bring Janus."

"Oh, yes. Janus insisted on coming to see you."

Robert turned toward the helicopter. Admiral Whittaker was standing in the doorway.

"You asked to see me, Robert?"

Robert stared at him, unbelievingly, and there was a red film before his eyes. It was as though his world had collapsed. "No! Why—? Why in God's name?"

The admiral was moving toward him. "You don't understand, do you? You never did. You're worried about a few meaningless lives. We're worried about saving our world. This earth belongs to us to do with as we please."

He turned to stare at the woman in white. "If you creatures want war, you're going to get war. And we'll beat you!" He turned back to Robert. "You betrayed me. You were my son. I let you take Edward's place. I gave you a chance to serve your country. And how did you repay me? You came whining to me to let you stay home so you could be with your wife." His voice was filled with contempt. "No son of mine would ever do that. I should have seen then how distorted your values were."

Robert stood there paralyzed, too shocked to speak.

"I broke up your marriage because I still had faith in you, but—"

"You broke up my—?"

"Remember when the CIA sent you after the Fox? I arranged that. I hoped it would bring you to your senses. You failed because there was no Fox. I thought I had straightened you out, that you were one of us. And then you told me you were going to quit the agency. That's when I knew you were no patriot, that you had to be eliminated, destroyed. But first you had to help us with our mission."

"Your *mission*? To kill all those innocent people? You're insane!"

"They had to be killed to stop them from spreading

panic. We're ready now for the aliens. All we needed was a little more time, and you've given it to us."

The woman in white had stood there listening, saying nothing, but now her thoughts floated into the minds of those standing in the field. *"We have come here to prevent you from destroying your planet. We are all part of one universe. Look up."*

Their heads turned toward the sky. There was an enormous white cloud overhead, and as they stared up at it, it changed before their eyes. They were looking at a vision of a polar ice cap, and as they watched, it began to melt, and the water came pouring through the rivers and oceans of the world, flooding London and Los Angeles, New York and Tokyo, and coastal cities around the world in a dizzying montage. The vision changed to an enormous vista of desolate farmlands, with crops burnt to cinders under a broiling, merciless sun, and the corpses of dead animals strewn across the landscape. The scene before their eyes changed again, and they saw riots in China, and famines in India, and a devastating nuclear war, and finally, people living in caves. The vision slowly disappeared.

There was a moment of awed silence. *"That is your future if you go on as you are."*

Admiral Whittaker was the first to recover. "Mass hypnosis," he snapped. "I'm sure you can show us other interesting tricks." He moved toward the alien. "I'm taking you back to Washington with me. We have a lot of information to get from you." The admiral looked at Robert. "You're finished." He turned to Frank Johnson. "Take care of him."

Colonel Johnson removed his pistol from his holster.

Susan broke away from Monte and ran to Robert's side. "No!" she screamed.

"Kill him!" Admiral Whittaker said.

Colonel Johnson was pointing a gun at the admiral. "Admiral, you're under arrest."

Admiral Whittaker was staring at him. "What—What are you saying? I told you to kill him. You're one of us."

"You're wrong. I never have been. I infiltrated your organization a long time ago. I was looking for Commander Bellamy not to kill him, but to save him." He turned to Robert. "I'm sorry I couldn't get to you sooner."

Admiral Whittaker's face had turned ashen. "Then you'll be destroyed too. Nobody can stand in our way. Our organization—"

"You no longer have an organization. At this moment, all the members are being rounded up. It's finished, Admiral."

Overhead, the sky seemed to be vibrating with light and sound. The huge mothership was floating down directly above them, bright green lights flashing from its interior. They stared in awe as they watched it land. A smaller spaceship appeared, and then another, and then two more, and another two, until the sky seemed to be filled with them, and there was a great roar in the air that became a glorious music that echoed throughout the mountains. The door of the mother ship opened and an alien appeared.

The woman in white turned to Robert. *"I am leaving now."* She moved toward Admiral Whittaker, General Hilliard, and Monte Banks. *"You shall come with me."*

Admiral Whittaker drew back. "No! I won't go!"

"Yes. We will not hurt you." She held out her hand, and for an instant nothing happened. Then, as the others watched, the three men began slowly moving in a daze toward the spaceship.

Admiral Whittaker screamed, "No!"

He was still screaming when the three men disappeared inside the spaceship.

The woman in white turned to the others. *"They will not be harmed. They have much to learn. When they have learned, they will be brought back here."*

Susan was holding Robert tightly.

"Tell people they must stop killing the planet, Robert. Make them understand."

"I'm only one man."

"There are thousands of you. Every day your numbers grow. One day there will be millions, and you must all speak with one strong voice. Will you do it?"

"I'll try. I'll try."

"We are leaving now. But we will be watching you. And we will be back."

The woman in white turned and entered the mother-ship. The lights inside began to glow brighter and brighter until they seemed to light up the entire sky. Suddenly, without warning, the mother ship took off, followed by the smaller ships, until finally they all vanished from sight.

"Tell the people they must stop killing this planet." *Right,* Robert thought. *I know now what I'm going to do with the rest of my life.*

He looked at Susan and smiled.

The Beginning

AUTHOR'S NOTE

In researching this novel, I have read numerous books and magazine and newspaper articles citing astronauts who had reportedly had extraterrestrial experiences: Colonel Frank Borman on *Gemini 7* supposedly took pictures of a UFO that followed his capsule. Neil Armstrong on *Apollo 11* saw two unidentified spacecraft when he landed on the moon. Buzz Aldrin photographed unidentified spacecraft on the moon. Colonel L. Gordon Cooper encountered a large UFO on a Project Mercury flight over Perth, Australia, and recorded voices speaking languages later found to belong to no known earth language.

I talked to these men, as well as to other astronauts, and each assured me that the stories were apocryphal rather than apocalyptic, that they had had no experiences of any kind with UFOs. A few days after my telephone conversation with Colonel Gordon Cooper, he called me back. I returned his call, but he had suddenly become unavailable. One year later, I managed to acquire a letter written by him, dated November 9, 1978, and discussing UFOs.

I telephoned Colonel Cooper again to ask him if the letter was authentic. This time, he was more forthcoming. He informed me that it was and that on his journeys into space, he had personally witnessed several flights of UFOs. He also mentioned that other astronauts had had similar experiences that they were warned not to discuss.

I have read a dozen books that prove conclusively that flying saucers exist. I have read a dozen books that prove conclusively that flying saucers do *not* exist. I have run videotapes purporting to be photographs of flying saucers and have met with therapists in the United States and abroad who specialize in hypnotizing people who claim to have been taken up into UFOs. The therapists say that they have handled hundreds of cases in which the details of the victims' experiences are startlingly similar, including identical, unexplainable marks on their bodies.

An Air Force general in charge of the Blue Book Project—a United States government group formed to investigate flying saucers—assured me that there has never been any hard evidence of flying saucers or aliens.

Yet, in the foreword to Timothy Good's remarkable book *Above Top Secret: The Worldwide UFO Cover-up,* Lord Hill-Norton, Admiral of the Fleet and British Chief of Defense Staff from 1971 to 1973, writes:

> The evidence that there are objects which have been seen in our atmosphere, and even on terra

> firma, that cannot be accounted for either as man-made objects or as any physical force or effect known to our scientists seems to me to be overwhelming. . . . A very large number of sightings have been vouched for by persons whose credentials seem to me unimpeachable. It is striking that so many have been trained observers, such as police officers and airline or military pilots . . .

In 1933 the 4th Swedish Flying Corps began an investigation of mysterious unmarked aircraft appearing over Scandinavia, and on April 30, 1934, Major-General Erik Reuterswaerd issued the following statement to the press:

> Comparisons of these reports show that there can be no doubt about illegal air traffic over our secret military areas. There are many reports from reliable people which describe close observation of the enigmatic flier. And in every case, the same remark can be noted; no insignias or identifying marks are visible on the machines. . . . The question is: Who or what are they, and why have they been invading our air territory?

In 1947 Professor Paul Santorini, a leading Greek scientist, was asked to investigate missiles flying over Greece. His research, however, was curtailed: "We soon established that they were not missiles. But, before we could do any more, the Army, after conferring with foreign officials, ordered the investigation stopped. *Foreign scientists flew to Greece for secret talks with me.*" (Emphasis added.)

The professor confirmed that a "world blanket of secrecy" surrounded the UFO question because, among other reasons, the authorities were unwilling to admit the existence of a force against which there was "no possibility of defense."

From 1947 to 1952, the Air Technical Intelligence Center (ATIC) received approximately fifteen hundred official reports of sightings. Of these the Air Force carries twenty percent as unexplained:

Air Chief Marshal Lord Dowding, commander in chief of the RAF Fighter Command during the Battle of Britain in 1940 wrote:

> More than 10,000 sightings have been reported, the majority of which cannot be accounted for by any "scientific explanation." They have been tracked on radar screens . . . and the observed speeds have been as great as 9,000 miles an hour. . . . *I am convinced that these objects do exist and that they are not manufactured by any nation on earth.* [Emphasis added.] I can therefore see no alternative to accepting the theory that they come from an extraterrestrial source.

Recently, in Elmwood, Wisconsin, the entire town watched as flying saucers moved across their skies for several days.

* * *

General Lionel Max Chassin, who rose to the rank of Commanding General of the French Air Forces and served as General Air Defense Co-ordinator, Allied Air Forces, Central Europe (NATO), wrote:

> That strange things have been seen is now beyond question. . . . The number of thoughtful, intelligent, educated people in full possession of their faculties who have "seen something," and described it grows every day.

Then there was the famous Roswell Incident in 1947. According to eyewitness reports, on the evening of July 2, a bright disk-shaped object was seen over Roswell, New Mexico. The following day, widely scattered wreckage was discovered by a local ranch manager and his two children. The authorities were alerted, and an official statement was released confirming that the wreckage of a flying disk had been recovered.

A second press statement was immediately issued stating that the wreckage was nothing more than the remains of a weather balloon, which was dutifully displayed at a press conference. Meanwhile, the real wreckage was reported to have been sent to Wright Field. The bodies were described by one witness as

> like human but they were not humans. The heads were round, the eyes were small, and they had no hair. Their eyes were widely spaced. They were

> quite small by our standards and their heads were larger in proportion to their bodies. Their clothing seemed to be one-piece and grey in color. They seemed to be all males and there were a number of them. . . . Military personnel took over and we were told to leave the area and not to talk to anyone about what we had seen.

According to a document acquired from an intelligence source in 1984, a highly secret panel, code-named Majestic 12, or MJ-12, was formed by President Truman in 1947 to investigate UFOs and report its findings to the President. The document, dated November 18, 1952, and classified Top Secret/Majic/Eyes Only, was allegedly prepared by Admiral Hillenkoetter for president-elect Dwight Eisenhower and includes the astonishing statement that the remains of four alien bodies were recovered two miles from the Roswell wreckage site.

Five years after the panel was formed, the committee wrote a memo to then president-elect Eisenhower about the UFO project and the need for secrecy:

> Implications for the National Security are of continuing importance, in that motives and ultimate intentions of these visitors remain completely unknown. . . . It is for these reasons, as well as the obvious international technological considerations and the ultimate need to avoid a public panic at all costs, that the Majestic 12 Group remains of the unanimous opinion that imposition of the strictest security precautions should con-